I0760298

CHAINS OF OBSIDIAN

Book Four of The Crystal Halls

Thomas K. Carpenter

Chains of Obsidian

Book Four of The Crystal Halls

Hardcover Version

by Thomas K. Carpenter

Published by Black Moon Books

Cover design by
G&S Cover Designs

Discover other titles by this author on:
www.thomaskcarpenter.com

ISBN-13: 978-1-958498-21-7

THE CRYSTAL HALLS
Shadows in Amber
The Emerald Eclipse
The Sapphire Stratagem
Chains of Obsidian
The Bloodstone Rebellion

The Hundred Halls Universe
SEASON ONE

THE HUNDRED HALLS
Trials of Magic
Web of Lies
Alchemy of Souls
Gathering of Shadows
City of Sorcery

THE RELUCTANT ASSASSIN
The Reluctant Assassin
The Sorcerous Spy
The Veiled Diplomat
Agent Unraveled
The Webs That Bind

GAMEMAKERS ONLINE
The Warped Forest
Gladiators of Warsong
Citadel of Broken Dreams
Enter the Daemonpits
Plane of Twilight

ANIMALIANS HALL
Wild Magic
Bane of the Hunter
Mark of the Phoenix
Arcane Mutations
Untamed Destiny

STONE SINGERS HALL
Song of Siren and Blood
House of Snake and Tome
Storm of Dragon and Stone
Sonata of Shadow and Thorn
Well of Demon and Bone

THE ORDER OF MERLIN
The Order of Merlin
Infernal Alliances
Tower of Horn and Blood

Other Series:

The Dashkova Memoirs
Revolutionary Magic
A Cauldron of Secrets
Birds of Prophecy
The Franklin Deception
Nightfell Games
The Queen of Dreams
Dragons of Siberia
Shadows of an Empire

The Kingmaker Saga
The Stone Tree
The Crystal Bard
The Ghost Tower
The Champion's Prophecy
The Shadow Labyrinth
The Autumn Empire

The Alexandrian Saga
Fires of Alexandria
Heirs of Alexandria
Legacy of Alexandria
Warmachines of Alexandria
Empire of Alexandria
Voyage of Alexandria
Goddess of Alexandria

CHAINS OF OBSIDIAN

One

Pain was familiar to Camina. To become a waku meant a continuous dance with the agonies of training. The best made pain their friend. During her few short months in the Drops, she'd witnessed Duro working out in a cavern, running up a vertical wall, thirty feet high, then leaping to a hanging bar where he did a hundred pull-ups before dropping to his feet, then starting all over. Camina got bored long before he'd finished. It'd been a lesson that greatness did not come cheap. The stones, while powerful, were not a shortcut to glory. They were only the beginning of a long and torturous path.

The pain Camina was experiencing now was not meant to better her, but to break her spirit. She knelt in a pool of her own blood and sweat. Minutes became hours. Hours had become days.

To her surprise, they'd let her keep the opal and amber stones attached to her belly button. Under normal circumstances, she'd use the opal to heal her wounds, but drained of energy from the constant beatings, she had little left in the tank, and what was there, she was saving in case she needed to find an early exit. It was theoretical, of course, how to take one's life using one's own opal, whispered late in the night when they'd gathered at the Academy discussing the limits of their powers. But it'd been a practical discussion given that a competent torturer with an opal could injure and heal someone for months, or years on end. Camina wondered if they'd let her keep her stones to test her will.

When a door opened somewhere nearby—she could barely see through puffed-up eyes—Camina's arms started to shake in anticipation. They were clamped in manacles and hanging above her head, and the involuntary movement made the ache in her shoulders worse.

A set of expensive leather shoes approached her spot at the center of the room, staying outside the puddle of bodily fluids. Camina spat, wishing she could mar the shoes in a pointless act of defiance.

"Release her arms."

The voice was like honey mixed with glass. Even though she wasn't the target, she felt the compulsion layered within the tones. She was being visited by a maetrie—a city elf.

The clicking of locks was followed by the release of her arms, which fell to her sides, the blood rushing back in, bringing on a new round of agony. Camina whimpered as she bent over on her knees, the shame of vulnerability long since past.

"They tell me you haven't been very cooperative."

Camina flinched. The voice felt like she was being grabbed roughly and forced to pay attention.

"I don't know anything beyond the plan, which you already know about since it's over."

"That's not what I'm asking."

Hearing him was both sweet and bitter, rich chocolate mixed with eye-watering capsaicin powder.

"Where is Pandora?"

"I don't know. I told the others the last time I saw her was when we first entered the complex. I hoped she was right behind us when we jumped into the waterfall. Your patrol picked me up at the end of the canyon and here I am."

A long pause. "Look at me."

Her head was as heavy as a boulder. Camina squinted through one partially open eye to see the leader of the Alliance clan, Dominion Thule. Some called the maetrie handsome, but he made her stomach crawl despite his superior features. He should have been attractive, but something about the sharpness of his cheeks and chin and the deadness in his eyes made him ghoulish. He wore an expensively tailored suit, probably custom made, but it did nothing to hide the fiend beneath the clothing.

"I told you—"

"Where is Pandora? You're holding something back."

"I don't know where your *granddaughter* is," said Camina, feeling the urge to answer every question to make the tension of his presence diminish.

A hiss sucked through his teeth. "So she told you."

"Unlike your kind, we find lying and secrets to be abhorrent."

"A weakness to be sure, one I'm happy to exploit," said Dominion. "Who was she with last you saw? Or heard?"

The answer bubbled up her throat even as she fought to keep it down.

"Kuma went back to find her instead of joining us in the waterfall. If you don't know where they are, they must have gone out another way, or followed us in the waterfall later. I swear that's all I know."

The compulsion popped like a bubble and she took a shuddering breath. She collapsed onto her knees, sobbing even though she didn't have a reason.

The voice of a second person that she hadn't realized had entered the room startled her, but she quickly realized who it was based on descriptions she'd been given. Titus Cabone.

"There was no sign of either of them. They could have gone back over the cliff."

"Kavano would have seen them if they had."

"Not if they went before the fight."

Dominion hissed. "Or he's keeping this information from me."

"Would you like me to talk to him?"

Dominion laughed. It was short, like breaking glass. "And lose your head? No. As I said when this venture began, I don't want you interacting with him. He maliciously follows orders."

"Then why do you use him?"

"Because there is no finer warrior. He might be the greatest of the eleven."

"Nothing an enchanted bullet couldn't solve," said Titus.

"I recognize your time conquering other realms might have given you the misconception you are his equal, but you are not. Take no offense. It is only the truth. Which is why I want you to stay away from him."

Even without her amber, Camina could sense the bristling of the maetrie mercenary. She wondered if Dominion was purposely planting this seed in Titus' mind. She'd heard both mercenaries came at an extremely high price. Getting them to kill each other would be an easy way to cut costs.

"Go and search the Undercity again. Check all the usual haunts at the Terreno and the other settlements. Anyone or anywhere they might think to hide. I would like my granddaughter returned to me at the earliest juncture."

"Understood."

"Now where were we?" said Dominion as heavy footsteps went the other direction. He stepped into the pool of blood, placing a finger under her chin. Looking into his eyes from up close felt like staring at the sun. She worried she'd be blinded.

"So young and fierce. You'd be a wonderful addition to my cadre of waku."

Camina screwed up her mouth. "Never."

"You must seriously misunderstand that word," said Dominion, chuckling. "I've made my career overcoming the word *never.* Call it fault that when I hear it, I find myself awake at all hours, my mind working away at it like a sculptor finding the truth in a piece of stone."

He let her chin drop, and Camina found herself desiring his touch again, which made her sick to her stomach. A moment later, one of her guards was placing a small glass to her lips and tipping her head back. If it was poison, she didn't care. Camina drank it down before she considered what it might have been. The liquid created warmth in her chest, a spark that grew to a bonfire until she felt what she could only describe as adoration for her captor. Camina warred internally with herself as she wanted to throw her arms around his ankles and kiss the soft leather of his shoes.

"What is that?" she gasped reflexively.

"Menya," said Dominion. "It will help make you an obedient and loyal waku who will do anything I ask. Even kill your friends if it should come to that."

Camina looked up, intending to be defiant, but found herself craving his attention.

"Never," she choked out, the word lacking the passion she'd intended. She felt shame and heat rise to her cheeks. Dominion chuckled and turned to the guard.

"Put her through the program. I want her working as soon as possible."

A collar was placed around her neck and she was led from the room and thrown into a shower. The guard stayed outside while she stripped and climbed into the steaming water, which simultaneously hurt and refreshed. The entire time she leaned against the cold tiles, all thoughts consumed by the picture of Dominion Thule leaning into her vision.

"I hate you," she whimpered, knowing that the combination of his maetrie compulsion and the elixir had put his hooks deep into her mind.

Two

Kuma fell out of the portal onto rough concrete. Vertigo rocked his mind, leaving him curled on his side, trying not to lose the contents of his stomach. He felt like he'd been catapulted off the side of the universe and was still waiting to land. Warm hands pulled him to standing.

"We can't stay here."

Pandora's voice brought him back to reality. He managed to squeeze his eyes open, expecting more spinning, but their surroundings had him gaping with surprise.

"Where are we?"

A single pillar of obsidian stood sentinel at the center of what his mind interpreted as a garden even though there was no actual resemblance. Statues as tall as buildings surrounded the portal, connected by faint webbing glistening in the not-light. The figures were noble and horrifying, visages of maetrie in various states of battle. The sky above the garden was gray and ominous. It felt like it was pressing down upon Kuma while further out the city skyline gave him touches of vertigo.

"Don't stare," she said, grabbing his hand. "We have to move before someone sees us."

Kuma ran with Pandora, crouched and head on a swivel. They passed between the enormous statues. He felt like he'd been shrunk down to ant-size and was trying to escape a stone chessboard. They reached the edge of the garden and headed into a dilapidated street with oily puddles and broken concrete littering the area. She dragged him across to an alleyway as a new round of vertigo tried to tip him onto his side.

"What—"

Pandora clamped her hand over his mouth before he finished speaking. She found a boarded-up door and gently pulled the planks off until she'd made a hole big enough to squeeze through. Once inside, she put a finger over her lips.

He didn't so much hear the approach of the newcomers as feel it in his chest and in the balls of his feet. The rumbling made him think of a tank.

She crept to the front of the room. As far as Kuma could tell, they were standing in an abandoned living room. The furniture had turned to dust. She used the meat of her palm to wipe a tiny hole in the filthy window, revealing the street near the statue garden.

The creatures that entered his view defied expectations. They had the shape of horses, but could be nothing further from the truth, with crunchy glass bodies that ground together as they strolled. Riders in black armor with amber badging rode on the strange beasts, glowering at their surroundings. A tall maetrie with long black hair and an androgynous appearance dismounted and crouched to the shattered street at a spot that Kuma was certain that he'd passed by. The dusty window blocked his speech, which came through as vibrations. When he turned up his amber, he was met with the language of the maetrie, a speech so angled and sharp that it made Russian sound like a cushioned divan.

Kuma sensed the tension in Pandora as she peered through the gap, her teeth grinding like a millstone. He placed a hand on her arm, receiving a glare for his imposition. The maetrie in black armor climbed back onto the glass horse-like creature and led the patrol away, heading in a direction that made following their progress impossible.

The urge to speak was strong, but Pandora shook him off when he opened his mouth. He couldn't sense anyone nearby with his amber, but he trusted her judgement in the Eternal City. They waited in the dusty room for an hour before she motioned.

"They've moved on from the area. It's safe to speak."

"Are you sure?"

She frowned. "Surety is a self-inflicted poison for fools." Pandora glanced at the window. "But I think we're good, as much as I can tell."

"Who were they and what were they riding on?"

Pandora's nostrils flared. "The creatures are called stelynka. Unlike the human realms' concrete, steel, and glass, all of these can be given life, or occur naturally on their own. To ride the stelynka is an act of willpower as a single touch will flay the flesh. There are races involving riding them bareback."

"Shadows below," he exclaimed. "That's horrific."

"More than you can imagine, but the stelynka are not our problem. The Marchesa was here too quickly. Had we been a moment slower, she would have found us."

"The Marchesa?"

"The Marchesa of Pain. Sharikilla. She runs his estate while he labors in Invictus."

"You don't like her."

Pandora stiffened. "Loathe is a better word. She was one who pushed my mother to treat me like a maetrie child. Those scars you saw on my back could be contributed to her."

"Is the estate near?"

She bobbled her head. "Yes and no. The Eternal City isn't like our world, or most realms. Distance and direction don't work the same here."

"That makes zero sense, but I'll take your word for it." The ache in her gaze made him realize that coming back to a place that she'd once called home had brought back traumas from the past. Her forehead was etched with wrinkles and her jaw pulsed rhythmically. "What do we do now? Is there another way back to our realm?"

A flat gaze followed by a slow headshake gave him the answer. A cold emptiness filled his chest.

"We're stuck. Unless we could sneak back in once things have settled down. Maybe my uncle and Duro survived their fight with the maetrie assassin and we could go back at a later date when they're hitting the alliance."

"Kuma...they had no chance. There is no better warrior in all the realms. Even amongst the maetrie. There are only a few that could beat him, and even then, I'm not certain."

"Could we find one of those others and get them to help us get back?"

"Kuma, there's no point in going back right now. Face it." She hung her head. "I'm too tired to use the portal again. It took a lot out of me and we can't get back to the one in the garden without being caught."

"I know this place is filled with bad memories, but we can't give up. We have to try to get back. It'll take time, but we have to do it. For the sake of our friends and family. Anything could be happening back there. Don't you want to make sure Triana and Vasy are okay?"

"They're not," said Pandora with her eyes squeezed closed. "It was a mistake. A trap. We did his dirty work for him. He served up his clan leaders on a platter and now the rest of the alliance will look to him to protect them. I'm certain that he anticipated Daraja. I would bet my stones that he sent Titus to keep them from leaving. That's why we didn't see him in the complex. We were so stupid. So arrogant to believe we could beat him, and now he has complete control of the Undercity."

Despair had hollowed her out. She looked ready to collapse onto the floor. He wanted to say something comforting, but there was nothing he could think of. She was right. They'd been outmaneuvered. They were—

"Wait. Do you think Marchesa knew who she was looking for, or was that a patrol?"

Pandora wrinkled her mouth. "We probably triggered something when we left the portal garden. If they knew we were here, then they wouldn't have stopped looking. We'd have been captured already."

A tiny spot of light formed in his mind. "Then no one knows we're here. Not your grandfather. Not our friends and family."

Pandora looked ready to refute him, but she clamped her mouth closed and squinted.

"What's your point?"

"I don't know. I don't know enough about the Eternal City to know what's possible. Could we get help from someone who hates your grandfather? I can't imagine that he doesn't have enemies here."

"Enemies are cheap in the Eternal City. There are countless who would love to see my grandfather's head on a spike, but they'd rather use us as a bargaining chip than champion our cause. War is dangerous. It makes you vulnerable. No one is going to help us. That's not how maetrie society works. Going to one of his enemies would be the same as throwing ourselves at his feet and hoping for mercy. If we're unlucky enough to be caught, the only way we'll survive it is to make them believe it's not worth killing us or turning us over to him."

"Then we have to do it ourselves."

"You're delusional," said Pandora, grimacing. "I don't think you understand how bad our situation is."

"What choice do we have? I'm not saying that we're going to rush through the portal tomorrow, but isn't there something we can do? Are there other beings than the maetrie? Someone who might help us?" Her eyes lit up momentarily. "You've thought of something, or someone."

Pandora crossed her arms and paced away, shaking her head the entire time.

"I doubt he would want to see me. I already failed once. I don't imagine he's the kind of teacher that allows for second chances."

"Who?"

"Hylakane. The Steel Sun."

The name sparked a memory of when Pandora had told him about her training.

"He was from the Ebony court? But that's been wiped out now, right? That would make him inclined to help us."

"Not at all. Without a court, you're more vulnerable. He fled the populated areas or he would have been killed. Now he lives so far away as not to be bothered."

"Without a court? How did your grandfather survive then?"

"Being unaffiliated and never having been attached to a court has minor advantages. Call him a free agent. On the other hand, it's why he spent most of his time in our realm. Safer and more opportunities."

"Could we ask Hylakane to train us? At the very least, it would give us something to do, and if he agreed, we'd be better equipped to return home."

"I don't know..."

"Pan," he said, capturing her hand, forcing her to look into his eyes. "Look. I know this place is filled with painful memories, but for the sake of our friends and family, for the sake of ourselves, we have to try something. You've already said we can't stay here, but it not here, then where? Why not go to Hylakane, ask him to train us? If he doesn't, then we'll make a new decision, but we need purpose. We need a goal. Otherwise, we might as well march back through the portal and put ourselves at your grandfather's mercy."

"It's a long journey... but you're right." She hung her head momentarily before meeting his gaze. "I didn't realize how many painful memories would surface when I returned. This was not a happy place."

"So we'll go to Hylakane?"

"When I was sent to him before, it took weeks in the back of a carriage pulled by shadowbeasts. On foot will take us months and it'll be through dangerous areas without easy access to food or shelter. We might not even make it to Hylakane."

"Better than sitting here."

"Kuma." She lifted their clasped hands. "If we're traveling through the Eternal City, we're going to have to be at peak efficiency. Every moment we'll need to expect to be attacked. We can trust nothing and no one. Everything in the Eternal City wants to kill us. This realm is the embodiment of survival of the fittest."

"I understand. Stay on my toes."

"More than that." She shook their clasped hands. "We can't have this. It's a distraction. It'll get us killed."

The warmth in his chest deflated. Despite the circumstances, part of him was looking forward to spending time with Pandora. He would be lying to himself if he said he hadn't hoped to rekindle their relationship.

"I'm not even sure you'd want me in the state I'm in." She looked away. "Returning hurts more than I expected."

"I will resist all urges to seduce you," he said with a cocked grin.

Pandora rolled her eyes as she released their hands. "Remember, death and disfigurement lurk around every corner."

Kuma touched the spot beneath his eye. "I'll keep the amber running constantly. Nothing can sneak up on us."

A heavy sigh released from her lips. "To Hylakane then. Even though I'm fairly certain he's going to reject me. Us. It'll be a long trip for nothing."

"It won't be for nothing. It'll be for hope."

Three

A grunt of frustration, followed by a rock smashing against the wall, brought Choo-Choo back to the camp. Yara paced around the clearing at the back of the ghost-eye field looking ready to tear her hair out, while Tick was crouched against the wall, stroking his pet snake's back. The reptile had curled in his lap in fear of Yara.

"It doesn't help to be a lookout when you're making a racket back here," he said.

"I'd welcome the fight. Something. Anything. We've been here four days, eating mushrooms and staring at our dicks all day! I can't do this anymore."

"What do you suggest?"

She threw her hand in the air. "I thought you said we were going to be the resistance."

An ache formed in his chest. The words had sounded good when he said them, but putting them into practice had been another thing. The few times they'd crept out to raid the patrols, they'd found themselves outnumbered overwhelmingly, so they'd slunk back to their makeshift camp in hopes of finding a better target later.

"We will, but we need to find a better place to call our base and we need supplies and weapons. We have two blades and a flying snake between us."

Yara curled her hand into a fist. "We have these. And those ass-holes have the stuff we want. Let's hit 'em and get the supplies we need, damn the odds."

"We could try going back to the Pajot," suggested Tick.

A tightness formed in Choo-Choo's chest as he thought of his mother and sister. "There's no Pajot to go back to. Hopefully they were able to get away, which means it's just us here."

"Then why don't we head to the city above for the stuff we need?"

"And how are we getting there, genius?" asked Choo-Choo. "All the exits are controlled by the Alliance."

"I know," said Tick, hanging his head. He whispered softly to the snake and stroked its diamond-shaped head.

"Give me both blades," said Yara, snarling. "I'll find some stupid Alliance waku and slice his fucking throat and then we'll have more weapons."

"I have a better idea," said Choo-Choo. It was a thought that had been brewing for days, but he feared to speak it because it might mean they would have to go through with it. "What about the Terreno?"

"Neutral ground don't mean shit when one clan holds the entire Undercity," said Yara.

"That's not what I'm suggesting. We'll have to sneak in, but I was thinking about what's going on right now. The Alliance is probably consolidating their little empire, and they lost a lot of waku when we hit the complex. They're not going to have the numbers to watch everywhere, and the Terreno is the least important area in the Undercity right now. They're going to have their guards at the mining sites, or Big Dave's, but not the Terreno. Not many anyway. We need food, weapons, and most importantly, information. We don't know shit about what's happening. I know we'd all like news about our friends and family."

When no one spoke, he knew he had a good idea. Or at least it wasn't terrible enough to keep them from attempting it.

"I could use a burger from the Umbra," said Tick.

Yara smacked him in the back of the head, which brought a hiss from Kora in Tick's lap.

"We won't be able to walk right in, you wayhos. Not that we have money," said Yara.

"There are a lot of back alley places to hide. People who are out for themselves and won't care a lick about the Alliance."

"We could see Leesa at the Onyx. She knows everything about everyone," suggested Tick.

Choo-Choo shared a glance with Yara, who raised her shoulders as if to say, "Why not?"

"It's worth a shot. Let's go. We've got hours of travel ahead of us."

The three of them made decent time through the caverns and tunnels with three ambers to keep watch. When they weren't sure about the way ahead, Tick sent Koro flying into the tunnels. The airborne reptile gave Choo-Choo the creeps, but it was better than being completely blind.

There were numerous ways to enter the Terreno. It was one reason it had stayed neutral ground, because it was impossible to defend. The porous caverns had countless hidden pathways, tunnels that were used by the various clans to move around unseen. Choo-Choo led them to a tight passage that Navos and he had used on a few occasions that came out behind the apartments near the Pale Sun.

When Choo-Choo reached the end of the tunnel, he knew something was wrong right away. Extending his amber brought none of the noise that he was expecting from the busy settlement. He crept to the edge, which gave him a narrow view into the main street, which even on its deadest days had a few clan members wandering around.

He gave them the sign for "stay here" and moved ahead until he could see the entire Terreno. The Bogo, which normally was a busy pachinko parlor, had boards across the front. The lights of the sign had been partially broken, leaving the dim neon "O" hanging by a wire.

"No one's here," said Choo-Choo.

"No one?" asked Tick incredulously, with Koro peeking over his shoulder. She'd made the journey wrapped around his neck.

"Let's hit the Onyx then," said Yara, leaning forward, her forehead hunched with thought.

Choo-Choo knew she was thinking of her father. Since the raid, they hadn't heard what happened to the others. Some of their fates they knew because it'd happened while they were in the complex. He harbored a secret hope that they'd find them and together make a more formidable band.

"First, Tick, you need to put that snake away. You'll give the girls a heart attack," said Choo-Choo.

"You're not just a snake, Koro," said Tick as he coaxed her into the backpack after giving her a kiss on the forehead.

"If we get spotted and it's more than a few waku or soldados, turn and run back here and we'll lose 'em in the tunnels."

"I think it'd be worth the fight for a greasy burger," said Tick.

Yara smacked him in the back of the head.

Choo-Choo led them into the Terreno proper with his amber on high. He was surprised when they reached the door leading into the Onyx, since nothing had been easy for them lately, but maybe they were due a minor win.

The interior of the hostess bar looked the same as always upon entrance. Light jazz played over the speakers and the glittering ball on the ceiling spun lazily, reflective sparkles traveling across the walls. The only difference from normal was there was no one inside. No customers. No hostesses. No one.

"Did everyone just fucking leave?" asked Tick as he approached the bar.

A tickle formed between Choo-Choo's shoulders, but he couldn't figure out why. There were no visible signs of danger. He kept checking around them expecting someone to jump out.

"I don't like this," said Yara, scowling.

"What's not to like?" said Tick, slipping beneath the barrier and appearing again behind the bar. "What would you like to drink? A Bloody Invictus? Or maybe a shot of D'Agastine Whiskey?"

"Tick. Quit fucking around," said Yara.

The diminutive waku rolled his eyes as he put three glasses on the bar. "Come on, guys. We've been hiding in a cave for four or five days. No one's here. Let's take a break."

The shift of a sliding panel opening had Choo-Choo reaching for his blade. He expected a group of waku, or some businessmen that had been sitting quietly, but not the battered form of Leesa stumbling into the room. Her lip was bloodied and her left eye was blackened as she limped into the space. She was halfway across the club before she recognized them, and rather than a greeting, she hissed out her words.

"What are you doing here? You have to leave, right now."

"But we just got here," said Tick. "And I haven't heard a single peep out of this entire club. No one else is here."

"Tick, you know better than that," she said, gesturing towards the back.

As soon as Leesa extended her arm towards the corner of the club where a set of double doors led to a hallway of private rooms, Choo-Choo understood their mistake. The back rooms were enchanted for silence. Not even their ambers could hear past their walls. Before he could even step towards the entrance, the sound of guns clicking off their safeties echoed in his ears.

"Well, lookie here," said a man striding through the double doors with two others behind. All three held automatic weapons in their fists, making escape impossible without eating a fistful of lead. "The boss offered a pick of stones for your capture, but I thought you wayhos were dead, or had run away into the light like the cowards you are."

The two men and one woman wore black clothing with an amber badge over the heart. The clothes looked new. Choo-Choo recognized the speaker as a member of Antimagus.

"Doran."

"I remember you, Choo-Choo," said Doran, sauntering towards them. He turned towards Yara, surprise widening his smile. "And you're Brazio's daughter. Oh, fucking hell, what a prize. The big boss is gonna lose a nut when he sees you."

Yara screamed at the top of her lungs as if she were a berserker ready to attack, but before she could take a step towards Doran, he shot her in the thigh and she collapsed onto the ground. Blood leaked everywhere, soaking into the patterned carpet.

"You, little fucker, get out from behind the bar now or I'll blow her brains out," he said to Tick, who scrambled back over with his hands up, knocking the shot glasses off with his foot.

As Yara rocked on the ground, holding her wound, she looked like she could literally bite Doran's head off.

"Hmm...that's a lot of blood," said Doran, shaking his head. "Won't do if we bring back a body, though I wouldn't mind. Mirca. Put a stop to the bleeding. You don't have to heal it all the way, you can let her hurt, but I can't have her dying if there's a reward to be had."

While Mirca knelt at Yara's side, placing his hands on her injured thigh, Doran placed the barrel of his weapon against her head. When Mirca was finished, Doran pushed Yara over with his boot.

"Stay." He walked to Leesa, who had her chin to her chest. "You tried to warn them, didn't you? Not very smart."

Doran slammed the butt of his weapon into her gut, bending her over, then he spun around, the heel of his foot catching her across the jaw. She slammed into the bar, collapsing onto the ground, blood streaming from her nose.

"I'll finish you later," he said, glowering over the fallen hostess.

Doran approached Choo-Choo with an arrogant saunter.

"Drops and Razor. It brought me immense pleasure when each of your clans fell. You were so proud, so self-important with your honor, but it was what brought you down. You couldn't imagine an Undercity without you in it. Now you're scrabbling at the edges, trying to survive. Kneel."

When Choo-Choo didn't move, Doran cocked his weapon. "Kneel."

Choo-Choo slipped to his knees.

"Now take out your stones. All three of you. Quickly. And throw them to me."

When Choo-Choo hesitated, Doran said, "I'll shoot the hostess if you don't follow directions."

Hands trembling with rage, Choo-Choo unhooked the amber and topaz stones from his nipples and tossed them at Doran's feet at the same time as the others.

"Suzanna. Wire his wrists. Double the normal amount. He looks strong enough to break them even without his stones."

The moment his arms were bound behind his back, despair set in. They hadn't been in the Undercity but four days and the first time they tried to do anything; they were captured. What a shit leader he was.

"Okay," said Doran, placing the cold barrel of the gun against his head. "Where are the others? It can't be just you three sneaking around."

"Others?"

Doran cracked him in the forehead with the barrel. The pain sent stars into his vision.

"Your friends. Kuma and Pandora."

A spark of hope formed in his chest at the news they hadn't been captured.

"We haven't seen them."

Doran squinted. "Hmmm...I think you're telling the truth." He slammed the barrel on Choo-Choo's head.

"What was that for?"

"For not knowing where they are." He grinned at the others. "I guess it's asking too much for us to capture all of them. Prize enough for now."

"Hey, the little guy has a backpack," said Suzanna.

Doran leaned his head to the side as he examined Tick. "Take it off. Suz. Bind him up. Then the prickly bitch."

Tick slowly slipped out of the backpack. He set it gently on the carpet before dropping to his knees with his hands on his head. Suzanna approached the backpack rather than Tick, using the tip of her weapon to poke.

"Did it just move? What's in here?"

"Rope," said Tick, straight-faced.

"Open it," said Doran. "He's lying. Probably a weapon or something valuable. If it is, we can split it three ways."

Suzanna spun the automatic weapon to her back with the strap and leaned down to unzip the bag using both hands. With everyone's attention focused on it, Choo-Choo tried to pull his hands loose of the wire, but his wrists were wrapped too tightly.

The zipper made a loud noise as the bag was opened. Suzanna had a slight frown as she peered into its depths.

"I don't think that's a—"

Koro leapt out of the backpack like an angry spring. The snake bit her in the cheek, sending her leaping backwards, her high, reedy scream puncturing the near-silence. Before Doran could shoot Tick, the smallish waku leapt to his feet and ran behind the screaming woman with a snake attached to her face.

Choo-Choo exploded from his knees, slamming his shoulder into Doran's gut. He had no idea what his stones besides amber were, but he'd rather go down fighting than be captured. The Alliance waku bent over, so Choo-Choo brought his head up, cracking him in the jaw. Before he could bring his head around, Choo-Choo broke his knee with a side-kick and followed up with a roundhouse that knocked him out cold.

He turned towards the third Alliance only to see a gun barrel pointed in his direction. Yara had tried to knock him down but she'd been too far away to reach him before he'd slammed her in the face with the butt of his gun. Choo-Choo flinched when he heard an explosion, thinking he'd been shot, only to open his eyes to find the guy lying on his side with a hole in his head.

Tick was sitting on the ground with Suzanna's rifle in his hands. The woman was still screaming. The snake hovered over her head using its leathery wings to stay aloft. Suzanna's face was puffy and she couldn't see out of her eyes. Tick aimed his weapon to put her out of her misery, but Yara spoke up.

"No more noise."

She retrieved her blade and cut the woman's throat. She slumped to the ground.

Choo-Choo ran towards the entrance. "I'll check to see if anyone heard."

He peeked out the double doors. No one was moving their direction. When he returned, a battered Leesa was behind the bar pouring them four shots of vodka while Yara bound the unconscious Doran with wire. Choo-Choo retrieved his stones, his trembling hand revealing the ache of their absence.

The alcohol went down easy, warming his belly and diminishing the pain in his forehead from getting cracked by the gun stock. He leaned on the bar, shaking his head as Koro flew around the establishment searching for more threats.

Tick coaxed Koro back onto his shoulders.

"I take back what I said before," said Choo-Choo. "I love snakes."

Tick gave the snake a peck on the forehead. "She says she appreciates it."

"You can understand her?"

Tick lifted one shoulder. "Not exactly, but I can sort of feel what she's feeling through the tiger's eye."

"Is anyone else here?" asked Yara.

"The other girls are in back, probably cleaning up after their visit," said Leesa grimly, pouring another shot for herself and throwing it back. The normally elegant hostess looked like a post-apocalyptic survivor.

"Tick, you want to keep watch on the entrance while we chat?"

When he was through the first set of double doors, Choo-Choo leaned on the bar.

"What can you tell us about what's going on?"

Leesa stared into the middle distance, risking a covert glance at Yara, who was examining weapons she'd taken from the fallen, looking for replacements.

"Nothing good. I heard about your raid, but word is that Dominion let his clan leaders be slaughtered so he could take full control, which he's done, quickly and efficiently." She squeezed her lips tight. "I was surprised when I saw you three walk in here."

"Thought we were dead?"

"No," said Leesa. "They've been looking for you three, Pandora, and Kuma. No other names that I'm aware of."

Yara surged towards the bar with two blades in her fist. "My father?"

Leesa hesitated to answer, checking back to Choo-Choo for support. He gave her a nod as he moved towards Yara.

"I'm sorry, Yara. He's dead."

Before anyone could stop her, she grabbed the vaguely conscious Doran and started punching him in the head with the full force of her topaz. Choo-Choo tried grabbing her arm, but within the first two strikes, his face was caved in and covered in thick blood. She continued to strike him for another dozen hits before screaming in rage, her arm shaking, knuckles bloody. Yara turned to him, lower lip trembling and eyes searching for help. She looked completely unhinged, with blood splatters across her face. Choo-Choo dragged her into an embrace as she sputtered, bubbles of spit forming on her lips.

"He was all I had. I've no one else. No one. Everyone's fucking dead. Or betrayed me. Even my fucking cousin disappeared into thin air. I'm alone, so bloody fucking alone."

Choo-Choo grabbed her head with both hands, forcing her to stare into his eyes.

"You have me, Yara. You have me. I'm your family now. And Tick. And somewhere out there is Kuma and Pandora."

"I've got your back," said Leesa, holding up a shot glass and throwing it down as she wavered on unsteady feet.

"Leesa's your family too. We're all your family, Yara."

"I'm alone," she muttered. "I'm alone."

"You're not alone. I've got you." He hugged her to his chest, almost to the point of crushing until she let out a rising sob and broke down in his arms. He held her for a long time.

When she finally started to calm, she pushed herself out of his arms, wiping the blood and tears from her face with the back of her hand.

"I'm sorry my father killed your sister. Your family didn't deserve that."

"It's okay. I understand now. I was being selfish when I couldn't accept why it'd happened. Your father didn't want to kill her either."

"I hate to break this up," said Leesa, pouring another shot for herself, "but others might come along any moment. I can probably explain what happened, but not if I'm seen here with the bodies."

"You should come with us," said Choo-Choo.

Leesa let out a deranged laugh. "I'm no good with camping. I'd rather take my chances here. The other girls need someone to look out for them."

"Where are the owners? Or the guards?"

"Fled or dead. As far as I'm concerned, this place is mine until someone comes back."

"Anything you know that might help us?"

Leesa leaned heavily on the bar. "I heard they captured everyone from the Pajot as they tried to escape the Undercity. Put some to the sword, others were sent to Alliance HQ, and others to the mines. I heard from our dead friend below the bar that they're wanting to increase the faez crystal sales a thousandfold."

"Wouldn't be that hard with everyone out of the way," said Choo-Choo, shaking his head.

"It'd be the best place to hit them," Yara said coolly.

"Possibly." He looked up. "Any supplies we can take?"

"The old owners kept a bunch of crap in their office in case they had to flee into the Undercity. Guns, camping equipment, and the like. You're welcome to it."

Choo-Choo and Yara hurried into the back, finding a jackpot of gear and dried rations that would keep them supplied for weeks. They hauled it to the front.

"There's a secret passage out of here in the supply closet behind the stage. It'll take you to...well, I don't actually know where it goes. You'll have to figure it out yourself."

"Thanks, Leesa. You're a lifesaver. What are you going to do about the bodies?"

She took another shot, and then another, before coming around from inside the bar.

"I need you to knock me out."

"What?"

"I can lie about a lot of things, but I need to have physical proof."

Yara grabbed the bottle of vodka. "Aren't you worried about their ambers?"

"I've been working in this club for years and not a single waku with an amber has accused me of lying to them. The key is that I have to be able to believe it. Knocking me out will go a long way towards that."

"Let me do it," said Yara.

Leesa chuckled drunkenly. "I know you've always hated me. I guess this is as good a time as any."

Yara took a swig from the bottle before approaching the hostess. "I've always been jealous of you. And a little mad that you always paid attention to Kuma rather than me." She leaned in and gave the hostess a kiss on the cheek, which brought a spat of laughter. "Plus, if you let Choo-Choo hit you, he'll break your jaw."

"That's a good—"

Before she could finish her sentence, Yara knocked her out cold with a single punch.

"I hope she's right, otherwise they're going to flay her alive."

Choo-Choo didn't say anything, because he had the same thought. They found the secret passage easily and within a few minutes were back in the tunnels of the Undercity. Yara quickly identified where they were, which helped them move far away from the Terreno in short order, because once the bodies were found, they'd send patrols after them. They needed to get far away and hole up for a short time until they could figure out how to get back at the Alliance, and he had a good idea where they could go that no one would find them.

Four

The broken houses, windows knocked out and doors boarded up, looked like battered faces staring at them as they passed through the shadows, boots tromping through oily puddles. The city was watching her. It was the thought that chased Pandora in and out of her dreams. A nightmare becoming real.

They'd barely spoken since the first day when they arrived. Fear of being discovered or attracting attention from one of the many dangers that lurked in the streets had kept them silent. Pandora had pulled them into abandoned buildings at the first sign of danger. Progress had been slow, but they hadn't yet encountered a single other being. A win in her column.

But those days were coming to an end.

"My grandfather's paranoia has served us well since we arrived," she told Kuma as they crouched in an alleyway behind the carcass of an old carriage. "He keeps his fortress at the edges of what the maetrie call the *aphena*, which translates roughly to arena."

"Like a stadium?"

"Sort of. You can win any battles if you're not in the fight. It's more about proximity to your enemies. The courts are squarely in the aphena, locked in endless intrigue. My grandfather chose to be near but not in the arena so he could affect it when he wanted, but not be subject to their constant warring. Especially since he's spent so much time in Invictus. But to get where we need to go, we need to pass through the aphena before we can head to the *mertvzemli*, which are the dead lands where Hylakane resides."

"I thought you said travel in the Eternal City relied on intention? That you didn't have to follow our world rules."

Pandora sighed.

"The courts are like a gravity well. They're constantly trying to pull you back in. It's hard to explain, but we can't entirely avoid the main city, which means we're going to be exposing ourselves to the troubles that exist there for a few days. Once we pass through the aphena, things will get better for a time, and then they'll get worse."

Kuma lifted his head, staring into the distance.

"So strange how the buildings move and locations are relative to their importance to each other."

"It's a realm of high magic. Though you can't see it, faez is imbued in everything. My sapphire works better here than in the Undercity." She hung her head for a moment. "But my point is that for the next phase, you need to listen to what I say without question. Run when I say run, hide when I say hide, and if we have to fight, well, we're probably dead."

Kuma chuckled, undiminished by their surroundings. "It's like the faerie tales when they say not to go into the forest, but here we are, headed right into the heart of it."

Pandora resumed the lead when they left the alleyway. The smells of the city permeated her nose, bringing back memories from her childhood. Once as they were crossing a street, she spotted a chunk of colored glass and flinched, checking with Kuma to see if he'd noticed, but he was looking the other way.

On the fifth day since their entry into the Eternal City, Pandora spotted their first dolgants. A trio of the bulky humanoids had captured something small near a building and were stomping on it with their heavy boots. They had workman bags thrown over their shoulders.

"Dolgant?" whispered Kuma.

She nodded, appreciating that he'd been paying attention to her explanations and warnings. He started to shift down the alleyway, but she grabbed his sleeve.

"We need food and water and, most importantly, information."

They'd been subsisting off edible fungi that grew in the cellars of the abandoned houses, and drinking from old fountains directly after it rained, which was most nights. Her gut was hollow, and if they were going to make a long journey, they needed supplies.

"Stay behind me and be ready to scrap. If we have to, don't let them grab you. They're impossibly strong. Almost topaz-like."

Pandora hated that her first encounter with other beings in the Eternal City might involve violence, but there was no other way to get what she wanted. Kindness was weakness. Strength was power. If she wasn't ready to kill them, they'd sense it and take advantage of her softness, but she also didn't want to give in to the maetrie side of her heritage after working for years to embrace her humanity.

The dolgants had finished murdering whatever they'd found and were laughing about the experience. When they spotted her approach, the olive-skinned humanoids bristled with anger, their ridged foreheads becoming more pronounced as they made themselves bigger in anticipation of a fight.

"You weaklings," she barked in the common language of the city. It was a derivative of the maetrie, as everything in the Eternal City was. "I require your gear."

The largest dolgant strutted towards her with a bowlegged stride.

She slammed him with a Push, knocking him backwards, and snarled.

"You fight like a brick, ridge-head. I bet your creche leader uses you like bed," she said in their language, attempting to use an accent that spoke of noble upbringing.

But the dolgants looked at each other as if they didn't understand, or she'd said something outlandish.

"You're not maetrie," said the big dolgant.

"I bet your creche leader uses your ass like a tool holder," she spat, receiving laughter from the dolgant in back. The big one slammed him in the shoulder and bared his teeth, before turning back to her. Pandora could see the indecision in his gaze, the correct identification that she wasn't truly maetrie, but probably close enough that it concerned him.

Then Kuma stood too far to the side, not staying in her shadow as she'd told him. The big dolgant's knuckles cracked in anticipation. Humans were rare in the Eternal City, but not an unknown.

"Flesh bag."

Though it didn't translate well, it was an insult. But Pandora didn't care about the slur. The big dolgant had fixated on Kuma and his shoulders were hunching upward, a sign that he was soon to attack.

Pandora quickly assessed the situation. They could take the three dolgants, but there was a decent chance that one of them would be injured. While she could heal most wounds with her opal, at their already diminished state it would only make them more vulnerable. She took the one action she saw would best eradicate the danger.

Her blade passed through the dolgant's throat. The thick flesh was no match for her opal-aided strength, and she was careful not to let it get stuck in the heavy spine. The dolgant's eyes widened with surprise before he fell to his knees. Pandora knocked him over with a Push.

"I require your gear," she said again, intoning the words with as much menace and anger as she could muster. Despite her fumbling over the wording, the remaining dolgants understood the danger. They threw their bags at as her feet.

Pandora turned to Kuma, rage tainting her lips, and gestured towards the equipment.

"Pick them up."

She said it in their language, but when Kuma stared back perplexed, she repeated it in English. Despite the rudeness, he grabbed the three bags.

Pandora turned back to the two dolgants. She wanted information, details about which court was ascendant, possible dangers ahead. Anything to help them traverse this dangerous stretch, but the words wouldn't come. She was locked in a prison of her own making.

"Seventeen," she muttered, then gestured at the dolgants. "Leave!"

As they scurried away, checking over their shoulders to see if they were being followed, Pandora marched away with her head down and her teeth grinding.

A few blocks away, Pandora deflated and the flood of adrenaline leaving her system had her shaking. Kuma tried to ask her a question, but she pushed past him, knocked down a door with her sapphire—not caring about the noise—and collapsed on her knees when they entered the abandoned building.

"What's wrong?" he asked, hovering over her.

She waved him away with her eyes closed. "Let me be."

"I don't understand. You dealt with them easily and we have their bags."

Pandora looked up at Kuma with water filling her eyes. "But I did it their way. The maetrie way. Show strength. Stomp out weakness. Always attack. Always. Always. Always. No matter what. I've been telling myself these last few years that I'm more human than maetrie. Three-quarters to be exact. But I'm here a few days and what did I do? Cold-blooded murder in the middle of the street to take what I wanted. I might be three-quarters human by blood, but I'm three-quarters maetrie by training. I'll never escape it. Not if I'm stuck here. It's only going to make me worse."

"I'm sorry," said Kuma, glancing back the way they'd come. "I didn't think of it that way. Wouldn't they have killed us if given the chance?"

"Yes, but that's not the point. The dolgants are the slave class of the Eternal City. They'd probably just finished with a thirty-hour shift working for some maetrie overlord deeper in the city. They're like that because the maetrie make them like that. Just as they made me."

When Kuma couldn't seem to find any words, she said, "See? Even you can't dispute it. I'm like them. I'm a fucking serial killer under all this. Just like I was when I first entered the Undercity. I got that poor kid from Blue Daggers flayed alive because I needed someone to pin the blame on. His death still haunts me."

"No. No, that's not why I hesitated. You're not like them. To be human is to hurt, or doubt. If you were truly maetrie, you wouldn't have had a single bit of remorse about your actions, but you're here, hurting in every way possible."

"It fucking sucks."

A chuckle slipped from his lips. "It does. Being human sucks sometimes."

Pandora wiped her eyes with the back of her hand before approaching the three bags. Focusing on the contents helped soothe her aching mind as long as she didn't allow herself to remember why she had them.

"Some food and water," said Kuma, holding up a slick black leather pouch.

"That's not water, it's like a potent version of grain alcohol. It'll knock you on your ass. The dolgants suck it down while they work. I don't think it affects them much."

Kuma started to toss it aside, but she said, "Hold onto it. We can use it for trade later."

After dumping the useless junk, they combined the rest into one bag, which Kuma tossed over his shoulder. If it were later in the day, she'd plan on resting for the night, but they had many hours of gray skies ahead.

"Are we ready?" he asked.

"No, but when has that ever mattered?"

"Good point."

Pandora led them back into the streets of the Eternal City, knowing that what had happened that day was only the beginning.

Five

The bucket slipped out of Vasilisa's sweaty fingers, crashing to the ground and spilling rocks over the cavern floor. She crouched to a knee, quickly picking up the spillage with her single hand and hoping no one had noticed.

"You. Girl. No one said you could rest."

The alliance waku glowered over her. She hadn't even heard him approach. She knew the voice. They called him Laird. He'd been a Crow but now he was alliance.

"The bucket slipped—"

He pushed her over with the bottom of his boot. "No one said you could speak, One Hand." Laird jammed the toe into her side, making her cry out. "Get up and get to work before we cut the other hand off."

Vasilisa scrambled back to her knees, throwing the rocks back into the bucket as quickly as she could while he watched. Carrying the bucket after getting kicked in the ribs was painful, but she kept her lips clamped shut and gritted through the pain until she reached the conveyor and dumped the load onto the belt. The workers at the other end were checking for stones with a black light that had been enchanted to highlight them. They were the best jobs at the pit, but she knew from her mother that the women working that end were sleeping with some of the waku.

With no one watching, Vasilisa checked beneath her shirt to find her side already blooming with a deep purple bruise. *Laird.* Vasilisa fixed the name in her mind. If she ever got hold of a blade, she'd cut him, balls to throat.

The empty bucket was a relief. Vasilisa returned to the mine slowly to catch her breath, making it look like she was struggling with her charge. When she made it back to the wide hole at the center of the cavern, an olive-skinned woman that had come from the alliance workers handed her a new bucket overflowing with rocks that had come from the mine. The thought of carrying another was exhausting. She'd been working for hours and her arm was numb from the strain. The woman gave her a weak smile, an acknowledgement of her condition, but neither of them could do a thing about their current situation.

Checking to see no one was watching, Vasilisa stayed near the hole to catch more resting time. While she waited, another bucket was brought from below using a series of pulleys. A brief scream was followed by a muffled slap and angry yelling. Vasilisa decided she'd rather carry the bucket than listen to one of the miners getting beaten for whatever infraction they'd committed.

When she returned, a woman was being dragged from the hole by Laird, adding kicks along the way. She was covered in dirt. Her helmet had fallen nearby and the headlamp spotlighted Laird's face. Vasilisa froze near the entrance with her empty bucket, hoping not to be noticed.

"You thieving little cunt!"

Laird held something small between his forefinger and thumb. His face was beet red.

"I wasn't trying to take it. I was cleaning it with my shirt. I was about to bring it to the foreman," whimpered the woman.

"The rule is you bring it immediately! No cleaning it with your shirt, or anything. This stone is worth more than your life," said Laird as he pulled out a handgun and cocked it at her head. "Let's see if you try to take any more stones after I blow your brains all over these rocks."

The woman on the ground wailed, holding her hands up, begging not to be shot.

"Laird!"

A woman with short black hair, smoking a stubby cigar and carrying an automatic weapon on a sling, marched up to Laird.

"Quit fucking around. We need them to dig. You know how much product the boss wants. We're not going to reach those quotas if you keep killing the workers."

"I—"

"I don't want your excuses, I want you to follow orders, or do you want me to have to explain to Titus why we missed our targets?"

Laird lowered his chin. "No."

"Good, then stop acting like a fucking child."

As she turned away, Laird barked, "You're in charge only because you were fucking Deacon before he got sent away."

She was in his face in the blink of an eye. "What did you say?"

"Nothing," said Laird, not daring to meet her gaze.

She sighed, shaking her head. "What's gotten into you, Laird? We used to be friends, remember? Things are going great. We've got the Undercity under our control. Business is about to be nuts. Focus on the bigger picture."

He tilted his head, knocking his dirty blond hair out of his face.

"Sorry, Syn. You know I still ain't over how Deacon treated me on that raid."

"Deacon's the least of your problems. And I wouldn't hold a grudge. The boss sent him to the EC to train up. He was already better than you before he left—you don't stand a chance once he finally gets back." She rested her arms on her rifle. "Why don't you take a break. I'll watch the pit."

After Laird left, Syn poked the fallen woman with her boot. "You ready to work?"

The woman sobbed, still processing her near-death, which left Syn to exclaim, "Fucking Laird."

"I'll take her place," said Vasilisa, surging into the cavern with the bucket in her hand.

Syn puffed on her cigar, blowing out a big cloud before answering.

"I'm not sending no ten-year-old girl with one hand into the pit. We need people who can get things done."

"I'm almost sixteen and I can work."

"Why?"

"Why what?"

Syn frowned. "Why do you want to go into the pit to dig? It's shit work."

"So is carrying a bucket, but at least digging for stones is interesting. I can at least strap a pickaxe to my other arm, but I can't do that with a bucket."

Syn dropped her cigar and ground it out with the heel of her boot as she blew a final cloud of smoke.

"Fine. The job's yours. Don't make me regret it."

Vasilisa hurried to the hole, dropping the bucket by the woman and taking her hard hat and pickaxe that she'd dropped by the edge. After hooking herself to the safety line, Vasilisa climbed down the knotted rope until she reached the shaft where the others were working.

Dust motes hung in the air amid the sound of metal striking rocks. A soldado with a rifle hung on his hip stared lazily at the four workers—three women and one man—who were working the walls, knocking rocks from the wall and then examining them for signs of stone with a hand-held black light before tossing them into a bucket.

"Where's Jasmine?" asked the guard.

"Laird almost shot her, so Syn sent me down here in her stead," said Vasilisa.

"Great. A one-armed worker."

"One hand."

He frowned. "Do I look like I give a shit?" He gestured towards the buckets. "You can haul them to the rope. You know how to work a pulley, right?"

"Of course."

"Great. Don't fuck it up."

The work with the bucket and pulley was hard, but not as bad as carrying buckets to the crusher. She moved at a steady pace, keeping up with the output of the miners even though her arm was screaming from the all-day effort. Vasilisa figured that if she could prove she belonged in the pit, she'd have the job again in the future.

Towards the end of the fourteen-hour workday, one of the miners needed a break. Since Vasilisa was caught up with the buckets, the guard sent her to fill the spot where the miner had been working.

Swinging the pickaxe was easier than carrying the bucket, but there was less downtime and her arm muscles were already torched. But she kept up the hammering, hoping to prove that she wasn't a useless fifteen-year-old.

Vasilisa hadn't been digging for more than five minutes when she broke free a hunk of rock, revealing a glittering vein of multicolored crystals.

"I found one!" she shouted right away, bringing the other miners and the guard.

"Shadows below, that's a good one." He nodded towards the broad-shouldered male miner. "Take over for her and make sure we don't lose a single stone."

"Hey! But I found it," said Vasilisa.

The guard leaned into her face. His breath smelled like rotting cabbage.

"You found it. Be happy with that. If you keep your mouth shut and work hard, you might find yourself with a better job."

Vasilisa inclined her head and took the guy's spot on the wall. She dug more slowly, frustrated that she hadn't had a chance to nab a stone.

The chance of escaping without a stone of her own was almost nil, but if she could get one like a topaz or emerald and attune to it in private, maybe she could get away. The only problem was that a single stone wouldn't help her mother, who was working in a different mine, somewhere else in the Undercity.

At night, they returned to the old Academy barracks in the Pajot. Most of the settlement was empty. They were using it as a staging point for the mines nearby with at least a dozen guards to watch. Vasilisa had spent her entire childhood dreaming of the day she'd get to enter those dormitories, but it wasn't the same as a prisoner. Nothing was. She'd cried the first night after they sent her mother to another camp. The next day, she'd watched an older woman get beaten until she was unconscious for sobbing uncontrollably after being yelled at. She was hauled off to the infirmary, never to be seen again. Vasilisa assumed her body had been thrown into the canyon of ghosts for the scorpics. She vowed not to let the pressures of her new existence get the better of her. She had to survive and find a way out for herself and her mother. There was no Choo-Choo to save her. No Pandora. None of them. They'd all died in the raid on the alliance. It was only her.

The next few days she returned to the mine, working the pulley, carrying buckets, and filling in for the others when they needed a break. The vein of faez crystals that she'd found had dried up. No more stones were found, even as they dug deeper into the earth. The pit was hot and each night she spent her two minutes in a cold shower scrubbing off the grime, wishing for a chance to nab a stone.

Her chance came on the sixth day in the mines. She was carrying the bucket when she noticed a glint of crystal on the side of rock after the contents had shifted. It was towards the end of a long, fourteen-hour shift, and the miner had missed it. Vasilisa shoved the rock in her pocket and quickly thought about how to dislodge the stone, which was about half the size of her fist.

"I need to piss," she told the guard, who nodded towards an older shaft that had been abandoned years ago by the Drops.

Vasilisa grabbed the bucket they used for human waste. The guard watched her enter the other tunnel, which was across from the one they'd been digging in. When she was getting ready to pull down her pants, she gave him a look, and he turned back around.

She threw her pants around her ankles and squatted over the bucket as she pulled the rock out of her pocket. In the blinding light of her headlamp, the crystal looked a mix of purple and blue, which could mean either a topaz or sapphire. Her heart raced with the possibilities, but there was no way to remove the crystal, nor could she bring it back with her to the dorms, because they thoroughly searched them at the end of every day. After she finished using the bucket, Vasilisa hurried to the wall and shoved the rock in a crevice for later.

The next day when they returned to the mine, Vasilisa managed to take a small chipping hammer with her when she used the bucket. When the guard turned around, giving her a moment of privacy, she leapt to the crack and pulled out the stone. As lightly as she could, Vasilisa tapped on the rock, trying to break it without making too much sound. It was hard to gauge how much noise would be heard over the steady hammering of pickaxes. She made small progress and then before the guard got suspicious, jammed both hammer and rock back into the crack.

On her sixth bathroom break for the day, the guard said, "What's with you?"

Vasilisa held her crotch. "A UTI I think. Nothing feels right."

He sighed and nodded backwards. Vasilisa grabbed the rock and hammer immediately, not bothering with her pants or the bucket because she was so close to freeing the crystal. She crouched on the floor and tapped the rock with three quick strikes, exploding the marble-sized piece and releasing the crystal.

She nearly missed that the guard was turning around to check on her, but she happened to glance up in time to kick the hammer behind the bucket and with the crystal in her palm, yank down her pants. When he saw her half crouched, he turned back, giving her a chance to sigh.

Hovering over the bucket, Vasilisa examined the stone. It was getting to the end of the day. She didn't know how to smuggle it out because they checked everything, including inside their mouths. There were places she could shove it but the stone was dirty and she didn't *really* want a UTI. Remembering the story about how Kuma had bitten the ruby stone off the ear of the Crow waku, she placed it in her mouth and after generating some saliva, swallowed the stone. She hoped she could get it later when it came out.

The attunement vertigo didn't hit her until that evening when she was lying on her bed. She woke to a full-body sweat, feeling a thousand degrees inside. Sleep was impossible. It was only in the depths of her shivers that she thought about the possibility that she'd swallowed a faulty stone. She'd heard about the horrors of what happened to waku testing new faez crystals. A few had disappeared into the Undercity never to be seen again—or maybe they'd died, and their bodies had been quietly disposed of.

Vasilisa knew that in the morning if she was looking bad, they might suspect what she'd done. It was a part of her plan that she hadn't thought through. So she got up to use the bathroom. Like the mine, they always had a guard stationed with them. She gave the man with the automatic weapon a low wave as she passed him, entering the bathroom with a bout of dizziness that threatened to knock her over, but she had to pretend nothing was wrong.

The crippling vertigo was awful. She wondered how her siblings could have survived it. It was the one part of being a waku that no one liked, but everyone was willing to tolerate for the prize at the end.

After squatting over the floor, not wanting to lose the stone to the deep well that served as a toilet, Vasilisa cleaned up and returned to her bed. She had no idea how long it took to pass a stone, but she was determined to be vigilant.

The next day was torture. Bouts of dizziness and nausea came and went like waves, but she couldn't show any signs of her symptoms. She worked through the agony, carrying buckets, digging in the wall—everything had to be done with a smile on her face. When the guard wasn't looking, she leaned against the rope. Once she managed to vomit into the corner without anyone noticing.

On the third day, she had stomach cramps in the middle of the night. When she got up, the guard frowned at her approach.

"Go to bed, girl. You've used up your bathroom visits for the night."

She held her guts, crouched in fear of losing control before she reached the bathroom.

"No. I think I have diarrhea. Please. I have to go. Might have been the rat at dinner. Wasn't cooked so great."

The guard shook his head. "I don't trust it. You've been hitting the bathroom at a high rate lately. I heard your pit guard say the same thing."

"Please. I'm about to crap my pants," she said.

It wasn't hard to give him an expression of agony, because the pain was real.

"Fine. But I'll be watching the entire time."

Forced to smile and nod, Vasilisa hurried to the toilet in a waddle with the guard right behind. When she tried to pull the curtain closed, he knocked it back open with his rifle.

"What kind of sicko are you? Wanting to watch a girl use the bathroom."

"It's no party for me either, but you've been acting real weird lately." He frowned. "I've already seen a few of my mates get skinned for not paying attention. That ain't gonna be me. So either start going or return to your bunk."

The guard didn't quite stare. He was turned to the side, checking her out with his peripherals. There was no option for her as she crouched over the toilet. Her guts had had enough of the vertigo and it felt like she'd voided her entire system. When she was finished, the guard chuckled.

"I guess you really did have to go."

Vasilisa stumbled back to her bunk in shock. The moment she'd finished, the vertigo had disappeared. She'd passed the stone and there was no way to retrieve it in the deep well. She fell onto her bed and cried herself to sleep.

Six

The sharp rock bit into Choo-Choo's palms as he pressed them against opposite walls, holding himself near the ceiling of the tunnel. His skin was calloused but the rock was sharp enough to slice through the outer layer. Blood ran down his wrist.

He would adjust, but Yara had signaled him a short time ago that the patrol was on their way. Choo-Choo kept his breathing shallow and light as not to be heard by any of their ambers. They'd picked a spot with plenty of ambient noise. An old crack in the ceiling of the cave passed air through from an unknown source, making a whistling sound at times, which had earned it the name of the Whistling Cave. The location was east of the Pajot on a path that led to the wastelands where numerous mines were located. They'd been covertly watching the patrols to understand numbers and levels of protection. Most were around six members with at least two waku. There were larger groups of a dozen, but they were mules for delivering stones after they'd been mined from the ground. Yara had wanted to hit one of those, but Choo-Choo argued it was best to start small. With only the three of them, they couldn't afford a single loss.

His topaz meant he could stay aloft for hours, but not with a piece of stone sticking into his flesh. He tried taking the weight off his hands by pushing down with his right foot, but the wall was less stable and a piece chipped off, crashing to the floor.

Two heartbeats later, a line of Alliance waku and soldado appeared beneath his legs, fifteen feet below.

"Did you hear that?"

"I can't hear nothing over that fucking whistling. It's like a burr in my ear."

Choo-Choo couldn't see how many of the patrol had arrived as only three of them were past the archway. They weren't using a light, which meant at least a few of them were ambers. The third in line, a woman with a shaved head and dark lustrous skin, held an automatic weapon casually on her hip.

He stared down at them between his legs, mentally urging them to move on because he was supposed to land behind them once the last member had continued past the archway. The wetness on his palm had grown and he spotted a drip of blood about to release from his wrist and land on the head of the second patrol member.

The drop let go from his flesh.

As it sailed downward, Choo-Choo anchored himself by pushing outward and used his right foot to catch the droplet before it made it to the patrol. The agony in his right hand was eye-watering, but he maintained his position.

"Must've been my imagination," said the lead patrol member.

As they continued forward, Choo-Choo prepared to release from the ceiling. When the sixth member passed through the archway, he waited a half second to see if there were any more coming. Satisfied that was the last, Choo-Choo dropped from the ceiling, landing hard on the rough ground. The crunch of gravel immediately gave him away, but he was already moving forward. He kicked the last member, sending him into the rest of the group like a set of dominoes.

Then he threw himself backwards, dodging around the archway as bright lights and sound echoed through the cavern. Bullets ripped through the patrol. The first three fell immediately, while those in back returned fire.

Choo-Choo grinned because there'd be no one to shoot at. Yara was supposed to unleash a few quick sprays of bullets to kill the first few members and then fade back. With their attention focused forward, he spun back through the archway with a handgun, squeezing the trigger three times. At close range, it was easy to avoid their armor and take them in the back of the head. The last patrol member was half turning, as he'd been the one kicked, but he didn't make it completely around before his brains exploded onto the rocks.

"Clear," called Choo-Choo as he watched for signs of movement.

"Clear," said Yara from the far side of the cavern, strolling in with her rifle on her hip.

"Clear," said Tick with Koro hovering above him. He'd been positioned behind the patrol in case there'd been any stragglers.

The adrenaline of the battle had Choo-Choo wanting to holler, but sometimes patrols were right on top of each other and another group could be upon them soon.

"That was too easy," said Tick.

Choo-Choo used his knife to cut a piece of fabric from a pant leg to wrap around his hand.

"I'll take easy over dead every time."

When Yara arrived, she took out her blade and cut the throats of the dead patrol members.

"That's gross," said Tick.

"Making sure we don't have to fight them again."

"Grab their gear. We need to be moving," said Choo-Choo.

The three of them scoured the fallen, taking weapons, armor, and the other little goodies they found on them. With their packs loaded, Yara led them southwest, through a series of winding tunnels and caverns. They had to traverse two freezing cold streams that were deep enough to reach their knees. They were taking the long way, but didn't want to leave traces that could lead to their hideout.

They came to the edge of a cliff that overlooked a basin that glowed with the faint light of fungi. A knotted rope, anchored at the top of the cliff, provided an easy descent. Choo-Choo went last after adjusting his bandage. As he climbed down the air grew warmer and wetter.

The bottom was covered in plant life, tall fronds that hid their surroundings and colorful fungi that claimed any bare section of rock. When they reached their camp, Choo-Choo slipped out of his backpack, relishing the release of weight from his shoulders.

"Fuck yes," said Tick, plopping down on his bedroll as Koro took off into foliage to hunt. He leaned forward and turned on the camping lantern, which provide a low, soft glow that was impossible to see from fifty feet away.

They'd chosen the Deep Basin as their camp because it was easy to hide in the greenery, and by climbing in with rope, rather than using the long ramp on the opposite side, they made it harder for anyone to detect their presence.

Tick pulled out a small bottle of whiskey from his pack and rocked it side to side. "Lookie what I found."

Choo-Choo's first instinct was to tell them it wouldn't be prudent to drink whiskey after their first successful hit on a patrol, but they'd spent weeks studying the patrols and figuring out their plan. It would be nice to have a little party.

"Don't be shy. Take a drink and pass it on," said Choo-Choo.

Yara immediately took out a sharpening stone and started working on her blades. She hesitated when the bottle was passed to her, but eventually took a swig, following with a half grimace.

"It's not terrible."

"With control of the Undercity, they have the pick of spoils," said Choo-Choo.

Yara resumed using the whetstone. "Did anyone see the two in back?"

"What about them?"

She frowned. "Fresh-faced recruits with a tan. They came from above."

"Not surprising. After absorbing the Crows, Dominion's probably looking for more guards and people to run his empire. With the faez crystal trade unleashed, he has the cash to spend on recruitment."

"Do you think what we did really mattered?" asked Yara.

The question put a stone in his gut. "What gives? You were all ready to spill blood after the Terreno."

Yara accepted the bottle and took another swig. "I want to kill every one of those motherfuckers, but that's not my point. They can recruit faster than we can kill them and eventually they'll decide we're a problem and send people after us."

"I wish I had an answer for you," said Choo-Choo. "But for now it felt good to finally hit them back."

"I'll second that," said Yara, leaning onto her bedroll with her arms crossed.

Choo-Choo lifted the bottle of whiskey. "Eventually I'd like to find Vasy and my mom and free them. But we'd need to figure out where their mining sites are and how to take down a larger, better armed and defended group. Hitting a patrol in an area we've picked out ahead of time is one thing, but going after a mine will be another level of difficulty."

He leaned over to pass the bottle to Tick only to find him deeply engrossed in a magazine. The advertisements on the back suggested it was a porno mag.

"Where'd you get that?"

Tick seemed heavily distracted. "Uhm, oh yeah, this? From one of the patrol." He closed the magazine and faced the cover towards them. "*Mages Gone Wild.*"

"What in the shadows is that?"

Tick cleared his throat as he resumed his investigation of the interior.

"Looks like they spell some porn stars into looking like famous mages and then film them having sex. It looks like this is just the stills from the movies."

Yara kicked Tick's foot. "Now I remember why you're friends with my cousin. You're both perverts."

Tick frowned as he turned the magazine at strange angles looking both disgusted and excited. "They really made them look like the real deal. This guy looks like the old Head Patron Invictus, except he's hung like a Tyrannosaurus rex."

"Grow up, Tick," said Yara as she closed her eyes.

Tick threw the magazine by Yara's feet. "I have to water the plants. Feel free to peruse the mag."

"Never," said Yara.

The smallish waku disappeared into the foliage. Choo-Choo took another sip of whiskey, enjoying the warming of his chest. He caught a single open eye from Yara.

"If you don't, I am," he told her.

She sat up and grabbed the magazine before he could, frowning as she opened it up. Her eyes widened.

"Oh wow. It really does look like him. Weird. I don't even know how to describe this next one."

Choo-Choo took position next to Yara, looking over her shoulder as she paged through the magazine. Each page had naked porn stars acting out famous scenes from recent years, including some that had been transformed to look like maetrie or human-like demons.

"Ha!"

Tick threw himself back into the clearing. "I knew you two couldn't resist."

Yara cracked a smile. "I guess this is proof that I'm going mad from being alone with you two wayhos."

She threw the magazine back, and he caught it deftly. Tick started to look at the pictures, then rolled up the magazine and tucked it into his stash of gear behind his sleeping bag.

The magazine was a reminder of the normal lives being led in the city, even if the contents of it were strange to him. Choo-Choo wondered what it would have been like to have grown up in the light, not in a clan. Just a normal guy trying to make a living doing whatever they did above ground. Would he be the same person? He loved the clan, but if they'd been in the city, they'd still be alive.

"Do you think things will ever return to how they used to be?" asked Tick as he settled onto his sleeping bag.

Choo-Choo glanced up, distracted from his thoughts. He gave it some consideration before answering. "No. There's no going back. Even if we could kill Dominion by snapping our fingers, the Undercity is changed forever. Before the stones, there were only scattered pockets, small settlements that probably only added up to a few thousand people who were just trying to survive down here. I bet those numbers have doubled or tripled since then and will continue to grow. The discovery of the faez crystals changed everything."

Seven

Kuma never really figured out where the light was coming from during the day. Dark gray skies seemed too thick to let light pass through. The only sign that sorcery was at work was the lack of shadows from the buildings.

"Is there a sun above that?" he asked, nodding upward.

They'd been walking in silence for half the day, creeping through the alleyways and jogging up streets to avoid threats he never quite spotted ahead of time. It became clear to him that without Pandora he would have died a dozen times over already.

"I asked one of my grandfather's guards that once. After getting smacked in the head for my stupid question, the guard admitted that a few millennia ago the cycle of night didn't exist. Only after the maetrie learned to create portals to other realms did theirs mimic the day-night cycle." When he gave her a strange look, she added, "I told you, it's a realm of high faez. It doesn't work like you think it should."

"It doesn't make—"

Before the words left his lips, Pandora grabbed his hand suddenly and they were rushing down the alleyway. When they reached the next street, she threw them behind an old steel dumpster.

Kuma knew not to ask what had spooked her. Silence was imperative. He crouched beside her, heartbeat thundering in his ears. The steady clomp of hooves eventually reached his amber-aided hearing. He dared a peek through the alley to catch a glimpse of dark skeletal horses pulling a gilded black carriage that glided behind the beasts. The moment he laid eyes upon the vehicle, he felt the urge to reveal himself and beg for forgiveness. Pandora grabbed his arm before he could make it up from the crouched position, digging her fingernails into his flesh hard enough to break the compulsion.

"Thank you for keeping me from being an idiot," he said, long after the carriage was gone. "Who do you think was in there?"

"Based on the fact that you were ready to reveal yourself from a brief glimpse of the carriage, I would say that it was a high-ranking maetrie from one of the courts. The longer they live, the stronger their aura." She sighed. "Its appearance means we've reached the area I warned you about. From now on, we have to be vigilant."

"I thought we'd been..."

Shadows passed across her gaze. The corners of her mouth creased with a frown.

"I worry this is a mistake. I'm starting to think it'd be better to throw ourselves at the mercy of one of the courts in hopes of trading information for passage back to our realm."

"Then why don't we?"

"Because the courts don't see our world in the same light as my grandfather. They'd just as likely kill us or give us back to him. The only way we'll survive an encounter is with luck and a bit of subterfuge."

Kuma brightened. "We're due for some luck and you're more clever than you give yourself credit for. You infiltrated the Drops without much fuss."

Pandora frowned. "No offense, but humans are like children when it comes to deception. Trying that here would be like sitting down to play poker with a table full of pros when you've only beaten your weekly neighborhood game."

"Are we that screwed?"

Pandora flattened her lips. "I hope I'm better than that, but it's why I say avoidance is best. But if we get into something bigger than us, I'm going to have to bluff our way out."

"Ahead it is then."

Pandora nodded. "Before we go..."

"Again? You're as bad as Duro."

"It's not for you, but me. I worry I've led us into a situation we can't get out of."

Kuma put his hand on her forearm, giving it a comforting squeeze. "You've led us well so far."

"So far. But what if we get separated? Or I die. You'll be alone."

Standing so close to her brought a warmth to his face. The time they'd spent in each other's arms in the back of the Onyx Club rose to the forefront of his memory, but her earnest expression reminded him of their precarious situation.

"The dolgants should be avoided if possible," he began. "Not because we can't beat them in a fight, but the commotion might bring other dangers. Most will avoid us, because they're smart enough to know when they're outclassed, but a few will test us. If we're forced into an encounter, run if there are more than ten—any less than that, strike fast and without mercy.

"The second danger are the faeila. They're small but come in huge clouds like locust and can take down a large dolgant in a few minutes. Avoid and run. If we can, find a building to hunker down in until they find someone else to bother.

"Third are the maetrie. If we're spotted, let you do the talking and

I should not make eye contact, or speak. I'll be your body slave. Unless it's one of your grandfather's soldiers and then we run as fast as we can.

"Fourth are the smoke-eaters. Which don't sound dangerous, but based on what you said, they're to be avoided at all cost. The rest of the dangers, we should be able to handle with our blades and stones, at least until we reach the hinterlands, and then we'll have a whole new list of dangers to worry about like the wraithhawks, which sound cool, but you say can be more dangerous than a smoke-eater."

"Don't worry about those for now. If we're lucky enough to encounter one, it'll mean we've made it through the aphena," said Pandora, anguish in her gaze.

As he followed her down the street, he worried their precautions wouldn't be enough. Given their unkempt appearance—dirt-smudged clothes, and faces haggard from a lack of food—any maetrie who caught sight of them would know didn't belong.

When they paused at corners, Kuma liked to look into the distance. It always seemed like skyscrapers lurked on the horizon, but now they were larger. He could see details not visible before, including buzzing neon lights and beacons that flashed near the top floors. He caught a glimpse of a stadium made of bone, but didn't have a chance to ask Pandora about it before they were hurrying to a new location.

The streets were busier. Dolgants lounged beneath the awnings of taverns, grunting in their rough speech. As long as they stayed on the opposite side, no one seemed to want to bother them, though they were watched the entire time. Once, a larger dolgant started to march across, but Pandora sent a wave of trash tumbling his direction using her sapphire and he got the message, turning back to his compatriots.

As they turned onto an empty street, Pandora paused, holding him back. A crimson neon sign buzzed on a building to their right, the red glow casting blood-like shadows across the cracked asphalt.

"What do you sense?" she asked with urgency.

Kuma poured his attention into his amber and the buzzing became a hurricane. It took a moment to partition the noise and continue his unmoving search. He caught a faint tinkling sound, like chimes softly bumping in the breeze.

"Nothing. The street is empty."

"Are you *sure*?"

He searched his thoughts. "Yes."

Pandora examined the street from the safety of the alleyway.

"What does that sign say?" he asked.

She chuckled lightly. "Nothing. Not anymore."

"That doesn't make sense."

"At one time it did. It was probably a bar, or fighting club, or both. But the city moved on, and the streets in its wake fade."

"So it doesn't say anything?"

She squinted. "Best I can guess, the Garnet Smile. Probably not that, but something similar." Pandora checked both directions. "Come on. Let's get to the other end quickly. Something doesn't feel right."

Halfway down the street, Kuma sensed the change. He thought it was wind, whipping up the trash and old leaves clumped next to the sidewalk. A mural on the bricks of an old building depicting a plump maetrie smoking a cigar and drinking a glass of amber liquid started disintegrating as the chips of color leapt from the wall and took flight.

Kuma didn't even realize he'd slowed until Pandora grabbed his arm, eyes wide with fright.

"Run! Faeila!"

The cloud of colorful insects mesmerized him until he remembered they were made of living glass. Kuma tapped into his ruby so they could share their emerald and sapphire. They ran with Lightness, leaping ridiculous distances with a sapphire-aided Push before briefly cycling Heavy upon landing. The regular travel had taught them to work in tandem without needing to speak. Pandora led them through side streets, and within a few minutes of full-out running, they'd outpaced the faeila. He slowed when he no longer saw the cloud of colorful glass creatures following.

"Now we know why that street was empty," said Kuma, checking over his shoulder.

Pandora paused, gesturing towards a lump on the far side of the street. A pile of bones lay mixed with leaves. A few glittering reflections of dead faeila made it clear how they'd met their end.

Kuma heard them before he caught sight of them. Pandora must have been using his amber, because her head rose as well. A second cloud of faeila, this one twice as large as the other, flowed over the buildings like a murmuring of sparrows.

"Run!"

As soon as they turned, they found the other cloud hadn't given up, trapping them between the two. Pandora identified a door across the street. He followed her at a headlong sprint as the faeila descended upon them. She blasted some back with a Push, but there were too many. It was like getting caught in a sandstorm made of insects. He felt their sharp edges flay his flesh as they tried to escape.

Pandora threw herself through the door, knocking it off its hinges. He followed as she tried to place the wood back against the hole, but too many faeila had gotten through and were attacking exposed flesh. Leaning against the door was like trying to push back on a hurricane. It sounded like a thousand knives being sharpened in the street as the two clouds of faeila hammered against the blockage.

"Hold this!"

While he made himself Heavy to keep the door from being pushed back, she turned and rage-screamed with a heavy Push that blasted the faeila against the far wall, turning them into sand upon impact.

A crash announced the cloud had broken through a window. They ran towards a set of stairs, bounding up in two leaps before throwing themselves into another room, but the faeila crashed through the second-story window and they had to continue to the third and final floor.

"Oh no."

The windows had been blown out long ago and a pile of moldy clothes lay in the center of the room. The clouds pushed into the room and the air was alive with color and pain. A slice right beneath Kuma's eye had him squinting. He swiped at the faeila but there were too many and they were so small.

She grabbed his hand, dragging him to a room he hadn't noticed. The door was cracked. It led to a tiled bathroom. Pandora slammed the door and flung herself against it, using her body to block the gap. The faeila threw themselves at the door. It sounded like the wood would splinter from the constant blasting.

"Ahhh!"

Pandora's pained voice rose to a crescendo as the faeila attacked her flesh through the small crack. Kuma held the door but could do nothing about her pain, then he looked into her black eyes and saw nothing but the darkness of the past reflected back.

Eight

The flesh of her left hip burned as if it'd been lit on fire. Pandora kept her body pressed against the hole, because to let them past was to be flayed alive by ten thousand faeila made of glass. The agony brought back visions of being trapped in a small, dark place, her back exposed against the bars. The number of faeila had been quite small, but their attentions had been brutal. She remembered after one long period, an attendant had to dig a faeila out of her back because it had burrowed in. Anesthesiology was a foreign concept to the maetrie, so she'd had to endure the pain without relief.

"No, stop," she whimpered, forgetting where she was.

Her peers, who were much older than she was, expressed their scorn, the insults cutting deeper than the knife. She'd been thrown to a pack of hyenas and had been expected to fight her way out.

"Eleven cracks. Thirty-seven times I failed to cross the field. Two parents."

Pandora paused after the last, eyes squeezed against the pain, trying to hold it back even though every part of her screamed to shift away from the door.

"No. One parent."

She smelled pancakes sizzling on the grill in their tiny Chicago apartment, remembered her father's bright smile and the fear in his eyes at the world she had to exist in. He'd loved her with all his heart, but it hadn't been enough to protect her. The world, like the maetrie, was cruel and capricious.

A faeila had dug into her hip, pushing against the bone. She could hardly breathe. When Pandora opened her eyes, she found Kuma staring. He held her hand.

"Let me take your place."

It was hard to talk, but she managed. "I can't. If I move..."

His face was etched with worry. The faeila near her hip bone nestled deeper, leaving her stunned. Bright lights formed in her vision. She endured her sentinel duty, holding back the faeila with her hip even as blood ran down her leg. How long she stood there was a mystery. It could have been minutes or hours. Visions of her previous time in the Eternal City flashed before her deluded eyes, scenes she'd avoided remembering, or buried beneath her training entirely. In the depths of her hallucinations, Pandora wondered if there really was a person beneath the things that had been done to her or if she were all scar tissue.

Pandora only became aware that the trial was over when Kuma helped her to the floor. She lay on her good hip, as the other was a pulped mess, her clothes shredded and soaked in blood.

"One of them is still in your hip. I can see it," he said, holding out his blade. "I'm going to have to dig it out."

"Do it."

Somehow it hurt worse than the entire episode. Her mind had built walls against the worst of the pain, but once the faeila had left, her defenses had been brought down in exhaustion. Pandora bit the strap of her backpack, eyes filling with water.

"Almost there. I think I can grab it."

She wanted to scream at him not to give her the play by fucking play. She was painfully aware of every touch.

When it was over she collapsed onto the tile as Kuma stomped the faeila into dust, then he cut the end of his pant leg and used it to stem the worst of the blood flow from her hip.

"I don't know how you did that. I don't think I would have been able to hold it like you did. You saved us."

Pandora was too exhausted to answer. She lay on the cold tile, relishing existence. In time, she was able to sit up and sip water. Her throat was parched from screaming. Her hip was tender, but she managed to get upright without making it bleed more.

"I think we'll stay here for the night, or however long it takes you to heal. I'm going to look for something to block the crack and something softer to lie on."

Pandora feared the faeila were waiting for them to reveal themselves. She knew stories of overconfident travelers who'd thought they'd escaped the faeila only to find themselves trapped in a cloud of small deaths. If they had to block the door, she wasn't sure she could do another round.

But Kuma returned a short time later with a bag of old clothes and a thin mattress he'd found on the lowest floor. He stuffed the ratty pea-green shirts into the gaps of the door while she lay on her good hip admiring the way he worked.

"You look like you're starting a new fashion with one pant leg higher than the other," she said.

Kuma smiled back at her. "It sounds like you're feeling better." He checked down his leg. "A few more encounters like this and I'll be wearing knickers."

"That's a fashion I'd like to see at Court. Pretentious, preening nobles wearing shortened pants," she said with a smirk from her prone position.

Kuma sat across from her with his legs crossed. His forehead was hunched with concern.

"I don't think I really understood what you meant when you described them before. How are they alive?"

"In the same way the fae realms are alive with nature."

He screwed up his face. "Do they reproduce? Or are they made?"

Pandora chuckled, which made her hip ache. "I have no idea. Only the city knows."

He hung his head briefly before meeting her gaze. "When you were holding them back, you started mumbling. Talking, shouting sometimes. It sounded like you were being punished. You said, '*No, Mother*,' a few times. What did she do to you?"

"Tried to make me into her. She'd survived maetrie society by stripping away her humanity, believing everything my grandfather fed to her."

Kuma stared the wall. "I wonder what happened after we left her with Dane and Phillip."

"Oh shit," she exclaimed. "I'd forgotten. But I fear that my grandfather anticipated us in that too."

Kuma shook his head. "So many lost. When will it end?"

"It ends when we either give up, die, or beat him."

He raised an eyebrow. "We're not doing a lot of winning right now."

"No, but we're alive and that's all that matters."

"Will you be able to walk tomorrow?"

"I'll be fine."

"That's not what I asked."

She chuckled. "If I can't then you can carry me."

"I seriously doubt you would let me do that. But I would."

"I know you would, Little Bear."

Kuma held out his hand, which she took despite herself. The warmth of his touch reduced the sharp edge of ache in her hip.

"I wish you'd had parents like I had."

Without opening her eyes, she said, "Me too. Me too."

Nine

Two weeks. Camina stood guard at the bottom of the elevator with a short blade on her hip. The cavern was full of the clan—*her new clan.* Her thoughts were like double images in her vision. Trying to remember herself as a Drops or Razor brought short breath and the feeling of being suffocated.

"I'm Alliance, I'm Alliance," she reminded herself, and the fear went away.

What have they done to me?

The awful mixture they made her drink each morning left her mind muddled. Minor decisions felt like trying to lift a boulder with her pinky.

Only obedience mattered. Dominion Thule's last words into her ear were the code running in the background of her mind: *protect the clan, but protect me over all.*

Camina had heard of women trapped in abusive relationships in the city and had always wondered why they didn't put a blade in their tormentors' bellies, but now she understood. An awful, illogical fear commanded her limbs whenever she tried to consider other alternatives. It didn't matter that she knew she was drugged.

A bout of laughter as a group of soldados left the Eleventh Gonka, the greenish neon lights casting odd shadows, made her flinch towards her weapon expecting a fight. One of the men glanced in her direction. She remembered scrapping with him in the complex, cutting his arm, but a fellow waku had gotten in her way before she could finish him off. He gave her a missing-tooth grin, elbowing his friends before he continued into the crowd. She'd been neutered. A drone in a busy hive without thought or agency.

Camina couldn't believe how packed it was in the cavern. It seemed like dozens of new members were joining every day. She assumed he was getting them from the city. They had tans, wore sunglasses, and talked too loud—the signs of a lighter. She'd heard rumors of an expansion to the west where they used to keep the workers in a smokey grotto.

The guard duty was generally pointless without any other clans to oppose the Alliance. She'd heard that the name would change soon, but no one explained what the new one would be. Not that she cared. She was still Drops deep in her heart.

The bleached blond hair of Navos caught her eye from across the cavern. He was returning with a patrol, laughing at one of their jokes with a pistol on one hip and a sword on the other. He looked comfortable in his new role. The group headed into a bar further down the cavern, and for a brief moment, he glanced up and made eye contact. If something passed between them, she wasn't sure, and he was gone before she could make the smallest acknowledgement.

Was it all gone? Had they lost? It was hard to think otherwise. She'd seen Adrenalynne two days ago with a different patrol. The piercings, short hair, and tattoos were unmistakable, but she'd passed by as if they'd never known each other.

The day they'd escaped through the waterfall was still fresh in her mind. The currents and rocks had almost killed her. She'd practically knocked herself out on the canyon wall, maintaining enough consciousness until she found herself washed up on a pebbly shore being poked with a rifle by a patrol. As far as she knew, the others had gotten away. She'd seen no sign of Choo-Choo, Tick, Yara, Pandora, or Kuma. Of course, they could be dead. There was no guarantee that their absence meant they were alive. They could have drowned in the river, or been killed at a later time, their bodies dumped in a deep hole.

A change in the tenor of the cavern had her stiffening to attention even though she didn't understand the reason. Bracketed by guards and with the towering maetrie mercenary at his side, Dominion Thule made his way through the narrow street, glancing at vendors or recruits with pinched disdain. His fitted gray suit and jet-black tie stuck out amongst the looser clothing. No one made eye contact with the new clan leader. Most bent at the waist, backing away as if they were afraid to turn their back on the new emperor.

Camina didn't realize how much she was hoping he wasn't headed to the elevator until he turned and she knew she'd soon be faced with his presence. She thought about the blade at her side. One thrust. She could cut his throat faster than his guard could stop her. It wouldn't be hard once he reached the elevator doors.

He approached with a casual confidence, a quiet smirk suggesting he could read her mind. The closer he came, the more her heart rate soared. Camina put her palm on the hilt and wrapped her fingers around the thick end, prepared to strike. She just needed a moment of clarity to end his rule. She flexed her muscles, ready to yank the blade out and thrust it forward.

Then he was before her.

Dominion Thule.

His gaunt, gray features filled her entire world. He leaned down and touched the top of her hilt with his finger, then swiped it across her jaw as he entered the waiting elevator.

The source of her pain and obedience was rising above her before she could get control of her thoughts again. While he'd been standing in range, her muscles had been at war. A bead of sweat rolled down her forehead, then leapt from her chin. Nothing. She could do nothing. The urge to pull her blade and cut her own throat was strong, but the compulsion wouldn't let her because death would make the clan weaker.

Please, make this end. I can't be here any longer.

Camina repeated the words in her head as a mantra, but there was nothing she could do. The Alliance had won. Her side had lost. There was nothing left but obedience.

Ten

Pandora felt like a bowstring pulled taut. The constant alertness wore on her mind, but Kuma looked worse. After the faeila attack, he startled every time a minor breeze rustled a leaf or a piece of trash.

They were only halfway through the most dangerous part of their journey. The streets were busier. Dolgants loitered beneath the awnings of neon bars, drinking too much and laughing in their loud, barking voices. Since she'd been back, she'd wrapped the demeanor of a hardened killer around herself, which was usually enough to keep them away. A few times, some of the larger dolgants developed enough courage to approach, but a single sapphire Push usually dissuaded them from further entanglements.

The occasional maetrie was a different story. Pandora couldn't tell if they were unaffiliated like her grandfather, or spies gathering information. As far as she could tell, they were headed through a section of the Ruby Queen's territory. Lady Amethyte was a notorious gangster. She'd never met her, but the rumors of her brutality were enough to make their passage perilous.

Pandora wasn't sure if she should be surprised or angry at how quickly she returned to her maetrie ways. She tried to tell herself it was reflex, and the need for survival. That it wasn't truly her. She wasn't a cold-blooded killer. She had room for growth and love. Yet the looks of the hulking dolgants as they hurried back across the street upon witnessing her anger was enough to disprove this false image of herself.

"We're being watched," said Pandora underneath her breath as they came upon a knot of dolgants carrying their work sacks, passing the other direction with their heads down. Kuma twitched to the side as he tried to identify the source of the observation.

"I don't sense anything," he responded in the same hushed voice they'd been using for the past few days.

Pandora reviewed her thoughts, trying to understand why she'd said what she had. She knew she was right. Instinct was the early warning system in the Eternal City. It'd saved her life more than once when she was younger. She checked back to the dolgants.

"They've been told to act natural, which is like telling a four-year-old boy not to think about the piece of candy on the table." She covertly checked the rooftops and shadows for others. She didn't see anyone, but that didn't mean anything. "Which means...their job is to block our retreat."

Kuma stiffened with the readiness to action, but she made the signs for "Stand down" and "Follow my lead." She didn't want to say more because there might be others listening. As a tickle formed between her shoulder blades, Pandora knew they were surrounded.

"Slave," she spat at Kuma. "Do not walk so close. I tire of your inattention."

Kuma's eyes widened briefly before he inclined his head submissively, a tiny smirk forming at the corner of his lips. Then she shifted her posture, eradicating the slinking forward advance and replacing it with a purposeful stride. It'd been years since she'd spent time in the Eternal City, but the resting arrogance that was required in maetrie society came back faster than she would have liked.

The approach took longer than she expected. Pandora didn't know how to read it. Were they unsure and wanted to observe her longer, or was she not as important as she thought she was?

When it finally happened, it brought a measure of relief much as the last day for a prisoner on death row. They were given no chance of escape. One moment, the street was empty, and the next, there were three sets of maetrie approaching from different directions. Pandora didn't even need to glance behind them to know the dolgants had blocked the entire street.

She recognized them as the Ruby Queen's personnel right away. Sometime in the past, they'd picked up the 1920s' gangster look, or their fashion choices had leaked into the human realm around that time. They dressed sharp, and androgynous, with little difference between the male and female maetrie. Slicked-back hair and gawdy jewelry on their fingers was the norm.

"Why are you in my way?" she asked the first one as he moved to block her. The verbal attack put him on his back foot, but surrounded by his mates, he had to lean forward, regardless of the dangers they implied.

"Your presence being requested at da Forgotten Midnight," said the maetrie in broken English, revealing an entire mouth of gold teeth as he spoke.

The other maetrie seemed oblivious to what he'd said, suggesting the spokesman was the lone maetrie who could speak her native language.

"I've no time for distractions," she replied in the language of the Eternal City, receiving surprise and concern from the maetrie who had surrounded them.

"Her Ladyship, ahh, farcically requests your presence," said the maetrie, fidgeting with his jewelry.

"Formally," she corrected in English. "Very well. I would not deny her a chance meeting."

They were led through the streets, surrounded as if they still might flee, but Pandora understood the concern. The best way to never have your head removed for disobedience or failure was to follow orders exactly. The only thing she wasn't sure about was why these lesser goons had been sent, which suggested what was thought of her, or that no one else who spoke her language was available on short notice. Pandora decided she would consider the number of guards a sign that she wasn't considered insignificant. If she was wrong, well, then it would be a short visit with the Ruby Queen.

To reach the Forgotten Midnight they went into an alleyway and descended a set of concrete stairs to a plain steel door. The only sign that something was beyond was two maetrie bouncers that looked like they could bench press a delivery truck.

The interior of the bar was a revelation after weeks on the streets of the Eternal City. Lights, music, and the chatter of a packed venue left her mind whirling with information. The décor matched what she'd once seen in a magazine for a high-end smoke bar in Invictus—the kind of place that sold magical experiences inhaled from a bag of designer fumes. Between the rich woods and reflective crystals sat small groups of maetrie, enjoying drinks while what appeared to be a human performer sang jazz ballads rewritten in maetrie, which left Pandora with an odd sensation upon hearing.

A secondary room that she briefly got a glimpse of revealed gambling tables, but unlike what was expected in her world. She knew the brutal games they played only by reputation. Most were based not on games of chance, but on mutual dares. Strength of mind and courage was prized more than a deep knowledge of statistics. A group of maetrie and one well-dressed dolgant wearing too much gold jewelry had their hands on a table while scorpion-like creatures crawled around. Whoever kept their hand in the "arena" the longest would win the bet. Depending on the level of competition, the scorpions could be anywhere from obscenely painful to deadly. They passed the entrance too quickly to see the conclusion of the match.

At the top of a set of mahogany stairs was a balcony that overlooked both sections of the Forgotten Midnight. A maetrie woman built like a shot-putter with spikey blonde hair and unusually rosy cheeks smoked a cigar and observed the action below with the resting amusement of a pit boss. Her attire was different than the others', with a high collar and low neckline. A pair of black suspenders over a white button-down with gold cuff links made her approachable, though Pandora knew she wasn't anything of the sort.

"You've a lot of nerve wandering through my territory without permission," said Lady Amethyte in a husky voice as she stabbed the end of her cigar onto the railing, flicking the ashes onto the floor below. She spoke confidently in English with no trace of stumbling.

Pandora inclined her head before the Ruby Queen, hoping that Kuma's training in Razor had taught him to bow even deeper given his status as her body slave.

"My apologies, Lady Amethyte. My long absence from the city resulted in a series of mistakes, leading me through your area. I promise to pass quickly and without disturbing your operations."

A single finger was placed under her chin, forcing her to meet the queen's gaze. Her touch was surprisingly warm for a maetrie.

"You're Dominion's brood. The mongrel girl."

"I am."

The corner of the queen's lips curled upward. "What's that slimy bastard doing these days? I've stepped on slugs less oily than your grandfather."

"He's focused his attentions on the human realm, where he sees much profit to be had," said Pandora, hoping that his absence from maetrie society had left his motives less concrete.

"A waste of time," said the lady. "I've dabbled in the realm, but found that it bored me. He should forget them and return to the city. I had good luck with his services."

"I shall inform him upon my return. He will be pleased to know that he served you well."

Lady Amethyte examined them both as if she were picking out a rug. Her gaze rested on the holes in their clothing and the visible wounds that had closed, but still bore the reddish flesh of healing.

"Difficulties," she said, chuckling. "I see you ran into a cloud of faeila."

"Two to be exact."

The lady's eyes glittered with amusement. She gestured towards an attendant who'd been lurking nearby, giving an unspecific order.

"I should send you to the gladiator pits for intruding on my territory without permission."

"It would be your right, but as you said, my grandfather can be useful at times. It would make him less inclined to work with the Ruby Court if his favorite granddaughter was put in the pits. On the other hand, I would find the experience quite enlightening. It would be good to try my hand against challenging opponents again after years in the city of sorcery."

The attendant returned with three glasses of liquid that appeared to glow with a slight greenish aura. Pandora accepted the glass as Lady Amethyte took her own.

"My body slave has never drank arosenthe."

Lady Amethyte raised her glass towards Kuma, who collected the drink without making eye contact.

"He wears your grandfather's sigils. What better time to try?" said the lady.

Pandora had drank arosenthe in her youth a few times. The liquid was hallucinogenic to humans, the effect varying depending on the constitution of the imbiber. Her experiences had been varied though it'd been many years. She threw it back, relishing the mix of cold and hot as it collected in her stomach.

Lady Amethyte stared at them both after finishing her glass. "Why bring a body servant if you have nothing more than a single bag to carry?"

The question caught Pandora off guard. The Ruby Queen stared as if she'd caught her in a trap. Still reeling from the impact of the arosenthe, it took a moment to formulate her response.

"Our gear was lost upon escaping the faeila."

"Should I question your servant to determine the truth? I'm sure he would speak more clearly, given the drink and his pathetic human condition."

Kuma wavered on his heels, eyes unfocused and mouth slightly agape. He looked like she could knock him over with a breath.

"Or would you like to tell me why you're really here?" asked Lady Amethyte, her earlier friendliness banished by heavy frost.

Her gaze was like a spear to the chest. Pandora had heard tales of Lady Amethyte binding those she was unhappy with to a game table while scorpions slowly stung them to a painful death. She found she couldn't meet the queen's gaze as she tried to formulate a reason for their misstep. There was a saying in the maetrie world: paint your wounds in gold and sell them to the highest bidder. But no answer came to her arosenthe-muddled mind.

Lady Amethyte gestured to a rough-looking maetrie in the back wearing a black suit with the sleeves rolled up revealing dozens of scars along his upper arms. They were a sign that he'd been a stelynka racer, and had been successful enough to be promoted into her personal guard. The willingness to endure such pain on a regular basis revealed everything about his character.

"Zoltv. Take the human to the ring. He'll be a brief amusement for our guests before he dies."

Pandora almost said the word *please*. It was a human reaction and it would have only hardened the queen's mind about them. She needed to be maetrie, the part of herself she hated the most. The guard grabbed Kuma, whose eyes betrayed his fear and confusion as he was wrapped in a cloak of hallucination.

She ignored Kuma's plight, facing the queen with resolve but deference.

"Lady Amethyte. I fear I have not been as honest with you as I would have liked."

The queen raised her hand, stilling the guard. Kuma breathed heavily as he stretched his jaw.

"Not about him. If you must entertain your guests, then please. I'm sure he would make a thrilling fight with one of your guards. As you so deftly noticed, without gear to carry, he's mostly useless for my task," said Pandora.

The human part of her was screaming not to risk Kuma's life in this way, but the maetrie part knew that she had to tread a narrow line for the two of them to survive this chance encounter. The Ruby Queen was a mobster, not unlike the gangs of Invictus, who only respected power and profit. She wasn't honorable like the clans.

The queen's eyes turned to slits as she parsed the situation for a hidden barb, but there was none. Pandora was playing out the situation as best as she could without ruining the ruse that she was in the Eternal City on her grandfather's behalf.

"And?"

"That's it. But I'm telling you what you already know. The only thing I can reveal is that my task has nothing to do with the Ruby Court."

The queen stepped to Pandora, the heat of her gaze a bonfire. The casual but pristine nature of her clothing shimmered to crimson armor as the glamour revealed the truth beneath.

"Do not dare to test me in my own club, mongrel."

It took all of Pandora's self-control not to flinch, or look away. When a maetrie queen focused their attention, it was like getting crushed by a mountain.

"Maybe we could settle on a wager, if it pleases the queen," said Pandora.

A half cigar appeared in the queen's lips, the glowing embers crackling with heat. She blew smoke into Pandora's face as a broad smile formed.

"The mongrel has gall. Let's see if it's earned." The queen placed her hands on the railing as her voice boomed into the club. "Good evening. A special guest has offered a match between her human servant and Zoltv."

A hiss of mirth filled the club as the guests looked up to the queen with excitement, raising their glasses. She puffed on her half cigar, her thick body reverberating with laughter.

"To the arena!"

Pandora thought they might head to a different club, but the queen headed to a third railing in back, where a glamour fell, revealing a fighting ring. The guests hurried into the other room, abandoning their contests to get a good view of the battle.

As Kuma was led away, Pandora asked the queen, "Do you have an antidote for the arosenthe?"

Lady Amethyte smirked. "You should have thought of that before you allowed him to drink it."

As the crowd gathered around the arena, Pandora joined the queen at the railing overlooking it. Pandora's heart rate soared, leaping around in her chest. There were all manner of contests that could be invoked, including a fight to the death. While she was a stranger to the clubs of the maetrie, as she'd either been in training or at her grandfather's estate during her time in the Eternal City, Pandora was aware of the events that amused the city elves. They preferred games of pain and willpower like the stelynka races or the scorpion matches, either of which would be to Zoltv's advantage.

Kuma and Zoltv, who made sure his scarred arms were easily visible by holding his clasped hands in front, stood beneath the railing basking in the queen's attention. She puffed on her cigar, amused by the scene.

"Tonight's contest"—the queen let the moment drag out, glancing surreptitiously at Pandora as if they were compatriots sharing a secret—"will be the hanging game!"

Pandora's stomach dropped even though she didn't know what the contest entailed, mostly because the crowd cheered enthusiastically while Zoltv smirked at Kuma, who was still reeling from the effects of the earlier drink.

"Did you grandfather ever bring you to a club like this?" asked the queen as the two combatants were led into the ring while other attendants brought implements that looked like pulleys and two beds of nails.

"I was lucky enough to witness the stelynka races as a child, but no, I was too busy training for clubs like these," said Pandora.

"This will be quite instructive to the difference between our two kinds." The queen gave Pandora a once-over. "Though maybe not as much to you as you stand in both realms."

"Despite my mongrel heritage, I am a maetrie at heart."

The queen puffed on her cigar and motioned to a servant for more drinks.

"We'll see about that. When this contest is over, you'll tell me why you're *really* in my territory."

"I'll tell you no matter the result."

This surprised the queen, who turned with the cigar in her teeth, smoke radiating from her mouth. She stared for a moment before returning to the rail.

"But when I win the wager, you'll let us return to our task?"

"That's it? Nothing more?"

Pandora inclined her head. "For the crime of trespassing, I believe that's a fair trade to be allowed to leave your territory without incident."

The queen regarded her with heavy-lidded eyes. "You amuse me, girl. Don't let that change. But when your servant loses, I want more than the truth of your task."

"Whatever you desire." Pandora turned her attention to the arena. "How does the contest work?"

"The two combatants will lie on a bed of sharp spikes that are connected by a series of pulleys. Their bodies will be suspended in place, but the bed will push upward based on the weights added. Either combatant may request more weights to be added. The one who lasts the longest wins."

"I see," said Pandora.

Kuma's stones would be of little help, she realized, as the emerald required balancing of Heavy and Light. What he needed was to borrow her sapphire or opal, but he was too far away for his ruby to matter.

"May I attend my combatant's side of the arena to encourage him?" asked Pandora.

"No."

Pandora inclined her head. "Very well."

As Kuma was laid upon the bed of spikes, she caught his grimace, which did not bode well for the contest. The hallucinogen could either help him or make the agony worse, depending on his state of mind. As she'd learned in the two cities of her upbringing, pain was a contest of wills.

"Tonight's event will be slightly different than our normal arrangement," said the queen with the cigar between her thick fingers. "Instead of the two in the arena deciding how many weights and how long they'll remain in agony, it will be myself and my guest deciding for our champions."

A round of applause followed the queen's announcement, and she winked at Pandora as if they were old friends. She spoke so only the two of them could hear.

"After all, it's really you and I who are battling. You say you're maetrie, but how far are you willing to risk your *servant* to win?"

The word *servant* was said as if the queen knew that her tale had been a lie. Feeling caught in the jaws of the trap, Pandora had no course but to chew her arm off. Or in this case, watch as Kuma chewed his.

"Ready?"

Pandora nodded.

"Begin!"

The gasp that slipped Kuma's lips made her whole chest tighten, even as she fought to show no sign of weakening. Pandora made her fingers unclench from the railing. *This is no different than Duro's or Brazio's training*, she told herself. But it felt different.

The maetrie guard Zoltv lay on the platform of nails as if it were a waterbed, while Kuma was clearly focused on his breathing.

"Shall we add another weight?" asked Lady Amethyte.

"How about two?" replied Pandora.

"My thoughts exactly." The queen raised her voice. "We've agreed upon two more weights!"

The crowd cheered as the queen chuckled. "How is your mother?"

"Dreadfully sure that I'm a disappointment," said Pandora, feeling no need to obfuscate. Beneath the railing, attendants carried two heavy weights onto the scale, increasing the pressure on the contestants.

"Is she still trying to prove to the world that she's worthy?"

The cutting but accurate analysis of her mother surprised Pandora.

"I wasn't aware that you knew her. A pity." She tried not to pay attention to the pain Kuma was under, focusing on her conversation with the queen as if they were two old friends having tea. "The more she carves herself away, the less interesting she's become."

"A brutally accurate analysis. You're nothing like your mother," said the queen, eyes glittering with amusement. "Shall we add two more?"

"Agreed."

The moan that slipped from Kuma's lips almost had her ending the ruse right then, but she knew that if she did the queen would be furious. But what did it say about her that she was willing to put Kuma through this agony while she stood by watching?

"You remind me of your grandfather. His blood runs true in you," said the queen.

It might have been the most devastating thing anyone had ever said to her but she smiled and accepted it as if it were a divine compliment.

"I wish I were more like him. He sees the levers which need to be pulled to get what he wants and acts without remorse. My sight is cloudy."

The queen leaned over conspiratorially. "When I was a young maetrie, before all of this"—she waved randomly at their surroundings—"I thought I wanted to be a soldier and take orders, which would free me from the agony of choice. I couldn't imagine how those in charge could understand which decisions to make, how to navigate the cutthroat world of our kind. It was daunting." Her ruby red lips creased flat. "Do you know how I got over it?"

"How?" asked Pandora, honestly curious.

"I didn't," said the queen, lifting her chin regally. "I came to the conclusion that no one really knows what they're doing, and everyone's bluffing all the time. The key is to occasionally show them how far you will go, how ruthless you're willing to be, to remind them never to cross you."

It was said with such sweet style that Pandora didn't take it as directed at her even though her mind was screaming.

"There will come a day," said the queen, "that you will decide to take your grandfather's place, just as I had to kill my mother to become the queen. After that moment, no one will ever doubt your resolve or question your motives. They will have seen it with their own eyes. Do you understand?"

"I do. Thank you for your advice."

The queen sighed heavily. "Shall we add two more?"

Pandora looked upon the scene. Kuma lay on the bed of nails, his arms and legs suspended, their sharp points penetrating his skin. Blood ran through the gaps, dripping onto the arena floor as the crowd jeered him. She could keep him on the nails for much longer if she needed, but she realized the queen would never relent. There was no choice for her. She could not back down, or they would see weakness and come for her much as she had her own mother.

"No. I concede. It is clear your champion will last much longer than mine."

The corner of the queen's lips twitched slightly. Pandora couldn't interpret the emotion because she'd turned to the crowd.

"The match is concluded! My champion is the victor!"

The crowd raised their glasses, cheering with aplomb, and for the first time, Pandora saw them for what they were. They were the nails upon which the queen had to lie, enduring their weights and the pain, to show her dominance. The queen, for all her regality and power and ruthlessness, was trapped.

With the weights off of Kuma's body, he was helped from the bed of nails, covered in slick blood and limping.

"My prize," said the queen with a single eyebrow raised.

"We're headed to the hinterlands to find Hylakane to resume my training."

"And why is that?"

A weight settled on Pandora's shoulders. It was the truth she'd been presented with when they'd assaulted the complex, but now that the others were dead and the mission failed, the task was left to her, and her alone.

"I must kill Dominion Thule."

The queen gestured for her to walk alongside while the other maetrie made themselves scarce.

"If we ever chance to meet again, do not dare to speak falsehoods to me, or I'll rip your tongue out and let the wraithhawks drain you for weeks."

"Understood."

The queen placed her finger under Pandora's chin as her eyes glittered with amusement. "But if you are successful, then remember our little discussion today. I like your grandfather, but I think I like you more." Before Pandora could respond, the Ruby Queen barked at one of her assistants. "Find them supplies for their journey. They have a long trip ahead."

Eleven

Kuma's flesh screamed as if it'd been lit on fire as he was pulled from the torturous contraption. Countless tiny wounds where the nails had gone through the outer skin littered his back. Kuma limped next to the attendant as he was led through a back door, spying Pandora speaking quietly with the Ruby Queen upon the balcony.

His mind oscillated between "how could you do this?" and "will we be let free?" He knew their position was precarious but it didn't release him from his anger at her. Pandora got to chat with the queen, having a nice conversation while he was tortured for the amusement of the crowd.

The doorway wavered when he tried to pass through as his mind was still under the effects of the hallucinogen. The maetrie attendant grabbed his hand and dragged him through, forcing him to walk faster, which made his pain worse.

"You cost me a valuable blade," said the maetrie woman.

Kuma blinked. They'd stopped in a room, and he couldn't tell if it was a torture chamber or a medical facility.

"What?"

He focused on the maetrie woman. She was angled and sharp like a runway model. Attractive, but in an alien way.

"Drink this."

He feared it was more arosenthe, but found it a golden mixture with bubbles rising lazily from the center. He put the chalice to his lips. The drink warmed him from head to toe, bringing a euphoria that bordered on manic.

"What was that?"

"Udovol. It heals and provides pleasure in balance to the level of pain you endured. Hopefully it doesn't kill your weak human body."

"What is your name?" he asked.

"Lisette."

He reeled as he rolled the name around his tongue. "It sounds like a human name."

"It is. I took it when I began to study your kind. My real name would likely be unpronounceable to your uneducated tongue."

"Studied humans?" he asked in a drunken slur. The world was revolving around him and he felt at peace with the world. It felt like he was sitting in a warm bath.

"Strip," said Lisette.

He hesitated.

"I can cut your clothes off if you prefer. I do enjoy a bit of knife play."

Kuma pulled his bloody shirt over his head, then removed the rest of his clothing. The only thing he kept on were the golden bracelets. Lisette pulled out a bucket of oily liquid and a white rag that looked like bendable coral.

"This will help close the wounds so you don't get any infections."

Lisette dunked the rag in the bucket and then placed it on his chest, carefully scrubbing the sweat and blood from his flesh. He knew he stunk from weeks of travel and the competition, but she didn't seem to notice.

"Why are you doing this?"

"It's my job. I tend the combatants to ensure they can return to the fight later."

The fact that she spoke English and knew how to care for humans suggested that he wasn't the first of his realm in their arena. She cleaned him entirely with the rag that was slightly abrasive. He wasn't modest, but between the hallucinogenic and healing draught, he felt no shame about his nudity.

The pleasure had him closing his eyes, leaning back to enjoy the attention. Between the two drugs coursing through his body, it was hard to pay attention. At one point, he opened his eyes to find her cutting into his right forearm, but then he blinked and it seemed he was mistaken.

"Interesting," she said with her hand grasping him between the legs as he came to again. He felt himself grow excited by her touch. "Now that are you are clean and sterile, I would let you pleasure me. Nothing's more exciting than watching you bleed in the arena."

Her black eyes glittered with excitement as she continued to move her hand around his crotch. Kuma was nailed to the spot with pleasure, and a moan slipped from his lips.

"Yes. I mean no."

He shook his head.

"Why?" asked Lisette, grasping him more firmly.

He wanted her like he'd never wanted anyone before. The cocktail of drugs running through his system made him blissful. Every touch sent waves of ecstasy through his system.

"I...don't know."

Lisette frowned and released him from her grasp.

"It's the mongrel. Your master. You desire her."

Unbound by inhibition, he answered, "I do."

Lisette grabbed him by the jaw, pressing herself against his naked body. "You humans are too caught up on your mating rituals. Besides, your mongrel girl Pandora would understand because she is maetrie. The best tonic for time spent in the arena is the release of pleasure." She bit his jaw lightly. "Let me show you how we fuck in the Eternal City. Think about it. She got to enjoy watching you suffer in the arena. Now it's your turn for pleasure."

Kuma found his hands on her lithe hips. It was almost too much to bear. When her lips found his, he indulged himself as his mind reminded himself that Pandora had cleanly ended their relationship a few months back. But since they'd come to the Eternal City, he'd harbored hopes that they might rekindle it.

"No. I can't."

He pushed her away. Lisette bit her lower lip mischievously.

"Shame. I wanted to give her the knowledge of our encounter as a parting gift."

His desire faded quickly as he realized Lisette was playing with him like a cat plays with an injured mouse. She stalked to a table and threw him a towel.

"Clean yourself up."

Kuma checked around the room. "Where are my clothes?"

"I burned them. But don't worry, you'll find new ones in the next room when you're finished." Lisette winked. "I would have made it worth the trouble."

She left him reeling against the table. Kuma collected himself before using the towel to gently wash the oily mixture from his limbs. As he cleaned his flesh, he noticed that the wounds from the nails were already closed; only angry pink puckers remained, showing how recently he'd received them.

In the next room, he found a set of clothes neatly folded next to his weapons, which had been cleaned and sharpened. Kuma ran his fingers across the fabric, which was smooth like silk, yet hardy like well-crafted leather. He wondered how it would withstand a blade. There were two layers, a loose-fitting set of pants and shirt, much like his uniform at the academy, and a heavier cloak that could cover his entire body when pulled around the front. Both were made of a material that seemed to absorb the light.

Kuma donned the outfit, feeling strangely alert despite the drugs still in his system, and slipped his blades into the interior catches that would keep them hidden. The clothes made him feel himself again after weeks of trials and heartbreak.

When he entered the next room, he found Pandora waiting for him, similarly clad in the same shadowy clothing. Her hair had been cleaned and brushed and her lips had been brushed with deep purple. Tension, like physical rod, rose between them.

"I'm sorry," she said.

Her expression flickered with confusion. Undercurrents of emotions he couldn't filter.

"It's okay. The drug she gave me made up for the pain." He smoothed his hands across the fabric, relishing their touch. "I assume that since we've been given these, they're not going to chop our heads off."

"No," said Pandora, strangely sad.

He turned his head, making it hard to see her. Only when he was looking at her did he view her completely.

"What is it?" he asked, indicating the fabric.

Her forehead knotted before she said, "I forget the maetrie word for it, but shadowweave would be the best way to describe the fabric." Pandora gestured towards two backpacks made of the same material sitting on a table. "They've prepared supplies for our journey and there's a carriage outside waiting to take us to the edge of her territory."

Kuma inhaled deeply. "It's good to be clean again."

"It is. We should go before the queen changes her mind."

Outside the building, a black carriage waited for them with two darkly colored stelynka on the yoke. The strange horse-like creatures made of glass invited an examining touch, but Pandora waved him off.

"Not unless you're trying to get fixed again," she said a little too harshly.

In the back of the carriage, Pandora took the other side of the cushioned bench. The velvety surface was luxurious and he sunk into its embrace with a sigh.

"Finally, a bit of good luck."

"Yeah," she said absently.

As the carriage rumbled forward, the buildings passing at a pleasing rate, Kuma pulled the hood from his head.

"Why?"

Lost in thought, it took Pandora a moment to rouse to his question. Her face creased.

"Why did she let us go?"

"Because I told her I was going to kill my grandfather."

He recoiled. "That's fucked up." When she flinched, he added, "That she would encourage that, not that you want to do it."

Pandora ran her hand along the velvety curtain, briefly peering at the city.

"The longer I'm here, the more I'm slipping into my old maetrie ways."

Pain was etched into her limbs. She appeared taut like a coiled trap, one that would break apart upon triggering.

"Not from where I'm sitting."

Her black eyes sent daggers his way, bringing him sitting forward.

"Why are you treating me like that? You sent me to get tortured in the arena and now you're acting like it's my fault."

"You didn't have to," she barked.

The serene feelings of relaxation were banished instantly, bringing back the memories of endless pain.

"Didn't have to? You said trust you and follow your lead. When they led me away, I kept thinking you'd say something and have me freed. That it was a bluff."

"It *was* a bluff. But the queen called it. There was nothing I could do. I didn't decide *anything*." She crossed her arms and pushed herself into the corner as far away from him as she could get. "Not like you."

Kuma opened his mouth before he realized what she meant. It wasn't pain and confusion in her eyes, but jealousy, which was a different form of those emotions. The healer Lisette must have told Pandora that they'd had sex in the back, something that had almost been true. When he started laughing, she grew angrier.

"Why are you mocking me?" she asked, cinching her arms around her chest tighter.

"I'm not mocking," he said quietly. Kuma shifted near her position, but was careful not to touch her, for fear of receiving a blade in anger. "You care about me."

Pandora snarled. "Of course I do."

"No. You *care* about me. Despite what you told me in the Pajot not long after I got there. I get why you pushed me away then. Everything was in the balance. Tensions were high and not everyone would understand why we were together if they'd found out. But why are you hiding it now?"

Her eyes widened as if he was brandishing a dagger at her heart. Kuma reached out to peel her hand away from her chest.

"What are you doing?"

"Trying to hold your hand."

"What?" she snapped. "After what you did?"

He let a soft smile climb to his lips. "But I didn't. No matter what Lisette told you. I didn't sleep with her. She tried, and I'll be honest, with these drugs running through my system, it was hard not to. Especially after she'd cleaned me from head to toe with a rag."

"You didn't fuck her?"

Kuma managed to capture her hand and slowly peel it away until he had it clasped between his, gently stroking it in hopes of calming her heart. It didn't take his amber to see the pulse on her neck beating furiously.

"No."

The tension broke, leaving her to collapse. Shoulders dipped and her jaw softened.

"Kuma—"

He didn't let her finish the sentence, pulling her towards him for a passionate kiss. A moan slipped her lips as she climbed atop him in the back of the carriage. The sway and gentle rocking added to their motions as they quickly stripped out of their glamoured clothing.

His pleasure climbed to heights he'd never thought possible. Between the drugs and the long absence of touch, he was primed for a quick release, but managed to hold off until she reached those peaks with him. When the climax hit them, he tapped into his amber and as far as he could tell, blacked out or at least wasn't aware of his surroundings for a long time.

When he came to, she was cradled to his chest, caressing the back of his neck. Words were unnecessary as they spoke in the language of touch, relishing the return of their connection.

"I'm sorry I pushed you away," she whispered.

Kuma squeezed her tight. They stayed that way as the carriage carried them through the dangerous streets of the Eternal City. For a brief time, they were safe. Touch eventually led to a renewal of their connection. Twice. Three times. Kuma lost count. They curled against each other on the bench, traveling to the edge of the Ruby Queen's territory. Soon they would have to leave the safety of the carriage and their benefactor's implicit protection, but in that moment, Kuma had never felt as contented in his life as lying there with Pandora in his arms.

Twelve

Two months to the day of when she'd been captured was when Vasilisa learned about the rebellion.

A few weeks after the failed attempt at stealing a stone, she was sent to a supply depot in the old Machi, which had been the home of the Razor before they'd been wiped out by the Crows. Now there were no other clans except the Alliance, which wasn't even an alliance anymore, but a monolith of control throughout the Undercity. A guard from the mining site had recommended her for a better job because of her hard work. She never learned which one, not that it mattered—she'd still put a blade in his gut if she could, especially because it took her away from the objects of her desire.

When she arrived at the Machi she was surprised how different it was than the Pajot, which had always felt like an otherworldly garden to her. The home of Razor seemed like it didn't belong in the Undercity, but in a quiet corner of the Japanese countryside. While the Crows' brief ownership had damaged some of the buildings and let other aspects fall into disrepair, it was a sign of Niran Santos' previous good governance that the entire place still looked mostly livable.

Vasilisa was sent to a small group that prepared food, water, and mining equipment for the digging sites around the Undercity. When she arrived the first day, she was met by a familiar face.

"You're Triana's youngest, aren't you?" asked Elani, who'd been the head of maintenance and construction in the Pajot. A jagged scar bisected her jaw and she didn't move her left arm naturally as she moved a box onto the table.

"I am."

Elani glanced at the window of the building. Outside, two clan soldados stood guard, chatting quietly.

"Vasilisa?"

"Vasy," she replied.

"I saw your mother a few days ago. Their mine had collapsed, killing three. They sent them here until they could be relocated."

"Where is she?" asked Vasilisa, surging to the table.

Elani lifted a single, apologetic shoulder. "I wish I knew. They move everyone around regularly. She left in the middle of the night. Never got to say goodbye."

The older woman didn't have to say why, because Vasilisa understood. They didn't want anyone to get too comfortable and start an uprising, or sabotage operations. Even at the mine, the people rotated in and out of the positions every week or so.

"You're a smart girl. Can I trust you with some challenging work?" asked Elani.

Vasilisa nodded enthusiastically. "I'll be your best worker."

Elani smiled wistfully. "I'll need you on my inventory team. We get punished if we don't have accurate numbers of our goods, but leakage happens everywhere. Between poor counts and our guards sneaking stuff for themselves, I can't keep up. I need someone who can count, who's organized, and who I can trust. I know you can do that because Triana braged about you when we used to get together for drinks."

"You did?"

Elani smirked. "Adults have lives too. They're not just parents."

Vasilisa blushed. "Right. Sorry. What can I do to help?"

"Come with me."

Elani led her from the building in a limping stride. The older woman had sustained an injury to the right side of her body that clearly hadn't healed. It was something Vasy imagined an opal could heal, but she knew they rarely used those stones on non-clan members, and only under dire conditions.

Soldados with automatic weapons stood outside the buildings, smoking cigarettes and laughing at their private jokes. They seemed to get younger as the clan recruited more bodies from the gangs in the city. It made her sick to think that the clans like Drops and Razor were being replaced with people who didn't understand honor.

The warehouse was guarded by a trio of soldados that barely acknowledged Elani as they entered the building. It smelled like old piss, mold, and smoke. The right corner was taped off as the ceiling had collapsed under circumstances that weren't readily visible. The back half of the warehouse had neat rows of shelves containing full bins. The partially see-through containers revealed shadows of what was inside.

"Here's where we prepare the shipments," said Elani as she touched both her ear and eye and nodded towards the front to indicate they would be eavesdropped on. Vasilisa hadn't realized the guards outside were waku, given their fresh faces, but things had been changing quickly in the Undercity. It was hard to keep up.

"This clipboard will contain the orders," said Elani, pulling it down from the wall next to a hanging lamp. "You'll get a stack of them which you'll need to fill. There's a cart somewhere around here that you can use to push through the aisles and collect the goods."

The older woman grabbed a piece of paper as she was speaking, scribbling on the front.

"This is an example order sheet. If you see here—"

Elani poked the paper, which read: *Some Drops waku live. No idea who. Hit mines and patrols. Want to help?*

"—the shelf numbers and bins are listed with these numbers. Once you've filled the order, you place it near the front, where it'll be picked up. After it's filled you can burn the sheet so we don't get it mixed up with the new ones."

A kernel of hope formed in Vasilisa's chest, sending her heart to bounce around like a jackrabbit. She nodded enthusiastically. Elani's smile suggested that it wouldn't be easy but she didn't try to talk her out of it which meant that the rebellion was desperate. The older woman took the paper, dropped it into a brass brazier, which was still smoldering, and blew on it to convince the fire to wake. In a few moments the sheet of paper with the damning words had caught flame.

"Got it."

"Shall we fill a few practice ones?" asked Elani.

Vasilisa nodded. For the next half hour, Elani walked her through the orders. Not everything was clear-cut as some supplies were in another building. After an air supply generator fell on the warehouse when the moisture lines clogged, they'd had to relocate those goods.

Once she had the routine down, Elani led her to the sleeping quarters—a single house for the warehouse workers. Vasilisa was intrigued by the sliding doors and wooden floors, which were more open than the tunnel living in the Pajot.

"I'll introduce you to the others when we eat later, but for now, you can return to the warehouse. A new set of orders should be arriving any moment and you'll be busy until dinner. Any questions?"

"What happened to the previous worker?"

Elani's flat gaze was answer enough. "Focus on the work."

The older woman limped towards the front, leaving Vasilisa alone. As soon as she reached the warehouse, a boy who was around her age that she didn't recognize ran up with a fist full of papers.

"They want these pronto," said the boy, grinning as if they were old friends. "You the new one?"

"Yeah."

"Good luck!" he said, running back the other way.

Vasilisa took the stack of papers inside, attaching them to the clipboard, which she hung on the cart. Using her hand and stump, she pushed her way around the warehouse, loading up the box until it was complete, then she brought it to the front, setting it on a table with a label showing where it was supposed to go. The majority of the orders were simple items she'd seen during her work in the mines: hammers, pulleys, dried rations, etc., but occasionally they included explosives which were kept in a separate building and involved being escorted by a guard who had the key. The guard would check her paperwork and confirm no extra explosives were taken from the building. Everything was recorded doubly to ensure no leakage.

She quickly got the hang of the work, memorizing the layout and making a game of filling the carts as fast as she could. The guards never bothered her, though a few peeked inside to see what the fuss was about when she would whoop when she beat a previous time. It was when she saw them that it reminded her that the work wasn't for her old clan but this new monstrosity, which slowed her pace.

The stack of papers proved larger than she expected and the work went much longer, especially as she tired towards the end of the day. By the time she was finished and could return to the little house in the center of the Machi, she was exhausted. After a brief meal by herself, Vasilisa collapsed on her mat and fell asleep.

The next few weeks became routine as she worked in the warehouse, filling orders and waiting for Elani to explain how she could help the resistance. At night, she ate with the other men and women, all of whom were much older, though none of them spoke about anything other than their job. They neither excluded or accepted her, which felt like the former from her point of view.

After that initial day, she didn't see Elani except from a distance as she limped through the cavern on her way to another emergency. Vasilisa began to worry that her answer had been misunderstood, so when she saw her, she ran across the bridges despite needing to get to the warehouse to start work for the day.

"Hey, Elani."

The older woman grimaced at her approach. "I'm busy. Get back to work."

"I was wondering—"

Elani blanched, her scowl turning red hot. "Go. Get to work. Now. Before I report you."

Shocked, Vasilisa ran back the other way, confusion on her brow. The whole way back she tried to figure out what she'd done wrong. When she reached the warehouse, the guards were chatting amongst themselves. The tall one named Andelei stepped in front, blocking her from the entrance. He had pimples on his forehead and was constantly smoking.

"What's wrong?"

No answer came to her lips.

"Not causing trouble, are you? Do we need to take a trip to the Room?"

Mention of the Room sent her heart rate soaring. The other workers had spoken in hushed tones about the place they sent suspected partisans for interrogations. Vasilisa was aware of what a skilled waku could do with their stones, especially the mix of amber and opal.

"I'm, no—"

"Then what's wrong? You're late. Why?"

Vasilisa hesitated before grabbing her gut. "I'm having cramps."

It wasn't true. She was still a few days away, but she also knew bringing up her womanly issues would quickly dissuade further discussion. As expected, Andelei backed away, gesturing inside.

"Sorry I asked."

It was three days later when she received her first job for the resistance. She'd expected something involving sneaking around or passing messages. Instead, when she received her stack of orders for the morning, there were two extra sheets in the middle that had been folded so they stuck out from the others.

The first order sheet had a list of equipment including explosives, trigger wires, and a detonator. At the bottom someone had scribbled: *place behind the warehouse near the collapse*. The second order sheet was the same as the first except a different note had been attached to it: *place only the boxes in this one.*

The intent of the double sheet made her heart rate soar as she realized that she'd have to fool the guards. The idea of being the resistance had sounded great until this moment. Vasilisa got to work filling other orders while she worked up the nerve to make a trip to the explosives building.

When she was halfway through the stack, she decided to make the run, just to get it over with. She'd been practicing casual conversation in her head in case the guard wanted to chat while they walked over to the building, which happened occasionally, but nothing sounded normal. She hoped the guard wasn't talkative.

"Hey, Andelei," she said, waving the paper at him.

The tall waku stubbed out his cigarette, shooting a grin at his fellow guards. "Wouldn't want to blow myself up."

The explosives building was about a hundred meters away across a single bridge. Andelei whistled softly.

"You do pretty good work," he said as they crossed the bridge. "Especially for a girl with one hand."

"Thanks," she said tersely, hoping he'd get the hint.

"How old are you again?"

The way he said it annoyed her. As if he'd asked before.

"Sixteen."

"I'm seventeen."

She was surprised by his young age as she'd assumed he was older because he wore the stones of a waku. He stared as if he expected an answer, but she wasn't sure what he wanted to hear.

"That's nice?"

"I know this ain't been easy for you. You know, bein' a Drops and all. I joined Blue Daggers last year. Before that I ran with N-Streets up top."

He paused again, so she gave a noncommittal, "Uhm."

"Right. So yeah." He scratched the back of his head. "I was thinking. Maybe we could grab a bite sometime? I like climbing that ledge on the far side of the cavern during lunch. It's a great view. Makes me feel like I'm somewhere else. Maybe you could join me?"

"I—"

"You know if we were friends, like *really* friends, I could help you. Get you more privileges. I can tell by how hard you work that you're supportive of the alliance. I know I'm new to the Undercity, but I really like the way the older clans had honor. I'm probably not supposed to say this but I admired them, even when I was in my old gang."

She forced herself to smile.

"That'd be nice. I could have lunch with you."

The last thing she had on her mind was dating, especially one of the Alliance, but she didn't want to make him mad. Not with so much on the line.

"Awesome. I can't wait."

Inside the building, she gathered the supplies listed on the order sheet and put them in the cart. Andelei grinned to himself the entire way back. When she went inside, he winked at her and the other guards elbowed him.

As soon as she was out of sight, she removed the items from their boxes and piled them below the table until she could find another container to place them in. Vasilisa was setting the triggers next to the explosives when she heard footsteps. She quickly rose and closed the boxes to make them look normal when she saw Andelei stroll around the corner.

"Hey."

"Hey."

Vasilisa's hand trembled so she shoved it below the edge of the table and pushed the explosives forward so they were out of sight in case he came around.

"I forgot to ask..."

"Yeah?"

"What do you like to eat?"

No words could come to her lips. She could only think about rumors of the Room and what might happen if she were caught.

"Pork bellies."

"Huh?"

She closed her eyes. "Sorry. I was just thinking about what my mom made sometimes for breakfast. Eggs and pork bellies with nice verde sauce. But that's a stupid thing to say for lunch."

He lifted one shoulder. "I get it. Comfort food. I like to eat fries with mustard whenever I get depressed. It's how my dad ate them when he was alive."

"Oh."

"He had cancer. After that, I was homeless, until I found this," he said, wagging his eyebrows at their surroundings. "I'll think of something for our date. See ya."

As soon as he left, she thought she was going to pass out. Her face was numb and tingly. The contents of her stomach rolled over and bile rose in her throat.

With a trembling hand, Vasilisa loaded the contraband into a separate container and snuck it out to the back of the warehouse where the note had said to place it. When she was finished, she put the empty boxes in a different container and pushed it to the loading area, which made her wonder what would happen when someone opened them. She hoped whoever had written the note had that plan in mind.

When her shift was over, Vasilisa returned to the group house, ate her meal in silence, and climbed into bed. She'd been dying to do something for the rebellion, but now that she had, all she could think about was that she was going to get caught.

Thirteen

It was their fourth ambush this week. Yara thought they were pushing their luck, hitting another patrol after the others, but Choo-Choo had been insistent.

We can't let them rest, especially with all these wayhos they're bringing in. Fresh meat for the grinder.

It wasn't that Yara disagreed, but she imagined the Alliance leadership would try harder to protect their patrols, or track them down more diligently than they had so far. She'd argued for a pause in their efforts. Besides, she was exhausted. For four months since the raid on the complex, they had been alone, fighting a guerrilla war, sleeping on thin sleeping bags on hard stone, and eating a mix of forged and stolen foods.

Yara crouched on the ledge, waiting for sign of the patrol with a carbon-fiber compound bow in her hands. It was part of the gear they'd gotten from the former owners of the Onyx. She had no idea why they'd thought a bow was a good idea in the Undercity, but it'd proved to be a valuable and silent weapon. She only wished she had more arrows, with just four left in the plastic quiver.

A flicker of red light from across the cavern made her crouch. Choo-Choo was in the far tunnel, watching for signs of the patrol's approach. The signal meant they were on the way, but using red meant that there was a problem. Yara slipped the notch of the arrow from the bow as she checked over the edge. Eventually the weaving lights of headlamps entered the far tunnel. She immediately understood Choo-Choo's caution as the patrol was twice the size of the regular ones.

I guess they've noticed us, thought Yara.

She tapped into her amber, and the quiet conversation of the patrol from a two hundred feet could be heard as if she were right next to them.

"Dumb bitch thought she'd cut me, but I buried it deep."

A round of laughter followed.

"Anyone know when we're getting another break? I could use some fun at the Onyx. Or at the very least a burger from the Devil's Lipstick. Never had one better. Fuck me, they must be enchanted."

"Shut up, Neon. You just had a break. It ain't no vacay in the shadows. I know you new and all but this ain't the city. We do things different here."

"Come on, man. I'm just talkin'. I get bored with this patrol shit. Same ol', same ol'. Should have joined the army. At least in my old gang we got to shake down people. Down here I just feel like a fucking courier."

"I wouldn't talk like that, Neon. If fucking Deac hears that he'll cut your tongue out."

Yara had only been half paying attention. The collective dick-wagging of the newer Alliance clan members grated on her ears. It only made her mad that those assholes had been the ones to take over the Undercity. But as soon as she heard the name "Deac" she sat up tall.

"Who the fuck is Deac?"

The laughter of the group died. Yara peeked over the edge to see the patrol of eight paused at the center of the cavern. Headlamps flashed every which direction.

"He's OG. Came from Crows, helped break Razor clan, and then was sent to the Eternal City. He just came back a week ago. I knew of him before, but he different now. Colder, harder. Like those creepy city elves. I think they made him like them. I wouldn't cross him, or mouth him. He's real."

Yara dug her fingers into the rock until her nails hurt. Deacon. The name brought rage. With the patrol distracted, she lifted her signaling penlight and covertly flashed Choo-Choo the color green, but as soon as he got it, he returned with red. She muttered obscenities under her breath. If one of the patrol had news of Deacon, she wanted to know. She could take one down in a way that would leave him out of commission but able to speak afterwards so she could question him. Another flash of green in Choo-Choo's direction was returned with red.

She didn't care. Yara gave him one more signal and stood above the rocky ledge, nocking and pulling back the arrow until the fletching was tickling her ear. Inhale. Exhale. Yara marked her targets, letting a calmness come over her until felt one with the bow.

She released the taut string. The arrow hadn't yet found its target before she'd nocked a second. A surprised gurgle from the soldado in back had the rest of the patrol erupting in chaos. Yara took the guy who hadn't heard of Deacon in the eye socket.

The third arrow was readied when the first squeeze of gunfire lit up the cavern, flashing lights distracting, but she concentrated on her target and released. The projectile hit the waku in the shoulder, a few inches left of his heart. She cursed under her breath at the miss as she reached for the fourth and final arrow.

"Someone's up there!"

A pointed finger was followed by headlamps rotating her direction. As rifle barrels aimed on her location, she let the final arrow fly and the soldado flew backwards, his headlamp spinning off his head as his neck was pierced.

As bullets sprayed across the ledge, Yara threw herself onto the rocks. There was no doubt that the remaining patrol members would converge on her location. She pulled a cannister from her pouch and tossed it over the edge. The concussive boom was followed by thick smoke. When she heard nearby coughing, Yara sprung to her feet, switched to Lightness, and leapt using her topaz.

Yara traveled through the air without being able to see where she was going to land, but she'd scouted the cavern well before the ambush and had picked her landing spot beforehand. She hit slightly off-center, tumbling over and switching to Heavy to compensate for her long leap.

When she reached her feet, she had her blades in hand. Yara rushed towards the confused patrol members, hitting them at the same time as Choo-Choo. While they had ambers in their group, they weren't as familiar with fighting without sight and their headlamps in the smoke only made their vision worse. Yara stayed low and sliced through them like a vengeful ghost. The last waku, the one who'd been talking about Deacon, pulled a handgun when he spotted her. Before he could pull the trigger, she threw her weapon at his head, hitting him between the eyes with the heavy hilt. The shot went wide. She reached the fallen waku before Choo-Choo, holding up her hand to keep him from killing the patrol member, then knocking him out with a rabbit punch.

"What the fuck, Yara?" asked Choo-Choo. "I flashed red. Which last I checked meant no-go."

"We won, didn't we?"

"But we took a big chance. We had to go hand to hand at the end. One of these days, someone will get lucky."

They both spun around at the sound of footfalls, relaxing the moment they saw Tick running into the cavern with his flying snake Koro over his shoulder.

"Did I miss all the fun? I thought we weren't hitting this one," he said.

Choo-Choo jabbed his thumb her direction. "It was her."

Yara put her foot on the unconscious waku. "He was talking about Deacon."

"Oh."

Choo-Choo got quiet. They both knew her animosity, having heard her rants during the long hours in camp between raids.

"He's back in the Undercity." She tapped her foot on the unconscious man's chest. "He knows."

Choo-Choo looked around. "We should get out of here. Those gunshots could have traveled far. The Earth Well is near here. Let's head there before we move on."

"I'm on pickup!" said Tick.

Yara slipped out of her backpack, pulling out a length of rope. "I'll carry him." She nodded to the ledge. "Grab my bow. I had to drop it up there."

The other two caught up to her near the Earth Well. They weren't going to go near the old well of power, but they were close enough they could smell the rich faez in the air. Her nose tickled. She finally got to scratch it the moment she dropped the guy onto the ground.

"Wake up," she said, slapping him lightly in the face.

When he finally roused, his eyes were wide. "Please!"

"Shut the fuck up," said Yara, nicking his cheek with her blade. "This is gonna go two ways. Either you can talk and receive a nice quick death, or you can drag this out, and I assure you that we can keep you alive for weeks while we slice bits from your body."

He curled his lip in an attempt at a snarl even as she could sense the animal spirits raging in his chest. He wasn't equal to their weakest members at the Academy, which only made her angrier. She'd take him apart with her knives but knew the price she'd pay for letting herself be drawn into her worst impulses. She already knew she was losing her humanity, out here at the edges of Undercity society. If she went much further, she'd never be able to get back.

"Use your amber on me."

His forehead hunched, so she hovered the tip of her blade before his right eye.

"Now."

He went from wavering defiance to a boy trapped in fear in an eye-blink. His eyes closed as his lower lips trembled. He'd seen in her heart and knew what she was capable of.

"I swear," said Choo-Choo, "it's a fucking insult, the weak-ass waku they're letting loose in the Undercity. You fucking wayhos wouldn't last a day in our time."

Yara pressed the edge of her blade against his throat and spoke in a quiet voice.

"Tell me about Deacon."

He blinked. "Deacon?"

"Yes. He and I are old friends. I was very interested to hear he'd returned."

"I, uhm, he came back from the Undercity. They were training him. He's much different now. I knew him from before. Not well, but he was around. Reminded me of a lot of cocky gangsters from the city, but now, not so much. I ran into him in Big Dave's. He stared at me with the cold eyes of a fucking snake when I said 'whatsup.' Was the creepiest fucking moment. I don't know what they did to him, but he ain't the same. He was smart and ruthless before, but now he's like a serial killer."

The news made her heart harden. He wouldn't be an easy fight, even if she could get to him.

"What did they do to him?"

The Alliance waku screwed up his face. "Fuck if I know, but I heard from some others he has wicked scars on his arms. Looks like he shoved them in a barrel of razors. Rumor is that a few days after he came back, someone gave him lip and he sliced the guy's face off. Faster than a fucking cobra. Word passed pretty quick after that. Don't fuck with Deacon."

"Where is he usually? You saw him in Big Dave's. Is that where he's stationed?"

The guy blinked, then shook his head. "No. He's a bigwig now. Spends a lot of time in the Nest with the big boss. He's in charge of the waku. Been cracking down on the silly grab-ass stuff that'd been going on in his absence."

Choo-Choo nudged the guy with his toe. "What about the maetrie? Titus and Kavano?"

"Titus is around. He's in charge of the mining operations. Security and all that. The other one? Dunno. Haven't seen him since the raid, but I'd hate to be the poor fuckers that had to scrap with him. Heard he chopped 'em in half."

Yara's arm jerked, spilling blood as Choo-Choo screamed for her to stop. The alliance waku choked on his blood while she stalked away with her hands on her head.

"Yara. He had more to tell us."

"He was talking about my fucking dad!"

Choo-Choo's chin dipped to his chest. "I know. I'm sorry."

"I'm going to kill them. I'm gonna kill them all."

Choo-Choo nodded his bald head. "I know, Yara. I know." He checked over his shoulder. "We should get moving. We're not too far off the main trail to the Machi. Let's head to the Great Arch."

As Yara stalked away, Tick tried to reach out and console her, but she brushed past, heading the way they'd have to leave. Not only was her father dead, but Deacon was alive and better than ever. A part of her had pitied him when he first came to Razor, seeing his cocky attitude and gold chains as a way to overcompensate for his deficiencies. Now he was one of the top members of the Alliance. She didn't know how she was going to do it, but she was going to kill him. If it cost her life, she didn't care. Deacon had to die.

Fourteen

Travel since they'd left the Ruby Queen's territory had been easy enough that Kuma had almost forgotten they were in the Eternal City, especially since they'd renewed their relationship. There was danger, but nothing that they couldn't handle. Occasionally, critters looking for a meal would approach, but they were easily dealt with, and the odd maetrie or dolgants they came across swiftly recognized from their clothing that they were not to be interfered with.

"I feel like we've been walking for years," said Kuma.

"Months, but I get your point," said Pandora. "But that's coming to an end and you might wish for these relaxed days of travel back once we reach our destination."

"Relaxed?" he snorted. "I don't know what that monstrosity of concrete and steel was back a few days ago, but it made me nick a blade. Took me hours to buff that back out."

Pandora rolled her eyes.

"Seriously. We're hitting the hinterlands now."

Kuma craned his neck. "How can you tell? Everything looks like bombed-out city after a long war. Sometimes I wonder if I'm wandering through the same streets on repeat. After a while, these broken-ass buildings look the same."

Pandora extended her arm towards the horizon. The sky was a constant gray with the only difference being night and day or the occasional rain shower.

"I don't see anything."

"Use your amber."

When he tapped into the stone, he saw what she was referencing. A section of the sky ahead seemed darker than the others, like a reverse spotlight was shining on the underbelly of the clouds. He thought he saw small shapes moving in patient circles, like vultures waiting for their next meal.

"What is it?"

"Hylakane's Spire. Those are wraithhawks circling above."

"Aren't those dangerous?"

Pandora shook her head. “Not to him. No idea why, or how. But I saw one land on his arm like a trained falcon once. Any other person, maetrie even, it’d suck them dry.” She frowned. “I know things have been good these last few months, but we should go back to before.”

The words were a shock to his system. “What? Why?”

Pandora reached out and touched his hand. “Not that. But we should be taking turns keeping watch at night. As we get closer to his area, we’re going to encounter others.”

“Really?”

Pandora nodded back the way they’d come. “You remember how we had to pass through the Ruby Queen’s territory while trying to leave the main city? His area is the same. His force of personality creates a gravity well that draws others in. There’s a whole settlement around his tower of sycophants, outcast maetrie that want to be trained by him, runaway dolgants, and the like.”

“Do you think he’ll remember you?”

A stiff wind whipped around the buildings, blowing her silky black hair around her face as she considered his words.

“That’s what I’m afraid of.”

Their journey over the next three days brought them closer to Hylakane’s Spire. Because of the similarities in name to the Spire in Invictus, Kuma had this idea that it would be a grand, towering building that overlooked the surrounding area like a lone sentinel.

The truth was far from this ideal, and he cursed himself for even thinking it otherwise. This part of the Eternal City had moved on long ago. Hylakane's Spire was named as such because it was the tallest building in the region that hadn't yet fallen down, but as Kuma laid his eyes upon it, he couldn't imagine that it would last much longer.

The lower half of the building was skeletal, with the steel girders and concrete pillars completely see-through, while the upper half sagged to the side suggesting its end was near. Dark shapes winged through the sky above it and trailing smoke from fires dissipated into the air around it. The smaller buildings, either created that way, or because the upper halves had already tumbled over, were lit with flame. The inhabitants of the settlement clustered around the Spire waiting for their master to show favor.

"Keep your hood up and be ready to scrap," she said when they turned onto a street that brought them directly into the thick of the settlement.

The loss of peripherals was compensated by his amber. He smelled the unwashed bodies of dolgants or vagrant maetrie even before they hit the shantytown that filled in the center of the street between the cratered buildings. Their rough language was less grating after months of hearing it and spending the travel time learning from Pandora. He could understand it better than he could speak it.

"Spotters in that metal tower on the left, and another in the building on the right," he said in a hushed tone.

"I see."

"Was it really like this when you were here last?"

Her pace slowed. "Feels different. At the edge of collapse. I don't like what that means."

His chest tightened with the thought they'd come all this way to learn that Hylakane had died or left. He knew it was foolish to place any expectations into the maetrie, especially one as esoteric as Hylakane, but hope had a way of blooming in unlikely places.

The shantytown forced them into contact with the inhabitants. Makeshift tents and huts made out of old materials lined the street, their residents sitting on dirty blankets. A maetrie woman with an arm missing and a cut on her jaw that looked recent sat on a chunk of concrete with her hand out. When Kuma looked over, she yanked down her shirt, showing an emaciated chest.

"Got anything to eat for an old woman? You can do what you want with me. Cut me, fuck me, I don't care. I'm hungry," said the one-armed maetrie woman.

Kuma found himself staring until Pandora pulled him along. "Don't linger."

"I...I wasn't expecting this," he said, pulling his cloak around his shoulders. "Couldn't they have healed her?"

"She might have lost the arm out here. Who knows why she was banished, or fled, but if you can't fight for yourself, there's no place for you in society."

Sometimes he thought humans could be cruel, but the maetrie felt like the worst excesses of his world.

A short while after the one-armed maetrie woman, a massive dolgant with no shirt and sores over his body stumbled into the street and grabbed Pandora's cloak. She spun around, slicing him across the chest. Not a deep cut, but enough to make the dolgant roar in rage. Before it could rear back and punch her, she knocked it over with a Push. Kuma stayed back while keeping an eye out for other attackers. It appeared he was the only one.

"It's like a leper colony," he said, wrinkling his nose at the unwashed bodies. While he knew they stunk as well, the stench in the area was significantly worse because it contained sickness.

A block from the entrance to the shantytown, the quality of residents improved along with the buildings. A shack with a broken unlit neon sign perched above the door read: The Golden Fist. The street continued with other buildings that had been cobbled together out of the wreckage, but this one looked more stable than the others. Kuma peered over the top to see the Spire a few blocks away.

"Yeah," said Pandora, catching his hesitation at the entrance. "Looks like as good a place as any. Better to understand what we're getting into."

A rickety door creaked upon opening, leading into a dim space lit with a couple of lanterns hanging around the area. Figures turned their direction, a mix of maetrie, dolgants, and other creatures. Kuma sensed their apprehension, anger even. A few shifted towards their hidden weapons. He wasn't sure he wanted to battle an entire bar full of enemies, but if it came to that, he was ready.

The bartender had his arms crossed when they arrived. It appeared his throat had been cut in the past and had never quite healed. The thick white scar was like a second, perverse smile around his neck.

"Go away," he said with a rough voice.

The maetrie aura briefly washed over Kuma, but after many months in the Eternal City he found it didn't hit as hard as it had when he'd first arrived.

"We're just passing through," said Pandora. "On our way to see Hylakane, the Steel Sun."

The bartender started laughing, which carried to the crowd in the Golden Fist. Within seconds, nearly the entire place was in full uproar, which made Kuma's stomach sink into his knees.

"The Steel Sun don't take no visitors no more. Not even sure the prickly bastard is even up there anymore, but no one been in the tower to check. Nor wants to. You come a long way for nothin'."

"We don't scare easy," said Pandora.

"Good for you. But it won't make a difference."

Pandora spoke to the bartender because she was fluent in their language, while Kuma examined the room further. He sensed hidden weapons being gripped tighter, nothing imminent, but with the wrong trigger, they'd be in a full-scale battle. The only being in the Golden Fist that didn't look like they wanted to kill them was a smallish figure muttering to themselves in the corner as they played with a strange device that looked like a puzzle cube with gears and shifting sections. The giggling and quiet laughter suggested the individual was flat mad and of no use to them.

"Come on," said Pandora, leading him out of the Golden Fist.

"What's the plan?" he asked outside.

"We go talk to him. Idiots are probably too scared to bother him."

The inhabited section of the area seemed to be at a distance from Hylakane's Spire. It was like a ring around the structure, placed at that spacing due to the potential collapse, or something else. They learned the reason when they cut through the burned-out buildings, crossing pockmarked streets to find a field of energy ringing the lower part. The closer they got the more it hurt Kuma's ears. A secondary ache formed in his right forearm, which made his fingers twitch. The noise was like an electrical transformer out of balance and getting ready to explode.

"That's awful," he said, squinting. "What is it?"

Pandora halted about thirty feet away. Moving any closer seemed like suicide.

"No idea. Some kind of eldritch magic. The older maetrie can do strange things with their powers. I never really understood it as they don't talk about it as not to give any advantage away."

Kuma scooped up a chunk of concrete and tossed it at the barrier. About ten feet away, a field of electricity wrapped around the solid material and turned it to dust before it reached the wall.

"Noted," he said. "Do not approach the barrier."

"Let's see if there's a gate or something," said Pandora, craning her neck at the leaning structure.

Circling the tower took them over an hour. They found no gaps, gates, or other suggested ways of entering. Discussion about leaping the barrier ended when he threw a rock high over top to see it get annihilated like the first one.

"Let's head back, see if anyone else can help us," said Pandora.

Kuma spotted him first. Blades leapt to his hands in reflex, which prompted Pandora to do the same.

"Planning on stickin' me with one of those?" said the smallish maetrie that had been in the Golden Fist. He spoke in English and wore the sleek style that Kuma recognized from the Ruby Queen's bar. His features were softer than most of the maetrie he'd met.

"Why are you following us?" asked Pandora, sliding her blades back in their sheaths.

"Not following." He wagged his eyebrows upward. "I live in this building."

Kuma surveyed the structure. It wasn't the worst in the area, but that wasn't saying much. It looked like a building that had survived a near direct strike from a missile but only the windows and doors had been blown off.

"How do you know my language?" asked Kuma, following Pandora's example.

"Your petty human tongue was quite the fashion a few centuries ago, and now it's come back. You should feel honored."

"You don't look like the rest of them," said Pandora.

"What? I have all my teeth and still bathe on occasion. I'm flattered you could tell the difference."

"Very funny. What's your name and why are you here?"

He gave a flourishing bow, extending his arms wide. "My name is Lvivsantank."

Pandora sucked air through her teeth. "How?"

The strange maetrie gave an odd smile. "A mistake, or perhaps not-mistake at my birth. Are you going to explain to your friend, Pandora Thule?"

Pandora pulled her blades again, angrily stalking forward. "How do you know my name?"

"I'm not a fool. I may be hiding out in the hinterlands, but it's by choice, not exile. Do not worry, I won't tell anyone who you are. The bigger question is why you want to see the Steel Sun."

"That's our business," spat Pandora.

"What's wrong?" asked Kuma quietly.

"It's an eleven."

"What?"

Pandora frowned. "His name. Eleven letters. It's—"

"Bad luck?" asked Kuma.

"Not really. I forget the term."

"Lucktwister," said the strange maetrie, inclining his head. "Which now that I say it in your language, I see it has eleven letters too. What a lovely coincidence."

Kuma knew about the maetrie fascination with primes, especially the number eleven, which had a fateful meaning that he couldn't quite understand.

"It's bad form to give a child a name with eleven letters. It's like tempting the fates," explained Pandora.

"Then how did it happen...?" asked Kuma, hesitating to pronounce his name.

"You can call me Jester, which I believe would be the closest translation of my name. And it happened because my mother misspoke during my naming and since she died right after, it was never corrected."

Pandora shot him a look that suggested she had reservations about talking with the unusual maetrie. With a name like Jester, he had to agree.

He was practically screaming that he would try to mislead them.

"Why are you here, Jester?" asked Kuma.

"I came to study Steel Sun, the last member of the Ebony Court and wielder of the famed weapon Zhinzi."

"Hard to study someone who won't let anyone see him," said Kuma.

"Oh, he'll let those worthy enough visit him. We've met many times over the last few years, and whenever we do, he questions me intensively about the city and the courts and what's happening in his little region of influence. Once he even let me hold Zhinzi, which was an honor I'll never forget."

"Then he will see us," said Pandora. "This isn't the first time I've met him."

Jester pursed his lips suggestively. "Do tell."

"When I was young, my grandfather sent me here to train with Hylakane, but I failed. I've come back...we've come back to seek his help."

"That's not the kind of story that's going to get you noticed," said Jester drolly.

"How do we know you're telling us the truth?" asked Kuma. "You could be lying to us about your connection to Hylakane."

"Proof is so boring," said Jester, striding between them towards the eldritch barrier of magic. "But if you desire it, this should suffice."

The smallish maetrie approached the humming barrier, walking right up to it without injury and then heading back to them.

"How did you do that?" asked Kuma.

Jester flipped up his lapel, which revealed a small circular stainless steel pin.

"He gave this to me so I could come and go safely, but we're not due for another discussion for another week, so I must amuse myself in the meantime."

"Why does he make you wait so long?" asked Pandora.

Jester shrugged. "If I knew that I wouldn't need to study him any longer. His enigma is part of the appeal. Otherwise, I probably would have gotten bored years ago." He gave a short curtsey and started heading back into the dilapidated building. "Anywho, I have things to do. Passing the time and all."

"Wait," said Pandora, hurrying after. "Can you get us an introduction? We've traveled for months to see him."

Jester paused at the corner. "I'll think about it." Before either of them could say another word, the smallish maetrie disappeared into the building.

Fifteen

Pandora found a suitable building away from the other inhabitants to make their home. The third-story space had a single workable staircase that they blocked at night and a view of the tower while still being far enough away that the humming vibration didn't drive them mad. Fresh water wasn't easy to find. They had to head to the outskirts of the old city after avoiding a small cloud of faeila that flitted around the buildings like a murmuring of starlings. A stream in what had been an old park in the former city bubbled up from the ground. Statues of famous maetrie of old littered the area, their heads knocked off or completely toppled and corroded with time.

"Do you know who they were?" asked Kuma, crouched by the stream refilling his water while keeping his eyes on the sky.

"The statues? No idea," said Pandora, making a slow revolution.

"Did you not learn them in school?" he asked.

"The maetrie aren't big on the past. Unless they're studying how someone got taken down, they don't care about the individuals themselves. The past is something the winners get to decide after they've trampled over the present."

"What about your time here?" he asked as he twisted the lid back on the bottle. "Was all this the same?"

"As far as I remember, except for the barrier around the tower. But then again, I came here in a gilded carriage protected by guards to meet a teacher who was expecting me. We never stopped in the streets and for the brief time I was here, I stayed in his spire, which looks much better on the inside, but isn't exactly a five-star luxury hotel either."

Pandora sighed as she examined their surroundings. She picked up a pebble and tossed it down the road. Reaching this place had felt like the answer to their problems, but now that they had arrived, she worried she'd misread her own past and had placed meaning into a teacher who had never wanted her as a student in the first place.

"You're tense," said Kuma from a crouched position.

"I worry this is a mistake. Hylakane barely wanted me the first time and only because of the payment from my grandfather. Why would I think he'd want me back?"

"Do you have another idea?"

Pandora launched the pebble into the overrun garden. "No."

A tickle between her shoulder blades announced the arrival of their watcher. Kuma rose to a standing position as she turned to find Jester approaching through the broken statues, tossing the pebble she'd thrown. For a brief moment, she thought she saw someone else in his stead, but her vision quickly confirmed the strange maetrie.

"Spying on us?"

"Not hard to. The two of you act like you're impervious to the dangers of the hinterlands."

"We're not without our protections," said Kuma, revealing the blade in his coat.

Jester looked out of place amid the ruins dressed in the fineries of maetrie society. His high collar and jeweled cuff links glittered without an obvious source of sunlight.

"And dressed in shadowweave that stinks of Lady Amethyte," said Jester. "Are you sure you're not assassins sent on her behalf? She's always desired to finish what she started when she sent her son to destroy the Ebony Court. I would be very cross if you eliminated my focus of study."

"I assure you that we're here on our own behalf, but you're correct, these clothes came from Lady Amethyte after a chance meeting and a contest that earned us the opportunity to leave her realm," said Pandora.

"A story I might like to hear," said Jester, mouth cocked with amusement as he leapt upon a hunk of concrete, balancing with ease.

"One I'd love to tell if you'll give us an introduction to Hylakane."

Jester flicked the pebble into the air and caught it behind his back, bowing as if he were performing before a large audience.

"In time, perhaps."

Pandora wished she had an amber to read the inscrutable Jester, but the way Kuma frowned at the strange maetrie suggested that he was a contradiction of interior thoughts.

"What would you require for this introduction?"

"Trimmings from Lady Amethyte's exquisite hair," said Jester, looking far too amused with himself.

"I thought maetrie grew more powerful and wise in time," said Kuma. "Not childish and brat-like."

"That's no way to gain my trust, human boy." His eyes glinted. "But perhaps my request is too challenging for the likes of you two. Maybe I should ask for something more immediate. Simple."

Sensing that he was playing with them, Pandora nearly left the garden, but they had nowhere else to go and Jester was their only way to gain access to Hylakane. She cursed their twisted luck that they had to deal with him.

"Near the Golden Fist lies an old courtyard that once contained a fountain where the residents drew water, but a building collapsed upon it. Remove the old concrete and steel from the fountain and I'll make that introduction to Hylakane for you."

"A fountain? Why do you care?" asked Pandora.

"If you're wondering, I've not suddenly sprung a human ethos of compassion. The return of the fountain will improve the spirits of the camp, which in turn will make my stay more pleasant. Besides, trekking to the edge of the old city for water is becoming tiresome, especially avoiding those cursed faeila that always seem to know where you're trying to go."

"Why don't *you* free the fountain?" asked Pandora.

Jester held up his gray-tinged hands. "And mar these beautiful instruments of writing? I'm a poet, not a dolgant."

"And we are?" spat Pandora.

"We'll do it," said Kuma, stepping forward and tilting his head at her.

Pandora didn't like being manipulated, but she knew Kuma was right in accepting it. It's not like they had anything else to do while they waited.

"You could at least do the honorable thing and not enjoy this so much," said Pandora as she moved towards the other area.

"What would be the fun of that?" said Jester with a smirk, bounding after them like a mischievous satyr.

He followed them back, citing the dangers of the faeila to stay together, but disappeared as soon as they neared the Golden Fist. Probably for a drink or to amuse himself with the patrons of the establishment. Using the directions he'd given them, they went to the location but only found a mound of crumbled concrete at least thirty feet high with barbs of steel sticking out at all angles like a disheveled porcupine, with no sign of the fountain beneath.

"That lying bastard," she said. "This isn't a small pile, but a fucking mountain. There's no way the fountain can be operational under all that. Fucking Lucktwister."

Kuma climbed onto the chunks, pushing his ear to the pile. After a few seconds he lifted his shoulders.

"I can hear the fountain underneath, or at least the water running. It doesn't have to be pretty, just functional."

"You want to move all this?"

Kuma peered at the mountain of concrete. "Not really, but—"

"What else do we have to do?" she finished for him.

He removed his shadowweave cloak and stripped off his shirt, laying them on a patch of unbroken concrete, but keeping his blades on his hips. With a heavy sigh, she stripped down to her smallclothes and cracked her knuckles, approaching the pile with the reluctance of Sisyphus squaring up to his boulder.

Sixteen

Vasilisa saw her first hanging two months into her station at the Machi. She wasn't told why she was being brought from the warehouse. Andelei had stuck his head around the corner, the mask of duty on his face, and told her to go to the main building where the alliance waku were stationed.

She finished her order, placing the cart near the entrance with the others, and headed across the white gravel and curved wooden bridges a few dozen strides behind her captors. Andelei walked with his fellow waku, but he glanced surreptitiously in her direction a few times with an idiotic grin on his lips. She smiled in return even though she had no feelings for him. They'd gone on a single "date" which had consisted of them sharing an apple on a boulder on the south side of the Machi and him talking about his excitement for the direction of the clan, oblivious to what that had meant for her family. But it was clear to her that he'd made himself believe that he could offer her a better life, if she was willing to be his girlfriend, a role she was only entertaining because to refuse him might be dangerous.

It wasn't the first time the gallows had been used at the main building. Other hangings had occurred during the first few months of occupation, long before Vasilisa had arrived. The entire walk she worried that Elani's role had been discovered in the resistance, which would imperil her own, but when she saw the older woman standing with the knot of other workers she allowed herself to take a breath.

The gallows, which had been erected near the main building, towered above the low roof, making it stick out. Vasilisa took a position near Elani, resisting the urge to grab the woman's hand in solidarity, not wanting to confirm more links between them.

Standing near the empty rope was the broad-shouldered maetrie in Kevlar body armor that had captured her and the rest of her clan as they tried to escape the Undercity. Titus Cabone. She hated him more than she hated the alliance waku. Probably even more than Dominion Thule himself, as he'd been the one to kill Daraja before the clan.

Vasilisa checked with the other workers, trying to figure out who was missing, but given the rotation, about half of them were new since she'd arrived. The people she immediately thought about had been moved to another area recently.

Andelei shot her another covert smile, which only made her angry because someone was going to die and he was treating it like a joke. She gave him a little wave of her hand, hating how it would make her look to the other workers. He'd been asking about another date, especially since he said he was due to be moved to either the Terreno or Big Dave's Town, but she'd managed to come up with plausible reasons that she couldn't meet him.

"Today did not need to happen," said Titus Cabone in a booming voice. "The Alliance has been good to you. Good to all of you, feeding and caring for you, giving you worthy jobs, protecting you from the denizens of the Undercity, which would happily spill your blood should we withdraw our support. Since the end of the clan wars, there has been no more pointless bloodshed, no more petty duels or honor killings. The Undercity is becoming a safer and more prosperous place, worthy of your valued lives. But not all of you see it that way. Some of you might even harbor beliefs that if you rise up together you can take back the Undercity, put it back to the fractured state that it was before Dominion Thule created order. I'm here to tell you that your ideals are misguided and there's not a chance beneath a thousand suns that this will happen."

The bulky maetrie put his fingers to his lips, whistling shrilly. Two guards appeared with a boy around her age in their arms. He was limping and looked barely put together, with two black eyes and blood soaked through his shirt. Vasilisa recognized him instantly. He was the runner that had passed her notes and she assumed had carried explosives and other contraband to other locations. The naked fear in his eyes brought a tightness to her chest as she thought about his end. The guards maneuvered the kid beneath the rope, slipping it around his neck and tightening the noose.

"Our young friend here claims he was acting alone, blowing up the mine near the wastelands with stolen explosives, and stealing faez crystals for himself with the intent of selling them when he could escape. He withstood a surprising amount of *questioning*, and while he never named any accomplices, I have my doubts. Let it be known that the next time we find someone working against the Alliance, we'll pick three others, chosen at random, to swing with the perpetrator. So if you're thinking about carrying on his mission, know you'll be caught and that you'll be sentencing others to your fate."

Titus turned away, swiping his hand downward. The guard on the gallows pulled a lever and the boy dropped fast, jerking to a stop at the end of his rope. Vasilisa flinched. A woman to her right burst into tears, while nearly everyone else watched blankly. When the hanged boy was no longer swinging, they were released to return to their duties.

Vasilisa resumed her work in the warehouse, but went through the motions like an automaton. He'd been a kid. Her age, which meant that if she screwed up they wouldn't hold back. She'd always wondered what it was like to be a waku, headed into battle, knowing that you might not walk away, and now she understood. Fear could paralyze if you let it. Thinking about the worst things that could happen only ensured that they would, but Vasilisa couldn't shake the feeling that she was headed down that same path.

Seventeen

Removing the steel and concrete from the old fountain took over a week. Their work became a curiosity to the other inhabitants, who occasionally watched from afar, shaking their heads incredulously. Pandora had argued to use her sapphire, but doing so would only endanger the fountain beneath the mound, which meant it'd taken arduous labor to remove every chunk.

When at last it was clear, Kuma leaned on the old crumbled wall, heaving with breath. His hands and arms were nicked from the rough material and a patina of sweat covered his head. Dust from their work had settled over the area, creating a thick blanket.

"Wasn't expecting it to be in such great shape," he said between breaths. "Though that doesn't help how ugly it is."

The fountain was made of a black material that seemed to absorb light. The wide base collected the water spitting from the central spout, which came out of the mouth of a horrific looking maetrie with gaunt angled features and blades for fingers. The style of clothing and modifications suggested the inspiration for the fountain had come from the distant past.

Standing in loose fabric pants and a stained sports bra, Pandora ran her hand through the murky water in the basin. She splashed some over the edge, clearly trying to remove the soot that had collected.

"This statue could be from centuries or a millennia ago," she said, catching water in cupped hands and using it to wash off her limbs.

Kuma checked over his shoulder when he heard the scuff of a foot. His blades were sitting on a blanket, not far away.

"Whoever you are, show yourself. I can hear you," he said.

A few seconds later, the well-dressed Jester appeared strolling through the wreckage with a darkwood cane under his arm. He was wearing a new outfit, which included a black top hat and bloomers.

"I guess we don't need to track you down now," said Kuma, dusting off his hands. "The fountain's clear. Might take a few days to wash out the basin, but you can collect water straight from the spout."

Jester ignored his comments and made his way to the fountain, looking up into the horrid expression.

"Nasty fellow. Some say we maetrie never change, but this fountain is proof of that. He looks like something out of a human nightmare," said Jester.

"Not a maetrie nightmare?"

"We don't dream, thus no nightmares," said Jester, running his fingers through the water as Pandora stared at him. "Which probably explains our fortunes as we cannot have hope like you pathetic humans."

"We finished your job, Lucktwister," said Pandora, who wasn't looking in the mood for conversation. "Time to pay up and speak to Hylakane for us."

"Oh," he said, dropping the cane from under his arm and catching it deftly. He swung it around like Charlie Chaplin, placing the end on Pandora's chest. "He remembers you. The scared little girl who couldn't complete even the simplest of tasks."

"He wanted me to walk through a field of wraithhawks. I wouldn't have lasted ten seconds once they got a hold of me," said Pandora.

Jester spun on his heel, pointing to Hylakane's Spire where dozens of wraithhawks roosted on the upper floors. Their shadowy figures could be seen as a blotch of negative light.

"Clearly the old man knows a trick or two, or he would have been sucked dry a long time ago."

"Well he didn't impart those secrets to me," she said angrily, pacing away from the fountain. Pandora halted midstep, shaking her head. "Or

I was too young to understand."

"Stop messing with us," said Kuma. "Does he want to meet us or not?"

Jester tipped the top hat from his head, flourishing it briefly before tossing it into the air and letting it land back on his crown.

"I'm really quite good at this," said Jester. "Maybe I could teach you both how to be both dashing and elegantly refined at the same time. It's a wonder that I can accomplish both. Truly marvelous. A worthy audience would have applauded already, but you two bores are completely devoid of interesting qualities."

The flippant way Jester addressed them brought anger up from Kuma's depths.

"Or maybe we're really fucking tired from ten days of hauling stone from a creepy old fountain and were expecting you to honor your part of the bargain."

"Which I have. But—"

"But what?" asked Kuma.

Jester rolled his eyes as he hobbled forward in faux injury. "Hylakane isn't quite sure he wants to talk to you. He has an inkling that you want him to train you again and doesn't think you're up to the task this time either."

The strange maetrie was inscrutable. Kuma's amber gave him only a faint impression of frivolous whimsey, rather than any deep read, which was rather unusual. He was used to sensing intentions more clearly.

"Liar," spat Pandora. "You didn't talk to him. I'm not even sure you can really get into his area. Whatever we saw before was a trick, wasn't it? I don't know how or why, but you're not being honest with us."

The edges of her Push made Jester stumble backwards. "Isn't that rude after I completed my half of the bargain."

"Pandora," said Kuma before she angered Jester further. He held his hands out, keeping them unmoving until she looked like she was backing down. When she relented, crossing her arms and sulking, he asked, "What else did he have to say? Or was that it?"

Jester eyed Pandora as if she were a snake that might strike again, backing away and holding his cane before him like a shield.

"He had a small request—"

Pandora stomped forward. "I knew it! He's lying to us."

"Let him finish," pleaded Kuma.

Jester held out his hands. "I believe he wants to know if you've improved enough to be trained again. That was my impression. It could be wrong, or very right. Who knows? But I know he's a hard man who listens only to his own counsel. Defying him won't get you anywhere."

Pandora growled as she stalked to Jester with fists at her sides. "What is it?"

Jester's pinched expression suggested an onerous task as he hesitated to answer, rare uncertainty from the strange maetrie.

"Hylakane, The Steel Sun, wielder of the famed Zhinzi, one of the eleven tears of the gods, requests that you prove your worthiness by capturing the cloud of faeila that haunts the city with your bare hands."

As soon as Jester finished speaking, he leapt nimbly away before Pandora could strike him, apologizing profusely as he dodged through the piles of concrete. When it was only the two of them, Pandora frowned.

"What do we do? Clearly he's trying to get rid of us. Or do you think Jester is lying? Making fun of us, or getting us to do stupid tasks as a way to entertain himself all the way out here?" asked Kuma.

Pandora had her eyes pinched closed. She looked like a spring at maximum tension and turned slowly, showing her scarred back, which looked like she'd slept on a wicker mat.

"We have to catch the cloud."

"How?" he asked.

Shadows passed across her eyes. "I haven't the faintest idea."

"Is there no clue from when you were here last? He wouldn't ask this unless it was possible. It's possible, right?"

He heard the panic in his own tone. If Hylakane had no interest in training them, but didn't want to say so, then he might place impossible tasks before them, letting their failures be his answer. Pandora didn't answer, letting her silence rise up like a tomb until Kuma wondered if they'd ever escape the Eternal City.

Eighteen

The tunnel was low and narrow, winding though the rock as if a meandering worm had eaten its way through. Choo-Choo crawled behind Tick, who'd taken the lead due to his smaller size. The stench of body odor from up close was the least of his worries. Choo-Choo kept banging the back of his head and the curve of his back against the sharp ceiling, cursing under his breath at each bump. Most of the inhabited caverns in the Undercity existed on the same plane for reasons of geology and magic that had never been satisfyingly explained to Choo-Choo, but some existed outside of those parameters, but they were harder to navigate and more prone to hold strange and dangerous critters, which was why Tick was in front with his tiger's eye. He'd already chased a knot of glistening black spiders away.

"Fuck me," cursed Choo-Choo as he cracked his head against the stone for the umpteenth time.

"You've got to be the clumsiest waku in the Undercity right now," said Yara from behind.

"I'm not clumsy, I'm big. You try fitting these shoulders through these gaps."

"That's why I'm behind and Tick is ahead," said Yara. "In case we have to drag you through a narrow section."

"If I get stuck, please leave me for a few days while I take a nap. These reverse ambushes are getting old."

They'd intended to hit one of the patrols near the wastelands south of Big Dave's Town, but Tick had sniffed out an ambush. There were nearly twenty members of the patrol lurking behind a wall, waiting for their attack.

"I'm just glad we have Tick and Koro, or we'd be dead a long time ago," said Yara.

Choo-Choo had his head turned, so he wasn't paying attention to what was ahead until he ran into Tick's leg.

"What did you say, Yara? Was that a compliment? You couldn't do this without me?" asked Tick from the front.

"Fuck," said Yara. "I should have known you'd hear me. Don't let it go to your head. You're still the brat that put spiders in my bra, and hid in the shower to get a peek at me when I was naked."

"I did not hide in the shower. I had a boner that wouldn't quit and couldn't leave until it'd gone down. It wasn't my fault that you were early."

Choo-Choo nudged Tick with his hand. "Come on. I'm dying to stretch out at camp. I'm even thirsty enough to drink one of those disgusting watermelon chili fizzies that we stole last week."

"You're welcome to let me have them all if you don't like them."

"I don't, but they're something different than bug-infested rock water," said Choo-Choo.

"Hey, we're almost here."

Tick climbed out of the tunnel into a cavern that was a little east of their camp. But the diminutive waku didn't move out of the way, prompting Choo-Choo to tug on his ankle.

"Let me out. I'm tired of crawling."

"Hush," said Tick, intently focused ahead. His flying snake, Koro, was nowhere to be seen, which meant she was scouting. Tick dropped into a crouch and motioned for Choo-Choo to make room in the hole, after which he crawled back inside feet first.

"What's wrong?" whispered Choo-Choo.

"They found our camp. Two dozen alliance are arrayed in the cavern, waiting for us to show up."

Choo-Choo let his head rest against the stone. He was tired. Exhausted. Sick of sleeping on stone and eating crickets for dinner when they were between ambushes.

"How do they keep finding us?" he asked aloud.

"They had a creature with them that looked like a cross between an anteater and a wolfhound."

"Seeing through Koro's eyes again?"

"It was fleeting, but enough. I'll deal with the migraine later," said Tick.

"What are we going to do now?" asked Yara.

"They're tracking us by smell," said Tick.

"We need to hold off on ambushes for a while. Find a place we can hole up and wait for them to get bored," said Choo-Choo.

"Where? If they can track us, then it's going to be hard to find food."

"I have an idea, but it's not going to be easy. I think we should return to the Terreno. After carefully scrubbing our scents before we reach it, of course, but we need a place where we can eat and sleep for a while without the danger of being caught."

"The Terreno?" asked Yara. "There are tons of alliance waku that visit all the time. We'd get caught for sure."

"I don't think so. Not if we have someone else bring us food and water. Help us stay out of sight."

"Leesa," said Tick.

"If she's still okay," said Choo-Choo. "It's been months since we've seen her. There's a chance we make it back only to find she's gone, or things are different, but I'm willing to take the chance. Are you two in?"

"You had me at sleeping in a bed and not having to scrap for my food," said Tick.

"I don't have a better idea, so yes," said Yara.

"Great. Now let's crawl back out the other way," said Choo-Choo.

After an arduous traverse they made it back into the regular caverns. Choo-Choo made them strip and bathe in the cold stream that ran towards the wastelands in hopes of reducing their stench before they traveled the tunnels. Under normal circumstances, trekking to the Terreno should have taken them less than an hour, but they moved at a glacial pace and tracked through multiple streams to hide their passage.

Five hours later, Choo-Choo stepped into the tunnel that led into the back of Club Onyx. He was relieved to find the door to the back unlocked, but his mind quickly conjured ill-fated reasons. He placed his ear against the wood, sighing with relief when he heard the nasally sound of someone singing karaoke on stage.

He brought them into the supply closet, which was stuffed with mop buckets, cleaning supplies, and other maintenance goods. A cylindrical water heater hummed.

"Might as well get comfortable. Not going to be able to do anything until it's closed," Choo-Choo told them, finding a corner for himself.

Choo-Choo didn't remember falling asleep, but he woke to the sound of silence, fearing he'd missed his chance to talk to someone in the club. As he climbed to his feet, his friends woke as well, Tick looking particularly disoriented.

"I haven't slept that good in...I can't remember," said Tick.

"Where's Koro?" asked Yara as she stretched her arms.

Alarm bells rang in Choo-Choo's mind when he noticed the door to the closet was slightly ajar.

"Did anyone open that?"

Tick startled upright. "It was hot in here. But I don't remember, unless I did it in my sleep. I was pretty out of it."

Choo-Choo produced his blades and stuck his head out the closet door, checking the area behind the stage where extra equipment, old dresses hung on wardrobe racks, and portable karaoke machines waited. He sensed quiet murmuring in the main area. Only female voices.

"Be prepared to run," said Choo-Choo over his shoulder.

When he stuck his head out from the door next to the stage, he found a cluster of hostesses by the bar cooing over something around Leesa's neck. She wore a glittering black dress with silver edging and had the air of a woman in charge. It wasn't until he stepped into the interior that he realized it was Koro around Leesa's neck.

"Emilio!" she said, waving.

His heart jackrabbited around in his chest as he extended his senses to check for others. He glanced to the private rooms, which brought a headshake from Leesa.

"It's okay. It's only us," she said, stroking the snake's head gently.

"Koro?" asked Tick as he stumbled into the light.

"She came out a short time ago while we were cleaning up. Caused a stir but I remembered her. She's a sweetie."

Tick stretched his arms out and the winged snake slithered over to his shoulders, where he hugged the reptile to his neck.

"She's welcome to visit me anytime," said Leesa. "Would someone grab them a drink? They look like they could use one."

"Is it safe?" asked Choo-Choo, finding it hard to relax around others.

"We closed an hour ago. I lock the door each night after we've swept the club for stragglers. That's how we found you in the supply closet. I left the door open because it was hotter than Hades in there, and I guess Koro came out to explore."

A crystalline glass of reddish-amber liquid was shoved into his hand. The burn as it went down his throat soothed his chest, helped him breathe again.

"Wow. That's better than sex."

Leesa bunched up her lips. "You three look like hell."

"We've been living at the edges for months, but our luck is finally catching up to us. They tracked us to our camp. We need a place to lay low for a while."

"You're always welcome here. The ladies and I won't forget what you did," said Leesa, taking a drink from her glass.

"It didn't get you in trouble?"

"A little, but when we threatened not to work and close down the Onyx, they backpedaled. It helped we still looked pretty beat up when they came to collect the corpses."

Choo-Choo glanced between his feet, remembering the scrap and looking for old blood.

"What's been going on?" asked Yara as she clutched the glass of whiskey to her chest.

Leesa ushered them to a booth after instructing the others to reopen the kitchen. She went on to explain how the alliance had been consolidating control of the Undercity, bringing in new recruits, expanding their mining operations by taking people from the city above and putting them to work. The three major business areas—the Terreno, Big Dave's Town, and Lazona—were back to normal and Dominion was using them to entertain new business partners. During the explanation, someone brought out a few plates containing teriyaki pork skewers and fried crickets, which were devoured in a matter of seconds. The longer she spoke, the more disheartened Choo-Choo became as he realized they were doing very little against the alliance.

"They're recruiting faster than we can kill them," said Choo-Choo, sucking the sticky teriyaki from his fingers.

"It explains why their patrols have gotten so much larger," said Yara.

Leesa's forehead rippled with concern. "I'm not going to lie to you. While I know the alliance clan members are scared shitless about running into the three of you in the shadows, they also believe it's only a matter of time before they catch you. I heard Deacon himself talk about how they were going to find you sooner rather than later."

Yara nearly came out of the booth. "Deacon? When? What was he doing?"

The conversation had been subdued up until that point, but Leesa seemed genuinely upset when they brought up his name.

"I didn't know him well from before. He wasn't in Razor long enough for me to get a good read on him, but he wasn't that much different than the rest of you. Now?" She gave a tiny shudder. "If I never have to be around him again, I'll be happy."

"Why?" asked Choo-Choo.

Leesa took a long drink from her glass and set it down too hard, rattling the ice.

"I heard they'd sent him to the Eternal City for training. But that ain't just training. He's different. Colder. More maetrie like. His eyes are ringed with shadows. They say he doesn't laugh or joke anymore. When he was here, it was only to evaluate the club. He didn't interact with the girls, or sing karaoke. I've heard enough whispers from his waku that he's faster than sin. A younger up-and-coming waku tried to challenge him to a duel. They say he dismantled him so fast that no one had a chance to blink before it was over. No one saw that young waku again."

The news brought Yara back to earth. She sat quietly against the back of the booth, staring into the middle distance. Choo-Choo put a hand on her leg.

"We'll find a way to get him back. Everyone is beatable."

The look from Leesa wasn't encouraging, but she was deft enough not to say anything further. Choo-Choo cradled his drink and tried not to think about how fruitless their efforts were.

"It's over, isn't it? They won, we lost. I feel like we're swimming against a tsunami."

"Until it hits the shore, a tsunami doesn't look like anything more than a regular wave," said Leesa.

"Thanks, but you know what I mean."

"Despite what you think, you're doing a lot. We always hear the alliance talk about you three. You know what they call you?"

Choo-Choo sat up with the others.

"They call us something?" asked Tick, grinning. "I hope it's cool." When Yara hit his leg, he said, "If we're gonna die, I at least want to know that we were memorable."

"The Ghost Shadows."

"The Ghost Shadows?" asked Choo-Choo. "What kind of name is that?"

"If you heard them say it, you'd hear fear in their voices." She smirked. "But now that you mention it, it does sound kind of ridiculous."

Tick spun his glass around in his hands. "Ghost Shadows? That'd be like the Wizard Mage, or the Samurai Ninja." He let his forehead dip down until it was resting on the table. "We let these assholes beat us. It's almost worse."

"The problem is, we'll never be able to do anything in the Undercity," said Choo-Choo.

"They don't know your names, or at least not that I've heard," said Leesa. "That's why they use that name."

"Small mercies," said Yara.

Leesa offered a hesitant smile. "What are your plans now? I was kinda surprised it took this long for you to return."

"We're hoping for some help in hiding out. We're tired, hungry, thirsty—"

"Stinky," said Leesa.

"Stinky," agreed Choo-Choo. "And we need time to figure out what we're doing next. But we can't do that running around avoiding alliance patrols. We need a place to hide and rest." He threw a small bag on the table filled with the stones they'd collected from the waku they'd killed.

"We have these as payment if you need cash."

Leese stared at the bag skeptically. "Those are useless to me. If they found out I was selling them, they'd think I was somehow stealing from the mines, or in league with you. Those are a death sentence. You might as well take them back, save them for someone who can help you." She cocked her mouth to the side. "You know you've inspired others to sabotage the alliance."

Choo-Choo almost had his glass to his mouth when he let it drop. "We have?"

Leesa nodded enthusiastically. "There've been explosions at mines, soldados showing up dead, other acts of rebellion. A lot of it's attributed to the Ghost Shadows, but it happens all over and I know you three aren't everywhere at once. In fact, as far as I can tell, you've stayed to the northeast quadrant of the Undercity."

"If you could figure that out, no wonder we've been having trouble," said Choo-Choo, shaking his head.

"But I can help," said Leesa. "There's an old room up top that had a water leak last year and part of the roof collapsed. It's been fixed since, but we haven't needed the extra room since because there haven't been any new girls brought in. It's yours but you have to promise me that you'll do everything I say. This is my club now and I'm in charge of protecting everyone. If you get caught, they'll kill everyone in the club. It's a fate those girls don't deserve."

"We agree," said Choo-Choo.

"I need to hear it from Yara," said Leesa, lips tight. "I'm sorry. I know your temper. Can you control it? Don't make these women pay for helping you."

Yara stared back as if she'd been punched in the gut. She gave a slow nod.

"I'll control it."

"Good. Thank you," said Leesa, placing her hand on Yara's and giving it a squeeze. "I know it's a lot."

"Thanks, Leesa. You're a lifesafer, literally."

She let out a quivering sigh. "There's one other thing that I think you might want to know. But you can't go rushing off, because it's old news and it might not be correct anymore."

The way Leesa looked at him made Choo-Choo sit forward. "What?"

"Do you promise not to act rash?"

"I promise."

"I think I know where your mother is."

Choo-Choo's entire body tensed up. Despite his promise and without knowing her exact location, he wanted to rush out of the hidden passage in search of her. Triana and Vasy were the only reasons he'd continued the resistance, long after reason faltered.

"Where?"

Leesa's mouth wrinkled. "Like I said, I don't know if it's valid anymore. It's just something I heard from one of the soldados who visited the Onyx. If you give me time, I can confirm if that's where she's at currently, but you have to follow my lead. I don't want my girls to lose their lives because you rushed off without proper consideration."

"It's my mother," he pleaded.

"And I knew exactly where the three of you idiots were operating out of without stepping into a single cavern. Do you think you'll continue to survive out there if you don't stop rushing into danger?"

He forced the tightness in his chest to relax. "You're right, as much as I hate to admit. Our early successes made us blind to their adjustments."

Leesa put a hand on his arm. "I promise. Once I can verify where she's at and how you can get her out, I'll let you know. But until then, stay here, heal up, relax a little." She cocked a smile. "And please, for all our sakes, take a shower."

Nineteen

Acquiring enough fabric took them a week. It wasn't like there was a regular supply route from the main city to the hinterlands. They'd had to barter with the locals, trading labor or food that they'd caught. A few, like an older maetrie woman who lived in a makeshift hovel, handed over a roll of extra fabric she had stashed as thanks for them unburying the fountain.

"An old woman like me doesn't like to travel that far, especially when faeila are in the air," she'd told them. It was one of the few times that Kuma had seen an older maetrie as a matronly grandmother rather than a cruel elder race. He wondered if not all the maetrie were the same, but given her status as an outcast, he assumed that those that went against the grain were a small minority.

"Do you really think this is going to work?" asked Pandora from his right. The sound of her voice was muffled from the wrappings. He turned slowly, the thick fabric around his legs making movement stiff.

"You look like a desert raider who got stung by a thousand bees," she told him.

He chuckled from beneath the wrappings. "I've never been so turned on before. All your ambiguous shapes and lumpy limbs."

"We could give the phrase bumping uglies a real run for its money," she said.

"When I was a young boy, on the cusp of training to be a soldado, my mother found me crying behind the house. I told her I was worried about becoming a warrior like them, because what they could do seemed so extreme, so powerful, I thought they must have some secret supernatural heritage that hadn't been passed along to me.

"She smiled, kissed me on the forehead, and explained the secret to training. Start simple, grow more complex in time. It's not like it was the first time I'd heard that, but then she took me to the open area nearby and pulled out two short rods. She set them on the ground about a foot apart and told me to jump over them. Which I did. Then she moved one an inch further apart. She kept moving them until I could no longer jump over the two rods. Then she told me to train every day, leaping over the gap, and making it slightly wider when I was successful."

The lumpy form of Pandora touched him on the shoulder. He didn't feel it but he saw her extend her arm.

"That's sweet, Kuma, but how's that going to help us when it comes to the faeila? It's not like they're friendly butterflies looking for a place to land."

"That's it. I don't know. Just like I didn't know how to jump five feet back then, but by the time I was in the Academy, I could jump further. Much further."

"The first thing is we have to find them." She wobbled forward. "I'm just glad we waited until we got here to wrap ourselves like mummies."

They ambled around the area they'd previously gotten water from, as the locals said it was the place they were most likely to encounter the faeila. He'd seen them a few times from a distance, usually flitting through the buildings or circling wide through the sky. From a distance the faeila could be quite beautiful, especially as they caught the light that somehow slipped through the ceiling of dark clouds, creating a scintillating burst of rainbow colors before fading to black.

"Shall we wait or walk?"

Kuma craned his neck to get a view of the upper skeletal buildings with vines clinging to their empty structures. He nearly tipped over, but caught himself with a jammed back right foot.

"I'd be afraid of the consequences of trying to move around. Besides, this area, besides the faeila, is safer due to the frequent visits from the locals," he said.

The layered fabrics grew unbearable over time. While the Eternal City was never really too cold or too warm, the cocoon of materials had Kuma drenched in sweat after hours of standing around. Whenever he had the urge to tear it off, he imagined Duro or Brazio chastising him for giving up so easily.

"Kuma," Pandora said, low and intense.

He immediately scanned the skies where she faced, catching the glint of movement. The shifting cloud moved in a schooling manner, ebbing and flowing through the air. Bulges of the flying critters expanded before the rest caught up as they shifted between the buildings.

His heart rate increased as he waited for the faeila to notice them. The cloud passed through the windowless buildings, dancing around the square, but never indicating they might come down.

"Should we do something?" he asked.

Pandora's answer was given as a heavy Push that knocked over a fragile stone wall, the moss-covered rocks tumbling over each other. The cloud darted towards them like an arrow. Kuma's confidence in his plan dropped precipitously and he reached to his face to confirm the piece of glass he'd installed as a pair of makeshift goggles would protect his eyes. When the cloud hit, he felt like they'd been caught in a chittering dust storm. His previous interactions with the faeila had been from a distance, or from behind a door as Pandora groaned in agony. The living pieces of glass surrounded them in a cyclone, searching for exposed flesh. Their dire beauty had him transfixed. Kuma held out his arm, which initially took damage as the passing critters tore holes in the fabric, but a single faeila landed on his curled hand, flexing its colored wings. The resemblance to a butterfly was unmistakable, except the faeila was made of razor-sharp glass that would flay his skin if he tried to touch it. Kuma opened his palm, hoping to coax the creature, but it released itself into the air to join the rest of its brethren, and a few seconds later, the cloud moved on, shifting towards the sky having satisfied its curiosity that there was nothing to destroy.

"Was that what you were hoping for?" she asked when they were alone.

"I...don't know."

Pandora approached him. "Your outer layer is a little shredded. No skin showing, but we'll need to repair it for next time."

§

The next few weeks were spent as motionless mummies waiting for the cloud to notice them. Each day, they managed to coax the creatures to visit them a few times, surrounding them like an angry swirl of razor-sharp death. Their outer layers had to be repaired frequently, as the attentions of the faeila were destructive.

Kuma grew discouraged as they failed to make progress. He'd hoped the faeila over time might see them as less threatening and roost on their protected limbs, but they continued to attack them until they were satisfied that they couldn't be hurt before winging back into the sky. It was a stalemate of sorts. Kuma began to hate wrapping himself in the stinky, holey fabric each day. To her credit, Pandora never complained, and only occasionally offered suggestions.

"Start simple, but grow more complex over time," said Kuma with a sigh. "It sounded reasonable, but now I don't know. Maybe this is a mistake. Maybe there's no way to capture a cloud of faeila with our bare hands."

"I saw Hylakane himself with wraithhawks roosted on his arms," said Pandora.

"Was it a trick?"

Pandora shook her head. "Would you ever accuse Duro or your uncle of tricks?"

"Good point." He leaned against the partially standing wall. "We can give up if you want. This feels like a waste of time."

"I believe in you, Kuma. I think your plan is good, but maybe we're missing something. Let's keep going."

His chest was tight but he nodded agreement.

§

They saw the cloud make a kill a few days later. Pandora had suggested they move to a nearby clearing between the buildings to change things up. There was a concrete platform and old pillars without a roof that suggested a pavilion in the distant past. Kuma imagined angry young maetrie rallying their peers against the atrocities of the Courts, but he knew he was projecting his human ideals upon the city elves.

The killing started with a shriek of pain. Between the unstable buildings covered in plant material, Kuma spotted a figure running down the street looking over his shoulder. It was a bare-chested dolgant with an iron bar in his fist. Kuma expected to see the cloud of faeila in pursuit, but when a dark shape swooped out of the nearby building, passing over the dolgant and making him cry out again, Kuma realized it was a wraithhawk on the hunt. He started to move forward to help, but Pandora put her hand out, stopping him.

"Not unless you want to join him. And I'm not sure we could reach him in time."

The dolgant turned for the second pass, swinging the iron bar at the wraithhawk, but the weapon went right through the shadowy creature. The dolgant stumbled, casting about for another escape route, which he found by running through the open building to another street. The maneuver confused the wraithhawk, which landed on an old lamppost, its black head turning slowly and silently like a sentinel.

Kuma's chest started to unwind as he thought the dolgant had made a valiant escape, but then he caught the shifting colored light careening around the corner.

"Oh, what bad luck," said Pandora.

The dolgant, oblivious to the faeila, stumbled out of the building right into the cloud's path. The end was not so kind. Kuma was relieved that they were too far away to see the details of the gruesome death but the horrifying cries were enough to give him nightmares for a time.

§

Kuma's patience had become thin and ragged. While he'd learned to stand motionless for hours at a time in the Undercity while on guard duty, the frustrations of their task burned bright in his mind. When the faeila cloud winged away from them for the umpteenth time, Kuma couldn't bear to face another failure.

"Shadows below," he cursed, using the wrapped fingers of his left hand to grab an edge of cloth that had been exposed, ripping off the outer layers until only a thin piece remained.

"Kuma," said Pandora, sensing what he was about to do.

"I have to try something."

Kuma borrowed Pandora's sapphire to send a gentle Push after the cloud, catching the trailing edge. The creatures bunched up defensively, becoming a ball of swirling razor-sharp death, then shot back at him with a vengeance. He steeled himself for the impact, using Heavy to restrain himself as he calmed his mind, thinking of the exercise as a bit of training that Duro had dreamt up to test him.

The faeila bounced off his chest harmlessly, as if they'd run into a cushioned mattress, but then circled him. He held up his arm, where the fist-sized hole in his protective shell had been whittled down to a single layer of fabric.

The faeila were attracted to the movement, pounding themselves against his arm to find a way through the cloth. A big faeila with the colors of a rainbow dipped in ink found the almost-exposed section. Sharp feet bit through the cloth, but he fought against a reaction, reminding himself that he'd invited the faeila to return and shouldn't begrudge them their desires.

The deep cut sent blood dripping into the cloth, collecting around his forearm. The big faeila tested other parts of his flesh, the thin cloth providing no protection. Kuma kept his mind calm and his arm steady. The creature continued creating slices either by accident or attention, while Kuma focused on the beauty of the living glass attached to his arm.

He heard the rip of fabric behind him, which suggested Pandora had followed his lead. With mincing steps, Kuma rotated until he could see her. A cluster of faeila had landed on the thinner area, blood blooming through the fabric. Pandora's eyes were white with fright, but she maintained an outer calmness. He wanted to console her as he knew how painful the touch of the faeila were not only physically, but as a reminder of her brutal past.

As she blinked heavily and her breath grew more shallow, he knotted his forehead, trying to get her attention. When they matched gazes, he tried to will her to relax, and after a few heartbeats she began to breathe normally again. Pandora gave him a curt nod, signaling she'd regained her composure.

After a minute of painful examination, the big faeila on his arm settled and the wings stopped flitting maddingly. Kuma used the moment to slide his arm towards his chest so he could examine the creature closer. It didn't fly away, leaving Kuma enraptured by the glinting light. He picked out tiny veins in the colored glass, shifting with what he could only imagine as a kind of silica blood. As he thought about caressing the faeila's glossy wings to understand their makeup, the creature burst away from his arm and the cloud rose with it, ascending into the sky and catching a beam of unseen light, glittering with strange and fell beauty.

§

The faeila didn't come back that day, requiring a return to solidify the idea that Kuma had settled upon as a method of subduing the dangerous faeila. Using a different part of his arm, he coaxed the creatures to land, keeping his mind and heart as calm as a lake on a day with no wind.

After the initial bloody investigation, the small knot of faeila stopped their beating wings and preened themselves in the city air. Their silent communion lasted longer than the day before and ended with a great lifting into the sky.

Start small and grow more complex with time. The saying from his mother was the beating heart of their exercise. Day by day they stripped away their outer layer, allowing more and more faeila to land on them. They met the end of each encounter with nicks and cuts, blood oozing from the wounds, but despite the increased number, their injuries were not growing in size.

By the sixth week, Kuma had his entire left arm exposed upon their arrival with only a thin layer of cloth across the rest of his body. Only his head and eyes remained protected completely. The faeila had come to expect their visits, arriving not long after them, taking their roost for a few minutes of quiet contemplation and then winging back to the skies in search of less willing prey.

Until that point, Kuma wasn't sure what it was exactly that was helping with progress. His first real clue came on a day that a small creature called a knavth—it reminded him of a jackrabbit with tiger stripes and fangs that stuck out its elongated mouth—came to investigate the pavilion right before the faeila cloud returned to the sky. He tensed up as he saw the creature come out from behind the broken pillar and his sudden internal change was rewarded with a bout of new pain as the faeila roosting on his exposed arm dug their feet into his flesh. He nearly cried out, which would have been a mistake, drawing others to him, but he focused on his breathing and forced himself to forget the pain.

The faeila made quick work of the knavth, leaving a bloody hunk of meat where it'd been caught. After the glassy critters returned to the sky,

Kuma examined his arm, which was marred with numerous small slices.

Pandora stood over the unfortunate knavth, a frown hooked to her lips. "Did you notice they flew away the moment it died? As if they could no longer feed on its pain."

He rolled the idea around in his head before replying. "Then why'd they leave the day they tore into your side?"

Her mouth hung open briefly. "I don't know. Maybe those were different because they were in the Ruby Queen's territory, while these are wild and untamed."

§

Many months after they entered the broken buildings, wrapping themselves in a cocoon of borrowed linens, they returned to the Golden Fist with their arms covered in fluttering faeila. Kuma entered first. All eyes fell upon them, followed by a collective in-breath. The rest of the cloud had fluttered away once they reached the cluttered avenue, but the few dozen that remained put fear in their hearts.

"What madness is this?" said the bartender in his gravelly voice as he backed away from the serving counter.

The terror in their eyes seemed foreign to Kuma after endless days of meditation on the pavilion, letting the faeila roost upon their exposed flesh. His skin was nicked with scars, but there was no blood today on either him, or Pandora.

The patrons of the bar reached for their weapons but none made a move to pull them out, clearly fearing an attack of the razor-sharp creatures. From the shadows of a dark corner rose the well-dressed Jester in a purple coat. He set the strange puzzle cube onto the table and approached tentatively, showing more fortitude than the others.

"I'd wondered if you'd returned to the aphena." His black eyes flitted over the faeila as he raised his hand as if he might try to touch one, a smile held firmly in his teeth. "But it appears you've been busy."

"You'll tell him what you've seen."

"Show him yourself," said Jester with a curt laugh.

"We don't know if he's in there."

"I'm sure he is doing things that maetrie like him do, being mystical and obtuse, a real pain in the arse."

Jester lunged towards them and the faeila burst away, flying chaotically through the bar as its patrons shouted and waved their hands to keep them away until they escaped through the openings that served as open windows. Once the creatures were gone, the patrons cursed Jester, but made no move to physically rebuke him.

Despite the sabotage, Kuma didn't find himself enraged like the others. Time with the faeila had taught him an internal calmness he never thought possible. The same was true for Pandora, whose past had made the interaction more difficult, because it reminded her of the brutal lessons her mother had forced her to endure when she was a child.

"You'll speak to him as soon as possible."

Jester's eyes creased with mirth. The expected quip wasn't offered. Instead the strange maetrie bowed deeply with an extravagant flourish and skipped out of the Golden Fist, leaving him with the meager hope that they might finally get to see Hylakane, the Steel Sun.

Twenty

Club Onyx became their home and prison for the next few months as Leesa tried to chase down the location of Choo-Choo's mother and sister using her network of information. Yara relished the comforts of the private room above the club, even as the noise from the endless karaoke and the return of the next-door pachinko parlor made relaxing during most hours difficult.

Tick, to her surprise, was the least annoying of her companions as he read the endless supply of romance novels that the hostesses provided while his flying snake, Koro, lounged around his neck or hunted mice in the back rooms. Choo-Choo, on the other hand, never seemed to be able to relax, twitching all day until the evening when the Onyx closed and he could question Leesa about any news, which never proved fruitful.

Yara spent her time practicing with her stones, doing endless push-ups, or watching out the tinted window at the scenes in the Terreno. The place had returned to its former glory, the streets filled with alliance members sampling the delights offered. The fresh-faced waku that strutted around the streets with their chests puffed out, stones prominently displayed in their ears or even some on their nose or lip, made her sick to her stomach that they'd been overtaken by them. They had neither the discipline nor the honor that had once existed in the Undercity.

When the Onyx was closed, Yara liked to spend time in club drinking with the hostesses as they unwound from their long shift. Most of them had been around before the alliance takeover, so they spent their time drinking heavily and complaining about the waku having no respect for the old ways. Yara found it relaxing to listen to their grievances, pouring whiskey and saying almost nothing.

After a particularly rough day when a couple of soldados had gotten into a fistfight over who was next for karaoke and had knocked one of the hostesses off the stage, giving her a bloody nose, Leesa returned from the back with a worn expression and plopped next to Yara in the booth. Tick was on stage singing tunes popularized by Ashnod's Theater, and Choo-Choo was behind the bar serving drinks for the hostesses.

"Fuck me, this job gets worse every day," said Leesa, putting her fingers to her temples and massaging. "Sometimes I wish I'd fled when the alliance took over. Took a job in the light. Switched careers instead of being babysitters to waku who don't know the first thing about their own stones. I've got a whole wall to repair 'cause a dumbass waku who just got his topaz the day before put his head through the back, nearly taking out a support beam. Fucking wayhos."

Yara listened intently while putting new ice in Leesa's glass and pouring whiskey until it was nearly full. Leesa stared suspiciously at the offer, before scooping it up and draining half of it.

"When did you become *our* hostess?"

The thought had been one Yara had been mulling for weeks, never really settling on any one answer, but Leesa's words made it harden in her mind.

"I guess for the first time in my life I'm not trying to prove anything to anyone, or have some big purpose. I know eventually we're going to get back out there. We need to find Triana and Vasy at the very least, but after that, I don't know."

"What about Deacon?"

"I hate him with every inch of my being, but it's hard to maintain that anger when you never see him. I also worry that he outclasses me now."

"Caution and restraint from Yara Santos? I never thought I'd see the day," said Leesa with a wry smirk, holding out her glass.

Yara clinked hers against it, throwing back a mouthful of whiskey and relishing the warmth as it traveled down to her belly.

"I've never not had something to do. I've always been training or preparing for something big. Throwing myself at every new problem in the same way my father did, never believing myself good enough. Now that I've had all this time to myself, I'm wondering what I'm actually doing anymore. With no clan, no family left, not even my asshole cousin, I don't know who I am."

Leesa put her hand overtop. "I'm your family."

Yara nodded tightly, not daring to speak for a few moments. "I want to help Choo-Choo find his family, but after that? I don't know. Maybe I'll leave the Undercity, find a new life." She lowered her voice. "Don't tell the others but part of me wants to join the alliance, if only to have that structure that I didn't realize I craved. When one clan knocked out another, the survivors would swear to the new one. Is this so different?"

Leesa searched her with her eyes, the corners rounded with sympathy.

"I'm not actually serious," said Yara. "For one, I'd never let Deacon have the satisfaction, and I still want to put my blade in his chest, but you know, it'd be nice to have that feeling back. I never realized how much the clan defined me. Whether it was Razor, or Drops. To think, Choo-Choo was my enemy for as long as we were alive, and then we were clanmates and now we're the only thing each other has left."

“What about Tick?”

They both looked to the stage as the smallish waku crooned his song, leaning into the microphone as if he were on a stage before a crowd of thousands rather than two polite hostesses who were watching and clapping with glee.

“He’s family, sure, but he’s weird. Lately, he’s been talking to Koro as if she has her own thoughts. Been wondering if that tiger’s eye is messing with his head.”

Leesa snorted. “I overheard him talking to the cricket cage in the kitchen as if he were Koro, picking out the tastiest insect for consumption. He actually threw a live one in his mouth, but then spit it out when the insect grabbed onto his tongue. I nearly peed myself with laughter.”

“He’s a dork, but at least he hasn’t been masturbating in the bathroom next to the room anymore. Those walls were too thin not to hear that fapping.”

“That’s because Darina’s been inviting him to her room. They’ve been going at it like two dogs in heat.” Leesa rolled her eyes. “I can hear *everything.*”

“Really?” asked Yara, laughing despite herself. She checked over to see how enthusiastic Darina was in cheering Tick’s singing. Yara had thought it pity, but now she saw it for what it was.

“It sounds like he knows how to please her, so there’s that.”

“Who would have thought? I thought he was a kinky perv,” said

Yara.

"I think that's why Darina likes him. They share the same fetishes."

Yara held out her hand. "Which I'd rather not know about."

"What about you?" asked Leesa as she collected her outstretched hand and held it between her palms. The warmth was soothing.

"What about me?"

"A partner to share a bed with."

"Me?"

The intensity of Leesa's gaze made her blush. "Yes, you. When you're not so angry you're quite stunning."

"I... Thank you, Leesa. I really appreciate the offer. I wish it was something I was interested in, but you know I've always been a fan of the Big D."

Leesa kissed the back of her fingers and released her hand. "Understood. I didn't know, but I didn't want to leave it unexplored if there was a possibility."

"There's one thing you can do," said Yara.

"Anything."

"Find where Triana and Vasy are. Choo-Choo's going to go mad if he's stuck in the Onyx much longer, and I'm not sure all this time with myself is the best either. I'm not going to be much of a waku if I don't get back in the action."

"I thought you were enjoying not having something to do?" asked

Leesa.

"I am. It's been nice. More than nice. But I think that time needs to be over soon."

"For Choo-Choo?"

"For myself. When Deacon drugged me, thinking I might follow him over after he wiped out my clan, it made me furious, because it made others wonder where my loyalties lay. Made me want to kill him, no matter what it took. I think this break has changed that for me. There's no one left to doubt me now. We're a clan of three, or clanless, however you want to think about it."

"But you still want to kill him?"

"More than ever. Because he fucked with my family."

Twenty-One

Camina found it hard to remember her old life before she was co-opted into the alliance. Details of being a member of Razor or Drops were hazy and distant, a direct result of the drugs she had to take on a daily basis.

Forgetting made it easier to make friends with her fellow waku, who'd seen her as an outsider for the first half year of her existence in the alliance. Over time, her status shifted as they forgot where she'd come from as much as she had. They started inviting her to the bars when they were on break, or including her in practice sessions, especially because she was much better than them in every way. At first she beat them without comment, letting her actions speak for her skills, but in time, she started offering suggestions, hating herself at each one, but then growing more used to it.

Word of the attacks on patrols or mining sites made her anxious, but she knew how little they were accomplishing, as the alliance machine was growing larger each day. Even if those few knots of resistance killed three times the numbers, they still wouldn't keep up with recruitment. She saw how futile their efforts were, and this reality, combined with the drugs, made it hard for her to remember what it was like before she'd been coopted into the alliance. She hated the contempt she felt for her old clan mates.

When Deacon came back from the Eternal City, she didn't know about it until he showed up at a sparring session. Camina was explaining how to use an amber to detect twitches in the opponent's muscles to predict where they would strike. Since many of the new waku had come from the light, she explained it as a batter learning how to read the pitcher's body language to guess where the ball was going to be thrown.

"You have to be able to read by instinct. If you're thinking about it, you're too slow, so you should have your amber on all the time, getting used to seeing inside people, knowing them better than they know themselves. Only then will you be able to use it with speed in a scrap."

Camina hadn't realized Deacon was there until she sensed the tension in the others. She spun around to find him striding towards her, wearing a black suit and tie with a gray shirt beneath. Menace haunted his gaze. It wasn't so much that he was angry with her, but there was something raw in his expression as if he were tapped into a font of baleful energy.

"Camina."

When he'd been a member of Razor, his voice always had a thread of sarcasm to it, but now it was changed. Nuance had been wrung out it, replaced with weighty intensity. She started extending her amber to Deacon, but retracted it instinctively, the conditioning from the drugs interpreting the use of her stone negatively.

"What are you doing?" he asked, standing over her. Without the tracksuit, gold chains, and slicked-back hair, he seemed much older than she knew he was.

"Offering advice to the younger waku. They're barely using the stones they have. I could beat all of them despite their superior stones."

Deacon surveyed the other waku, who couldn't meet his gaze with their own. She knew without looking what he saw: a group of kids who were long on bravado but short on cunning and skills.

"Show me."

Camina hadn't meant to insult the waku she was training, she'd only been answering Deacon honestly, but she saw in their expressions that they were going to give it their all against her. In addition to their ambers, they had two topaz, one sapphire, and one emerald. The sapphire would be the biggest problem.

With her blades in her fists, she turned her head slightly. "Conditions?"

"No killing, but make it count. Just like old times."

The curl of a grin was the first time she'd seen a hint of the old Deacon, the one who'd sent her to the hospital after a sparring match in which he'd beat her until she was unconscious. That should have been her first clue that Deacon would do whatever it took to survive and get ahead.

"May the shadows keep you safe," she told the five waku, who had lined up in an arc ten feet from her location. They looked back at her with confusion on their brows. The ceremonial words had never been taught.

"Begin!"

Camina shifted to the left, placing two waku between her and the sapphire. They moved like a mob, getting into each other's way as they tried to come at her en masse. She kicked out, connecting with a knee with force, hearing the cry of agony as she continued circling. She felt like a sheep dog wrangling, forcing her opponents into a tight knot. If the fools would have spread out they would have stood a better chance, but the only fights they'd probably been in had involved fists and brute force.

The sapphire, getting frustrated with never having a good shot at her, slammed into the backs of his fellow waku with a healthy Push. It was an inspired, but selfish decision, with little thought past the first move. Camina had sensed the change and when the two tumbled forward, she filled in the space, making two shallow cuts across the man's cheeks, then kicking him in the chest, sending him onto his back.

With the sapphire on the ground, holding onto his bloody face, Camina slammed the butt of her blade into the fifth waku, knocking him out. When she spun around, she found the five waku on the ground, none of them appearing willing to continue the fight.

The cold glare from Deacon suggested an upcoming outburst of rage, but he remained silent for a long minute.

"Go," he said, gesturing to the young waku. "Take yourselves to an opal."

The waku with the busted knee had to be helped from the room. When they were gone, Deacon turned to her, his jaw pulsing.

"You're angry with me."

"No, Camina. Completely the opposite. You've shown me that our training isn't working. We're bringing in too many new waku who aren't worth a smudge of shit on the bottom of my boot."

She hated the way the acknowledgement was pleasurable, a brief euphoria brought on by the drug, which only conditioned her further.

Deacon paced away, cupping his jaw in his hand. "So much has changed since I've been gone. Dominion has placed me in charge of the clan's waku, but I'm no trainer. I didn't spend my life in a clan Academy, and what I learned in the Eternal City, well..."

Emotions raged within Camina. She knew what he was contemplating and craved it. More than she wanted to admit to herself. But she knew once he offered and she took it, it would only deepen her ties to the new clan, erasing her life before.

"I accept."

He spun on his heel. "I haven't offered it yet."

"It's logical. We both know a fourteen-year-old kid from old Razor or Drops could take any one of those waku even without a stone. They preen and puff up their chests, but they don't know shit. While I'm no Brazio, I'm the best you have, and you don't want the job."

"If that was meant as an audition, it was quite convincing." He pursed his lips and looked away. He was changed from his experience in the Eternal City, but he was still Deacon beneath the harsh new exterior. "The job is yours. But if I find a whiff of the old Camina interfering with alliance business, I'll cut your throat and dump your body in Canter's Folly."

"Understood."

Deacon left without comment, making her wonder if she'd made a terrible mistake, but the drugs coursing through her system had her constantly wondering who the real Camina was anymore.

Twenty-Two

It took nearly a week for Jester to return with an answer from Hylakane. They'd been sparring in an empty square, mixing up their routine with non-stone matches, or using each other's weapons—anything to keep the training fresh since they only had each other. They'd just finished a round that Kuma had won when he'd used a borrowed Push to knock her enough off-balance to land a "killing" blow. Pandora leaned against a stone wall next to Kuma, chugging water they'd brought from the fountain, letting some spill down her shirt to cool off.

"We were beginning to think you'd run off because you really didn't have a connection to Hylakane," said Pandora.

"My apologies," said Jester, touching his fingers to his forehead in what could be interpreted as a mocking version of the waku salute. "As I've said before, my visits with him are prescheduled, making it difficult to get the word to him in a timely manner."

"Do you have news?" she asked.

Jester grumbled under his breath, glancing askew. "I do. I'm afraid the Steel Sun wasn't as impressed as I was when you walked into the Golden Fist with handfuls of faeila."

Heat rose to her cheeks as she surged forward. "What do you mean, not impressed?"

"He, well, the Steel Sun requests another test of your skills. But I imagine this one is much simpler, or perhaps shorter, though much like the other, I'm not sure how it can be accomplished."

The hiss of a blade being removed from its sheath filled the air. "If you're lying to us, or playing games and making up these challenges to keep us from finding out that you're not really connected to Hylakane," Kuma said, "I will start slicing off any dangly bits, starting with your nose and ending with whatever lurks between your legs."

Jester backed up, holding his hands up and nervously replying. "Please. There will be no need. I swear to you on my honor that I am being truthful. This request came directly from the Steel Sun. Not me." He pulled a handkerchief from an inner pocket of his velvet purple coat and dabbed his forehead with it.

"Is this the last request before we can meet him?" she asked.

Jester screwed up his face. "I cannot say."

"Get on with it then. I'm anxious to get started."

The strange maetrie extended his right arm towards a nearby building. Besides Hylakane's Spire, it was the tallest structure in the area, though the upper floors looked on the verge of collapse.

"His Grace, the Steel Sun, wishes you to leap from that building and land without injury. Together, of course." Jester squeezed his eyes shut with a grimace. "If you're going to start chopping off bits, please be quick about it."

Laughter bubbled up from Pandora's chest unexpectedly, catching fire in Kuma as well until they were both wiping away tears. Jester stared at them with naked confusion.

"I don't understand. Did I say something funny? Or have you finally gone mad> It's understandable. The Eternal City can be quite trying on weak human minds. If you'd like I can offer a tonic that might help. There's a chance it could kill you, but such is the danger of good medicine."

"No. It's not funny. Not on the surface anyway," said Pandora. "Or that you could have guessed. But for the first time, the task is not insurmountable. In fact, I think we'll get to completing it right now, if you'd like to join us."

For the first time since they'd met the strange maetrie, he seemed at a loss for words. The journey to the building wasn't difficult, though climbing it was for Jester, who had none of their abilities to leap or climb. Not all the levels were connected by stairs, requiring an emerald-aided leap through holes in the concrete. After which they would extend a hand down and pull the stylishly dressed maetrie up.

The wind at the top of the old building proved to be fierce, sending Pandora's hair, which had grown quite long, around her face. She quickly tied it behind her head and approached the edge, feeling a knot in her stomach despite the knowledge that they could accomplish this task quite easily.

"Quite a view," said Jester, holding onto his hat rather than letting it blow away.

Hylakane's Spire was two blocks from them, but towering over their location. Otherwise they had a good view of the abandoned city, which stretched much further than she'd first suspected, or noticed during her first time visiting when she was younger.

"Why all this waste?" asked Kuma, frowning at the empty distance, littered with buildings on the verge of collapse. "And does it really go on forever?"

Jester lifted both shoulders. "No one knows. A few foolish explorers have left in an attempt to catalog the past, but they've never returned to tell the tale. This region is one of the furthest known inhabited areas."

Pandora could understand his question. She'd had the same when she was younger, but no one had given an answer she understood. Mostly they made comments that would be the same as answering why the sky was blue in their world. It just was. That was it.

Motion from across the way had her head bobbling up. The wraithhawks on the spire had lifted into the sky, circling around the upper level.

"We shouldn't dally here," said Jester, staring at the wraithhawks with a pinched expression. "If they deem to notice us we will not have a good end to our day."

"No," said Kuma, deadpan. "We shouldn't."

Pandora knew instinctively what he meant and stepped to Jester's right while Kuma bracketed the other side. The strange maetrie quickly scanned his surroundings, sensing their presence, but before he could move away, they each grabbed an arm. For a moment, she felt Jester's strength as he tried to pull away, but then it faded. She couldn't decide if it'd been her imagination, or just the surge of adrenaline that had made him temporarily stronger.

"What is the meaning of this?"

Kuma met her gaze over Jester's head, a wry smile on his lips.

"We thought you might like to experience Steel Sun's trial. After all, you've got to be quite bored, day after day waiting for his appointments with little to occupy your time except that puzzle cube you're always playing with."

Jester clutched his arms to his chest, alarm in his eyes. "But I have nothing—"

The words meant to follow were swallowed as Pandora felt the light hum of Kuma's ruby activating, followed by a tickle of Lightness. They leapt together, dragging Jester over the edge. The twenty-story fall went by quickly. Plummeting like a meteor, they sped towards the cracked concrete, and for a split moment, she worried Kuma would activate his emerald too late. Their speed never changed, but suddenly she felt as airy as a bubble and they hit the ground at speed, but without the deadly impact.

The strangest thing about the fall was how calmly Jester took it. She released his arm, expecting cursing or fright, but he merely craned his neck towards the sky.

"That was a neat trick. Can we do it again?"

"If it'll get you to take our message to Hylakane sooner, then I'd be happy to give you another ride," said Kuma.

Jester swallowed heavily again. "My apologies, my next visit with him isn't for another two weeks. You'll have to occupy yourselves until I can return."

"Bullshit," said Pandora, crossing her arms. "Tell him right now. I know you're lying."

Kuma tilted his head but she shot him a glance not to interfere. There'd been something about Jester that had been bothering her since they met him and it wasn't until they'd made him take the fall with them that it occurred to her what it was, even if she didn't understand *how.*

"Two weeks, I'm afraid. We could pass the time pleasantly in the Golden Fist. Drinks will be on me," said Jester, backing away with his hands up.

"No. You showed us the first day you could walk to his barrier without injury, which means you can go through and talk to him. Now. Or are you a liar and have been messing with us, sending us on dangerous and pointless expeditions?"

"You survived, and that's all that matters," he said petulantly.

She extended her arm like an owner giving a dog instructions to return to the house.

"Now."

Jester tried to move towards the city, but Kuma moved into his way, forcing him towards the spire.

"You know he's prickly, dangerous, possibly homicidal. He'll probably take my head, leaving you with no avenue to reach him."

"Then I guess you'd better be convincing about why we should see him now rather than later. But I don't think that's necessary at all. I think he's quite aware of us. Up close and personal."

Kuma's head craned briefly as if he thought Hylakane might be nearby, but that's not what Pandora meant. Before Jester could dart away, she slammed him with a Push, knocking him on his back.

"What rudeness! My jacket is ripped," said Jester, checking to his rear as he lay near an oil-kissed puddle. "And my trousers are stained. You know how difficult it is to keep things clean here!"

Blades appeared in her fists. She stalked over to Jester, stood over him.

"Stop this nonsense. I want to speak to Hylakane. No more games. We met your tasks. The fountain. The faeila. The leap. It's time. Show yourself."

The impeccably dressed Jester looked on the verge of tears. He edged backwards on his rear.

"Pan?"

"It's good. Everything's good."

Kuma approached, concern on his brow. "Are you sure?"

Before he could stop her, Pandora slammed her blade into Jester's chest. The tip would split his ribs in half. There should have been nothing he could do about it, given his unremarkable nature.

His eyes flashed black.

Pandora found herself flying backwards through the air. She landed thirty feet away, managing to get her feet under herself. The prone form of Jester no longer lay on the cracked concrete, surrounded by oily puddles. In his place stood a powerful looking bald maetrie with broad shoulders and a jaw that one could break a two-by-four over. He wasn't quite as large as Titus Cabone, but his inner intensity was as if he was hiding a nuclear power plant in his chest.

"What...?" exclaimed Kuma, stumbling backwards.

Pandora kept her blades in her fists even as she knew they'd be meaningless against the Steel Sun. Hylakane looked ready to charge.

"The mongrel returns."

"I want to complete my training."

Hylakane spun towards Kuma, kicking him solidly in the chest. The blow should have caved in his chest, but he flew through the air with Lightness, landing with his blades out.

"Why?"

The question caught her off guard. Not that she didn't have an answer, but she knew that it wasn't an answer for him. Hylakane wouldn't accept that she had no other options. That wasn't the kind of maetrie he was. Not that she knew him well, as she'd only been in his care for a short training period, but he saw events through an unblemished window.

"I want to be the best."

"Liar!"

Even though he'd been thirty feet away, he was on her in an instant, throwing fists and feet, blocking her blades with his hands, and within three moves sending her spinning into the concrete wall of the building behind. The air fled from her lungs and her head spun from the impact.

"You can never be the best, even if you train your entire pathetic life. The best is a fool's dream, a quest that would damn you to irrelevance. Why?"

Pandora climbed to her feet, snapping her arms forward with blades ready.

"I have to stop my grandfather."

The corners of his eyes creased, and for a brief moment, she thought the answer had been good enough, but then he came at her like a windstorm. She never saw a single blow. Pain cascaded through her body.

She woke on her back, Hylakane standing over her with his fist ready to drive into her chest. It would be a killing blow. Pandora looked for Kuma but saw him dozens of feet away climbing to his feet unsteadily.

"Why?"

A thousand answers ricocheted through her mind, competing with each other. Pandora had thought the months in the Eternal City, traveling and training—meditating in the clearing waiting for the faeila to notice them—had helped her understand herself. Find the truth at the center of her being. Her entire life had been at the mercy of others' decisions. When her father had died, she'd been whisked away to the Eternal City, thrown into a life she'd been completely unprepared for. No one had shown her kindness and every day had been a struggle for survival. Many nights she'd worried the maetrie her age would finally find a way to kill her without being caught. She wasn't sure her grandfather would have even cared if it'd happened. A tool was only as good as the work it performed, and she was a poor tool.

"I have nowhere else to go. We escaped to the Eternal City without an ally in the realms. I hoped that in coming here, I might find enough strength to continue. We're trapped, and even if we could return to our home, I don't know if anything is left for us."

The blow that never came turned into an open hand. The anger rippling through Hylakane's body calmed as if the storm passing over the lake had moved on, leaving the waters smooth and glassy like a mirror.

"Good," said Hylakane, helping her to her feet. "Training can begin."

Twenty-Three

Leesa had gotten word about his mother's location that morning when she overheard two waku talking about the mining operation in the western caverns south of the air well.

"If you can get her away, bring her back here. I think we can disguise her as one of the workers from the Bogo, returning to the city for prizes and other materials."

"What about others?"

Leesa had shaken her head. "It'll be hard enough for one. I'm sorry, Choo-Choo. If you want your mother safely out of the Undercity, it can only be her."

It'd been months since they'd been in the tunnels. They assumed the alliance was no longer looking for them, as they'd lain low long enough to let the search dissipate, but that didn't mean they could be incautious. The alliance still controlled the entirety of the Undercity and patrols could cross their paths at any moment.

"It's good to be back," said Yara when they were fifteen minutes west of the Terreno. "I don't know if I could have stayed in that room another day."

Tick looked less pleased about the return to the hunt. They'd woken him from Darina's bed. Koro had hissed at them from her perch on the bed frame.

For Choo-Choo, heading into the tunnels to find his mother was more than a rescue mission. He was beginning to doubt the purpose of his life, hiding in the old spare room above the Onyx. Without Drops clan driving his daily schedule, or acting as the rebellion and sleeping on hard stone, he didn't know what to do with himself. Tick had Koro and Darina, while Yara had taken to reading books or training alone behind the stage when the Onyx was closed. Choo-Choo had come to realize that he didn't know who he was without his family, which included Navos, who'd been captured by the alliance during the raid. In the quiet times of the morning before the Onyx opened and when his roommates were still asleep, he sometimes thought about giving up their opposition and joining the alliance. What other choice did he have? Unless he wanted to escape the Undercity entirely, but he knew no other life. He worried he'd make a fool of himself in the light, where people lived entirely different lives.

"Emilio."

The use of his real name snapped him out of his trance. He hadn't realized Yara was speaking to him until she'd switched away from his nickname.

"What?"

Their wide-eyed glances were followed by a wash of emotion, which he easily picked up with his amber. Their auras were tight and uneven, likely because they were out of practice after months sequestered.

"Patrol ahead. Koro just came back from scouting. About a quarter mile. What do you want to do? Only five, no stone count."

Their expectations surprised him though he supposed they shouldn't have since he'd been the one to lead the group before they escaped to the Terreno. The time away had made him soft. He could feel it, and it scared him. Before that, he'd been in constant training and he'd felt honed, like a blade carefully sharpened. Now he felt like a carelessly kept weapon that had become dull from misuse.

"How far out from the mine?" he asked, hoping they hadn't noticed his indecision, but their auras flared, so they probably had the same questions about him that he had for himself.

"Not far, twice or three times that of the patrol," said Yara.

"It's either a courier group, or they're a patrol for the mine."

If it was the first, they could let it go and not worry about it for their hit on the mine, but if they were a patrol, then they might circle around at the worst possible moment. Killing them would be the safest answer. Blank stares followed his pronouncement.

"No idea?" he asked, looking to Tick, who lifted his shoulders. He almost said, *Is this a good idea?* He wanted to find his mother, get her to safety, but he worried they were out of practice. He hadn't used his stone in a meaningful way in months. "Let's hit the patrol then. We could use the practice."

Their semi-grins were acknowledgement that they agreed, which made him all the more reticent. He knew it was likely the patrol was filled with pups, fresh from the city, recruited with the promise of becoming a waku with little idea how to use their stones. They might have even read the mangas. While he didn't want a hard fight, when it was too easy he felt like he was killing children. The only reason they'd been chased from the tunnels before were the overwhelming numbers that the alliance had brought to track them down.

"Let's teach 'em who the Ghost Shadows are," said Tick.

"Don't fucking remind me," said Choo-Choo.

A patrol of five was a manageable number for a direct hit. The usual makeup was two waku and three soldados, which meant identifying and taking out the tougher opponents first. Though a lucky soldado could mean trouble if they had a happy trigger finger.

The caverns were unfamiliar but they found a good ambush spot. Tick reached for his handgun, but Choo-Choo waved him off and gestured towards Yara, who had her throwing knives already out. If there was one thing they had plenty of practice at in the Onyx, it was throwing blades into the structural pillar, which looked like a giant had taken a bite out of it.

Choo-Choo found a cluster of stalactites and stalagmites that had grown together from the constant dripping from the tips of the limestone. There was no illuminating fungi in the cavern, which gave them a slight advantage since the patrol was using headlamps.

Crouched with throwing knives in his hands, Choo-Choo calmed his breathing as to give nothing away to an enterprising amber. Tick had sent Koro near the ceiling to pick off any stragglers that weren't taken out with a flurry of knives in the first seconds of the fight. If all went well, the patrol would be dead before they'd realized they'd been hit.

Quiet conversation gave away the patrol's approach, followed by lights bobbing forward, illuminating the glistening rocks at the entrance. Choo-Choo used his amber to follow their progress. When they hit the appointed location, they would spring out and attack. He held up his fingers, signaling the start, but when he reached "two" a cry of alarm changed the calculation.

"Ambush!"

Choo-Choo's mind went red. Yara was throwing blades before he'd gotten a chance to spring around the limestone wall. Gunfire flashed in his vision, bullets slamming into stone around his body. He launched his blade as something punched him in the arm, spinning him sideways, but his topaz momentum brought him into the middle of the patrol.

The blade in his fist slipped out uncontrollably, and he slapped an alliance clan member rather than stabbing her. His opponent's eyes widened as she sensed the opportunity, bringing her blade around to slice open his belly. Choo-Choo barreled forward, putting his shoulder into her chest and driving her into the rocks. The crunch of impact was followed by the woman going completely limp.

He rolled off her to find a pistol pointed in his direction. Before the gun went off, the guy stiffened, a blade sticking through his neck. By the time he hit the ground, Choo-Choo was back on his feet. Only two other people remained standing, both of them his friends. The woman he'd landed on was gasping for breath and another was convulsing from Koro's venom.

"You're shot," said Yara.

Choo-Choo found his arm was a bloody mess. The bullet had gone through the meat of his biceps, leaving it incapable of movement. He let it hang at his side as Tick reached into the backpack for a first aid kit while Yara approached the woman who was still alive. She had tattoos on her face—not the kind some members of Drops had, but the ones seen in the city.

"Her spine is snapped from when you landed on her."

"Can she talk?"

Yara shook her head. "I don't even think she's sixteen. Fuck. I'm sorry." A quick slice and the gasping ended.

The apology surprised Choo-Choo, who'd never heard a moment of regret from Yara, but maybe the months away from fighting had brought a measure of self-analysis. He hoped that wouldn't impact their fighting prowess. Too much thinking in the middle of a battle wasn't good.

"That was a fucking mess," said Choo-Choo as Tick finished wrapping the bandage around his arm.

"They were all ambers and one topaz," said Yara, placing the stones in a little leather bag with a drawstring.

"Makes sense," said Tick as he placed the first aid supplies back in the bag. "They've been mining the hell out of the Undercity. They can afford to give everyone a stone."

"That makes our job harder," said Choo-Choo as he tried to flex his right arm, but the pain was too intense. "Fuck. I'm useless."

"Should we come back later?" asked Tick. "The mine is going to be worse. More numbers, better stones."

Yara was staring at the young woman who'd had her spine severed. "They fought better than expected. Someone's been training them. Those wayhos used to not be able to detect us if we were silent and not moving. While we were hiding out, either we got worse or they got better."

"Or both," said Choo-Choo. "But no, we're hitting the mine. I've been trying to find Mami for months. I'm afraid if we don't take this opportunity, it'll be many more months before I find her again."

After dragging the bodies to a location off the main path, they continued towards the mine. Choo-Choo's wound throbbed through the local that he'd been given. It would have been a lot easier if one of them had an opal, but they weren't that lucky. Camina had been captured before they could whisk her away to safety.

When they neared the site, Tick sent Koro ahead to scout without giving them away. As far as they knew from Leesa, the flying snake wasn't connected to them and dangerous creatures were common in the Undercity. A few minutes later, Koro returned, landing on Tick's neck. As Tick stroked her back, Choo-Choo could tell by his tight aura that the news wasn't going to be good.

"Eight guards and a crew of twenty workers. It's a big cave and the mine is on the side wall, heading down at an angle. They're walking down wooden ladders rather than being lowered. The processing equipment is near the opening and the guards are spread out in the cave."

"Did you see her?"

Tick screwed up his face. "I couldn't get that close. The view I got was brief, and Koro's vision isn't that great at a distance."

"Fuck," said Choo-Choo, grimacing as he tensed, making his wound burn.

"I don't know about this," said Yara.

Choo-Choo closed his eyes. He knew it would be risky, but he couldn't help it. Leaving her would only invite the chance that she'd die in a mine collapse, or from any of the other dangers. He'd already heard too frequently about workers dying to accidents, or aggressive guards.

"I have to," said Choo-Choo.

"I understand. I'm with you."

"Me too," said Tick.

"I don't deserve you two."

"Or maybe we're your punishment," said Yara wryly.

Choo-Choo chuckled. "Who are you these days?"

She sighed heavily. "If you figure it out, let me know. So what's the plan?"

"I don't know...yet. Whatever it is, it has to be soon. If that patrol is due back soon, they'll get suspicious when it doesn't return," said Choo-Choo. "They're too spread out to take down quickly, and I don't want to get into a gun battle. Shadows below. Eight guards. We can assume they're all waku, so sneaking up isn't going to be easy."

"Want to try a creature feature?" asked Tick.

"Anything nearby?"

He shrugged. "I don't know, but I can look."

For the next twenty minutes, they circled through the nearby caverns, looking for insects or critters that could cause a worthy distraction. Choo-Choo was about to call it off when Tick giggled like a little kid in a dirt pile as Koro returned to his shoulders.

"What is it?"

"Spiders."

Choo-Choo frowned. "We need more than a few creepy-crawlies to distract them."

"Not these spiders. They're iron-rippers. I read about them years ago. There were rumors that some had gotten loose in the Undercity. I've always wanted to find some."

"How do you know what they look like?" asked Yara.

"Oh, you'd know if you saw 'em. Let me coax them from their lair."

"Don't get Mami killed," warned Choo-Choo.

The lack of response worried him, but then again, Tick had his eyes closed. A few minutes later, Choo-Choo sensed their approach and it didn't even require his amber. Their feet made loud tapping sounds on the rocks.

When he saw them, he recoiled. As large as a small dog, the mottled-gray spiders skittered over the uneven landscape with frightening alacrity. Seven of the critters slipped past, leaving Choo-Choo feeling sick to his stomach. It was one thing to die from a quick blade, but those reddish fangs sticking from their mandibles were enough to give him nightmares.

Normally Choo-Choo carried Tick when he was in his creature-trance, but with the useless arm, Yara took the role. It wasn't that she couldn't carry him in the past—she had a topaz like him—but she complained about Tick always getting excited in more ways than one.

The procession made him feel like he was in a dream. Seven dog-sized spiders in a row with three humans following, one carrying the other, and the last with a dead arm. Choo-Choo kept the butt of his rifle shoved into his hip. If he had to fire, he wanted to keep it steady and not hit his friends. Yara stopped them about a hundred meters from the mining cave, setting Tick onto the ground and propping him up against the wall while the iron-ripper spiders continued their advance. Leaving Tick behind, they followed the critters, not bothering with staying quiet since the tapping from the spider legs was unusually loud and the sorting conveyor in the cavern ahead was noisy with mechanical motion.

Yara signaled him. *Let the spiders distract then move in on cleanup.* He tried to reply but answering with only one arm was difficult, so he nodded.

The spiders had gone directly across the cave, while they crept along the outside to avoid line of sight. At the rocky corner, Yara stepped over a patch of luminous fungus, leaning against the wall with her rifle held at an angle. The adrenaline he expected to feel so close to a fight was less prominent due to his injury. Choo-Choo closed his eyes, concentrating on his amber. He smelled the leaching chemicals from the mines, the oils from the equipment, and the body odor of workers who'd spent long hours beneath the surface.

The first shout was quickly followed by the rattle of gunfire and the pinging of ricochets. Choo-Choo sensed Yara counting internally in front of him, anticipating the moment of advance. His adrenaline spiked, the fight nearly upon him. When Yara surged forward, he stumbled after, the immobility of his arm making travel painful.

Muzzle fire flashed in the next cavern, revealing the iron-ripper spiders dancing across the rocks, avoiding bullets. When Choo-Choo reached the entrance, a few painful seconds after Yara, he watched as a spider sunk its teeth into the thigh of an alliance waku. A machete would have been cleaner. The screams ended when the guy caught friendly fire in the back. Stunned by the carnage, Choo-Choo flinched when Yara fired from his left, picking off the waku on the far side of the cavern and then two more who came rushing up from below.

The fight was over before it began.

Choo-Choo never fired a shot, nor was he sure he could have managed it. Four of the spiders had succumbed to return fire, and a fifth was twitching with a curved blade stuck in its back. The other two skittered out the opposite side, and a minute later Tick appeared, rubbing his eyes as if he'd been taking a nap.

"How'd I do?"

"Remind me never to make you mad," said Yara, staring at the waku covered in blood nearest them. The open-eyed stare contained the horrors of his final moments.

Choo-Choo made his way towards the entrance to the mine, keeping his weapon trained. He sensed bodies lurking below on the wooden ladder and hiding behind the processing conveyor, which was still running, dumping rocks into the buckets at the end. He could see two people crouched beneath it, sobbing quietly.

"You can come out. It's safe. We're not here to hurt you."

A moment later, he heard a rising, "Emilio?"

The woman that climbed from the ladder wasn't the mother he remembered. Around the Pajot, she was a vibrant woman who never stopped moving or talking, but had the warmest heart of anyone he knew. Choo-Choo didn't recognize her at first, covered in grime with a miner's hard hat, looking like something out of the Old West.

Her limping gait turned into a run, and he met her midway, capturing her with his one arm. She didn't smell like he remembered, covered in mine dust. Choo-Choo held her tight, kissing her forehead, rocking softly with their roles reversed.

"I'm sorry, Mami. I would have rescued you sooner, but we couldn't find you."

"It's okay, Emilio. I'm fine. Tired and sore, but nothing bad happened. To me, anyway." She pulled back, holding him at arm's length.

There was no need to ask the question.

"I haven't found her yet. But I'm sure she's good. Vasy's a tough kid."

Even as he said the words, he didn't really believe them. He'd seen what a few rogue alliance members had done in Club Onyx. What would keep someone from hurting his sister under the wrong circumstances?

She punched him in his good arm. "You have to find her. I can't lose another."

"I will."

"Hey," said Yara. "We have to get out of here. If another patrol shows up, we'll be the one ambushed."

His mother broke away from his arms and marched straight to Yara. He didn't remember until his mother was almost to Yara about their history. He'd been fighting alongside Yara for so long, he'd forgotten that her father had killed his sister. Yara never moved as Triana stopped cold in front of her and reared back her hand, slapping her across the cheek. The red handprint remained long after the echo faded.

"Mami—"

The words barely left his lips before his mother threw her arms around a stunned Yara, squeezing her like a long-lost sister.

"Thank you for keeping my Emilio safe." She pulled away, holding onto Yara's arm, squeezing tightly. "But your debt is not finished. You must save my daughter. My heart cannot take another."

"I will. We've been trying to..."

Choo-Choo had never seen Yara so out of sorts, but he knew the effect his mother had on people.

"Do better."

She gave Yara another slap, this time lighter, then turned back as if she hadn't just smacked her twice in short order. Yara stood mutely, arms hanging at her side, clearly working through what had just happened.

"I'm ready. Where are you taking us?" asked his mother.

The other men and women from the mine were clustered near the processing machine. Choo-Choo thought he recognized a few from his old clan, but they looked like beaten dogs, too numb to care.

"Mami. I'm afraid we can only take you. There's no way to get everyone out. The alliance controls all the exits from the Undercity, but we have a plan. A friend has a way out lined up."

Stubbornness ran deep in his family and it hadn't come from his father, may the shadows protect his soul. She crossed her arms and planted her feet as if she were a protester.

"If I go, we all go."

"Choo-Choo," said Yara, gesturing with open arms.

"Mami, we can't take everyone."

"Then I'm not going. I'm not leaving them here. You haven't seen what I've seen. If the mine doesn't kill us, they will. They have no honor, Emilio, not like the old clans. They're about profit, nothing else, no matter how much they wrap themselves in the clothes of the waku." She spat on the rocks. "The stones were a curse that doomed the old ways."

"But we can't get everyone out," said Choo-Choo. "You don't understand."

"I understand very clearly," said his mother calmly.

He checked back to the knot of workers. There were nearly twenty, too many to disguise and smuggle out through the Terreno. The Onyx wouldn't even be able to safely hold that many without being noticed. Leesa would be furious.

"Fuck," he said, putting his fist into an open palm.

"There is one way we haven't tried yet," said Yara, the red handprint still on her cheek.

"That's a good girl," said Triana. "Where is it?"

"It's the only one the alliance doesn't control. The place the Halls use to keep watch on the infernal realm. The Chamber, or whatever they call it," said Yara.

"We can't go that route. They put up more guards after we went that way last time. We'd never be able to get past them with just the three of us."

"I'm not suggesting that we fight our way out," said Yara. "Look at them. They need food, water, medicine, and a bath. I don't think they'll turn them away."

"And if they do?"

"Then we'll take them to the Terreno and figure a way out from there."

Choo-Choo grumbled under his breath. As always, his mother had imposed her will on others. The slap and demand to Yara had somehow placed her firmly on his mother's side, despite their history.

"Your friend speaks well. You should listen to her, Emilio."

He opened his mouth to argue, but realized the futility of engaging in verbal battle with his mother. She was the Duro of arguing.

"Alright then. Let's get moving. Tick, you take point. Yara, you make sure there are no stragglers. I'll stay in the front of the group."

The collective relief of the workers made him glad that he'd agreed, even if he didn't think that it would work. They were a few hours away from the Chamber, which would leave them at the mercy of random patrols. Progress was slow. Choo-Choo had to help some of the older members of the group across difficult terrain, and there were more than a few falls and skinned knees. But luck was on their side and they made it to the area where the infernal invasion had come through years ago.

They didn't bother hiding their approach as there was no point, and no feasible way to move that many people quietly. They came upon the guard station that they'd disarmed a year before, finding it doubled in defenses.

"Hello!" Choo-Choo called out before he stepped into view. "I'm coming out to talk to you. Please don't shoot, or do anything weird.

We're not a threat."

A husky woman's voice answered. "Go away. This is Hundred Halls' property. We are armed and lethal."

He knew it wasn't going to be easy, so he stepped into the cavern with his hands up. A half dozen weapons were trained on him from behind a half-wall covered in warding runes. The similarity to the wall at the Alliance complex had him smiling in remembrance.

"I told you to leave," said a woman in heavy Kevlar gear. "We *will* shoot."

"I have twenty men and women here who were enslaved by the Alliance clan, a group led by a notorious maetrie, who were using them to mine faez crystals from the earth against their will. I'm no fan of mages or the Halls, but I at least respect that the majority of you try to be honorable. We've no other way to get them out of the Undercity. The Alliance controls all the other exits. This is the only way they can get out safely. Otherwise, you're dooming them to death."

He hadn't requested any of the workers to step out, but his mother led a group of them into the light. They didn't have their hands up, but their pathetic exterior was enough to put a waver into some of the rifle barrels.

"We're not a charity," said the woman in charge.

"I'm not asking you to be. I'm asking you to let them ride up in your elevator and enter the city. Nothing more. Please. If there's anyone to talk to in there, ask them. I'm sure they would agree."

He heard her curse under her breath and then relay the issue to someone inside by a walkie-talkie clipped to her jacket. A few minutes later, a thin, unassuming man in a checkerboard sweater vest appeared.

"I'm Professor Sinclair of Coterie of Mages, a specialist in demonology. I want to start by informing you that if anything untoward happens during our conversation, I can make quick work of your entire group with a few simple spells. Do not test me."

Exasperated, Choo-Choo gestured with his good arm. "Do we look like a threat? I got shot during the rescue and everyone here is exhausted after a long day. We just want passage to the city and I know you have a nice elevator in there."

Professor Sinclair frowned sympathetically. Choo-Choo sensed his aura to be not as fierce as he wanted them to believe. He was trying to put up a front.

"How many of you are there?"

"Nineteen," called out his mother before he could answer.

Professor Sinclair closed his eyes momentarily, before nodding as if he'd come to an internal conclusion.

"Send one forward at a time. I want to verify they're not carrying any weapons or contraband. Once we have everyone assembled, I'll take them up."

The sense of relief nearly overwhelmed Choo-Choo, but he held himself together for the sake of his mother and the workers. She took charge, picking the oldest to go first, while the others gathered in the cavern.

"What will you do above?" he asked his mother.

"We have the stones from the mine," she said. "We'll find someone to sell them to and then find a place to live in the city. Once you rescue your sister, find a way to reach us. There's nothing left in the Undercity for any of us."

While he'd considered abandoning his home many times since the failed raid, hearing his mother suggest it hardened his heart against the idea. He couldn't imagine himself in the city where there was infinite sky and no honor. He'd probably end up in a gang, and while he was no stranger to criminal enterprise, he'd always felt like there'd been a twisted logic to how the Drops had conducted themselves.

"I'll see what I can do," he said, not wanting to contradict his mother.

She gave him a look that suggested she knew he was lying. "Emilio."

"You should go, Mami. We made a lot of noise and left a lot of tracks on the way here. We need to leave and make sure we've confused our trail before someone comes along."

"What about your arm?" she asked.

"I'll find someone to fix it."

Triana made him lean down so she could kiss his dirty bald head.

Then they hugged for a long time, until it was her turn to enter the Chamber. She gave a little wave before she disappeared behind the hidden door, and Choo-Choo left with his friends, returning to the shadows where they belonged.

Twenty-Four

The date wasn't their first, but it was easily the nicest. The Lime Duck was on the third level at the Lazona, where Vasilisa was currently stationed, managing logistics for the Alliance. Andelei sat across the table in his clan uniform, which wasn't that different than what Razor had worn. A basket of warm fries sat between them while they waited for greasy burgers to arrive. Vasilisa took a sip of lemonade, keeping her eyes fixed on her date.

"Best fries in the Undercity," said Andelei. "Don't you think?"

"I don't know, Andy. The ones in Big Dave's are pretty good."

"I haven't been there yet," he said, hanging his head sheepishly.

"Was hard enough pulling strings to get stationed here."

The first time they'd gone on a date, it'd been purely defensive on her part, not wanting to seem like an enemy asset as she passed explosives and other materials to her connections. But in time she found he was quite sweet, despite knowing what he stood for as a member of the Alliance.

"I'm glad you did, Andy," she said, smiling as he covered her hand. She meant it. She did like him. He was handsome and tall, and always brought her something nice whenever he visited. They hadn't fucked yet, but had messed around two weeks ago when he'd arrived in the Lazona. She knew what he wanted but given her situation she wanted to withhold that as a piece of leverage. Despite making herself invaluable with their logistics operations, she didn't feel like she'd be protected if something bad happened.

The owner of the Lime Duck, a half-maetrie named Najani, brought their burgers, dropping them onto the table and returning to the back of the bar. While there were more maetrie being spotted in the Undercity, Najani had arrived long before the Alliance takeover.

"You've really changed since last time," he said, eyes searching her hungrily.

It wasn't the first time he'd said it, but she understood. Her body had been going through changes the last half year, including growing two inches and other more important updates as far as Andelei was concerned.

"I've gotten the hang of the job," she said, purposely not acknowledging his comment. "I like it though it's not my first love."

Andelei brought his burger towards his mouth, and a piece of melted cheese dripped onto the table. The table vibrated from the nearby construction, creating tiny waves on the surface of their drinks. She'd gotten used to the noises from the elevator, but he stared at it with a frown hooked on his lips.

"You know they won't take you," he said, glancing towards her missing hand. "The Alliance Academy is pretty strict about their applicants."

"Strict?" she exclaimed. "I could beat half the new waku with my good arm tied behind my back. I'm a better knife fighter than most, Andy. Probably even better than you."

He flinched, before taking a bite, using the burger as an excuse not to talk.

"You know what I mean," he said darkly, glancing about as if he expected to be overheard despite them being nearly the only people in the bar.

"I know," she grumbled.

Since she'd moved to the Lazona away from Elani's influence, and with the passage of time making the idea of the Alliance being destroyed by a rebellion less plausible each day, she'd been thinking less about sabotage and more about how to find a life within the new structure.

"You're really good at your job. I've heard that from the others."

Vasilisa ran a french fry around her plate, making designs in the mustard.

"I always beat my mom and brother in this game we made called Undercity. Even though I was much younger. The only person who ever beat me was Pandora."

Andelei sucked in a breath, checking covertly around them. "Don't say that name."

Vasilisa froze. She'd forgotten that the Alliance had a standing order to kill or capture her, which made Vasilisa believe that she was still hiding out somewhere in the Undercity, or maybe in the light above.

"That's why they'll never let you in the Academy," said Andelei.

Rebuked and sullen, she focused on her burger, musing over the dual lives happening simultaneously in her head. After she'd moved to Lazona, she started thinking less about rebellion and more about finding a place for herself. The only thing keeping her back from committing entirely was the feeling of betrayal, as if she'd let down the memory the clan. At night in the comfort of her bed, she saw the faces of the Drops that had died to protect her. What had she done for their memories in turn? The few things she'd done for the rebellion seemed miniscule in comparison to a life given. But it was hard to be effective worrying about getting caught all the time. She thought about her failed attempt at stealing a stone. It gave her an idea. With a french fry dipped in mustard before her mouth, she asked in a whisper, "Any way you could get me a stone?"

His expression cracked. Andelei tilted his head. She could see his resistance, so she licked the mustard off the fry and then shoved the whole thing in her mouth. His eyes were as wide as moons.

"I'd be eternally grateful."

Andelei leaned forward. "I would but they keep a tight control on them, and what would happen if you got caught with it?"

"I'd keep it hidden. Since I don't work the mines, they don't search me anymore, and if they did, I'd never tell them where I got it. Come on, Andy. I know the clan is flush with them. I'm in charge of logistics, which means I get to see the manifests. The clan is making millions in the city every month. Almost too much because the price of some of them have dropped to almost nothing. An amber is cheap these days. No one would notice."

"I don't know, Vasy..."

She leaned back in her chair, slipped her foot out of her shoe, and rested it on his crotch, gently kneading.

"I'd be grateful," she said in a singsong voice.

The moment he went inward, she knew she had him. "I can try. I'm being rotated to the mines for the next few weeks. Everyone with experience has to take a turn now because of what happened."

Vasilisa sat up straight. "What?"

"Oh, you hadn't heard?"

"No."

Andelei frowned. "There was a bit hit on one of the big mines in the northwest quadrant. Eight waku dead, twenty workers escaped. They've had to beef up security since. Titus was pissed. He gutted the guy who'd been in charge of that quadrant, left him impaled on the wall."

The news spiked her heart rate. She couldn't believe twenty people escaped, but didn't want to ask questions that might make him suspicious. If she could get out, would she? Living in the city, where there was no comforting ceiling to keep you from floating into the sky, gave her the sweats. Sure, she knew that one could adapt. Others from Drops, including her brother, had been sent up to the light and had survived without going mad. But could she find a life for herself up there? Staying in the Undercity working for the alliance was more palatable than that idea. For now.

Andelei checked his watch, letting out a withering sigh. "Sorry, Vasy. I have to go. My shift starts in a few, but it was nice getting together again." He reached out and squeezed her hand. "Hopefully we can see each other real soon?"

The meaning was naked across his face.

"I'd like that," she said, squeezing back. "And maybe you'll have a gift for me."

He leaned down to give her a kiss before leaving. She grabbed him by the back of the neck and bit his lower lip suggestively before releasing him.

After he was gone, she finished her fries, musing on the meaning of the raid. Was there an active rebellion? Or had that been single act of escape? Since she'd been rotated out of the Machi, her life had seemed relatively normal. Vasilisa could almost believe that nothing had happened, that her friends and family hadn't been slaughtered by the alliance. But they had, so deep down, she couldn't resolve the double life that existed in her mind.

Twenty-Five

The strain was bone-crushing. Kuma supported a wooden platform with both hands and the top of his head. Above him, Pandora was working through a series of kicks and punches. He had to borrow her opal with his ruby to hold her up; otherwise, he would have collapsed a half hour ago.

It'd been four months since Pandora had forced Hylakane to reveal himself. Kuma had barely slept since. They'd moved into a lower level on the spire. Every day they woke before "dawn." Hylakane worked them every second, keeping them in constant motion.

The board shifted downward, forcing Kuma to rebalance. The top of his head screamed from the constant impacts. Hylakane was watching from somewhere nearby and when he was satisfied, he'd give them a brief break and then they'd switch. It couldn't come soon enough.

Kuma had thought they'd be working with their weapons when Hylakane took them as trainees, but they hadn't touched their curved blades since they'd arrived. The few times Kuma had asked about them, he'd received a withering glare and a rude comment about how children shouldn't ask to play with knives.

The board grew light, which meant Pandora had leapt into the air. Kuma tapped into his amber to ready himself for impact, grunting when she landed, but managed to keep the board level. Blood ran down his forehead, slipping around the corner of his eye, making it sting.

While the exercise was painful and exhausting, it wasn't the worst that Hylakane had put them through. That honor was reserved for the death crawl. At the back of the spire, Hylakane had them put down a field of broken glass, concrete, and steel, which they had to crawl through with their hands and feet tied behind their back. Squirming like a snake across the brutal landscape left them agonizingly bloody by the end. Then they had to use Pandora's opal to put themselves back together, a feat which seemed to amuse Hylakane every time.

There were other exercises, less vicious but nonetheless challenging, like the tower climb, the fire brick hold, and the knavth chase. The last made Kuma feel like a child, especially when Hylakane would snatch the critter in a millisecond, snapping its back with a twist of his wrist after they'd spent hours stalking it through the buildings.

"Are we tired yet?" asked Hylakane from behind.

Kuma had heard him approach. "No, Steel Sun."

"A pity. If you'd been tired, I would have let you stop. But since you're a stubborn insect who doesn't appreciate the meaninglessness of his short existence, I will let you continue."

"Thank you, Steel Sun."

The bald maetrie stepped into his view. He was built like a fireplug. While most city elves were slender and gaunt, Hylakane looked like he could run through a brick wall and come away laughing. There was a similarity in build to Titus Cabone, the maetrie mercenary that worked for Dominion Thule, but Hylakane didn't move like someone his size.

"Do you really want to waste your short life listening to an exile at the far end of civilization tell you what to do every waking second? You humans have such pathetic life spans, barely a blink of an eye. What's the use of training when you'll be dead before you make any significant progress?"

"Yes, Steel Sun."

"A shame. Really," said Hylakane.

While he spoke fluent English (and other human languages apparently), his accent was decidedly not the gravelly, honey mixed with glass tone that most maetrie had. It sounded like silk being pulled over steel, but amplified.

"I could offer—"

The sentence was never finished. Hylakane burst forward, sending his fist into Kuma's stomach. He'd managed to detect the subterfuge, but even still, he couldn't harden his gut enough to withstand the impact. The hit toppled him backwards, spilling Pandora off. She survived the shift with a backflip, landing on her feet, while he had to climb out from beneath the board.

"The mongrel and the insect. What a pair. Never before have I had such worthless trainees. Your presence insults me."

"Yes, Steel Sun," they said in unison.

"What's next? Shall we work on our crawling? Appropriate for an insect, but it bores me to watch you struggle with little progress. I'd hoped you would be able to cross the field in minutes rather than the hour that it takes you. Pathetic." Hylakane sneered from his position before them. "Have you regretted your choice to see me yet? Wish you could slink back to the city, beg your grandfather for forgiveness? I can see it in your eyes, mongrel."

Hylakane stood inches away from Pandora, who had to avert her eyes.

"I have much respect for Dominion. It takes cunning to survive without a court to protect you." He laughed. "You two look like the ass end of a dolgant. Get out of my sight. You have an hour and then I expect you at my quarters, clean and ready to fail your next challenge."

Neither of them looked up until he was gone. They'd made the mistake of relaxing too early previously, only to earn another round of whatever training they were currently suffering under.

Pandora raised an eyebrow when she glanced over.

"His quarters?"

"No idea. Probably a trick. He's just messing with us," said Kuma.

Many times before Hylakane had made it appear they'd have a day off or a long break only to show up and put them to work immediately. In the time they'd been under his supervision, Kuma felt like he'd never been able to relax.

They headed to the fountain, which was a short jog from the spire, and stripped bare, washing their bodies and clothes in the basin before returning to their quarters to grab fresh uniforms. A basket of local fruits waited for them on the table. The flavors were bitter and oily, but they provided sustenance for the long days of training. Kuma gobbled his down, licking the sticky fluids from his fingers, even as he hated the taste. A heavy sigh from Pandora prompted him to ask a question.

"Regrets?"

"No," she said grimly. "Worried what it means that we're headed to his quarters."

"I'll believe it when we get there. As for now, I'm expecting him to detour us back to the death crawl." He tossed the skins from the fruit into the empty basket. “Shall we?”

Pandora leaned over and set her head on his shoulder.

“Whatever happens next, I want to say I’m sorry for dragging you into this.”

The tone of finality surprised Kuma, but before he could ask a question, she was headed towards the concrete stairs that would lead to the higher levels.

Twenty-Six

The request to join Hylakane in his quarters was familiar as it was unsettling to Pandora. It'd been over a decade since she'd last trained with the Steel Sun, but every memory from her previous attempt had been with her since the beginning. While the tasks had changed, the sense of overwhelming physical and mental challenge had remained. Hylakane knew how to push them to their very limits—which was why Pandora was so worried about the next one.

Since they'd been given residence in the spire, they hadn't been allowed past the third floor, which was where their quarters were. It wasn't much beyond a pair of raggedy cots and a stone table. They were barely in the room except to collapse after each day to attempt to sleep despite the aches and pains echoing through their bodies.

Heading up the stairs made her right foot twinge—she'd ripped off the toenail from the big foot. It'd been hanging precariously for a few days, but the recent training had finally finished it off and she'd yanked it free at the fountain. They passed a level filled with brownish-orange plants from which the oddly colored fruits they'd been regularly eating were hanging.

A few levels later, they reached Hylakane's quarters to find him spinning through maneuvers using a weapon that she'd heard about, but had never seen before. Zhinzi, or Lifespinner, was a long pole with a circular disc at one end and a crescent on the other. She could tell he was moving slower than he would normally so they could see him in action. The dark weapon put off a low hum that made her teeth hurt. It seemed to be made of a material that had the glossy exterior of obsidian, but none of its fragility.

"The insect and his keeper are early," he said, letting the weapon freeze behind his back. Had it been either of them trying to use Zhinzi, the weight alone would have made the sudden halt impossible.

Hylakane regarded them silently before approaching the wall and setting the strange weapon upon two hooks. Pandora wondered why she was being allowed to see Lifespinner, when her previous visit she had not. No explanation was given, and Hylakane headed to the concrete stairs that led ever upward. She hurried to follow, knowing his moods from months of training.

His quarters were midway up the building. They followed him up, watching the other buildings of the forgotten city drift below them as they reached the highest floor. Every ponderous step brought Pandora closer to the trial that she'd known would come since the day she saw the dark shapes circling the spire.

Kuma sucked in a breath behind her when they crested onto the roof. Without walls to block their sight, the space was larger than she imagined, but it wasn't the emptiness she was paying attention to but the cluster of black shapes sitting on the far edge. Her heart was in her throat. Wraithhawks. The ethereal creatures could drain a person to a husk in minutes. The last time she'd been this close, Hylakane had asked her to walk through them, but she'd refused and that had been the end of her training.

Realizing Hylakane's eyes were upon her, she concentrated on her breathing. Slow in. Slow out. Letting her breath cycle like undulating waves until the fear wasn't fluttering around in her head.

"Despite what the Courts might think, wraithhawks are the ultimate predator in the Eternal City," said Hylakane with his hands behind his back like a human professor. "Not even Lady Zaire could withstand a flock of them draining away her essence. Magic does little to them besides make them angrier."

His casual demeanor had her risking a question. "What are they?"

The creasing around the corners of his eyes made him appear much older than he looked.

"Some think they're related to the smoke-eaters, but that couldn't be further from the truth. The reality is they are not originally from this realm, but refugees from another that long ago collapsed under its own chaotic weight."

"How do you know this?"

Hylakane arched an eyebrow. "Long before the annihilation of the Ebony Court made me an exile, I studied them. I kept a garden where they would visit and I would release disobedient slaves or other creatures for them to feast, allowing me to observe their behavior."

A tightness formed in her chest. He smirked in her direction.

"Maetrie morals disgust you."

She nodded.

"Yet you are one. Is that why you cannot reach your true potential? You hold yourself back as not to appear too different from the other half of your heritage."

Pandora shared a glance with Kuma, who was staring at her curiously.

"Are you?" he asked.

"No," she said emphatically. "I think."

Hylakane turned towards her and placed a thick finger into her chest.

"You are neither human, nor maetrie. You are something else entirely."

"A mongrel," she bit back.

A slow smile climbed onto his lips. "That is one description. But I have another." He faced the flock of wraithhawks that had been staring at them the whole time, an unsettling feeling. "What is stronger, iron or steel?"

"Steel," she said after a moment of hesitation.

"Why?"

She shook her head.

Kuma spoke up. "Steel is an alloy."

"Good, the insect has a brain," said Hylakane. "And why is an alloy stronger than regular metal?"

"The different metals overlap, or something like that," said Kuma, face pinched.

"An incomplete explanation, but it's close enough. Alloys are stronger because the mixed metals cover for the weaknesses of each. But an alloy that thinks it's a base metal is as useless as one."

"I don't think I'm a base metal."

"Really? Then why don't you use your maetrie aura to influence the weak minds of your world?"

"I don't have an aura," she said right away.

"Or you desire to be seen as human and not a ghoulish maetrie," said Hylakane.

She opened her mouth to refute him, but knew it was true. She'd had the same conversation with Kuma years ago.

"You came to me because your grandfather has taken over the world you'd cultivated for yourself. He destroyed that which you cherished. You'll never beat him unless you can embrace your maetrie side."

"I don't know what that means," she said, feeling her heart rate increase.

"I think you do."

His eyes flickered towards the flock of wraithhawks. "You passed the faeila trial. You can do this too. I placed a gift for you on the ledge, one that will help you with your grandfather, but you have to retrieve it yourself."

The idea that she would walk over to the wraithhawks and casually take an item from the ledge without them sucking her soul away seemed ludicrous, even as she knew that Hylakane could do it. Pandora took a step forward, and then another, until she was halfway across, but as the shadowy heads turned her direction like a bench of judges readying their decision, she found her legs would no longer move. She could see the object, but not what it was. Maybe it was a box, but she couldn't move any closer to find out. Pandora considered using a sapphire Pull to draw it near, but then Hylakane called out behind her.

"I wouldn't do that. If you do, it'll draw them to you and they'll feast on your soul and there'll be nothing I can do."

Pandora closed her eyes. She had to get her emotions under control, but the task only reminded her of how she'd failed the previous time. She managed to shuffle a foot forward, but then the flock rustled their ethereal wings, their attentions growing more severe. She kept imagining the entire group leaping into the air and descending on her before she could flee.

She wasn't sure how long she stood there, but after what felt like an hour, but had probably only been ten minutes, she returned to Hylakane and Kuma with her head hung low.

"Does this mean I have to leave?" she asked in a quiet voice.

"Not this time. The gift will remain on the ledge until you find the will to retrieve it."

Pandora found she couldn't meet his gaze, having disappointed him once again. She wasn't used to failure. Silence continued for longer than she expected. In fact, she assumed he would send them back to training, probably the death crawl. Instead, he spoke in a firm voice.

"Today's training is complete. You may have the rest of the time to yourselves." He chuckled. "Don't worry. It's not a trick. Tomorrow morning I want you to meet me in the field of statues with your blades."

Twenty-Seven

Freeing Triana brought a renewed sense of purpose to the group, after months of being sequestered in the upper room at Club Onyx. While Choo-Choo was constantly peppering Leesa with questions about things she'd overheard during open hours in hopes of learning where Vasilisa was located, Yara spent her time working out in the room, a mix of physical exertion and maintaining her faez crystal disciplines. It wasn't just the long-term goal of revenge on Deacon for his betrayal, but the fight at the mine had made her—and the others—realize that the alliance waku were getting better. They couldn't rely on their assumed superiority any longer.

When they weren't waiting for the news of Vasilisa's location, they prowled the Undercity, being careful not to repeat themselves or leave obvious trails that could lead pursuers to the hidden passage behind Club Onyx. In those months, they freed another couple dozen slaves, depositing them at the Chamber. And each time they were told not to bring any more.

To keep anyone from being able to follow them, Tick used his tiger's eye to confuse their tracks with the various creatures he could find. It was almost amusing to Yara to be sneaking through the tunnels with a pack of tumblers rolling behind them like living tumbleweeds.

Their target was a mining site near the wastelands in the southeastern quadrant, which was near Big Dave's Town. It would be their riskiest raid, but Leesa had heard that Elani was stationed in the area. The presence of the former maintenance leader of the Drops made it a must-hit, since they knew she'd been involved with many aspects of the Alliance clan's mining expansion. Leesa had overheard some of the waku discussing the problems associated with mining near the enormous canyon that had once been the site of other digging operations many decades ago. The deeper trenches were the home of many dangerous creatures that had already given them problems. Yara knew the stories of the early mages of the Halls performing arcane experiments in the depths, and the rumors of powerful artifacts lost to the shifting earth. She'd even heard that there were maetrie structures in the deepest section, but that seemed improbable. The occasional traveler that headed into those places made it clear they were more than rumors.

Yara sighed as she tried to balance all the concerns in her head. If they could get to Elani, they could not only put a major dent into the Alliance's operations, but hopefully find out where Vasilisa was located.

"Are we on the right path?" asked Choo-Choo for the fifth time since they'd left the Terreno.

"I know this area better than Tick knows his own cock," said Yara. "We were always expecting a raid from Drops, so our defenses were placed in these areas."

"I found it," said Tick, sticking his head around the corner.

"Your cock?" asked Choo-Choo.

"What?"

Choo-Choo frowned. "Sorry. Something Yara said. You found the entrance?"

"Yeah," said Tick soberly.

As they followed the smallish waku to the entrance of the tunnels Razor used for transporting goods and people across the Undercity safely, Yara couldn't help but notice how the last year of guerilla warfare and seclusion had changed him. While he still said the most outrageous things, he was more subdued during their excursions. More focused. Professional. He even had a little soul patch growing on his chin. If she didn't know any better, she'd think he was all grown up.

The entrance was behind a hidden wall at the back of a cavern. The only reason Tick had found it was because the wall had shifted at some time in the past.

"A good sign they're not keeping up with the maintenance," said Yara, running her hand along the rough edge. The fake wall had been constructed from two-by-fours, mesh wire, and spreadable concrete, then painted matte black and had dust and rocks thrown on it before the paint dried. It was a task the younger kids worked on when they weren't in school or training.

The stainless steel wheel squeaked heavily when they turned it. Had they not had two topaz, they probably wouldn't have been able to get it open. Yara dropped into the darkness first, using Lightness to land, while the other two had to climb down the rungs in the wall. The ladder was in a little cubby away from the main route. Using a headlamp, Choo-Choo examined the tunnel, running his hands along the hewn surface.

"So these are the famous Razor tunnels. I never thought they'd be so smooth. How did your clan manage a feat like this?" he asked.

Yara was examining the dust for signs of recent passage. The layer was thick enough to suggest no one had passed through it in months at the least, possibly longer.

"They made a deal with a talented Stone Singer back then. They needed help with a problem you don't bring to the police, and we needed tunnels."

Choo-Choo whistled softly. "Must have been some problem. I can't imagine how long it took."

"Six years," said Yara. "On and off. It was long before my time and everyone who probably knew about it is dead now."

"I heard it was the head of Stone Singers," Tick said as they headed in a southwesterly direction.

"That's bullshit," said Yara. "A rumor only without a shred of evidence. Nor did they kill the mage afterwards to keep the tunnels a secret."

"So much history lost when the Alliance took over," said Choo-Choo as they traveled. "Why haven't we used these before?"

"Because this is an older tunnel without much use for the Alliance," said Yara. "I'm assuming they use the ones from the Machi to Big Dave's or some of the cross-city tunnels, but this one is an offshoot of the others, only leading to the wastelands."

"Why?"

"There was a time when Razor was investigating setting up a base in the canyons, thinking they might take advantage of whatever was left after the excavations ended last century, but they learned pretty quickly that it's not a place to mess around. This was pre-faez crystals, so they had to battle some wicked stuff with blades and moxie alone."

"What do you think they were looking for?"

Yara shrugged. "No one knows. Powerful artifacts, I'm sure. In the early years of the Undercity, only the mages dared visit to study the wells or practice their forbidden magics in secret. Supposedly there are things lost here that could destroy entire cities, but that's probably just bullshit."

"What do you think's down there?" asked Choo-Choo.

"On the near side, there's a big lake. Heard from some older waku that the lake has jellyfish in it that'll make you go mad, and on a little island on the far side is a three-headed hydra the size of a dinosaur, but I'm not sure how they could have seen that. It's where the water well of power is. But on the eastern side of the wastelands, not far from the lake, the ground drops away and it goes down hundreds of meters."

The remoteness of the tunnel allowed them to converse during their journey, a different experience from their normal passage through the Undercity, which required constant attention. When Yara spotted a symbol etched into the wall with faded white paint, she held up her hand, indicating silence. For the next hundred meters they moved without sound, until they came upon a side passage with a set of rungs on the wall leading to an escape hatch.

The mining site was a couple hundred meters away from the tunnel. They could hear it right away, the thumping vibration of heavy machinery, reverberating in the soles of her feet. An intense whooshing sound brought hunched foreheads. It sounded like water was being sprayed from a fire hose. Yara pulled her blades right away, feeling strangely exposed. The nature of the operation meant the site would be well guarded. It'd seemed like a good idea when they discussed it in Club Onyx, but now that they were creeping forward with Koro on scout duty, Yara wondered if it was the right choice.

Tick discovered that it wasn't like the other mining areas. A small settlement had been set up. Two dozen tents and two wooden buildings littered the cavern next to the mine.

"There's too many people here," whispered Tick. "I counted a dozen guards and I couldn't even see the other side without risking Koro."

The heavy noise made speaking without fear of discovery possible. Choo-Choo was grinding his teeth, staring into the distance. His aura was thick and taut. Yara put a hand on his forearm. He twitched, then seeming to sense his own tension, exhaled through his nose, making his nostrils flare.

"There was something else," said Tick, furrowing his brow. "A big hose coming from another cavern. The thing was being held down with pitons, but it didn't look like it wanted to stay that way. I think it's what's making all the noise."

"What do you think it is?" asked Yara.

"No idea," he replied.

"There's too many odd things about this site. Is this a good idea?" she asked.

Choo-Choo closed his eyes momentarily. "I don't want to lose this opportunity."

"If we're dead then we can't rescue your sister," said Yara.

"I can't keep doing this," said Choo-Choo, his face etched with existential agony. "We've been lurking in the shadows for what, a year now? I don't even know. The longer it takes the more I worry that something will happen. I promised that I would get her back."

Yara squeezed her hand around the hilt of her blade. "We only need Elani. We're not hitting the mine. Did you see her, Tick?"

He screwed up his face. "No. I couldn't get too close."

"She'd be in the building," said Choo-Choo. "A tent wouldn't give her space to hang drawings. She's got to be in one of those two buildings. They're less protected. We could get her out without the rest of the mine knowing we're here. Whatever that stupid hose is, it will help us hide our approach."

It was a plausible plan, but Yara didn't like it. She worried they were pushing too hard. After the close battle to free Triana, they'd promised each other not to overstep and risk the final defeat.

"I don't know..."

"Please," said Choo-Choo. "Once we find my sister and free her, we can leave the Undercity, or whatever you want to do."

"I was thinking of setting up a supply shop in the Terreno," said Tick with a shrug. "Darina has the money to front me."

"Tick," said Yara, shaking her head. "They'd recognize you, or at the very least, Koro."

"I know, but..."

"Yara," said Choo-Choo emphatically.

She could feel the group fraying at the edges. Seeing a potential end in sight made them less cautious, but she couldn't make herself break Choo-Choo's heart.

"Okay, but first sign of danger, we're out. No fucking around. If I say run, you run."

Choo-Choo hesitated, which made her glare until he finally relented, nodding reluctantly.

"If I say run, you run," she repeated.

"I got it."

Tick's eyes unfocused for a moment. When he returned to awareness he said, "Now is as good a time as any. There are a few people sleeping in the tents, and two guards on our side. Be easy enough to take them out without alerting the rest."

"What's the plan?" asked Yara.

"Bug and throw?" suggested Choo-Choo.

"Good enough," said Yara.

They moved into position. Choo-Choo stood behind Yara around the corner while they waited for Tick's distraction. It took a few minutes for Tick to get his bugs into position. Yara listened with her amber, catching snippets of the guards' conversation as they watched two centipedes the length of their forearms fornicating on the rocks near the guard station. Yara was always amazed at how easily they could be distracted by such trivial sights.

She tapped on Choo-Choo's thigh and he grabbed her by the collar and belt as she shifted Light. With blades ready in her fists, she gave him a nod. He spun around the corner and launched her in a high arc. The guards never saw her coming. The first brought his head up when she was about to land, but it was too late. Choo-Choo's throw had been perfect. She landed between them, arms slicing outward, severing twin throats. The guards staggered to their knees, their gargling end leaving bloody pools amid the rocks.

Choo-Choo and Tick caught up to her as they crossed the cavern, stepping quietly between the tents. Halfway across she had a sudden urge to flee that she didn't understand until the door to the lighted building swung open, revealing a familiar figure.

Deacon had changed since she'd seen him last. He always had a cocky exterior—a resting smirk and playful twinkle in his eyes that said he was ready for anything the world could throw at him—in addition to the sharp edges that allowed him to survive in a world of cutthroat criminal enterprise. His time in the Eternal City had knocked off the smirk, but filled his edges until they were razor sharp. Something dark and ominous lurked behind his eyes.

Yara felt like a mouse spotted by a circling hawk without a place to run, but reason fled her mind as the rage in her soul came bubbling to the surface. She was sprinting forward before she had a chance to consider the consequences.

She never saw him draw a weapon, but a hooked blade was in his fist as she slashed in a series of rapid attacks. Yara was certain she'd never moved faster but Deacon blocked them easily, moving quicker than her eyes could detect. Had it just been the two of them, the counterattack would have been fatal, but Choo-Choo and Tick joined her in battle, the three of them combining with deadly strikes to put Deacon on his back foot.

They managed to drive him backwards a few steps, before he found an opening, kicking Tick hard enough to tumble him into a canvas tent. With only two on the offense, Deacon flipped the momentum, striking with his hooked sword with power. The impacts rung through her arms, making her feel like an anvil to his sledgehammer.

Yara shoved her foot under a loose rock the size of her head and kicked it into Deacon's chest, making him miss a counterattack. She brought her left blade around, knowing that Choo-Choo's forward thrust would force him to block. She thought she had a wide-open angle to his neck, but then he side-shifted, landing ten feet away. He staggered when he stopped, black smoke leaking from his lips then curling back into his throat like a living thing returning to its womb.

There was nothing more in the world that she wanted than revenge against Deacon, but the way he avoided what she'd thought had been a killing blow told her that they were outmatched.

"Run."

Deacon's eyes lit up at the prospect of the chase. Before Yara could take two steps, he'd cut off their escape.

"I've been waiting for this moment for a long time. To finally finish what Gregor and Titus couldn't. The final elimination of the Drops and Razor clan."

His dark eyes glowered with frightful energy as if he were readying a powerful attack, but before he could unleash it, a winged creature appeared in his face, forcing him to defend himself.

"Run," said Yara again, this time sprinting the opposite direction, collecting Tick from the fallen tent as Koro protected their escape.

They ran towards the mine, their appearance creating chaos, but before the guards could lift their weapons, they had slipped into a side tunnel. Bullets ricocheted on the rocks behind them.

But their escape was brief as they ran out of room, skidding to a stop at the edge of a deep chasm. The mine had been built on the edge of the wastelands and they'd trapped themselves against the expanse.

Deacon appeared first, slowing when he saw their predicament. Choo-Choo pulled his handgun before Deacon could close the gap, unloading the entire clip into his chest. The alliance waku staggered as the bullets hit him cleanly, but when the sound of gunfire no longer rang in the small space, Deacon was still standing. His skin was matte gray, but flashed back to its normal pale color.

Not only was Deacon faster and stronger than them, but he had a black diamond. They'd been so careful. Yara cursed herself for not avoiding the camp entirely.

"My biggest regret was that I didn't bring you with me, Yara. We could have been great together."

"Fuck you, Deacon. The fact that you thought I would come over to you tells me you never understood me. You stabbed us in the back. It might not have been your hand, but you killed my father with your betrayal."

"Kill or be killed. You should know it as well as I. Letting honor or family confuse you was your mistake. They were never going to survive once Dominion took over the Alliance clan. You have no idea how outmatched you are. I didn't understand until he sent me to the Eternal City. Once they decide they want to take over a place, there's nothing you can do to stop them. They live longer than us, are more cunning, ruthless. It's the whole package. I promise I'll make it quick. It's the least I can do."

The way Deacon approached suggested that he was in full control of the situation. Yara backed to the edge with her friends at her side. She checked over her shoulder at the yawning expanse, seeing only one possible way out of their situation. She hoped she correctly understood the purpose of the hose and what it was carrying. Yara sheathed her weapons.

"Grab onto my belt and hold on tight," said Yara.

As alarm appeared on Deacon's face and he surged forward to intercept, she locked her arms with Choo-Choo's and Tick's as they stared at her, not understanding. Before they could stop her, she leapt from the cliff, taking her friends with her.

Twenty-Eight

Vasilisa didn't see Andelei for nearly three months after their date at the Lime Duck. He was sent to the wastelands on guard duty for a special project that didn't involve faez crystals. She knew about the work because her logistics supply depot provided the equipment that had been brought down through the elevator at the Lazona. The Drops had been working on the easy access to the Undercity for years, but once the Alliance had taken control, the work renewed in earnest and it'd finished a few weeks after he'd left. She'd thought about trying to smuggle herself out in a shipment, but she'd seen how they thoroughly searched the crates and knew she'd never be able to evade detection. Besides, she was getting used to her new life and had been thinking about Andelei often whenever she wasn't busy. The owner at the Lime Duck asked her about him whenever she went in for a meal too.

When he appeared around the corner at the Lazona, a duffle bag slung over his shoulder, her whole body grew warm in anticipation. Andelei had let his hair grow longer and it was past his shoulders. She skipped towards him, resisting the urge for a full-out run.

After they embraced, he cupped her chin and pressed his lips against hers. They stayed locked in a kiss, hips agonizingly close. She squeezed his tight ass when they parted, which made him flush.

"Shadows below, I've missed you," he said.

Vasilisa let her tongue rest on her bottom teeth. She placed her palm against his chest, enjoying the firmness of his muscles, digging her nails into his flesh.

"It's been a long three months," she said, arching an eyebrow suggestively.

"I was hoping—"

"Yes, you can come back to my room."

Vasilisa led him by the hand. She'd worn a tight black outfit that clung to her body with a touch of floral perfume that she'd bought in the Lazona. The attendant had claimed it had alchemical undertones that would drive a partner mad, but Vasilisa thought it was marketing bullshit—besides, she knew after three months her presence alone would be enough for arousal.

The stairs to the fourth level was on the opposite side from the Lime Duck. She occasionally glanced back to Andelei, who was staring at her hungrily. When their boots rang against the metal flooring, he looked around.

"Where are we going?"

"My apartment," she said.

She led him through a hallway that went into the earth. A blue metal door opened to her key, revealing a two-room space that was larger than her family's place in the Drops. She'd managed to scrape together enough favors and cash for a couch and a glossy print of the city above that hung on the wall.

"How? When?"

Vasilisa pressed herself against him. "Last month. They said I'm doing a good job, so they let me move in here and I'm getting paid now too. Not a lot but enough for small things."

He cupped his hand against her back, which brought shivers down her spine. She'd been dreaming about this moment for months. With a shaking hand, she undid the front of his pants, letting them ride down on his slender hips. The kiss that came after was hungry, filled with pent-up need, followed with him tugging off her bodysuit. When she was naked except for her underclothes, he traced his fingers across her body, leaving trails of delight. Vasilisa shivered.

"Are you cold?" he asked, pulling away with concern in his brown eyes.

"No," she breathed, shoving him onto the couch and straddling him. She felt him straining through his underwear, and rocked against him, catching little moans slipping from his lips. They ground their hips together, until she couldn't take it anymore. The final layers were quickly tugged off and then they were back together, warm and wet, rising and falling in an undulating cycle that didn't last long.

"I'm sorry," he said, when they were sitting side by side, cradling each other on the couch. "It's been—"

Vasilisa put her finger to his lips, then grabbed his hand and placed it between her legs. She showed him how to pleasure her, and within a few minutes she joined him in quiet relief on the couch. Afterwards, she grabbed them a fizzy drink from the refrigerator and they cuddled for a while, which eventually turned horizontal, this time with Andelei on top. At first she was annoyed that the couch was squeaking as he thrust inside of her, but her thoughts quickly evaporated with the explosions of pleasure in her hips. Having already released once, he managed to last long enough to bring her to fruition before following her into ecstasy.

When they were finished, they were both lying on the floor. She barely remembered falling off. Andelei was on his back, while she lay on her side, hand pressed against his chest, which rose and fell like waves.

A tinge of guilt rose up as she thought about how different her life was from a year ago, when she was still in the Pajot, a member of Drops, and in school. Now she had a job, an apartment, and a boyfriend.

"I'm hungry," she said, sitting up after a long time on the floor. "Wanna get burgers at the Lime Duck?"

"I do, but—"

He crawled over to his duffle bag, which had been thrown into the corner when they first came in. She smacked him on the ass, enjoying the loud slap, and giggling afterwards. She couldn't believe how comfortable she felt naked around him, but it would have felt weirder to put her clothes back on.

When he returned to her side with a small box in his hands, her heart rate spiked and she felt suddenly exposed. He shifted onto his knees and presented the box.

"Andy, I don't think—"

Andelei's face screwed up with confusion, before he broke into laughter. It lasted for too long, and she punched him in the shoulder.

"What are you going on about, you wayhos?" she said.

He cocked a grin. "I guess I could understand your confusion." He popped open the box, revealing a tiny stone sitting in the center of a velvet catch.

Her heart soared with excitement. "Is that...?"

"Yes. An amber stone."

"Oh, fuck me," she exclaimed.

"Already did, but we can again."

Vasilisa laughed, then leaned over and kissed him hungrily, before returning her attention to the stone.

"How did you? Or do I want to know? I guess I'll have to hide it," she said, considering where to attach it on her body.

"You don't have to. I bought it. Made sure it was on the level and everything. I had to tell them who it was for, but you know, since you've been kicking ass here, they approved it. It's yours. You know, assuming you can attune to it."

Vasilisa hugged the box to her chest. "Oh, thank you."

Her dream as long as she could remember was to have a stone of her own. To be a waku like her brother and sister. To not just be the girl with one hand who "surprised people by how effective she could be." Holding the velvet box in her hand left her strangely empty.

"Is something wrong?"

Vasilisa shook her head. "No. Not at all. I'm just surprised. I really didn't think you'd be able to get me one on the up-and-up. Before, you know, when I was in the Drops, they said I'd never get a stone or join the Academy because of my missing hand. It feels weird to get one now." She sighed. "Though I still have to attune."

"Given your family's history, I'm sure it'll be easy."

The reminder hit her in the forehead, but she knew he meant well, so she gave him a weak smile.

"Thank you, Andy."

She leaned over and kissed him sweetly, cradling the box to her chest.

"Aren't you going to put it on?" he asked, eyes alight.

"Not right now. I don't want the nausea to interfere."

"To interfere with...oh," he said.

Before he could lean over to kiss her, she pushed him over, laughing, and climbed on top.

"Use your amber," she said.

"What?"

"Turn it all the way on. I want to thank you properly for my gift."

The grin on his face could have split the world. She tapped on his chest.

"Don't forget to return the favor after I'm attuned."

§

Vasilisa didn't hook the amber stone to her belly button until the next morning before she headed to work. Under normal circumstances, she would have put it in her ear to show her status, but since she didn't know if she would attune, and part of her couldn't quite believe she'd been approved for the stone, she wanted to keep it hidden. For now.

Her office was on the bottom floor of the Lazona, next to a converted bar that had become the warehouse. She had three people working for her, an older man who took care of the paperwork and two kids around her age that had originally come from the Machi. They kept the warehouse organized and loaded the carts for delivery. Most of what they supplied was food and water for the mining sites in the southwest quadrant, but they kept a few simple equipment repair items too.

"Andelei's return must have gone very well," said Nota, the older gentleman, who sat at his deck on the opposite side of the room with a stack of papers in his hands. "You're more zoned out than a drug addict."

"Oh, it was great," she said absently.

Nota furrowed his brow. "I sense more than great. You haven't admonished me for a single pun this morning."

She approached his desk and lifted up her shirt, showing her belly button.

"He got me a gift. An amber. Approved and everything, but I'm worried that I won't attune."

Nota whistled. "He must really like you. Those don't come cheap."

"He's a patrol leader now, but yeah, it wasn't cheap. I don't want anyone to know in case I, you know..."

Nota winked conspiratorially. "I won't tell those two knuckleheads, but you might want to focus, or they'll know something's up."

The reminder gave Vasilisa the kick to pay attention. The day passed faster once she'd thrown herself into preparing for the big shipment that would be coming in the next morning. With the elevator up and running, more goods were coming through the Lazona than Big Dave's Town. She'd heard her office would be expanding, but she didn't know if someone else would be in charge or if they'd let her grow with the position.

That night curled with Andelei on the couch after welcome-home sex, she admitted her concerns.

"I haven't felt a single thing yet. Not a moment of vertigo. Nothing. Never before have I wanted to feel sick so bad."

"It can take days for some people. More rare, but it's possible."

§

On the morning of the third day, Vasilisa didn't want to go into work. Andelei found her sitting on the edge of the bed, staring at the stone attached to her belly button. The flesh around the hook was still red. He placed his arms around her and cradled her to his chest. She leaned back and stared at the blank wall, a chasm of regret inside.

"It might still happen."

"No, Andy. It's not. And even if it did, that's not even the final step. Attunement is rare for those that don't feel sick right away. I heard my brother's stories about his Academy group. It's not going to happen."

"I'm sorry, Vasy. It's bad luck."

"No," she said. "Not bad luck. It's my fault."

"Don't say that." He cupped her jaw and turned her gently towards him. "Not everyone can attune. It's a fact of life in the Undercity."

"No. It's my fault. After the Alliance took over, I could only think about escaping. I managed to sneak an untested stone out of the mine by swallowing it. I was sick for days and then it passed into the toilet and I couldn't get it back. I know now that that long exposure probably killed my chance. I fucked up, Andy. I'll never be a waku."

She didn't cry as he held her to his chest. She was too empty for tears. A part of her had harbored the idea that once she had a stone, even a lowly amber, she might be able to resume her resistance to the Alliance. But now she didn't know. Not only had her new clan given her the very thing that she'd desired her whole life, the gift that the Drops wouldn't have allowed, but her disobedience was the reason it'd failed. As Andelei rocked gently, his arms comfortably around her chest, she vowed that she would no longer oppose the Alliance, not even in her heart. She would accept her new family with open arms, forgoing the revenge she'd once desperately desired. She was, once and for all, Alliance clan.

Twenty-Nine

The sword felt as light as a feather in Kuma's grip as he extended it forward at an excruciatingly drawn-out pace. If it weren't for the speed of this thrust, it would have reminded him of his youth when they played with sticks and pretended to be famous waku defending the clan's honor.

"Too fast. Even slower," said Hylakane from atop his pillar as he cooled himself with a hand fan.

Kuma forced his muscles to move at a glacial tempo as he balanced on the pillar opposite Hylakane. Pandora was behind him, performing the same maneuvers, but he had to focus, so he couldn't check on her progress. The only sign he had that she was still there was the slow cycle of breathing.

The sword tip swayed to the left, his arm bending at a ninety-degree angle to simulate a block, before he performed a kick forward—balancing on a single foot—while his arm propelled forward again. The deliberate pace strained his back and thighs as he had to maintain his position for longer.

"Catch."

The word was his only warning. Hylakane threw a pebble in a high arc. Kuma positioned his blade beneath the falling rock, accepting it on the tip without a single wobble. The last two attempts, the rock had slipped from the end, requiring him to start over.

"Flick it to Pandora."

She was behind him, but he could sense her location with his amber. He flicked his wrist, sending the pebble over his shoulder. The bright sound of rock on metal brought the creasing of a smile to the corner of his lips as he continued through the rest of the routine.

When he was finished, Hylakane stared back with heavy-lidded eyes. "Not bad for an insect. Now do it again. This time I want you to keep the pebble on the end of your blade the entire time."

He tossed Kuma a second rock. He shook out his limbs, set the pebble on the end, and began again. They'd been on the poles for the last three hours. His legs were tired, but not yet to the exhausted state that made exacting movements challenging. It took him ten tries to repeat the routine with the pebble on the tip of his sword, mostly because his right arm kept twitching unexpectedly, an issue he'd been having of late. Pandora managed it in three, but Hylakane made her continue until he was finished too. The hardest part was keeping it on the blade for the blocks.

When they were finished, they stood like statues on their pillars, waiting for the next instruction. Hylakane seemed almost annoyed that they'd managed to complete his tasks in a relatively short time compared to some of the other challenges he'd given them.

"Again, but I want to you to switch rocks when I give the signal."

This went on for another six hours. Each time they managed to complete the instructions, he increased the difficulty. When Kuma's legs shook and their attempts grew worse rather than better, Hylakane snapped his hand fan closed.

"Enough. You've managed to not be completely terrible today."

The bald maetrie squinted towards the sky as if there was a bright sun, but the Eternal City was cast in perpetual gloom, the gray-black cloud layer providing a solid ceiling that reminded him of his home. When Hylakane looked back to Kuma, he felt the Steel Sun's gaze like a surgeon's knife. Something heavy and dark passed across his eyes, but it was gone before Kuma could process what it meant.

"Clean up and meet me in my domicile."

The fountain was busy when they went to wash up. Two gap-toothed maetrie were filling their containers with fresh water. The taller one had a missing eye and the other moved with a hitch as if his hip had been broken and never repaired in the past. Kuma found himself overcome with the sudden urge to cut their throats to release them from their miserable existence. Their broken forms disgusted him and filled him with unusual rage. His right arm started to reach for his curved blade, but then he realized what he was doing and the feeling faded quickly, replaced by embarrassment. He admonished himself even as he couldn't figure out where it'd come from. The two maetrie seemed to sense his mood, grabbed their water containers, and disappeared.

Back in the spire, they found Hylakane lounging on a stone couch, wearing gauzy cream robes that left little to the imagination. A glass decanter of silver liquid sat on the stone table with three empty goblets.

Pandora's hungry gaze as she noticed the silvery liquid had Kuma curious, but he kept his mouth shut, knowing that Hylakane preferred them to speak only when spoken to. He gestured to a stone couch opposite, and as Kuma settled next to Pandora, Hylakane rose and lifted the decanter expectantly, which prompted them to grab their glasses and hold them out.

"Do you know what this is?" asked Hylakane.

"Vicisk," said Pandora, eyes wide with wonder. "I had it once, at my grandfather's table. It's quite...transformative."

The unusual description made Kuma curious. "It's not like the arosenthe, is it?"

"No better way to find out," said Hylakane, holding his glass in salute.

Kuma matched the gesture then looked into the silvery surface, spotting swirls of inky black that revealed themselves momentarily before disappearing. The liquid seem to have an energy of its own. He let it grace his lips, tasting it on the tip of his tongue, which immediately sent tingles of pleasure through his head. Encouraged, he took a big drink, reveling in the experience. Kuma barely was aware of his surroundings as he leaned against the stone couch, staring into the distance. The world seemed both infinite and small, with a warm cloak of contentment wrapped around his shoulders.

Lost in the pleasures of the vicisk, Kuma didn't realize Hylakane was standing over him with a knife until the blade had cut into the flesh of his forearm. Before he could jerk away, Hylakane held his arm fast. To his utter shock, the maetrie warrior stuck his fingers into his flesh, grasping something black and oily. A stab of pain shot through his body, but he was numb enough from the drink not to feel it other than as a distant problem.

When Hylakane yanked his arm upward, pulling something shiny and black from his forearm, Kuma thought it was his muscles at first and he was being dissected alive. But when the wriggling thing tried to wrap its tendrils around his forearm, Kuma realized that it wasn't a part of him. It looked like a miniature glistening ebony eel with a proboscis-like tongue. Hylakane threw it on the ground and stomped it with his heel until it was a black smear. Then he leaned over Kuma, running his fingers over the gash in his forearm until it closed as simply as pulling curtains shut. When it was finished, there was a white line surrounded by pink flesh and the dried blood from the once-open wound.

It took time for the strange liquid to wear off, but when it did, he found that Pandora and Hylakane were deep in conversation. Her maetrie constitution had shaken off the effects much faster.

"…there are no more left, the Black Butcher made sure of that, but it doesn't mean I couldn't cause her problems in the future." Hylakane smiled as he noticed Kuma sitting up. "How do you feel?"

Memories of what had happened came back, prompting Kuma to check his arm, which had a thin scar.

"Was that real?"

Hylakane nodded.

"It was the Ruby Queen," said Pandora. "Her physician put something in your arm."

"A typhid," said Hylakane. "It's part tracker, part mind control."

"Mind control?" asked Kuma in horror.

"It hadn't quite gotten to that stage yet. It was placed in your arm as a larva and had only recently grown large enough to start affecting your moods."

Kuma sucked in a breath. "I wanted to murder the two maetrie at the fountain. Their broken bodies disgusted me and I couldn't understand why."

"It was the Ruby Queen's doing. She was the one who caused the annihilation of the Ebony Court. That I still live is an affront to her sense of completion. She has long desired my demise, which was why she took the opportunity to place the typhid in your arm."

"I knew I shouldn't have trusted her," said Pandora. "I shouldn't have agreed to the fight."

"Do not regret your choices," said Hylakane. "Had you not been on your way here, she probably would have executed you, or tortured you for information about your grandfather. Knowing that you would be coming to see me meant that you were useful."

"How long have you known I was infected?"

Hylakane furrowed his brow. "Only recently did I figure out that it was a typhid, but from the moment you found me, I suspected that she would try something. At first, I thought you were willing conspirators to the plan she'd hatched, but then over time I realized you were unaware. It took me time to figure out what it was."

"That's awful," said Kuma.

"My race is short on compassion and long on grievances. Lady Amethyte does not forget, or forgive. She wiped out the entirety of my family because she saw us as weak. We dared to upset the norms of our culture by freeing our dolgant slaves and treating our workers with consideration. Nothing like the soft hearts of humans, but for a maetrie, what we were doing was blasphemy."

"Why doesn't she send her people to kill you?" asked Kuma.

"Because I make sure that no one actually knows if I'm truly here. Lady Amethyte isn't aware that I'd taught myself the art of shapeshifting. Walking amongst the settlement as Jester has helped me detect previous attempts on my life, which I was able to remove before word could get back to her. And she cannot penetrate my spire, because I protect myself with ancient magics that even she does not have access to."

Hylakane's eyes flicked to Zhinzi hanging on the wall.

"Your weapon?" asked Pandora.

"Indeed."

"Is that what that strange vibration is?" asked Kuma, staring at the dark weapon apprehensively.

The sober look from Hylakane was worrying. "You don't know?"

Kuma shook his head at the same time as Pandora, which surprised him.

"Plazkabog, or Tears of the Gods in your language. There are eleven of them. They were made long ago by our forebears, who had arcane knowledge we don't possess, despite being their superior in many other ways."

"Kavano has one," Kuma blurted out.

"The fact that you've met him does not surprise me since it is well known that Dominion manages to hire him on a regular basis despite his exorbitant fees. Many think there is some other link, or leverage, but no one knows. But yet, Kavano has one of the eleven. The Black Butcher has another. A few lie in the Eternal City, while the others are scattered amongst the realms, including one that is supposedly lost in yours. Each owner carries their burden in their own way."

"Burden?" asked Kuma, fearing the answer.

Hylakane approached Zhinzi, holding his hand near the circular blade as if it were a raging fire too hot to touch. The glossy black material seemed to absorb the light, and his nearness increased the tenor of the vibration as if it were waking to his presence.

"These weapons are proof of the maetrie's crimes against the realms. Mass destruction on a scale that even humans could not comprehend. They're made from an alloy of obsidian and *mágrithral*, which can only be found in another realm."

"Obsidian? Isn't that used for portals? I didn't think it could be combined with anything else due to its transient nature," Kuma said.

"That is the mystery the ancients conquered. A secret that should rest for all eternity, because its making was the start of a multi-realm genocide enacted by the maetrie." Hylakane returned to his stone couch. "Each weapon has the capability of destroying an entire realm and trapping the dead inside its cage in an awful half-life, thus powering even more destruction."

The idea was almost incomprehensible to Kuma, who shared his shock with Pandora. She curled her arms around her chest as if the thought was too horrible to consider.

"Your disgust is understandable. I should never be forgiven for what I did on behalf of my race. It was one reason that Lady Amethyte was able to destroy the Ebony Court, because I was too maudlin, too awash in grief to see her machinations."

"An entire realm?" asked Kuma in a voice that came out quiet, as if he were afraid to anger Hylakane.

"I don't know if the makers intended for it to happen. The idea was to use the arcane energy between places, the raw stuff of creation, to power the weapons. But to use that energy, one had to subdue the entire realm. Destroy it so it wouldn't fight back. Crush any rebellion with an iron fist. I hear their screams whenever I wield it. Even as I sleep, the flames rise in my mind. I annihilated whole cities using the power of the weapon."

Kuma had always known the maetrie were dangerous, but now he knew they were murderous on a scale that defied imagination. The strange vibration he could sense at the edge of his hearing took on a new shape, as if he could pick out the individual screams, the buildings collapsing, the flames licking at the edge of existence.

"Every weapon is a realm destroyed?" asked Pandora.

"Not all. Seven of the eleven by my count, though one of them was not used for an entire realm. Four are yet to be unleashed, including one that was lost to a thief in the recent past. Four more realms to be destroyed in the quest for ultimate power."

Kuma saw the Steel Sun as a war criminal who had launched a nuclear weapon without truly understanding the impact of his choice. Using the weapon had broken something inside of him, making him less maetrie, which was why the others had destroyed the Court that he served. They saw difference as something to be stomped out. Destroyed.

"Enough ruminating," said Hylakane, standing suddenly. "Return to your quarters and get some rest. We have much to do. Now that the typhid is destroyed we can truly get to work."

Thirty

The Eleventh Gonka was packed on Saturday night. A second story had been recently added, making it the largest bar at the Alliance headquarters. The music thumped, masking the racket from the boring machine cutting out new tunnels to the nearby cavern so they could expand.

Camina sat at the end of the bar drinking whiskey. Despite the shoulder-to-shoulder state of the interior, no one had taken the stool next to her. The brief friendliness she'd earned from her fellow waku had evaporated the moment she'd been named the head instructor at the Alliance Academy. The other waku either saw her as an authority figure to be avoided, or they were older and had coveted the position, leaving her as the odd woman out. She stared into the mirror behind the bar, wondering why she'd bothered putting on dark eye makeup and shaving the sides of her head. She hadn't gotten laid in months. The woman she'd been dating briefly during that time had died when guerillas had hit one of the mining sites, killing two guards.

She spotted Navos on the dance floor. His tall form was unmistakable. He was swaying with a beer in his hand, laughing with a group of waku that he'd become friends with. While his evasions could be understood since they'd only been clan mates for a few months, the way Adrenalynne actively avoided her left a hole in her heart. Camina had a pretty good idea that Adrenalynne thought she was a traitor for taking on the training role, which was funny, since they both were working for the Alliance, but she guessed there were levels and she'd crossed a line for the former Razor.

The whiskey didn't taste as good as it did on most nights. Camina threw it back, draining the glass and thinking about heading back to her apartment, when she sensed the change in the mood of the Eleventh Gonka. She expected to see one of the maetrie that made their home at the Overlook, the name that had been given to the complex above the cliff. There were more of the city elves around. Camina didn't like interacting with them as they were cold, aloof, and operated with a different set of influences, which she couldn't figure out. She might have been able to completely get on board with the Alliance if it weren't for them. The maetrie made her feel like a second-class citizen within the clan, even with her lofty position.

"Saving this seat for someone?"

Camina was surprised to find Deacon standing next to the empty stool, a bubble of emptiness around him as everyone moved as far away as possible. He wore a black suit with a black tie. The baleful energy in his gaze could have subdued a tiger, but she had enough whiskey coursing through her veins not to care.

"Sure," she said with a shrug. "We can both be pariahs."

"Better yet, let's have a private room."

"It's not like I have friends anyway," she said offhand, bringing a furrowing of his brow.

Deacon gestured at her glass and two more whiskeys were brought before they headed to the wall of private rooms. The sliding paper doors reminded her of Onyx, though the Eleventh Gonka lacked the personal charms of the hostess club. A group of younger waku were sitting at the table, but as soon as the door slid open, they fell over themselves scrambling out, and a waitress hurried in to clean away the glasses and half-eaten plates of food. The teriyaki skewers smelled delicious but Camina was suddenly not interested in eating.

"I assume this isn't a social visit," she said, leaning against the wooden back with her arm over the side. The interior of the paper doors had faint runes glowing around the outside that gave them a minor level of privacy and blocked the worst of the noise from the dance floor.

Deacon closed his eyes as he kept his hands around the glass of amber liquid. When he opened them, she resisted the urge to flinch. Only in the maetrie had she seen such wrath, and though she knew it wasn't directed at her, it still wasn't easy to witness.

"How do you stand it?" he asked.

"Stand what?"

He spun his glass, took a drink, then set it down. "The barriers. The loneliness." Deacon stared at the paper screen. "I'd decided to join the revelry. Have a drink, meet the waku in my retinue, but as soon as I walked in, I saw how they looked at me. I was about to leave until I saw you at the end of the bar, looking as pathetic as I felt."

"Thanks," she said.

Deacon cocked a grin, reminding her of the younger version of him she'd met when the Crows had allied with Razor.

"You don't treat me like the others. They look at me like a loose high voltage wire, afraid to get too close."

"I stopped caring when all my friends died," said Camina.

"You don't worry that I might think you disloyal with a statement like that?"

Camina lifted a shoulder. "You wouldn't have made me the head of training if you'd thought I was disloyal." She took a sip, deciding her tongue was already too loose. "When they stopped giving me that drug, the one that messed with my head, I thought I'd go back to the old version of me, but when nothing really changed, I realized that I had accepted my fate and my new clan."

She raised the glass in salute, which he matched. He downed his drink and she followed his example. With the glasses empty, he pressed a red button at the center of the table.

"But you don't like it?" he asked.

"It's not that. You said it yourself. The barriers and loneliness of leadership. But there's no challenge. The wayhos you send me from above, they don't know anything. A ten-year-old from Razor could kick their asses. I have to start with the basics. And then there are the older waku, the ones who were here before. They don't really listen to me. Sure, they go through the motions, but I can see it in their eyes. They don't understand why they're training. They say we won. A lot of them grumble about all the new faces and wonder why you're bringing in even more."

Deacon leaned back on his bench. The door slid open and a waitress dropped two whiskeys on the table.

"I'm glad I stopped in. This is good to know." He wagged his eyebrows. "Do you know why we're bringing so many in?"

"I hadn't thought too much about it," she said. "I assumed to keep the mines safe, or expand into other operations."

Deacon shifted his mouth to the side. "Both of those are true, but they're only the beginning. Dominion has big plans. He sees far. Very far. He wants to make the Undercity a destination, remove the stigma of this place *and* expand into the city. If it were just the stones and the drugs from the Pajot, there wouldn't be a need, but if we're going to move into the light, we need numbers, especially when the Halls decide we've gotten too big. He wants to make sure we're too large to stop by the time they notice—that's the reason for the influx of new members. You understand?"

Camina nodded as she considered the implications. She'd been so focused on her own duties, she hadn't thought about the bigger picture.

"He expects to go to war with the Halls?"

"Preferably not," said Deacon, spreading his hands. "He's a businessman after all, but he knows that to play the game, you need to have a good hand. A strong hand. Having a large crew of waku ready to do anything will make him a powerhouse in the city. Once we push into the gangs, taking their territory and businesses, things will get rougher. Right now we're in a lull as we expand down here, but it won't stay that way forever."

"Got it. Good to know, but I assume this is private information."

"It is."

"I think they might be more motivated if they understood the stakes."

He tapped his nails on the glass. They were painted black. "You'll have to find another way to motivate them. Surely there's some trick from Razor we can utilize?"

Camina broke into laughter at the memory of the ass-kicking she'd received from Deacon that had put her in the hospital. She tapped on the little scar on her jaw.

"Remember when you gave me this?"

He nodded. "I do."

"What if we put on a big tournament within the clan? Or maybe even opened it up to others as a way of recruiting. Put it out there so they have time to train and put a big prize on it to encourage them," she said.

Deacon raised an eyebrow. "An intriguing possibility. I'll have to run it by Dominion, but keep thinking about it in case he agrees."

"What's he like? Whenever I see him, I can barely think—either the old drugs, or his aura. He makes me feel like a worm crawling in the dirt, hoping I don't get stepped on."

"He's the most human of the city elves that I've met, but living in our world for the last four decades will do that. Yet. He's still maetrie through and through. The things I saw—"

"Like?" she asked, genuinely curious.

Deacon went internal, swallowing heavily before taking another drink.

"It was brutal. I was a child compared to them and they knew it. Made anything I dealt with training in Razor seem like a nap. I feared for my life at all times. The other students tried to kill me more than once. Shadows below, it was practically weekly. I took to sleeping in unusual places so they couldn't get to me when I was asleep. I still have nightmares."

"But it worked. You're stronger. I've heard what the others say about you. You could probably have beaten Duro or Brazio if they were alive."

"Maybe," he said absently, still lost in his painful memories. His mouth twisted. "It's not because I worked harder. Eventually they realized I wasn't going to be good enough." He loosened his tie and unbuttoned his shirt, revealing black metal attached to his pecs like individual scales of armor. He tapped, and the metal rang dully. "They gave me these. There are two more on my shoulder blades."

"What are they?"

"I haven't the slightest, but when they gave them to me, it was the most painful thing I'd ever experienced. Like being burned at the stake." He chuckled madly. "They're alive. I can hear them whispering when things are quiet. I think they're the essence of some creature from the Eternal City, maybe a smoke-eater or wraithhawk, or something else. Dominion gave a set to Gregor Anderson, but his body was too weak and the exertion killed him. Sometimes I wonder if I'll die from them, too."

Deacon carefully buttoned his shirt back up and retightened his tie.

"If you're offered the chance to have some, don't do it." He drained his glass, hammering the red button with the palm of his hand. "I have a question for you. Something you can help me with."

"Sure. Anything."

"A few months back, I ran into a couple of familiar faces."

Her chest tightened, but she feared to say anything.

"Three, to be exact. Yara and Tick, plus one I only knew by reputation from the Drops, Choo-Choo."

"Really? Where?" she asked, surprised to hear they were still alive.

Deacon explained the day at the mines, including the fight and their daring escape.

"Did they survive the jump?"

"As far as I could tell, unless something in the lake got them first, but we never found any bodies. I assume they made it back to wherever they've been hiding, and I haven't seen them since."

"What were they after?"

"That's what I wanted your advice on. It's not my job to track them down, that's Titus', but they have killed a lot of my waku and freed a lot of workers. They're not doing any real damage, but they're annoying and need to be taken care of."

"Why are they still fighting? We lost. They should just join the Alliance," said Camina.

"I'm glad to hear you say that. I can't understand their defiance either."

She'd said it to keep Deacon from questioning her, but there was some truth in it. Why keep fighting for a cause that was lost over a year ago?

"Do you have any idea why they might be fighting? Or how I might track them down?"

Camina drummed her fingers on the table. He would sense if she thought of something and didn't tell him. She was about to tell him that nothing came to mind, but then she remembered the fight between Choo-Choo and Pandora.

"What?" he said, before she'd even decided if she were going to speak.

"I don't know if this helps, but he had a family. A mother and sister that he felt strongly about protecting. His older sister had been killed by Brazio back in the day, before the stones. Maybe he was trying to get to them? I assume they're somewhere in the Undercity."

Deacon snapped his fingers and leaned back. "I knew it was a good idea talking to you. That has to be what it is. It would explain why they've been hitting the mines. He's looking for them. I should be able to track them down." He grinned, looking like the Deacon of old. "Thanks, Camina. I really appreciate it."

The sliding door opened with a new round of whiskeys. Deacon rose to his feet, adjusting his stylish jacket as he moved to leave.

"Sorry to run, but I need to check on some things. Thanks again for the intel. I owe you one. Anything you need."

"The tournament?"

"I'll talk to Dominion, but he's gone right now, so it might be a few weeks. But I love the idea. I'll give him my highest recommendation."

He left her alone in the booth with two whiskeys. She circled the one in her hand, listening to the ice shifting against the glass, feeling like a traitor to her friends, but the surprise of finding out that Tick and Yara were alive hadn't prepared her to lie. Not that Deacon wouldn't have detected it. She needed a way to warn them and pass along what she'd learned about his modifications, without drawing unwanted attention to herself.

Then she had an idea. If there was someone that would know how to get word to them, it was Leesa at Club Onyx. Since she'd taken over, the place had thrived. Camina had only been there a few times, but it never surprised her when she heard Leesa mention things that no one should know. A visit to the Terreno wouldn't be out of the question, especially if she combined some pleasure with the trip.

Thirty-One

Hylakane stood on a pillar across from her, one leg curled underneath like a flamingo, his hands hanging loosely at his side. Pandora held her curved blades at a forward angle. It was their seventeenth match and not a single one had gone in her favor. The pain of falling twenty feet to the hard concrete beneath the field of pillars made her reticent to begin. At least Kuma wasn't there to see her fail. Hylakane had given him a task in the city.

"Afraid?" asked the Steel Sun, an eyebrow arched mockingly.

"Not—"

Pandora disguised her attack within her response, sending a heavy

Push at his feet as she leapt to the pole on her right. She guessed correctly that Hylakane would leap away from her sapphire attack, landing on the pole opposite her. She struck three times, but he avoided her blades with minimal turns of his body.

"Is that all you have?"

His smirk infuriated her. She blasted him with a Push, forcing him into a backflip to land on the pillar behind, but she expected the maneuver and followed, slashing downward when he hit, but he used the palm of his hand to block her blade by hitting the flat side, sending a vibration through the metal that made her shoulder ache. Before she could swing her other arm, his agile foot knocked her legs out from under her.

The fall was halted by jamming her blades into opposite pillars, and using her sapphire to aid, Pandora flipped back onto the same level as Hylakane.

"You're learning." He gave her a wry grin. "But not enough. Open your mind, Pandora. There's a whole world you're missing."

He'd been mocking her with this line of analysis the entire day. She couldn't decide if he was being an asshole, or actually trying to teach her something. She leapt to the left, hitting him with a Push, but instead of advancing as she had been, Pandora returned to her original pillar for a second attack, which he stymied by kicking her thigh. They traded a few blows, before she tried to knock him off the pillar with a Push, but he sidestepped.

"Not bad, but it's still the attack of a mongrel," he said.

The constant refrain put a burr in her gut. She spat back, "But I *am* a mongrel."

Ignoring the height of the pillars and the failure of her previous attacks, Pandora threw herself at him like a hurricane, steel and sapphire assaulting him in a wave of intensity. She drove him back three pillars, her pace forcing him into frenetic defensive maneuvers and giving her hope she might finally land a blow—*finally*!—before he pirouetted past a blade and struck the pillar she was standing on hard enough to knock her off.

The sneer on his lips followed her as she fell. Pandora used her Pull to keep from slamming into the concrete, but the impact rattled her teeth.

"Fuck."

Eleven cracks in the pillar. Three bruises on her arm. Seventeen strikes that failed to find flesh.

After sheathing her blades, she monkey-climbed up the pole, returning to the same plane as Hylakane.

"A first for the day, a worthy attack."

Pandora bowed.

"But I failed again," she spat back.

"There is truth in failure. What did you learn?"

Pandora reviewed the fight sequence in her head, but all she could think about was how close she'd gotten to landing a blow. Thirty-one pillars. Nineteen broken windows in the building across from her. Forty-seven—

"Why are you counting?"

She exhaled through her nostrils. "It helps me..."

"It helps you what?"

"I don't know. Remain calm. Not scream, or rage."

"Why don't you? Your best attack was one in which you didn't think and came at me with rage and cunning," he said.

"It was sloppy and you knocked me off my pillar. I shouldn't have lost control."

"Why are you so determined not to be what you really are?"

"What? A mongrel?"

"Exactly. It's who you are. Embrace it." He glowered from his pillar. "What is stronger, iron or steel?"

"Steel."

"Why?"

"Because it's an alloy."

He placed his hands behind his back. "You know this yet you do not accept its truth into your heart."

"I don't know how."

"Or you refuse to acknowledge it. Despite your disagreement about your history, you are maetrie. You are a being of the Eternal City. Do you know why prime numbers are sacred to our kind?" he asked.

She shook her head. It was never something that was explained, only a reality that was hard to ignore.

"The Eternal City is much closer to the font of creation than your human realm. This place is akin to the Infernal Realm, a land of high magic and raw creation. But unlike the Infernal Realm, we found a way to provide structure, or we would have stayed as chaotic as that pitiless place."

"Primes," she said, the shadows of understanding casting across her mind.

"Yes, primes. They aren't just a superstition, or a lucky number, they are the underpinnings of our magic, our ways, and our power. It's why you rely on them in times of need, because part of you understands that it's the primes that drive your power."

"I don't feel powerful, but powerless."

"When you win a battle, do you feel more powerful or less powerful?"

"More."

He lifted his chin. "Why? You're the same person. Nothing has changed about you."

"But I won."

"An external event. A confirmation of the truth, but not the truth itself. You have not changed but in the most miniscule ways. Your feelings are not you. They're only one such interpretation of the world, a primitive one at that. To be a great warrior you must see the world as it is. You must act without regard to your feelings, which do not always have your best interests at heart. This is true for yourself as much as your opponent." He gestured towards himself. "In this case, a full-blooded maetrie exile who let his entire Court die because of his inattention. You have yet to see me for who I am, so you are doomed to fail."

See him for who he was. The thought infuriated her. She could barely understand herself, let alone another being, one who'd been alive for orders of magnitude longer than her.

Hylakane looked ready to wave her on for another round when he suddenly relaxed, his gaze shooting over her shoulder. Kuma was jogging up from the buildings.

"Did you find her?"

Kuma nodded, holding up a solid bottle that appeared to be made from stainless steel, though she knew it couldn't be since that type of material didn't exist in the city.

"The Marionette sends her regards and appreciation for letting her use it," said Kuma.

"Did anyone follow you?"

Kuma frowned. "There was one, but he stayed at a distance. I didn't see him upon my return."

"Come now. We have a task," said Hylakane, dropping from his pillar to land as if he were merely a feather. If she didn't know any better she would have thought he had an emerald, but the Steel Sun had strengths she could barely comprehend.

Dropping to the concrete using her sapphire to slow the fall, she followed as Hylakane marched back to the spire. In his quarters, he dug into a trunk until he pulled out a purple hat with a pale feather stuck into the band. By the time he'd slipped the covering over the crown of his head, he'd transformed into Jester.

"What's the bottle for?" she asked as they headed towards the eldritch barrier.

Jester spun on his heels. "Its purpose will be revealed in time, but until we reach our destination, remember that I am not Hylakane, Steel Sun and exile of the Ebony Court, but that annoying researcher who you've been forced to interact with."

They journeyed away from the settlement in the city, led by the mercurial Jester who chattered like an old girlfriend for the entirety of their trip. The skeletal buildings soon turned to rubble, leaving them to avoid the massive piles that had once been majestic structures. The heads of statues peeked out of the wreckage, reminding them of days lost. Pandora's thoughts trended towards Hylakane's comments, making her wonder if she truly was part maetrie, because nothing she did made her feel like she was. She tried to count the primes as they walked, but his observation had robbed her of the comforting pastime.

"We've arrived," announced Jester suddenly.

"This looks like the same pile of rocks we've been walking past for the last hour," said Pandora.

Jester opened his mouth for a rebuke, but remembered that he was no longer in his regular form. Instead, he tapped his nose.

"I can smell it."

"Smell what?" she asked.

"The smoke-eater," said Jester with a wink.

"Smoke-eater? Are you crazy?" she asked.

"Yes, but that's beside the point." He tapped his nails on the metal bottle. "That's why I needed this."

"I know a smoke-eater is bad, but why?" asked Kuma, glancing between them.

"They're holdovers from the early days of the Eternal City, before we'd organized ourselves. They are pure annihilation, feeding on anything living, reducing them to the fundamental of raw creation. They cannot be killed or reasoned with. They're like the great sharks of your realm, endlessly and mercilessly hunting, a relic of a time long past."

"You talk in riddles, Jester," said Kuma. "Tell us why we're here."

"The bottle. The Steel Sun wants us to take a sample," said Jester.

"Hopefully it involves using you for bait," said Pandora, enjoying herself.

Jester flourished the hat, returning it to his head. "I'm afraid I am not the warrior that you two are. This task will need speed and cunning, not the pompous erudition of a semi-retired researcher."

"Figures," said Pandora, crossing her arms. "How do we do it? You know, without getting returned to the atoms of creation."

"Simple, really. You'll need the smoke-eater to pass over the bottle. The container will do the rest."

"And where is the smoke-eater?" asked Kuma.

Jester extended his arm, pointing towards a large mound about a quarter mile ahead.

"It makes its home there."

Once they were out of earshot, Kuma asked, "What's this about?"

"I haven't the slightest idea."

"How was your training?"

"Terrible," she said. "He keeps trying to tell me I'm an alloy, but he might as well be telling me I'm the abominable snowman, because it amounts to the same thing."

"I think I'd know if you were the abominable snowman. My dick would have frostbite," he said with a smirk.

"Ideas on how to do this?" she asked.

"Set the bottle in the street and lure the smoke-eater over it?"

"I get that, Kuma. But how do we get rid of it once it's on our tails?" she asked.

Kuma glanced back the way they'd come with a grin lurking in his eyes.

"He wants us to do his dirty work for him like cleaning up the fountain, but what if we turned the tables?"

Pandora had a good idea of what he meant. "You know he's going to talk to Hylakane and get us in trouble."

"I'm counting on it," said Kuma. "Are you in?"

Pandora sighed. She knew she shouldn't...

"I don't know."

"You know you want to."

"Of course I do, but...oh, hell, why not? Count me in."

"Excellent," said Kuma, rubbing his hands together.

The mound was twice the size of the others nearby. Whatever building it'd originally been, it was probably the centerpiece of the surrounding city. To their surprise, the mound had a dark entrance at the bottom where they assumed the smoke-eater lurked, though they supposed it could be out hunting, which made their plan more perilous.

"It's in there," said Kuma as he crouched on his heels. "I can feel it."

The way he said it prompted a question. "What's it like?"

"Like standing on the shore as a category five hurricane is hitting the beach. Not that I've experienced it, but that's as close as I can describe."

As if summoned by their conversation, a black mist drifted out of the opening, spreading out into the clearing. The thick cloud moved with purpose, and Pandora almost expected to see crimson eyes in the middle. The baleful presence was like observing a serial killer who'd taken hundreds or thousands of lives. She stared into its depths wondering what primes hid beneath the surface.

"I'll lead it," said Pandora. "I'm faster. I'd rather not take any chances now that I've seen it."

Kuma checked to the skies, spying metal scaffolding that hadn't yet fallen. The tip was curled over.

"I'll climb up there. I can call out directions."

She waited for him to get in position. The metal creaked when he ascended, triggering the smoke-eater to shift in that direction. She hoped they weren't making a mistake by placing him up there. Once he gave her the sign for readiness, she trotted down and placed the bottle in the middle of the gap. Coming around the pile, Pandora was mentally readying herself for the chase, but found the clearing empty when she arrived.

"Fuck."

Pandora checked back to Kuma to see him gesturing wildly, pointing to a location near his perch. She tapped into her opal and headed towards him at speed, coming around the corner to find the smoke-eater approaching the base of the metal scaffolding.

"I don't think this was a good idea," called Kuma from above. "Unless it can't climb. Hopefully it can't climb."

The thick black cloud sent tendrils up the metal, curling through the gaps.

"It can climb," he said blankly.

Pandora ran to the edge of the smoke and waved her hands. "Hey! You want me! Come here, you gaseous bag of death!"

The smoke-eater seemed uninterested in her, so she hit it with a Push. The black cloud billowed, bunching in the center, but continued going after Kuma. She hit it with two more Pushes, until she was frighteningly close.

"Come get me, coal breath!"

The cloud shifted faster than expected. One moment she was twenty feet from the trailing edge, the next it was surging towards her like the tide rushing to the shore. The edges of the cloud brushed her arms, searing the flesh and sending bright pain through her body. Pandora leapt away using a Push as the smoke-eater flew after. In the blink of an eye, she was having to race for her life, the gaseous creature pursuing her with surprising speed.

"Go left! Go left!" shouted Kuma from his lookout position, but she was going too fast and had to leap the wall instead, soaring over and hoping the obstacle would slow the pursuit, but the smoke-eater shifted over the stone embankment, flowing after like a living wave.

Keeping ahead of the smoke-eater took every ounce of her skill, aided by frequent directions from Kuma, who kept her from trapping herself in the maze of materials. But she'd been escaping for long enough she had no idea where the bottle was, but hoped he was threading her back that way.

When she saw Jester sitting against a pile of rocks, picking his teeth with a piece of wire he'd rescued, she shouted, "Run!"

The colorful maetrie's jaw dropped open, and then he burst into a sprint alongside her, glaring the entire time.

Jester glowered. "This isn't how it was supposed to unfold."

"There was a complication," she said, trying not to laugh even as they ran for their lives.

Picking up Jester helped her figure out the path back to the bottle, which was necessary since Kuma was too far away for directions. They circled the piles, keeping the smoke-eater on their trail. When they ran past the bottle, she put her hands to her mouth and shouted, "Meet us outside of town!"

She allowed the smoke-eater to stay with her for a minute to give Kuma room to grab the bottle, and then poured on the speed. Jester ran beside her with his hat clutched in his hand. When they could no longer see the black cloud following, they stopped near a crater formed by the collapse of an underground area.

"My hat is ruined," said Jester, knocking it against his leg to uncrumple the edges.

"The perils of hanging with two of Hylakane's apprentices," she said.

"Apprentices? His pet idiots is more like it. You'd better hope he doesn't take it out on you for interrupting his thoughtful meditation," said Jester.

"You survived, and that's all that matters," she said with a smirk.

Jester curled his arms around his chest and visibly pouted while they waited. A short time later, Kuma appeared, out of breath, holding the shiny steel bottle, which had miraculously closed. He handed it to Jester, who treated it like a live bomb, setting it into his pouch.

"Neither of you deserve Hylakane. I'll be sure to inform him of that," said Jester.

"Actually, I think we deserve him quite well. Something of a perfect punishment, an exile without friends or family teaching two more exiles. If there's not a more perfect match, I don't know what is," said Pandora, finding she was having far too much fun.

Jester jammed his hands into his pockets, grumbling under his breath. The journey back to the spire took a few hours, and once they arrived, Jester disappeared.

"Think we made a mistake taunting him?" asked Kuma, glancing after the mercurial maetrie.

"Probably, but it was worth seeing his face when I ran up with the smoke-eater on my tail."

"Any idea why we had to take a sample?"

Pandora threw up a shoulder. "I suspect we'll find out soon enough. Let's go clean up in the fountain."

After eating from the fruits of Hylakane's garden, they relaxed for the evening, finding themselves with more time than usual. Kuma was snoring soon enough, leaving Pandora to mull over what Hylakane had told her that morning. Sleep evaded her and after a few hours of lying awake, she threw on her uniform and rather than heading up the stairs through Hylakane's quarters, she climbed the outside of the spire, using the cracks and exposed steel bars as handholds.

The flock of wraithhawks stirred when she arrived on the roof, fluttering their shadowy wings, their heads turning towards her like silent sentinels. Pandora crouched on the opposite side, returning their stares, trying to understand how Hylakane could walk through their midst without having his soul drained dry. Nor could she see the primes that he claimed underpinned this realm. They were a crutch, a soothing ritual, nothing more.

Pandora rose and took a step towards the wraithhawks. Each stride was like moving through molasses as her body didn't want to complete the task her mind had set her upon. She reached halfway, a few steps further than last time, and her limbs could move no further. She basked in the fear of their presence, hoping she could inoculate herself, but eventually realized her body would not allow her to move closer for fear of eternal death.

The climb down the spire help soothe the tension in her limbs, and by the time she reached their quarters, she found sleep was more tempting. Pandora curled behind Kuma, who was snoring softly, placing her arm over his body and letting her mind drift to dreams of shadows and smoke.

Thirty-Two

Leesa was sitting at a booth waiting for them with a bottle of whiskey and four glasses—already filled with ice—when they came down from their room. Her tight expression told Choo-Choo that whatever news she had was not going to be easy to hear.

She poured the drinks as they slid into the booth with her as the other hostesses cleaned up the bar after a long evening. It was probably five in the morning by the city clock, but time had little meaning for them in the shadows of the Undercity.

"I had a visitor," said Leesa.

Choo-Choo pulled his glass close and hesitated with it before his lips before letting a mouthful slip down his throat. The burn was soothing.

"Did Invictus come down to give you tips on hospitality?" asked Tick, stroking Koro's neck as she stayed wrapped around his shoulders.

"It was Camina."

The entire booth tensed. Choo-Choo only knew her from the few months that Razor had joined with Drops, but he knew she was a close friend of Kuma's and Tick's. They also knew she'd taken over as the head trainer for the Alliance Academy, which would have felt like betrayal if they actually had some semblance of a clan left to be betrayed.

"I assume this wasn't a social visit," said Yara, staring intently.

Leesa swirled her glass before taking a gulp. "She's stayed to the headquarters for the most part. I know she's been in the Terreno a few times lately, but this was the first time we've talked since the takeover."

"And?" asked Choo-Choo, expecting bad news.

"She had a lot to say. We spent an hour in a private room, and she wanted me to pass along this information."

Choo-Choo froze, checking back to the entrance, but Leesa shook her head.

"She doesn't know you're here. Only that I'm a person who knows people and how to get word to them. I never acknowledged that I could pass the information along, only that if I had the opportunity I would. Besides, if she knew you were here and was working for the Alliance in all capacities, you'd already be in chains, or dead."

"Fine. What did she have to say?"

"Deacon wants to take you down. He doesn't think Titus is up to it and wants to be the one so he looks good for Dominion."

Yara slammed her glass on the table. "We never should have let that snake in Razor."

"Hey," said Tick, giving Koro a kiss on the back of her scaly head. "Snakes are a much better class of being than Deacon."

"Yeah, sure," said Choo-Choo. "But what does that have to do with Camina?"

"She said he knows that you're looking for your mother and sister." Leesa shook her head before he could ask the question. "I didn't correct her error about where she was at, which confirmed to me that she's not completely gone over."

"Good to know, but we'd have to find her first," said Choo-Choo.

"Something tells me you'll learn something soon enough. A trap won't work if you don't know to walk into it." Leesa checked around the room. "There was something else. About Deacon and why he's so much faster and stronger since he came back from the Eternal City."

Leesa went on to explain the black metal attached to his chest and back, including the theories on what it actually was. When she was finished, Choo-Choo leaned back in the booth.

"I'm not sure how it helps us," he said.

"She didn't know either, but thought it might help."

"Feels like a trap," said Yara.

"Everything's a trap for us these days," said Choo-Choo.

"Camina told me to tell you to be careful. More than you usually are," said Leesa, frowning.

Choo-Choo normally didn't use his amber on Leesa out of respect, but he sensed her aura as taut with threads of concern.

"What? I know you have more to say," said Choo-Choo.

Her chin dipped to her chest as she bunched up her lips. "I don't want to lose what I have here."

"You want us to leave?"

Leesa closed her eyes momentarily. "You can't do this forever. And what are you really accomplishing? The Alliance is unstoppable now. You're three talented and dangerous waku, but you're one mistake from the ultimate end. And if Deacon's going to set up a trap using your sister as bait, I know you, Choo-Choo, you won't be able to resist, no matter how clean it looks. I love you guys. I was happy to provide shelter, but with things the way they are, I think that I'm not going to be able to much longer. I have all these girls who look to me to protect them."

"I thought you owed us," said Choo-Choo.

"I did, and I think I've paid that price," said Leesa sternly.

"Fuck," said Choo-Choo. "Do we have to leave right away?"

Leesa frowned. "Soon."

"Okay, fine. We'll get out of your hair. Give us a few days to figure out where we're going to go. Maybe it's time to leave the Undercity for good."

"Even without your sister?" asked Yara.

He closed his eyes. He'd promised his mother he'd free her from the Alliance, but it seemed like suicide to consider it if Deacon knew they were looking for her. Besides, knowing her, she'd found a way to thrive under the difficult circumstances.

"I'm not ready to decide that yet. Let's figure out our options." He put his hand on Leesa's, giving it a squeeze. "Thank you for the intel and for letting us stay here. We'd be dead otherwise."

"I'm sorry. I really am," she said.

Leesa slipped out of the booth, leaving the three of them with the bottle of whiskey. Choo-Choo refilled their glasses, which prompted Yara to say, "You'd make a good host if we went up top."

He threw back his drink. "This is the only life I've known. I don't know if I can start over. Nor do I want to."

Thirty-Three

"Another task?" asked Kuma incredulously.

Pandora had her arms crossed. "He's not coming this time either. I think we made him mad when we ran the smoke-eater up on him."

"It was accidental. Well, preplanned accidental. He should have been paying attention." Kuma sighed. "What's he want?"

"There's a gang on the far side of the city. He said they don't come near his spire, so we need to find them."

"And?"

"There's one of them they call the Fist. He wants us to bring him back here. Alive."

Kuma rapped his knuckles on the stone bench. "I imagine this Fist isn't going to want to come."

"Probably not, but we should get going. It's not far but it's getting dark soon," she said.

The city had become familiar enough they moved without comment, finding their way through the streets using landmarks and intention. Since they didn't know the exact location where the Fist and his gang lived, it would require a random search once they reached the target area.

A few times they spotted a cloud of faeila winging through the sky, slipping past buildings like a murmuring of starlings, shifting and pulsing. A deadly dance of wings and glass. After hours of searching, they spotted the glowing lights of burn barrels. Unaffiliated maetrie were dangerous in their own way. Without the formalities of the Court system to keep them subdued, they tended to act without regard to niceties as their existence relied on being the strongest. Using an old building to scout from, they determined the Fist and his gang was much larger than expected.

"At least twenty," said Pandora, shaking her head. "If they were dolgants I wouldn't be worried."

A whooping shout was followed by more yells, rising into the night air. A spark of eldritch magic crackled between buildings, followed by distant laughter. Their antics reminded Kuma of the city gangs, more interested in showing off than making their clan better. It meant they were undisciplined and prone to being incited to foolish decisions, which made them easier to manipulate, but also volatile and chaotically dangerous.

Using his amber-aided vision, Kuma managed to pick out the one known as Fist. While the maetrie near the Courts tended to go for the slender aristocrat with ghoulish appearance, the ones outside the aphena looked more like human gym rats, bulky and physically imposing with arcane modifications that made them more formidable. Fist looked like he could knock down a building with a single punch. Narrow silvery plates had been attached to his bald head with the spaces between filled in with shadowy tattoos.

"Maybe we could issue him a formal invitation," mused Pandora as she leaned against the concrete wall.

Kuma crouched on his heels, staring at the flickering lights of the gang's burn barrels.

"I have an idea," said Pandora, squinting into the darkness behind them.

The cloud of faeila was back that way. He knew what she was thinking.

"I don't know," he said. "That only worked when we were calm, not letting the pain get to us. But if we have to drag them into their midst, avoiding pain is going to be impossible. And then we have to get Fist out alive."

"Got a better idea?"

"No. Who gets to play the distraction and who gets to be bait?"

"I'm faster," she said right away.

"And you won't be around to borrow your sapphire. I feel like I'm getting the short end of the stick."

"It won't be long. They just need to be distracted for a short time until I can bring the faeila into their midst."

"And then?"

"We improvise in the chaos. I'm sure there will be plenty."

Kuma climbed down to the ground level after Pandora left, headed towards the location they last spotted the faeila. He moved at a deliberate pace, in no hurry to engage Fist and his gang on his own. They weren't keeping lookout, which made sense given this area was an apocalyptic wasteland, and there were few predators that they couldn't handle. He hoped that arrogance would keep them from killing him before Pandora and the faeila arrived.

He lurked in the shadows at a distance until the clock in his head pushed him forward. Kuma checked over his shoulder before squeezing through the old blocks of stone, making his appearance in the dim light of their fires.

"Greetings," he said in the maetrie tongue as heads turned his direction. Speaking their language made his throat hurt and he couldn't manage more than basic conversation, but he wanted to start with a diplomatic bent.

The hard jaws and muscles flexing towards their weapons were familiar to Kuma after a life spent in the Undercity. They were a rival gang and he was a lone idiot wandering in their midst. He wondered how Pandora had convinced him that this was a good idea. Their chatter was too fast for him to pick out the details, but the message was clear enough. *Look what wandered into our camp, let's have some fun.*

"What the fuck is a human doing here?" asked Fist. He'd been sitting near a fire with a bottle in his hand, but he'd joined the others in examining the newcomer.

Kuma sensed some of the gang circling around and cutting off his escape. He resisted the urge to check to the skies, not wanting to give away the plan, but it was growing harder by the second.

"This human brings a message from Steel Sun," he said in broken maetrie. The version of the word human was hard to say, because he knew it was more slur than description, translating roughly to *stupid bag of meat that surprisingly can speak.* He hoped mentioning Hylakane would calm their advance, but they gripped their weapons more tightly and checked to the skies as if they expected him to leap into their midst.

"That old fool would never send a human to bring a message. Maybe that idiot Jester who fawns over his droppings like a knavth eating its own shit. I think you're lost. Come here, human, let me show you the pleasure of our fire," said Fist.

Their laughter masked the hard glint of their gazes. They meant him harm. He was wishing he'd spent a little longer in the shadows before revealing himself. When he didn't move, Fist jerked his head towards two maetrie, who brought out iron bars they'd rescued from the wreckage. They looked like refugees from a war-torn region, who'd survived by killing without remorse. Their grayish skin reflecting the nearby firelight gave them haunted expressions as if they were the newly undead.

Kuma waited until the last moment to reveal his twin blades, giving the maetrie a moment of pause before they laughed derisively and attacked in a pincer maneuver, the choice showing they weren't as foolhardy as he'd thought while observing them. Kuma shifted to his left, avoiding their clumsy strikes and kicking out their legs, until both were lying on the cracked street, looking confused about their new position. Maybe not foolish, but certainly not practiced in the arts of combat. That was why they were on the far edges of maetrie society, where the pickings were easy and rarely fought back. He could have easily killed them, but didn't want to enrage the entire gang, forcing him into an outnumbered battle he had no chance of winning.

"Maybe he is a messenger from Steel Sun," said Fist, squinting. "But your presence is an insult."

The two maetrie on the ground quickly climbed to their feet as two others joined them, surrounding him on four points. Kuma kept his amber tuned, waiting for the twitch of muscle like a trap spider expecting the vibration of approaching prey.

The first maetrie lunged in a fake attack, which Kuma ignored, spinning past the swinging crowbar, slicing ribs and bouncing up the pile of rubble with Lightness. He could have made a dramatic leap, but wanted to keep his abilities less obvious.

"The human cut me," said the maetrie, holding his side, which was covered in dark liquid.

The perch he'd chosen wasn't as large as he would have hoped. Other shapes moved in the darkness, and in the blink of an eye, there were at least eight maetrie surrounding his location. Kuma heard the crackle of eldritch energy the moment before it nearly took his head off. Ducking the seething electricity unbalanced the rocks he was standing on, but he managed to regain his balance quickly, the muscle memory from countless days of sparring on the standing pillars coming back to him.

Fist approached his position with a wary eye, his muscled form hiding the cunning predator beneath. The leader's aura was bunched with menace and his movements suggested training far beyond that of the rabble in his retinue. Kuma had a good idea he'd been a soldier or guard in one of the Courts, but had to escape to the hinterlands after a crucial mistake.

"What does he want?"

Kuma drilled his amber into Fist. Was he being honest, or creating a distraction? The bulky maetrie hid his intentions well, which was another sign of his previous life in the Courts. To survive their machinations, one had to practice duplicitousness on a daily basis—or at least that's how Pandora had explained it.

"He wants to talk to you, and you alone," said Kuma in halting maetrie. "Come with me and you can be back here in the morning with a story to tell."

Fist turned his head as if he were searching for the real threat. He was correctly picking out that it was a trap, but he hadn't figured out where it was coming from. Kuma silently wished that Pandora and the faeila would arrive, because he was sure that Fist wasn't going to give him much longer to distract them.

"Kill him—"

The words had barely left Fist's lips when a cry from the back of the group sent waves of alarm through them.

"The sharp death!" they cried, amongst other names they had for the winged glass creatures.

As the rest of the gang descended into chaos, Fist stayed stationary, keeping his gaze on Kuma, who was doing the same from his perch. The cloud's approach sounded like glass being crunched underfoot. As the winged death surrounded him, he closed his eyes and meditated, ignoring the cuts and bright lines of pain appearing across his body. They were incensed by the maetrie gang, and dealing injury when normally they would have settled on his form like curious butterflies. Screams punctuated the night as Fist's gang ran in all directions to escape the cloud of faeila.

Kuma opened his eyes to see Fist staring back at him, stationary as a statue with a few faeila of his own bleeding him at points, while one of his crew was covered by the sharp creatures only a dozen feet away, wailing screams announcing the end of his difficult life. In the matter of a minute, the entire gang—minus Fist—disappeared into the broken buildings or met their end as lumps of bloody flesh.

"That went well enough," said Pandora, appearing out of the gloom.

"I thought Steel Sun wanted to talk to me."

"He does," said Kuma. "But you were never planning to come quietly. Not when a couple of talking meat bags were your escort. But I was surprised to see you knew how to avoid getting sliced to ribbons."

Fist cracked his knuckles by squeezing his hands. "I've seen you in the city with the faeila. I didn't understand until now, but that's not going to help you when I break both your necks."

"Come now," said Pandora, strolling into the clearing. "Do you really think that's going to work?"

The big maetrie leapt towards her, his fist raised, glowing with eldritch energy. He'd moved faster than Kuma expected, and he feared for a half-second that Pandora wouldn't get out of the way in time.

But as she slammed Fist in the chest with a heavy Push, slipping past him and leaving twin cuts on his ribs, he knew he shouldn't have been worried. Kuma hopped off his pile, casually positioning himself opposite Pandora, leaving the big maetrie with no way to easily defend himself.

"Steel Sun said to take you back alive, but not necessarily in good shape, or conscious," said Kuma.

Fist slammed his knuckles together, eliciting sparks. The metal strips on his head glowed with power, sending tendrils of electricity down his arms. Kuma wasn't sure what he said next, as the language was in high maetrie, which he barely knew a lick of, but whatever it was, it triggered a spitting rage in Pandora.

Kuma borrowed her sapphire, hitting Fist in the back with a Push, then twisting him with a Pull to keep him off-balance, while Pandora flew in with her foot coming around in a roundhouse right as the big maetrie's head snapped around. The two impacted like a sledgehammer on rock. Fist crumpled to the ground, the seething electricity crackling across his skull quieting.

"What did he say?"

Pandora was still staring at the fallen form of Fist. She barely noticed that he'd asked a question, finally grunting with acknowledgement after a half-minute.

"It doesn't matter. Who gets to carry him?"

"I saw some junk back by the burn barrel. We can make a carry-drag."

After scavenging materials, they managed to tie him to a makeshift cot they could drag back to the main area. As they pulled him through the broken buildings, they occasionally heard screams as the faeila cloud caught up to his escaping gang.

Fist woke around the time they brought him through the barrier. Hylakane was waiting for them inside, leaning on Zhinzi, glowering with menace. The big maetrie broke his restraints and fell to the ground. The arrogant posturing that Kuma witnessed before disappeared upon seeing the ancient warrior.

"Steel Sun," said Fist breathlessly, his tone suggesting apology, which was heresy amongst the city fae. He stayed on his knees, making himself small. Kuma had watched him remain calm while faeila left slices all over his body, but in the presence of Hylakane, exile of the Ebony Court, he looked like a suffering penitent.

"Rip the metal from your head and leave it at my feet," said Hylakane.

Fist brushed the metal on his skull with his fingertips. "I can't. It's all I have. They'll tear me apart without it."

Hylakane bumped Zhinzi on the concrete. The impact sounded like a gong ringing in a distant city.

"I was only a soldier following orders," said Fist, clasping his hands before him and pressing them against his forehead. "I would have been killed had I refused, and look at me now. I'm an exile too."

The weapon spun easily in Hylakane's grip, the circular end coming to rest a hair above Fist's head. A tap and the silvery metal rang.

"More than a soldier if you were given these. Magesteel is not cheap, which tells me you're still in Lady Amethyte's employ. You're here to observe and report back to her. I will give you one more chance to live. Rip the metal from your head and you can return to her with this message. *I will never relent.*"

"I would never make it back to the aphena without them. Removing them would be my end," said Fist, staring into the cracks of the concrete as if they were the impenetrable void.

Kuma never saw Hylakane move. One moment, Steel Sun had his weapon hanging over Fist, the next, the bald head was bumping across the uneven ground, eyes wide with eternal surprise.

Kuma wasn't entirely sure he'd seen it, but after Hylakane had taken the gang leader's head, the weapon Zhinzi flashed with eldritch light, and a wavering scream that sounded like Fist's voice echoed in the distance. He was expecting the Steel Sun to make a comment, or explain, but he returned to the spire in a slow stride.

"Want a drink at the Golden Fist?" asked Pandora.

Feeling like he'd witnessed a more horrific act than it appeared, he said, "Probably best."

Thirty-Four

Vasilisa hadn't been in the Terreno for years. The once neutral ground was a place her mother never wanted her to visit, except once when her older sister had fought an honor duel, she was given permission to travel with Emilio. Valeria had dismantled her opponent from Vipers, leaving twin scars on their cheeks before they begged for mercy. Vasilisa still remembered the thrill of waiting for her sister's decision, silently hoping that she'd refuse the request, but also relieved when blood wasn't spilled.

She'd been given the building that had once been the Rush, but had been abandoned a year before. The new role had felt like an honor when she'd received it, but seeing the disrepair made her worry that she'd been demoted. It didn't stop her from throwing herself into cleaning up the building, throwing out the trash where rats had been hiding, scrubbing the floor on her hands and knees.

The work helped her forget that Andy had been left behind at the Lazona. His assignment hadn't changed with hers, but he'd promised to get relocated as soon as he could. Whenever she paused, her thoughts returned to their last morning in bed as she ran her fingertips across his chest, then she threw herself back into the work to forget.

When the instruction had come to her at the office in the Lazona, she hadn't quite understood the purpose, since the Terreno was far from the mines. The only well of power it was near was the one the Halls guarded, which made it an unusual location for a resupply depot, but that didn't stop her from treating it like a major logistics hub. They'd given her a week to get set up, but she was finished in half the time, the shelves rebuilt and reinforced, ready for her first delivery.

Only when she was finished did Vasilisa permit herself to wander the Terreno, enjoying the flashing lights and the sound of the pachinko parlors. When she'd visited before, the tension between the various clans had given her a thrill, but now with only the Alliance in charge, it felt more like a gaudy amusement park.

"Roman's Raunchy Elixirs! Want to keep your dick harder than diamond skin? Or keep yourself as wet as Canter's Folly? Half price for new customers, and discounts for bulk buys!" called a street vendor as she passed.

The greasy, mustached vendor had set up shop near the alleyways where prostitutes of all kinds worked. Vasilisa passed a woman with furry arms and a tail like a monkey sticking from her frilly skirt. Not an amusement park. A freak show. The tastes of the Alliance waku, unhindered by honor and encouraged by the peculiarities of the maetrie, pushed the limits of what had been acceptable before.

As she circled the shops, wondering what it would have been like to have been here as a waku of the Drops, she drifted past the famed Club Onyx. Emilio had visited the hostess club on more than one occasion. Not that he'd told her, but she'd eavesdropped on him and Navos when they'd sequestered themselves in his room, whispering too loud about their exploits in the thin-walled apartment.

Near the center of the Terreno lay the dueling grounds where she'd seen her sister scrap. Empty cages lay scattered around the exit, where scorpic fights had occurred during the first days she'd arrived. When she'd been in the shop on her hands and knees scrubbing the corners, she'd heard the cheering and jeers, wishing she had the time to watch, but knowing she'd be too distracted to continue if she did. Better to finish her duties and take time once they were complete, but running her fingers along the metal-reinforced cages had her wishing she'd spent a little time to watch. As she turned to return to the shop, she thought she caught movement out of the corner of her eye. Someone had slipped behind a building. They might not have been watching her, but her hackles were up. Eventually, she convinced herself that she was mistaken and returned to her apartment.

§

A week after her first shipment of supplies arrived, Vasilisa was preparing a delivery. The materials were basic exploration supplies: batteries for headlamps, dried rations, water bottles, small pickaxes and the like, stuffed into three backpacks. She was expecting the patrol to swing by in the afternoon to collect them and ran her fingers along the edge of the cardboard box, wishing there was more to do. Travel supplies weren't the only things she had in the shop. There were uniforms for new waku, and the open clasps for attaching stones to the body. After her life in the Drops, it was strange to see how commoditized the faez crystals had become, but without competition, the Alliance had more than enough for its members.

The new job wasn't a demotion, she'd decided, but it certainly wasn't a promotion either. Unless they had bigger plans in the future that they hadn't shared with her, the purpose of setting up a logistics center in the Terreno made no sense.

"Hello?"

The front door had squeaked slightly, but not rung the bell hanging from a string, which meant whoever it was meant to be silent. The curved blade she kept in her desk was in the other room. Vasilisa grabbed the box cutter to investigate, wishing she hadn't foolishly spoken. *This is the Terreno. Nothing should happen here.* She didn't know why she was taking precautions, except that it was burned into her blood, a lifetime of living in a place that was trying to kill her.

Vasilisa stepped through the door, expecting to see someone in the main room, but it was empty. Had someone mistakenly started to enter her shop thinking it was a store and then changed their mind? It would make sense given that she didn't sell anything, but then again, there weren't many outsiders in the Terreno to make that mistake.

The scuff of a boot to her right had her lunging out with the box cutter. If she could initiate the first blow, she could escape the shop before they hurt her. A hand grabbed her arm, stopping the blade short of his throat.

"Andy!"

Dropping the box cutter to clatter on the wood, she threw her arms around his neck, pressing her lips against his, and then pulled away and punched him in the chest.

"Ow, what was that for?" he asked, laughing.

"You fucking scared me, you imbecile. I could have cut your throat. Imagine how that would have made me feel?"

She was mad, but not mad enough to refuse him as he tugged her back into his arms, kissing her gently on the forehead. Feeling him wrapped around her soothed the aggravation she'd been under since she'd had to relocate to the Terreno.

"What are you doing here?" she asked, laying her head against his chest, listening to the beat of his heart. The steady thump-thump eased her tension. She closed her eyes, wishing she could stay that way all morning.

"I have a day off."

"A day?"

"It's not long, but I couldn't stand not seeing you, Vasy. These two weeks have been forever."

Vasilisa frowned. "You didn't, like, come all this way by yourself?"

"The Undercity's not that dangerous anymore. I ran into three patrols on the way here."

"The fuck it isn't, Andy," she said, pounding her fist on his chest. "Something weird and hairy from the wastelands killed three miners before they wounded it and it escaped. Said it had claws like knives and bled weird green blood. There was a banshee sighting south of Big Dave's too. It's still the Undercity. People die all the time down here."

"I know, I know," he said, stroking her hair. "But it was worth it to see you."

She sighed and he leaned down, pressing his lips against hers. The kiss sent waves of desire through her. Vasilisa clawed his chest and wrapped her right leg around his. When a groan slipped out, he pulled away, hunger in his gaze.

"Is there anyone...?"

She glanced towards the door. The patrol wasn't due for a few hours, not that they couldn't be early. Vasilisa grabbed his hand, dragging him into the supply room. He smacked her ass playfully, and when they neared the desk, he grabbed her around the waist and lifted her onto the surface, knocking off papers.

Fingers dug into flesh, stripping off clothing, passions inflamed by grinding kisses. She pulled down his pants, loosening his cock from his underwear, a moan escaping his lips as she grasped him firmly.

"Oh, fuck."

"That's the idea," she said, letting her tongue rest on her teeth.

Andelei yanked off her silky pants. She guided him between her legs, gasping with pleasure as he pressed inside of her. Vasilisa bit his chest to keep from making too much noise. His big hands grabbed both her cheeks as he thrust repeatedly. After weeks apart, it was hard to let it drag out like they did in the privacy of her apartment and within a few minutes of scrambling to the back room, they were making muffled screams into each other's shoulders.

Afterwards, they sat naked on the ground against the front of the desk, running fingers over sweaty bodies, leaning against each other.

"I missed you."

He kissed her deeply, then fetched a water bottle for them to drink.

She placed the cool container against her forehead. Andelei noticed the room as they shared drinks.

"Smaller than I expected."

Vasilisa hung her head. "I can't figure out why they sent me here. It doesn't make any sense. They can supply the patrols from the other locations."

"I asked to be relocated, and I think I might get it. There aren't many spots, and they're boring guard duty without a lot of chances for promotion, but at least I'd be with you," he said, kissing the back of her hand.

After quiet conversation, their affections turned frantic and she was lying on the wood floor with Andy on top. He made sure to place his shirt beneath so she didn't get splinters, which made her want to bite him playfully again. This time, they managed to last longer, cleaning up in time for her to meet the patrol, while he wandered the Terreno to enjoy his day off.

§

In the days after his visit, Vasilisa bathed in a warm glow, anticipating when he would return. Andy thought he had a good chance of being relocated soon, which gave her hope that the new job in the Terreno wouldn't be so terrible.

Until then, the biggest problem was boredom. At an earlier age, the mystique of the Terreno was intriguing, but after spending time trying out its various delights she wasn't so impressed. The pachinko machines seemed like a waste of money, watching little steel balls bounce through a vertical pin maze in hopes of them landing in the right holes. The carnal delights available in the back alleys were of no interest, and even the few hostess clubs provided no appeal. She tried singing karaoke at one of the newer ones, but she couldn't get over how much it cost to have someone be her friend for an hour while she butchered pop tunes.

And none of the restaurants were as good as the Lime Duck, though she knew part of the enjoyment had been her burgeoning friendship with Najani. The waitstaff in the Terreno treated her professionally, but without the personal touch that she'd enjoyed in the Lazona. The only thing she found interesting was a poster for a grand martial arts tournament put on by the clan, but it wasn't scheduled for another few weeks.

After eating at the Pale Sun, Vasilisa headed back to her apartment, which was in the building behind the shop. On the way, she had a strange feeling she was being watched. Turning proved only that the streets were empty save for a few drunken waku meandering beneath the glittering lights hanging from the ceiling of the cavern.

When she made it back to her room, Vasilisa locked the door and then after a moment of contemplation, shoved the chair beneath the handle to keep anyone from forcing their way in. While she had no proof that she was being watched, little things kept adding up. It felt like every other day she nearly caught someone. She assumed she had a stalker, or maybe an enemy of the Alliance who saw her as an easy way to get back at the new clan. Things would be better once Andy moved. Until then, she planned on carrying a blade. It was the only way to be safe.

Thirty-Five

Pandora missed the moon.

The eternal gray skies of the city had no celestial bodies, and while it was night, the dim luminance that came from nowhere gave her the impression of moonlight. When she'd brought it up to Kuma, he stared at her blankly. Of course he wouldn't understand. He only knew the shadows of the Undercity. The moon was a foreign concept.

She'd only known it during a brief moment of her life when she lived with her father in Chicago. Pandora recalled waking in the middle of the night with the moon shining through the window onto her bed-covers. The silvery light was magical. On nights her father was patrolling the streets with his gang, she asked the moon to watch out for him, keep him safe and bring him back home.

Safety. An illusion that was shattered at a young age. Doubly so when her mother brought her to the Eternal City. Those first few months had been terrifying. The gaunt maetrie with their black-eyed stares had been like living in a haunted mansion.

Kuma shifted, his hand unconsciously clinging to her naked stomach as she lay upon her back. She smiled at the memory of their evening. They'd had no shortage of chemistry in their early trysts, but spending time with nothing else other than learning the language of each other's bodies had paid off in dividends. Pandora had made him sit on the edge of the bed while she'd stroked him, long and slow, drawing it out until he was begging for release. Seeing him so attuned to her touch had left her sopping wet, and once he'd recovered she'd straddled him until she'd joined him in bliss.

Pandora wondered what Hylakane thought of their exuberant noise-making. On the other hand, she saw him sneaking out to the settlement as Jester. There were opportunities for their teacher to find his own fun.

The comfortable nature of their training had Pandora wondering if they'd ever return to their realm. Not only did she have no idea where they might find a working portal, but even if they managed to make it back to the Undercity, her grandfather had had nearly two years to consolidate his power. What could she really do to stop him? She had no idea who had survived the raid on the Alliance complex. For all she knew her friends were all dead, which left her wondering why she'd want to return at all. There was no reason she couldn't stay with Hylakane, honing her skills for the entirety of her life. Her mother had told her stories about rogue warriors patrolling the edges of the Eternal City, imposing their will upon whoever crossed their path. Much as Fist tried to do, until Hylakane took his head. Was that what she and Kuma would become? Mercenaries? Or low-level criminals living on the edge of society?

She sat up, resting her bare feet on the cool concrete. No. This wasn't the life she wanted. If there was one thing she was certain of, it was that she wanted something greater. Even before her mother stole her away to the Eternal City, her father had told her that she could be anything she wanted, then he would ask what she was thinking of. She'd always refused to tell him, fearing that saying it might make it impossible to happen. He'd ask if she wanted to be a princess, or an astronaut, or a firefighter. She'd shake her head at each one. Pandora hadn't thought about those moments in a long time, but she remembered her desire as if she were lying in her little bed, staring at the moon through the cracked window.

Pandora had wanted to be the boss of her father's gang. Even before he'd died in the shooting, she'd known how dangerous his life was and wanted nothing more than for him to be safe. If she was the boss, then she could have kept him alive. As she glanced down at Kuma's sleeping form, his fingers twitching with dreams, she knew she still wanted the same thing. To keep her friends and family safe. To keep Kuma safe.

That was the paradox of her life. The stronger you were the more you invited challengers. But weakness tempted fate. The Undercity was proof of that. The stalemate between Razor and Drops had given the Alliance the opening to take control. In the eyes of the maetrie, family was a weakness too. Familial bonds could be exploited for gain. Your family's weakness was yours too. The only things that counted in the Eternal City were strength and cunning.

That was the rub.

To be human was to have family, connections you were willing to do anything for. But to be maetrie was to turn your back on your family, because they made you weaker. She couldn't be both. Not as Hylakane said, to be an alloy.

Pandora ran her fingers across Kuma's chest, feeling the little scars from years of training. The gunshot wounds healed imperfectly by an opal. The warmth and strength contained within his finely honed muscles.

Or maybe she *could* be an alloy? She would go to the ends of the realms for him. That desire to protect made her stronger. Those that had something to lose fought harder. She could be both cunning and kind. Strong and loving. Human and maetrie.

Pandora slipped into her uniform. She started to put her blades on, but quickly decided to leave them behind. The route up the side of the spire was familiar. She'd made it a dozen times, each one ending with her returning back to their room without the contents of the ornate box.

The cluster of wraithhawks turned their heads in unison. *Oh, you again.* She could see the thought in their bored expressions. Pandora stood on her side of the roof, hands at her side, feeling like she should be doing something different to be able to claim the box. Hylakane had demonstrated on more than one occasion how he could walk amidst them without having his soul sucked dry. At times she'd thought his connection to the famed weapon, Zhinzi, might offer protection, but he wouldn't ask her to attempt it if that were the case. Or maybe it was something about the pain that he held in his chest, the memory of an entire Court, his family, destroyed by the Ruby Queen. They'd passed the trial of the faeila by learning to accept pain. Was there a similar trick to the wraithhawks?

She thought about Hylakane. What was different about him that the wraithhawks felt no need to attack? She'd seen them take down dolgant and maetrie alike. There was nothing you could do once they'd gotten hold with their spectral forms.

"He grieves."

The words came to her lips as she remembered her earlier thoughts about her father. But it wasn't as simple as that. It wasn't the grief protecting him, but the lack of fear. Dying didn't seem that bad in the depths of that existential pain. Which gave her a moment of unexpected insight into the maetrie. Fear. She'd always thought they were immune, but if wraithhawks were attracted to fear, then no maetrie should ever be eaten.

"Or I'm an idiot," she whispered aloud.

But it felt right.

In the trial of pain, she'd learned to let the agony of having her flesh sliced open by the sharp edges of the faeila pass through her. She would have to treat fear in the same way.

Pandora took a step forward and then another. As her adrenaline kicked in, she paused, using the techniques she'd learned with the faeila to calm her beating heart. Fear. Pain. They were emotional siblings. Great warriors had to acknowledge them, but not let them cloud their judgement. She'd never seen fear in Brazio's or Duro's eyes. They'd met each challenge with clear-eyed purpose—knowing they might not make it out the other side.

She took another few steps until she was at the point that she'd given up on the last few attempts. The wraithhawks rustled with anticipation, their collective gazes making her feel like a buffet before a starving crowd.

When she moved, it felt like swimming against a tide. Her body was screaming not to continue further. How did one acknowledge fear without letting it consume? Her father had gone out each night, knowing he might not return, but also that to stay home and avoid the dangers of his streets would mean his little girl would starve. She took another step. The wraithhawks fluttered their wings, their silent stares like daggers dragging against her chest.

Fear was a powerful force, holding her back like an invisible wall. She started to close her eyes, thinking that the lack of sight would make the challenge easier, but before she took a single step she opened them again.

Why did the maetrie fear? Shouldn't that be a clue? The city fae, they of terrible eldritch powers, beings who'd conquered whole realms, felt fear? In a way, it didn't make any sense, except that fear was what drove them. Made them paranoid and prone to fits of rage. They feared the other maetrie, the Courts—they probably feared themselves. That was the difference of the Ebony Court. Hylakane had explained they were trying to forge a different way.

Fear drove the maetrie to be awful beings. In the depths of that emotion it was easy to believe your enemies would do the same, so why not strike first? Now she knew why Hylakane said she needed to be an alloy. Take the best parts of her heritage. Humans for all their flaws were less prone to unabashed fear. Their history was filled with brave and courageous souls overcoming challenges that seemed impossible.

Somehow, by being weaker, they were paradoxically stronger.

The hot emotions coursing through her veins quieted, calmed. She felt at peace for the first time since she'd stepped onto the roof.

"I am weak. A speck of dust in the infinite multiverse."

Her feet were moving before she'd thought about it. As she crossed the second half of the roof, the wraithhawks fluttered their shadowy wings.

When she was within ten feet of the flock, she wasn't sure how she would reach the box since they were crowded around the corner where it sat, but then they parted like the Black Sea. Pandora stopped in their midst, studying their ethereal forms. Up close, they weren't as distinct as observing them from a distance suggested. Their edges shifted like smoke and their black eyes contained galaxies. She could have stared into the depths of those glossy portals for hours, but sensed her presence was only tolerated.

Pandora placed her hands around the box. The wood was cool. She turned to return to her side of the roof only to feel a momentary spike of fear. Having the wraithhawks at her back where her imagination could do its worst made her struggle to hold back her feelings, but then she pictured their black eyes again and the mysteries contained within, and that infinite universe calmed her beating heart.

Before she knew it she was back on her side of the roof. Pandora collapsed on the far edge, cradling the ornate box in her lap. She traced her fingers over the intricate designs, which she assumed came from the Ebony Court. After many months of trials, now that she had the box in her lap, she was reticent to open it. Rather than spoil the surprise, she marinated in the success as she watched the unspecific glow that distinguished day from night in the Eternal Realm reveal itself.

"Don't you want to know what's inside?"

She'd heard Hylakane coming up from behind, but had been enjoying a sublime contentedness, and hadn't wanted to stir any sooner than required.

"It feels like a door and once I step through I'll be changed."

He placed himself before her, hands behind his back, robes hanging loosely around his sturdy frame.

"Your intuition is correct."

Without fanfare, she slipped the latch to the side with her thumb and lifted the lid, revealing a shadowy mask that made her heart catch. The resemblance was uncanny. Pandora feared to touch, but when he nodded, she scooped her hands inside, lifting the mask and revealing a solid object that would fit over her face. She sensed it contained terrible magics.

"A wraithhawk."

"It was mine once, an artifact of the ancients, before I understood the secrets of the wraithhawks as you do now too. But do not forget from which it came, or why it was made."

Pandora tilted her head. "Why?"

Hylakane glanced over her shoulder. Kuma had come up the stairs.

"I woke him before I came up. It's best if you both hear this at the same time. But first I must ask you a question."

"We're ready," said Pandora.

"Do you still want to stop your grandfather? Is it your intention to return to your realm and do battle with your kin?" he asked.

She wondered if he could somehow see inside her thoughts since she'd mused over that path just that morning. Pandora checked to Kuma, who gave her a tight nod.

"I do. It is. Even if I don't know how."

Hylakane held out two vials containing smoke and glittering silver dust. Pandora accepted hers as Kuma did the same. It was warm.

"What is it?"

"The two tasks. The essence of smoke-eater and the dust of mag-esteel. Together with other enhancements, they offer a way to return to the Undercity without giving yourselves away."

"Like Jester," said Kuma, wide-eyed.

"Yes, like Jester. I can take many forms if necessary. If you wish to learn, drink the elixir and then I can teach you how to change your appearance. It's not difficult. Only a few days of practice to master."

"But if we do, how do we get back? And what is the mask for?" she asked.

"I know a working portal that you can use. Probably guarded, but we can deal with that once you've decided. The mask is a gift to help you with your grandfather. You should understand if you think about it."

"Fear," gasped Pandora.

The trial with the wraithhawks wasn't only about her, but a way to give her insight into the mind of the maetrie—and specifically her grandfather. She would have never guessed that he felt fear, but it was a different kind than what humans felt.

"No mask for me?" asked Kuma.

Hylakane reached into his uniform, revealing a second mask. The snowy snout and fangs were unmistakable.

"A knavth?"

"Do not underestimate the power of being small, quick, and difficult to kill. They've been known to feed on faeila by tricking them into small spaces then devouring the remains of the creatures they shatter with their long teeth. In a fight between the faeila and knavth, it's the terrain that decides the winner. Once you have both learned the arts of shape changing, I have more tricks to teach you that will help solidify the mysteries of your masks."

"Thank you, Master Hylakane. I owe you a debt I cannot repay."

"When the time comes, you'll find a way," he said cryptically. "I assume this means you want to return?"

Pandora checked with Kuma, who nodded once. "We do."

"Then drink up."

With the elixir poised before her lips, she asked, "Is it going to hurt?"

Hylakane's lips stretched wide. "Assuredly."

Thirty-Six

Choo-Choo paced the room where they'd been sitting for the last three hours. He felt on the edge of a great chasm with no way to get across.

"I'm sorry," said Yara, sitting on the edge of her bed, hands clasped and forehead knotted. "You know it's a trap. As soon as we step foot in her shop, it'll be sprung. Better to wait until Deacon's gotten bored and forgot about your sister."

"We've been doing this for over a year and a half and this is the first time I've seen her! If I miss this opportunity, I might as well forget about her."

"She seems happy," offered Tick, flinching when Choo-Choo spun on his heels. "I'm sorry, but she does. Maybe it's us that should reconsider what we're doing. Leesa's not going to let us stay much longer. Once we leave here, I'm not sure how we can continue."

"What? You're giving up? Are you going to join the Alliance?"

"I doubt they'd take me after all we've done. Probably find a way to the surface. Darina said she'd visit me if I did. Not sure what I'd do, but Koro and I will figure something out."

Choo-Choo's world was slipping away. Everything he'd ever cared for, everything he'd ever done would be meaningless if he abandoned his sister and the Undercity. His chest felt like it wanted to cave in.

"I'll do it myself then. I don't need your help."

Yara met him at the door, grabbing his arm and yanking him around.

"I didn't say I wouldn't help. I'm saying we'd be idiots to rush out there now while he's watching."

"We haven't seen him," said Choo-Choo.

"You know that doesn't mean shit," she said, nostrils flaring. "Now stop acting like the impulsive waku you were when I first met you and start acting like the one that's kept us alive for all this time."

The comment shamed him. Choo-Choo dipped his chin towards his chest as his cheeks grew hot. He returned to sit on the bed, clasping his hands in front.

"How do we rescue Vasy without getting caught?" he asked.

Tick was at the window, peeking through a gap in the newspaper they'd taped to the glass when they first took ownership of the room.

"I think there's a party in a few days. I see workers hanging spark lights all along the streets."

"Shade's End?" asked Yara.

"I thought Dominion ended the holiday?" asked Choo-Choo.

Tick lifted his shoulders. "Looks like Shade's End to me. Maybe they're bringing it back now that the Alliance has complete control."

Choo-Choo looked to Yara, who was deep in consideration about the new information. Shade's End was the Undercity's version of New Year's Eve, but celebrated closer to summer. Not that the seasons mattered to those who lived in the shadows. There were a lot of rumors about why the holiday had been born: It fell exactly between the birth dates of the two longest existing clans, Razor and Drops. Or the Head Patron Invictus of the Hundred Halls had visited the Terreno on that date and given his blessing. Or that it was the date of a famous duel between Len "Moonblade" Santos and the Great Viper, also known as the Shadow Khan, but Choo-Choo thought it wasn't anything so storied. The likeliest explanation was that the Terreno needed to drum up business and invented the holiday to draw the clans into its caverns.

"I miss Shade's End," said Tick with a longing sigh. "The cheap alcohol, the special pachinko deals, scorpic fights, the ladies in their skimpy outfits."

"It would be a good opportunity," said Yara. "Be hard for Deacon to keep watch, especially with all the bullshit that goes on."

"Will it be as crazy?" asked Tick. "Without all the enemy clans in close proximity, it won't feel as tense. No duels. No unsanctioned fights in the darker caverns."

"Never underestimate the combination of youth plus alcohol, ramped to eleven with stones," said Yara. "Choo-Choo?"

He'd been staring into his palms. "Sorry. I was thinking about the last Shade's End when Pandora and Kuma dueled. Not really about then, but them."

"Wondering what happened?"

"Yeah. Everyone else, we know what happened to them. It's just kinda weird they up and disappeared."

"I miss them too, my friend," said Yara, nodding.

"So, are we making a move during Shade's End?" asked Tick.

"We are, but Deacon will be expecting something to happen," said Choo-Choo.

Thinking about Pandora helped him calm his mind. She was always so clear-eyed and quick to make the right decision. Even though they'd been around the same age, there was something about her that reminded him of his older sister, Valeria. He missed her as much as he missed Vasilisa.

"We'll need a distraction," said Yara, staring at Tick.

"Me?"

"Yeah, you. Is there someone else here that has an army of critters in their pocket?"

The smallish waku cradled his arms around his chest and grimaced. "But that'll mean I'll be out there in the middle of this chaos. They'll spot me for sure. And I'm not sure I can sneak back in here with a bunch of tumblers, or something, without getting caught."

"Can you just encourage the critters around here? Are there enough rats and mice and insects to cause a scene?" asked Yara.

"He's right," said Choo-Choo. "We need something bigger to cause a distraction worthy of Deacon."

"I know," said Tick, eyes alight. "There'll be scorpic fights during Shade's End."

"So? They're all in cages," said Choo-Choo.

"But what if they weren't?" said Tick, grinning from ear to ear.

"He's got a point," said Yara. "How hard can it be to open up a few cages and cause a little chaos?"

"Okay," said Choo-Choo, nodding. "We've got some work to do on that one, but what about my sister? How do we get her out without anyone noticing?"

"Or more importantly, how do we find her in the middle of the party? She'll probably be out and about," said Yara.

Choo-Choo put a hand to his forehead. "Why can't this be easy?"

Yara chewed on her lip in the silence. After a few minutes of quiet contemplation, she offered, "We should draw her to another part of the Terreno. Leave a note, or something official that she can't miss. Somewhere we can sneak her out."

"I'd say Club Onyx, but I don't want to leave Leesa with a mess after all she's done for us."

"The old Razor bar, the Umbra, or whatever it's called now, has some passages in the back we could use," said Tick.

"The Eleven Tears," said Yara.

"Is that another maetrie name?" asked Choo-Choo.

"Probably. They're turning this place into a pale version of the Eternal City," said Yara.

"Okay," said Choo-Choo as the plan started to take shape in his head. "Tick somehow opens the scorpic cages to create a distraction, while we lure my sister to the Eleven Tears, where we sneak her out of the Terreno and then to the Chamber, where we convince the Hall mages to let us up."

"Why would they do that?" asked Yara.

Choo-Choo pulled a small pouch from his pocket, shaking it lightly. The dozens of stones they'd taken from Alliance waku shifted in the bag.

"Use whatever it takes to get us to the surface."

"But how am I going to get near the scorpic cages? They know what I look like," said Tick.

An idea formed, leaving Choo-Choo grinning. "How do you feel about wearing dresses?"

Thirty-Seven

The room on the lower level of the spire was spartan. Barely more than a concrete space with few comforts. Kuma had spent little time in the room except to collapse exhausted from a long day of training with Hylakane. Nothing he'd done in Razor Academy had prepared him for the extremes that the maetrie warrior had put them through. Kuma felt like a different person than when he'd first come to the Eternal City. It was hard not to be changed by the realm, where a brutal death lurked around every corner.

"He wants us to meet him on the bottom level," said Pandora, entering from above, where she'd been talking with Hylakane for the last hour.

He'd been giving her instructions specific to her grandfather. Kuma was a little annoyed that he wasn't allowed to hear them, but it was probably for the best given the challenges that they faced.

"I feel a little, I don't know, guilty about leaving," said Kuma as he shifted his pack onto his shoulder.

"Why?"

Kuma pursed his lips. "I think for the first time in my life I recognize how little I know. After all this time with Hylakane, I'm just starting to understand what he's been teaching us and we're leaving."

"Our training isn't over," said Pandora with a wry smile.

"I know. Brazio and Duro never rested. I think I'm starting to understand them better. They seemed like mythical figures when I was younger, but now I understand what they must have felt. Despite their training, they weren't near the level they wanted to be. It's like going for a swim thinking that it'll be easy to cross the water only to find out you're in the ocean. I guess that's why Duro was putting himself through all those weird trials."

Pandora gave him a peck on the cheek. He followed her to the lower level, which was something of a wreck. Except for the stairs, he'd never spent much time there. Hylakane was waiting for them with nothing except two piles of clothing sitting on a chunk of concrete. The famed weapon Zhinzi was not present, which relieved Kuma. Since he'd learned what was contained within, he found it hard to not stare at it with horror and he didn't want to insult their teacher.

"Today is your last day in my care," said Hylakane simply, standing with his hands behind his back. "You may feel that you're not ready, but I assure you that you've come much further than I ever expected. The mongrel and the insect. Do not forget the lessons that you've learned here."

The old warrior gathered the two sets of clothing and handed them over. They were not martial uniforms as Kuma had expected, but styles that suggested minor nobility of the maetrie Courts.

"After today, you can no longer be Pandora and Kuma. You change your forms and don these outfits, becoming the personas we constructed during your training." Kuma closed his eyes to begin his transformation, but Hylakane cleared his throat. "Not now. It's best that if you're seen leaving the area it's not as your new selves."

"Won't they figure it out based on the fact we're no longer seen around the spire?" asked Pandora.

"Let me take care of that," said Hylakane, a glint in his black eyes. "Let's go over who you'll become one last time."

Kuma stiffened to attention, sensing Pandora doing the same at his side. It wasn't necessary but after years of training, the act was instinctual.

"My name is Lady Saha, an adjunct minor noble from the Jade Court who has been on her liebereisen for decades. I've been traveling with my human body servant, Aman. I acquired him on the plains of Brodaria after besting a warpriest of Ghoghali in individual combat. I'd considered returning to court, but heard rumors of Dominion's incursion into the human realm and thought it an excellent opportunity to further my knowledge."

"Why do you wear the wraithhawk mask?" asked Hylakane.

"It is a symbol of my minor house. We are known as fierce warriors, but less inclined to bother with the minutiae of noble politics, preferring gladiator pits or fields of battle to ply our trade. We are aloof but dangerous."

"Good," said Hylakane. "Now you, Kuma."

"In English or maetrie?"

"English is fine. You've spent little time in the Eternal City, so the reasons for your incomplete knowledge will be inferred."

Kuma sighed internally. He was less sure about this plan than Pandora, who had embraced it enthusiastically. Hiding and subterfuge was not his strength.

"You won't have to carry this deception," said Hylakane as if sensing his reticence. "The heavy lifting will be with Lady Saha."

"I am Aman Crownline. My mother was working for the Golden Helix, a mercenary company related to Blackstone Security. I was born in Brodaria." He paused. "I'm still not sure how I'm supposed to fool anyone about living there. I know nothing about them."

"Neither does Dominion, and besides, you'd feel quite comfortable with the Brodarians. They're an honorable race who feel it is their life's purpose to wage war. It is a holy thing for them. Fierce fighters and even more devious strategic minds. Never play a game with a Brodarian unless you are extremely confident in your abilities. They are ruthless when it comes to strategy. They'll come out on top even at simple games like crosses and blood."

"Won't Titus Cabone know I'm lying? He's a mercenary. Surely he's been to Brodaria?"

"Not that I'm aware of. He was more interested in looting and pillaging, which is frowned upon by the Brodarians. For them, victory alone is the prize. Entire battles killing tens of thousands have ended with both sides leaving content that they fought well, with the losing general serving tea to the winning one as his punishment."

"That sounds ghastly."

"As your rituals in the Undercity might seem that way to others. But do not be disillusioned—everyone in those armies was a volunteer. To be a warrior is an act of self-improvement."

"With a murderous penchant for tea," quipped Kuma.

He knew he'd screwed up as soon as the words left his mouth. Hylakane stiffened slightly, which prompted Kuma to incline his head.

"Tea is sacred to the Brodarians. If you're to keep up the illusion you must never disparage it," said Hylakane, then he visibly relaxed. "I think that should be good enough. Once you inhabit your new skins, you'll find the form will lead you to invent other aspects of your personalities. By the time you reach the portal, you'll forget who you really are."

Kuma wasn't so sure, but he wasn't going to disagree with his teacher.

"Keep the clothes until you've reached the end of the tunnels and have to surface again. Then you can ascend into the light as Lady Saha and her body servant Aman." Hylakane smiled. "Remember, you're on your liebereisen, a journey of discovery. This will give you cover to ask questions, be inquisitive, to be a little odd. Dominion will not question it."

"Assuming we make it back to the Undercity," said Pandora.

"There shouldn't be anyone guarding the old Ebony Court portal, because they are not aware that it still works. And I'll make myself seen during the next few days so any of Lady Amethyte's watchers will not bother to look for a couple of students who aren't the focus of her ire. Enough talk. Now is the time for action."

Hylakane gave them an Undercity salute which they crisply returned. The old warrior pressed his palms against a great block of stone and, with short grunts, shoved it out of the way, revealing a pit of darkness.

"A thirty-foot drop and then a two-day walk. Intention will be your guide. May the blessings of the Ebony Court be with you until the end of your days."

"Thank you, Hylakane-san," said Kuma, bending at the waist until his forehead nearly touched the cracked concrete. "May the shadows keep you safe."

Pandora matched his gesture.

As they gathered at the edge of the darkness, ready to drop below, Hylakane spoke one last time.

"And the light blind your enemies, mongrel and insect."

Thirty-Eight

Tick had been most worried about strapping his dick to his leg with tape. What if he got an erection? Would it hurt? Could he damage himself permanently? Those questions disappeared the moment he walked out the front door of Club Onyx in a small black dress, holding a pink parasol that matched the basket full of Club Onyx literature.

It'd taken hours longer than planned to get him ready. Darina and the other girls had worked on him with makeup pens, lip wax, and other accoutrements that he hadn't the words for. He came away feeling like a piece of taffy after it'd exited the stretching machine and a new appreciation for the ladies that worked at the club. He'd spent enough time with

Darina outside of her work hours to know that it took effort for her to transform into the consummate hostess, but going through it himself gave him a new perspective.

Don't tug at the skirt. Don't tug at the skirt. Darina had slapped his hands away a dozen times when he practiced walking around the room. They'd given him low pumps rather than high heels after the disaster of his first attempts. *Be calm. You're drumming up business for the club, not causing a scene in the middle of the Terreno.* He hoped no one was running their ambers, or they were too drunk to notice his little slipups.

Shade's End had brought crowds. More than the Alliance were in attendance. Workers from the mines, or the other settlements like Big Dave's or the Lazona wandered the area with wide-eyed glee. If he didn't know any better, the Terreno looked like it had in the days of old. A host of firecrackers went off nearby, sending Tick's heart into his throat, but he managed to get his breathing under control quickly.

A curt whistle was followed by a slap on the ass that nearly made him drop the parasol. Tick nearly sent Koro after the burly waku who had come up behind him unexpectedly, but then he remembered his companion flying snake was in the room with the others.

"Don't be shy, baby," said the wide waku with drunken heavily lidded eyes.

The tanned skin and slight beard marked him as a recent entry to the Undercity. Tick almost told him he would give him six inches the hard way, until he remembered that his voice wasn't quite high enough to get away with speaking, so he pulled a flyer from the pink basket and handed it over. It was an advertisement for a special karaoke party that evening, where the hostesses would put on semi-burlesque show.

"If you're gonna be there in something a little more revealing, you can count me in."

Tick barely knew what to think as the burly waku wandered off. The forward comments were startling. He found himself reviewing everything he'd said in the last few years. A few other waku walked past, giving him side-eye. *Walk, you idiot.* Tick started striding forward, but remembered to be demure and shortened his strides until he was taking mincing steps.

The fliers made for an easy exit when men tried to talk to him. He handed one over and made a tight-kneed curtsey before shuffling away before they could try to make small talk. Hands found their way onto his ass on a frequent basis, which he had less tolerance for. He'd spin around as if he were surprised and step hard on the guy's foot, before giving an apologetic shrug of the shoulders and skittering off.

As the time grew near, he made his way towards the central chamber of the Terreno where the scorpic cages were set up. In the past, he would have been examining each creature for signs of its fighting prowess with the intent of dropping a large sum of money on his selections, but this day he could only see the guards standing around, watching for trouble. Tick picked a cage with no one around. The plaque read First-hammer. The pale boney critter inside had a heavy stinger with a bulbous end that was probably the reason for its name. Despite sounding impressive, the thick end was probably the reason no one was excited about the scorpic—a slow stinger tail was certain death. Tick reminded himself he wasn't here to pick scorpics, but sabotage the cages. He reached into the bottom of his basket, beneath the papers, for the set of wire clippers. He was pulling them out when a hand settled on his hip.

"Shouldn't you be wiggling your ass and giving out fliers?"

The stink of whiskey made Tick want to retch. The waku with his hand on his ass looked like he could be knocked over with a breath. It was more than alcohol. His eyes glittered with purple lights and his lips were stained indigo. Tick gave him a slight shove with his elbow, expecting him to topple over, but he was as firm as a stone pillar.

"Come on, let me take you to one of the private room. I can show you how a real waku does it."

Tick almost kneed him in the balls. Not only for the leering advance but thinking he was a real waku. It was easy to see the man's off-kilter stance and the lack of calluses on the knuckles. Tick was certain he could kill him in one move. The drugged-up waku's eyes widened and he seemed to sober up as if he'd sensed the underlining menace.

"Are you…?"

"Leaving," Tick squeaked out, hoping he'd disguised his voice enough, yanking his arm away and moving towards another cage.

The man followed for a few steps until he was distracted by a walking vendor shouting about fresh pretzels, leaving Tick alone. After he confirmed that no one had seen the encounter, he returned to the cage, and using his body to hide the movement, clipped the wires carefully until they were about to break. He didn't want the modifications to be obvious. Then he found a second unattended cage near the Poinsettia and performed the same job. Tick was looking for a third but the crowds had packed around them since there'd be a match in less than an hour. Needing a distraction, he reached out to the first scorpic with his tiger's eye, inciting it to escape. Screams, followed by everyone rushing to that side as the creature burst through the broken wires, freed up the other cages for sabotage. Tick managed to clip three more cages, not bothering to make the modifications invisible. As he filled the entire group of caged scorpics with unending rage, Tick shuffled away from the central area, heading to a room Leesa had rented for him on the west side, where his weapons and clothes were waiting. Once he'd changed, he would meet the others in the hidden passages behind the old Razor bar. Tick couldn't help but grin at the chaos that he'd left behind.

Thirty-Nine

The kitchen staff at the Eleven Tears startled when Choo-Choo came barging through with Yara on his heels. The cook went for a butcher knife, but it only took a headshake to let him know it was a bad idea.

"We're just passing through," said Yara, patting the automatic weapon held to her chest.

Choo-Choo hadn't wanted to bring guns, because if they had to use them, then the plan was probably in shambles. Even if it couldn't kill Deacon outright due to his black diamond, Yara had been adamant about bringing it.

Everyone in the eating area was standing near the windows, watching the mayhem of scorpics running rampant through the crowd as drunken waku tried to kill the boney creatures. Not far from the window, a younger waku with a shaved and tattooed head was screaming from a stinger blow after she'd jammed her blade into the back of the creature.

At first glance, Choo-Choo thought that his sister hadn't made it to the Eleven Tears. Or had left early. But then he caught her side profile when someone gasped at Yara's weapon. It'd been two years since he'd seen his sister up close, and the passage of time had made a difference. She wasn't the annoying, flat-chested younger sister that never wore make-up and never shut up about becoming a waku, but a young woman with rich brown skin, rosy cheeks, and a calm pose that reminded him of their older sister. Vasy slowly turned, her expression a mix of surprise and confusion, until she ran across the restaurant and threw her arms around him.

Choo-Choo could have hugged his sister forever. He squeezed a little too tightly and she yelped.

"Emilio," she said as she pulled away.

"You're so tall," he responded, realizing she was his height.

"I got Dad's height. Sorry, brother." She checked over her shoulder at the chaos in the Terreno. "What the fuck are you doing here?"

"We came to rescue you."

"Rescue me?" she asked incredulously. "From what?" Her expression dropped. "No. Really? Have you two been..."

"We got Mami out a while ago. She made me promise to find you and bring you to the light."

Vasy pulled her hands away from his shoulders and clutched them against her chest.

"I'm not leaving. I'm happy here."

"Happy? With the enemy?" he asked, his voice rising with anger.

"Emilio. We lost. There are no Drops anymore. That's what we do. We pledge ourselves to the new clan and move on. Why haven't you?"

"New clan? The Alliance ain't a new clan. They're a gang. That maetrie bastard at the head doesn't care about the Undercity, doesn't care about his waku, or even you. He's just here to extract the stones from the earth, make his money, and then I don't know what. Probably move into the light and cause havoc there too."

His sister shrunk into herself. "Has that been you two? Ambushing mines and killing patrols? Andy's lost friends from your killing spree? Did you cause this out there? You know real people are getting hurt."

"Andy? Your Alliance boyfriend? What about the friends and family we lost when they took over?" asked Choo-Choo, his voice rising.

The rest of the restaurant was moving away, checking back suspiciously while Yara kept her automatic weapon trained on them. When an older man tried to shift toward the door, Yara merely shook her head and he returned to his spot along the window.

"Emilio! I'm not a child anymore to be rescued. I have a job here that people care about. Something I'm good at." She held up her missing hand. "This is what I got for all the wars between the clans. I don't think you understand. It's good that one clan finally took over. Yes, it was awful when we lost the Drops, but except for you and that murderous bitch who killed our sister over there, it's been quiet. Civilized even." Her face broke with emotion. "How can you be working with her?"

It'd been so long that he'd forgotten that Yara's father had killed Valeria.

"Yara didn't do anything, and what I learned, what I know…" He couldn't quite get the words out. "Fuck, Vasy. I'm here to rescue you. You need to come with me."

She shook her head. "No. I don't. I'm happy here. For once, I'm happy."

"Don't you want to be a waku? They'll never let you do that."

A short laugh tinged with madness slipped out of her mouth. "Shows how little you know."

"Choo-Choo, we have to go," said Yara, low and under her breath.

"Go, Emilio. This isn't the place for you anymore," said Vasilisa with her arms crossed.

"The fuck it isn't," he said, lunging forward and throwing her over his shoulder. "I promised Mami I would get you out, so I'm getting you out."

He carried her through the kitchen as she screamed and slammed her fist into his back. They pushed into the caverns behind the restaurant, using the passages to wind away from the Terreno.

"You need to shut her up," said Yara, glancing into the shadows as they broke into a larger cavern with faint illumination. A trickle of water from the back made light music.

"Put me the fuck down! I'm not going. I'm happy here!" shouted Vasilisa.

Choo-Choo turned his head to speak to Yara when a blur flashed through the space. The clatter of a weapon landing in the distance startled them both, followed by a warm light revealing a group of Alliance waku led by Deacon. He wore a black suit and white tie. His hair was slicked back, which made him more gangster than waku.

"I knew you'd never be able to resist," said Deacon. "But I didn't expect that she wouldn't want to come with you, which made it much easier to find which way you'd gone. Doesn't that feel terrible, Choo-Choo? That you worked so hard to steal her away and she doesn't want to come. Now I'll finish what Titus couldn't, and Dominion will know that I'm best suited to be his second-in-command. Thank you, the both of you, for offering me your lives as this gift."

Forty

Yara had expected rage. It wasn't the first time she'd seen Deacon since he'd wiped out Razor. Yet, she couldn't muster anything more than a regret that they'd fallen into his trap. Maybe it'd been Vasilisa's comments about the futility of their resistance. What good had it really accomplished? Were they anything more than terrorists? Another danger that lurked in the shadows of the Undercity? What made them any better than the scorpics that patrolled the canyon of ghosts?

"You don't have to do anything," said Yara, wishing she still had the automatic weapon in her hands to spray into the waku on his side, but Deacon had somehow ripped it away. That he could have killed them already was a blow to her confidence. "We're leaving the Undercity. You'll never see us again."

"It's too late for that, Yara. You've done too much damage, caused too many problems to get to walk away now. If you'd been smart, you would have come with me after we took care of Razor. Now you have to go out the same way as your father," said Deacon as he strolled forward, smoothing the lapel of his fitted jacket.

One of his underlings handed him the hooked sword when he held out his hand. The weapon glinted in the dim light. She understood the purpose of it now. A hook on the end of a blade was unwieldy, but it wasn't meant as an effective weapon, but as a horrifying one. Deacon had chosen it to scare. To put fear in his enemies as he tore off pieces of their flesh, oblivious to their counterattacks due to his black diamond.

Yara shifted to the side, putting the wall to her back. Choo-Choo followed her lead as he revealed his blades. She wouldn't go down easy, even if she thought their chances of winning were slim.

"You can't kill my brother," said Vasilisa, placing herself in front of them. "Please. I work hard for the Alliance. Let them go. She said they would leave. I don't want to watch you kill my brother."

"Get out of the way, girl. You served your purpose," said Deacon, making practice swings with his hooked blade. "I'm not here to kill a cripple."

From the passage from the Eleven Tears, a tall waku stumbled out, looking disheveled.

"Vasy!"

"Andy!"

Deacon growled at the interruption. "Get her out of my way."

The newcomer, clearly Vasilisa's boyfriend, looked conflicted about the situation.

"Come on, Vasy. You have to move," he said, approaching tentatively, holding out his hand while trying not to come between the two sides.

"I can't," said Vasilisa, anguished.

"Get. The Fuck. Out of my way," Deacon growled as he marched forward.

Vasilisa's boyfriend lunged forward to grab her hand, but made the mistake of going for the missing one. Yara used the distraction to pull out the C-30 Longfellow tucked into the back of her pants. The handgun had been designed to take down charging supernatural creatures at close range. She hoped it was enough to put a dent in Deacon. She sidestepped to avoid hitting Vasilisa and squeezed the trigger three times in succession. Vasilisa crouched at the knees with arms near her ears as the projectiles flew overhead. The impact staggered Deacon, ripping smoking holes in his jacket around the lower rib cage. He examined the matte gray flesh beneath as his skin rippled from the steelskin, then he raised his blade and charged.

Yara ran left, using Vasilisa and her boyfriend Andy as a distraction.

She fired once, aiming at Deacon's head, but he jerked his neck, avoiding the impact. Steelskin might protect him from death, but getting hit in the head would be extremely painful.

Her escape was brief. She thought she'd be able to make it back to the passage, which would give her a narrow gap to hold defensively, but Deacon cut her off. Yara froze, expecting the hooked blade to take off her head, but Choo-Choo tackled him in the midsection, throwing him across the cavern.

The other Alliance waku had clearly been told to hold back, but seeing their leader knocked down unleashed them. Despite being outnumbered, Yara felt some relief, knowing she and Choo-Choo outmatched them. Leaving the handgun in her left hand, she brought forth her blade in the other, dancing alongside Choo-Choo as they cut through the approaching waku. Their strikes were too slow, too sloppy. She cut them down as if she were harvesting wheat.

Sensing Deacon's return, she sunk her blade into the chest of a young woman with green hair and a dozen face piercings, and used her slumping form as a shield. The hooked blade chopped off the dead woman's arm, so Yara kicked the body into Deacon. Yara fired the C-30 Longfellow two more times into his chest, staggering him.

Before Deacon could reach her, the staccato pace of an automatic weapon firing erupted, flashing lights and hammering her eardrums. She'd be a little deaf after the fight if she survived. Choo-Choo had picked up a weapon one of the others had dropped and was unloading into Deacon, tearing his jacket to shreds. He stayed on his feet, grunting into the impact, until Choo-Choo emptied the clip.

"I'm gonna take you apart piece by piece!"

Deacon tore away the remnants of his jacket, revealing his rippled muscles beneath and the black metal fixed to his pectoral muscles. Camina's warning about the plates from the Eternal City came back to Yara, but she had no idea what to do with the information. She quickly replaced her clip with a fresh one while Deacon was removing his tattered clothing, but seeing the rage in his eyes told her the end was frighteningly near. Yara readied herself for a last stand.

Forty-One

There'd always been a part of Vasilisa that had wanted to be in a scrap. She'd grown up idolizing her older sister and brother—both formidable waku in their own right. And Yara, despite her feelings, was the daughter of the famous Brazio Santos, second only to Duro in fighting prowess.

But as the bullets rang out and people moved faster than she could see, the romanticized idea of battle was quickly dispelled. Blood splattered across her face as she crouched in the middle of the cavern. She wasn't so much frightened as stunned by the brutality of the violence and the speed at which people died.

Thing were unfolding so quickly, she didn't even know who was winning, only that her brother and boyfriend were still alive. But so was Deacon after taking multiple hits to the chest. She'd heard the rumors that he was a black diamond waku, but seeing his invulnerability herself made things even more real.

"I'm gonna take you apart piece by piece!"

The next part happened in slow motion.

Andy grabbed her hand. He'd stayed low with her and yanked her to the side to get them both out of the field of battle. Vasilisa happened to glance up to see the moment after Deacon had thrown down his tattered suit jacket, blown apart from gunfire at near point-blank range.

Deacon was fast.

He moved in a blur, faster than she could track, but she knew in an instant that Andy was leading her the wrong way. Right into Deacon. She tried to pull him back but he was too strong.

A wet squelch was followed by warm liquid hitting her face, splattering across her jaw and forehead. Andy's hand was no longer gripping hers tightly. It went slack. Then he stumbled to his knees. Deacon's hooked sword had ripped a gash in his chest. Vasilisa couldn't comprehend what she was seeing. The world dimmed and rotated around her, but she managed to crawl to his side as he lay on his back, breath coming in short, frantic heaves.

"No, Andy. No."

She gripped his hand. His eyes were growing dimmer by the second. She wanted to go back in time. Tell them it was a mistake. Maybe if she'd come with her brother quietly, Deacon wouldn't have found them.

"Andy..."

He was trying to speak, but his chest was a ruin. Blood was pumping onto the rocks at an alarming rate.

"I'm so sorry."

Andelei mouthed his final words and then stilled. She held his hand to her chest as gunfire rang around her. But nothing else mattered. He'd made her happy. So joyously happy. And now he was gone. Cut down in the middle of a scrap. What did any of it mean?

"Come back, Andy. Come back," she whispered, desperate to make the nightmare go away. "I forgot to say I love you."

Forty-Two

Deacon was going to kill her.

Yara knew there was no way to stop him. He moved too fast. He was too well protected. She hoped it would be quick. A swift, sharp pain and then a rapid descent into darkness. A return to the eternal shadows. She would have preferred a different end, fighting against an opponent where she might have had a chance, but there were no fair fights in the Undercity, only winners and the dead.

Then Vasy's boyfriend saved Yara.

Deacon had been headed straight for her when he'd gotten in the way, moving the wrong direction, and rather than delay, Deacon had cut him down.

Yara almost missed her chance. She'd been so sure that she was a dead woman standing. But the hesitation gave Yara a clean shot, but rather than aim for the head, she targeted the black metal on his right pec, thinking about what Camina had said about his modifications. The black diamond would protect his weak flesh, but not the additions to his body.

At that range and with Deacon momentarily stilled, she couldn't miss. Yara plugged him five times, hitting the black metal in succession, the thunderous impacts staggering Deacon until the surface shattered into glassy pieces that fell amid the rocks. Dark, sinewy smoke rose from the wreckage and his bubbling flesh, leaving him screaming with rage—and pain.

For a second, Yara feared the mist was coalescing into something real, and terrifying, but then it diffused. She reached for another clip as Deacon fought through the pain to remain standing. He took heavy steps forward, the bloody hooked blade in his grip, the effects of the injury wearing off. He would come for her soon.

Static buzzing in her ear had Yara questioning the injuries she'd sustained during the fight. Thinking it was the concussive sound of gunfire at close range that had damaged her eardrums, she put a hand to her ear expecting blood, but when it came away clean, she searched for the source. A shifting cloud of pale insects entered the cavern. She recognized them as the grasshopper-like critters that lived in the rocks and were served in the local restaurants.

Before Deacon could break free of his agony-induced stupor, the cloud of insects surrounded him, cocooning him, blocking his sight with glistening wings and tiny, prickly feet. He screamed and tried to swat them away, but there were too many. Deacon could kill any one of them with little effort, but he was no match for ten thousand crickets.

"What are you waiting for?" shouted Tick from the side passage, still wearing his black dress and the wig, though he'd discarded the matching pink parasol and basket. Koro hung around his neck and he had a backpack over his shoulder.

Yara thought about unloading the new clip in Deacon, but given his steelskin it wouldn't do a thing. As she stumbled away from the scene of battle, Choo-Choo grabbed his sister.

"You have to leave now. If you stay here, he'll kill you."

Vasilisa was covered in blood as she clung to the lifeless body. The shock of seeing her boyfriend slaughtered registered in her blank gaze. Choo-Choo tugged her to her feet while Deacon screamed at the top of his lungs, hell-bent on revenge but unable to do anything about it. Vasilisa stumbled after them as they ran through the passages, but eventually Choo-Choo convinced her to ride on his back and then they made good time.

"Where should we go?" asked Tick a few caverns later.

Without thinking too much about it, Yara said, "The Great Arch."

The proper place to go would have been the Chamber, in hopes of getting passage to the surface, but since she'd mentioned that to Deacon, she knew that would be the direction he sent his people after them once he was able to free himself from the cloud of insects. While reaching the Great Arch would be challenging, since they'd stopping raiding in those areas many months ago, she hoped it would be the last place they'd think to look.

Halfway to their destination, Vasilisa started beating on Choo-Choo's shoulders demanding she be put down. She looked like the survivor of a horror movie. Her dark hair was stuck together from the dried blood.

"I have to go back," she said.

"Vasy," said Choo-Choo. "He'll kill you. You know that."

"It's my fault," said Vasilisa, staggering on her feet. "If I hadn't been so loud, he wouldn't have found us. He just killed Andy. He was supposed to be on the same side."

"I tried to tell you, Vasy. They have no honor. It's only going to get worse. But I promise I'll find a way to get you to the surface. We can bribe someone at Big Dave's or something else. I don't know. We'll figure it out."

"No," said Vasilisa, shaking her head. "I'm not leaving."

"It's not safe here for you, Vasy."

The shock of her boyfriend's killing had either worn off or she'd buried it beneath her anger. When she spoke, the desire for vengeance threading through her words gave Yara the chills.

"I won't rest until Deacon is dead."

Forty-Three

Two days after they left the spire, Pandora exited the tunnels as Lady Saha, a minor noble adjacent to the Jade Court. The clothes Hylakane had given them were stiff from unuse, but their rigidness helped her slip into the new persona as she scanned the area with the quiet disdain of royalty. The high collar was set with gemstones that glittered from lingering enchantments, a sign of her station. A modestly jeweled scabbard hung from her hip. Within the protective covering was a weapon Hylakane had drilled her on for the last few months. In the human world, the weapon would be called a katana, but the Maetrie referred to it as a stalbyka—"steel smile" in their language. Unlike the face-forward stance of the famed samurai who wielded katanas, her fighting style with the stalbyka was different. Employing a heavy, metal-lined cloak on her back, she would use intricate flourishes and spins to disguise her attacks.

"I don't even recognize you," said Kuma, low and under his breath.

She gave him a haughty look. Aman Crownline was stockier than Kuma, with coal-black hair and a dusty skin tone that suggested his ancestors had come from the steppes of Rus and raided on horseback. The weapon on his hip was a heavy spiked mace, a terrifying weapon on the battlefield. They'd each had to learn new fighting techniques, because they didn't want to give themselves way by scrapping with curved blades as was customary in the Undercity.

"Hush, Aman. Remember, we have to be our new selves from here on out."

Kuma scanned the broken landscape where they'd come out. A solitary steel tower and two squat buildings were the only things standing in range.

"There's no one here."

"It doesn't matter. If we have to switch back and forth, we'll screw it up later. Better if we stay in character always."

Kuma sighed heavily, raising an eyebrow in her direction. His face was different, but his mannerisms were the same.

"Had I known that I would have made use of our time in the darkness."

She reached out and ran a finger along his jaw. "There's no reason a noblewoman can't have her way with her body servant. You are here to serve me in all ways possible, after all."

The Eternal City seemed less formidable after their training with the Steel Sun. While certain dangers like smoke-eaters or large bands of traveling maetrie could cause them issues, the problems that had plagued them on their way to his spire no longer seemed relevant.

Not long after they left the tunnels, the hazy light that existed as day dimmed and they found a standing structure, climbing into the higher levels to sleep. Kuma was brewing a pot of tea on a small fire while she watched out the openings. As she peered into the distance, she saw where they'd come from, the collection of buildings that made up Hylakane's settlement. It took her a minute to recognize what was missing.

"It's gone."

"What's gone?" asked Kuma as he tended the fire, checking the water for signs of boiling.

"The spire."

He joined her by the opening, scanning the horizon and following her outstretched arm.

"What happened?"

She squinted, shook her head. "Remember that shaking we felt the other night? That must have been when it fell."

"It wasn't that close to falling down."

"He destroyed it so our absence wouldn't be questioned." A heavy weight settled on her shoulders. "He upended his life there for our benefit."

After all she thought she knew about the maetrie, he'd surprised her with an act of self-sacrifice.

"Maybe he was sick of living there and being watched by Lady Amethyte's followers. A good chance to make a break with the past."

She elbowed him in the ribs. "Hush. I like my version better. He was a good teacher."

"Still is," he said.

Travel took on a familiar pattern over the next few weeks. Navigate through the wreckage during the day, avoiding others if possible, but if they had to engage, usually she could persuade them to leave either through her nobility or the prowess of her blade. Kuma made them tea at night, and as promised, she took advantage of her body servant in all the best ways. It was exciting to be someone else during their trysts. Sometimes, Kuma gave her strange looks, but she understood as she was often surprised by who was beneath her as they rocked on their bedrolls.

She grew used to being Lady Saha during the travel and more than once she found herself wondering what it would be like to actually be on a liebereisen—a journey of self-discovery. Or, she decided, maybe this trip to the Eternal City to train with Hylakane had been hers already. Short, in terms of how the maetrie viewed these trips. It wasn't unheard of for a liebereisen to last decades, and a few had gone on as long as a century. But it was easy for them to spend a fraction of their long lives on such a journey, while as part-maetrie, she had no idea how long her life span would be, and the addition of the faez crystals changed the calculation again. Mages of the Hundred Halls could live hundreds of years because of the influence of magic on their bodies, but faez crystals were new and a vast unknown when it came to their long-term effects.

"Do you really want to go back?" she asked Kuma one night as they were curled by the dim fire at the center of an old building.

"Hmmm? Back?" Kuma sat up.

"To the Undercity. What if we used the portal to go somewhere else?"

"I don't actually know. Probably not. But if we could?"

He lay back next to her, rubbing his fingers along the curve of her hip.

"It would be tempting for sure," he said. "Two wandering warriors on an endless quest for self-discovery. I think I'd actually like to meet these Brodarians, or some of the other known realms. It's a romantic idea..."

"But?"

She felt his tension, like his aura thickened. "Don't we have unfinished business in the Undercity? With your mother and grandfather and the clans? And after nearly two years will there be anything or anyone left that we recognize? Why go through all of this with Hylakane, the training, the masks and changeling elixirs to not go back?"

Pandora placed her hand on his neck, running her nails along the exposed flesh until he made murmurings of pleasure.

"You're trying to distract me." He rolled over, facing her. "What are you thinking?"

The words were held close to her chest. It took time to dislodge them, force them up her throat and into the air where they couldn't be taken back.

"What if we go back just to die? It all sounds good and romantic, two disguised warriors returning to seek their vengeance. I'd like to believe that it's possible..."

"Hylakane thought so."

Pandora squeezed her lips tight. "He has no idea what waits for us in the shadows. He only did what we asked. And maybe a little more. My grandfather is a cruel and cunning maetrie. Hearing the Ruby Queen speak kindly of him was a reminder that he is extremely formidable. And what resources do we have other than our weapons, our disguises, and our wits? He has everything else."

Kuma reached out and stroked her jaw, bringing a creasing around the lips that never quite turned into a smile.

"I don't think that's what you're worried about. You've never once in all the time I've known you been unwilling to throw yourself against overwhelming odds. I'd be lying if I didn't think we'd never make it to Hylakane's spire back when we first got here, let alone convince him to train us, or any of the other weird shit he had us do. But moving forward was better than curling into a ball and giving up."

Pandora grabbed his hand, squeezed it, and kissed his fingertips.

"I don't understand."

"I think you're afraid of winning. To take the mantle from your grandfather, to deal with the repercussions of your mother's betrayal. It would be easier to lose. To die. Then you wouldn't have to face those trials. To truly figure out who you really are. An alloy. The best of both worlds."

"Or the worst."

"I don't believe that," he said.

She settled into his arms, content to let him hold her, the weight of future decisions pushed away for the moment. She hated that he was right, because it forced her to consider what would happen when she was face-to-face with her mother and grandfather. What did it mean to be related to people you despised? Did it mean you hated yourself too because you came from them? Humans believed in the duality of nature and nurture, but the maetrie believed they were one and the same. The maetrie were stronger because they were ruthless, and that strength of purpose was in their blood.

As their travel brought them closer to their destination, Pandora felt like the weight on her shoulders was growing heavier. The more she thought about returning to the Undercity, the further away she wanted to run. Multiple times a day she'd almost convinced herself to beg Kuma to not go back, to find a way to another realm, and become the false personas they'd been inhabiting. It was better than anything that waited for her. But she never said the words, because she knew even if she did that, she'd never escape the feeling that she was supposed to be somewhere else. This was her liebereisen, but the journey had to take her back to the Undercity, to confront her mother and grandfather. Only then could she resolve who she really was.

"It shouldn't be far," said Pandora, one day as she spied an enormous archway standing sentinel amid the declining ruins. The structure was solid and huge. Bigger than the Arc de Triumph in Paris, a structure she'd only seen pictures of. The furthest edge of what should have been the lands of the Ebony Court. The stone structure had frescoes of maetrie warriors, figures from the past, though no one was left except Hylakane to speak their names.

The region beyond the archway was hazy. Not right away, but in the distance where the outline of a cityscape should have been the air grew fuzzy and impossible to penetrate. It was like someone had taken a painting of the region and wiped away the paint, leaving a smear.

No other region of the Eternal City had looked like that. Despite the low-hanging gray clouds one could always see a considerable distance.

"What is that?" asked Kuma, squinting.

"It's what was once the Ebony Court."

"I thought it'd be ruins, not...gone," he said, grimacing at the thought. "If this is what the tears do, I can't imagine it happening to an entire realm."

The thought made her ill, and not just because there was a faint buzzing in the air like static. She knew it was from the emptiness that filled the space where the Ebony Court once was. As if the world couldn't quite take not having that section of reality existing. It was a burr in the circuit.

"Come on," she said. "The portal can't be far. Let's get this over with. I don't like being so near it."

But they were faced with the emptiness ahead. The nearer they got, the worse the static grew until the buzzing was giving them both a headache. It was like standing before a waterfall, except instead of water it was the emptiness of a void crashing into the world. A vacuum of existence, trying to correct itself, while the place that had once been there now existed in a weapon back in their realm.

"We're being watched," said Kuma under his breath as they neared the area where the portal would be waiting.

"I know," she said without moving her head or her mouth. "Two in that old building to the left, one more on the right, but probably more that we can't see." Pandora kept up her stride, acting like nothing was wrong even as they walked into the trap. "Any idea who they are?"

Kuma expanded his senses. "Maetrie for sure. I fear they're part of a court. Something tugs at my memories."

A stone formed in her gut. "The Ruby Court."

His head twitched, but he kept moving forward. "Why? We left him long ago. What would they gain by interfering with us?"

"I think we're about to find out."

Two maetrie approached from the back. They'd purposely placed themselves to block passage to the portal, which meant they likely knew who they were. Pandora recognized the two maetrie from Lady Amethyte's bar. Her bodyguard Zoltv had his sleeves rolled up, revealing his scarred arms. The old wounds looked like he had ropes hidden beneath his flesh. At his side was the physician who had worked on Kuma and placed the tracker in his flesh. Lisette. She looked like a runway model through a funhouse mirror.

"Out of my way," said Pandora, using her haughtiest tone. "I have business in another realm and am already late."

Zoltv had a bully bar in his hand, the maetrie version of a barbed-wire-wrapped bat, while Lisette held a pair of short, thin blades that looked like enlarged scalpels. A half dozen other maetrie came out of the buildings, encircling them, while neither she nor Kuma reached for their weapons.

"Dispel your glamour. We know it's you, Pandora Thule and Kuma Santos. Our spies tracked you from Hylakane's spire."

"I assure you we are neither of those people," said Pandora. "I am Lady Saha and this is my body servant Aman. Unless you'd like to learn why the Brodarians called me the Breath of the Wraithhawk on the battlefield, you'd best step aside. I respect Lady Amethyte and would prefer her not to lose such valuable assets in a mistaken fight."

The two maetrie shared a glance, then spoke quietly to each other. She'd placed doubt in their minds, but wasn't sure it would dissuade them from attacking. It was better to learn they'd murdered the wrong people than to go back to the Ruby Queen with empty hands.

Kuma arched an eyebrow, his hand twitching towards the satchel on his hip where his mask was contained. She gave him a tight shake. The masks were for a different purpose.

Zoltv swaggered forward, swinging his bully bar casually. "I'm afraid we'll have to bring you back to the Lady's territory, where we can have a long conversation over drinks. I can vouch for your safety. I'm sure the Ruby Queen would love to hear about your travels, Lady Saha."

The circle tightened. While she was confident fighting against a couple maetrie, the odds were eight against two, not great for either of them. But there was no chance they would allow themselves to be taken back to the Ruby Queen's territory. Their changed appearances might fool these lesser followers, but Lady Amethyte was a powerful arcane practitioner and would see right through their disguises.

"I'm afraid my schedule will not allow it," said Pandora.

When they continued to advance, Pandora drew her weapon and flourished her cape, hoping the display was intimidating. Kuma unbuckled his spiked mace, twirling it expertly before placing his back to hers.

In the hesitation before the battle, a spike of adrenaline surged through Pandora as she worried that she was still too new to her weapon to be effective against a large group. That Hylakane's training had barely scratched the surface and she would falter at the first pass.

As a rail-thin maetrie holding a long spear lunged forward, her training kicked in. Pandora twirled her iron-lined cape like a matador before a bull, disguising the advance of her blade, chopping the spear in half, before kicking out, shattering a knee. The killing blow had to be pulled as two more attackers followed up, forcing her to spin through their weapons, parrying one and using the cloak like a shield against the other.

Behind her, Kuma's grunts were interspaced with a heavy crash against their weapons. One of his attackers got too close and took a mace to the face, screaming punctuating the scrap. Out of the corner of her eye, she caught Lisette slipping in with her scalpel-like blades, right in Kuma's blind spot. Pandora sent a sapphire spear of force into her hips, twirling her around.

The ebb and flow of battle continued like poetry in the dim light of the Eternal City. Cape and mace provided a whirling shield which the maetrie could not penetrate, and any mistake was punished with cut or smash. They whittled down their enemies until it was only two against two. She and Kuma versus Zoltv and Lisette, both of whom looked apprehensive about theirs odd. Their companions were bleeding out on the concrete, moaning in pain, or no longer moving.

"You would have been better off returning to your queen and beginning forgiveness," said Pandora. "Not even the ur-hounds of Brodaria dared to interfere with my travels."

The former stelynka racer, Zoltv, pulled a vial from an inner pocket and threw it back. His eyes glowed with eldritch light. He advanced with the arrogance of assumed immortality, a fact she was about to disabuse him of.

"Step away, Aman. I mean to teach this fool his final lesson," said Pandora.

Kuma bowed and retreated, leaving her in a one-on-one duel with the former gladiator.

The bully bar burst into bluish flame when Zoltv spit on it. He sneered as he advanced, moving in fits and starts, his body amped up from the elixir he'd drank. She danced with him as a partner, shifting when he lunged, using her iron-lined cloak to disguise her movements. At first glance, the fight looked weighted in his favor. She retreated from his attacks, and he grew more confident by the step.

Pandora let him take the initiative, keeping him guessing to which way she would shift as he swung his bully bar with the intent of smashing her skull. When she sensed his overextension, she yanked him forward with a heavy sapphire Pull, shoving her curved sword through his gut as she held back his arm holding his weapon.

The surprise on his face quickly slackened. Pandora placed her foot against his belly and shoved him off. He stumbled backwards and before he could register the change, she sliced through his neck. The head tumbled across the concrete, landing against an old shattered statue. Both sets of eyes were matched in their blankness.

The maetrie woman, Lisette, quickly realized she was outmatched and alone. She turned to run and Pandora thought that Kuma would go after her but he stood silently, a smirk on his lips.

The reason for his inaction became clear when a figure stepped out from behind a broken wall. The bald maetrie grabbed Lisette by the head, snapping her neck in one smooth motion.

"I sensed him halfway through the fight," said Kuma.

Pandora wasn't surprised that he hadn't interfered. He probably had wanted to see them fight, but it annoyed her that he'd used them as bait. Hylakane approached with his hands behind his back. There was no sign of his Zhinzi, but that didn't mean it wasn't close at hand.

"I thought we wouldn't see you again," she said.

Hylakane tilted his head. "Consider it your final test." He reviewed the carnage. "Not bad for a mongrel and an insect."

"You tore down your tower," said Kuma.

He shrugged. "Spending time with two insolent apprentices reminded me that there are a multitude of realms out there. I was staying in the Eternal City because I was grieving my family, but recently I realized that I had moved past that and that maybe it was time for my liebereisen."

"I thought a journey like that was for the young," said Pandora.

"In a way, I'm born again without a Court or purpose. Maybe travel will help me discover who I am now," said Hylakane.

"You could always come to the Undercity and help us with Dominion," offered Kuma.

"That would only complicate things," said Hylakane. "It would give Lady Amethyte a reason to interfere. No. If there was a reason to travel to your realm it would be to have a conversation with a certain individual."

"Revenge?"

Hylakane shook his head. "Nothing would ever bring them back, and as a fellow wielder of the tears, I know all too well the burden. There's a reason the Black Butcher fled to your realm. But I don't think it's yet time for the two of us to talk."

"Where will you go?" asked Pandora.

"Wherever the word *maetrie* has no meaning," he said. "Come, let us make the last few steps of this journey together."

They joined him on the walk to the portal. Hylakane offered a few suggestions based on his observations from the fight, but he seemed less interested in instruction than he had at the spire.

The pillar of obsidian sat in the center of an abandoned garden. Strange plants that looked too dangerous to touch had spilled onto the concrete, but the ring around the portal remained empty.

Hylakane approached the portal first. He stared at it with apprehension. It was strange for Pandora to see such open doubt on a maetrie, but after over a year in his care, she understood he was not like the others. That thought gave her hope.

"May the shadows keep you safe," he said.

"And the light blind your enemies," they replied in unison.

After matched bows, Hylakane turned, touched the glossy black stone, and disappeared.

"Where can we go?" asked Kuma near the stone.

"Not the place we left from, that much is for sure. But I know another portal in the Undercity. I visited it once, and made sure I understood its signature."

"Where is it?"

"The Great Arch."

Kuma nodded. "I know the place. It's a good spot. There are no passages that go near it unless visiting the arch is your purpose. We can assess the condition of the Undercity and make our way from there."

Pandora held out her hand. She gripped his tightly. Nearly two years away from the Undercity. A long time in which anything could have happened.

"Come, Aman. We have a revolution to incite."

§ § §

ABOUT THE AUTHOR

Thomas K. Carpenter resides in Colorado with his wife Rachel. When he's not busy writing his next book, he's hiking, skiing, and getting beat by his wife at cards. He keeps a regular blog at www.thomaskcarpenter.com and you can follow him on twitter @thomaskcarpente. If you want to learn when his next novel will be hitting the shelves and get free stories and occasional other goodies, please sign up for his mailing list by going to: http://tinyurl.com/thomaskcarpenter. Your email address will never be shared and you can unsubscribe at any time.

Continue Kuma and Pandora's adventure in Book Five of The Crystal Halls series

THE BLOODSTONE REBELLION

OTHER BOOKS BY THOMAS K. CARPENTER

The Hundred Halls Universe

SEASON ONE

THE HUNDRED HALLS

Trials of Magic
Web of Lies
Alchemy of Souls
Gathering of Shadows
City of Sorcery

THE RELUCTANT ASSASSIN

The Reluctant Assassin
The Sorcerous Spy
The Veiled Diplomat
Agent Unraveled
The Webs That Bind

GAMEMAKERS ONLINE

The Warped Forest
Gladiators of Warsong
Citadel of Broken Dreams
Enter the Daemonpits
Plane of Twilight

ANIMALIANS HALL

Wild Magic
Bane of the Hunter
Mark of the Phoenix
Arcane Mutations
Untamed Destiny

STONE SINGERS HALL

Song of Siren and Blood
House of Snake and Tome
Storm of Dragon and Stone
Sonata of Shadow and Thorn
Well of Demon and Bone

THE ORDER OF MERLIN

The Order of Merlin
Infernal Alliances
Tower of Horn and Blood

www.ingramcontent.com/pod-product-compliance
Lightning Source LLC
Chambersburg PA
CBHW030420310726
48979CB00009B/1535/J

* 9 7 8 1 9 5 8 4 9 8 2 1 7 *